REMOVAL

REMOVAL

A Novel

PETER MURPHY

25 years
NO EXIT

First published in 2012 by No Exit Press,
an imprint of Oldcastle Books Ltd,
P.O.Box 394, Harpenden,
Herts, AL5 1XJ

www.noexit.co.uk

A CIP catalogue record for this book is available from the British Library.

ISBN
978-1-84243-598-4 (print)
978-1-84243-599-1 (kindle)
978-1-84243-600-4 (epub)
978-1-84243-601-1 (pdf)

2 4 6 8 10 9 7 5 3 1

Typeset by Avocet Typeset, Chilton, Aylesbury, Bucks
in 10 on 13pt Garamond MT
Printed in Great Britain by Clays Ltd, St Ives plc

For more about Crime Fiction go to www.crimetime.co.uk / @crimetime.uk

The President, Vice President and all civil Officers of the United States, shall be removed from Office on Impeachment for, and Conviction of, Treason, Bribery, or other high Crimes and Misdemeanors.

– United States Constitution, Article II, Section 4.

Prologue

'The President wants you to know,' Dick Latham said, 'that you all have his complete trust.'

Not for the first time that day, Latham's hands were unsteady. His law school graduation ring kept catching the edges of the black binders as he took them out of his briefcase one by one. He was sure everyone had noticed.

'This is just a precaution. I'm sure you understand. You will find the confidentiality agreement behind tab one.'

Until recently, Latham had enjoyed his time as Attorney-General. A former prosecutor who had made a name for himself by breaking up a major drug supply network through Miami, Latham was flattered when President Steve Wade asked him to take on the top law-enforcement job in the country. His days seemed to be a never-ending round of meetings and phone calls, but he was getting good results and he felt he was handling it well. Recently, though, Wade had asked him to do certain things outside the scope of the Attorney-General's usual duties. Latham felt uncomfortable about some of them, such as calling Senators on the pretext of offering advice about the law. The Senators had their own legal advisers, and they were not fools. They knew his calls were pure political pressure, and had nothing to do with the law. Not that there was anything wrong with a little political pressure during an impeachment. It was just that Latham was not sure the Attorney-General should be the one applying it. His closest friend, a constitutional law scholar at an Ivy League law school, agreed with him.

Then, as if that were not bad enough, the President had initiated Latham into the Williamsburg Doctrine. Rather like God calling Moses to receive the Ten Commandments, Latham reflected in an irreverent moment, except that the Williamsburg Doctrine was considerably less edifying than the Ten Commandments. Latham immediately wished he could just forget about it. But it was obvious that Wade did not intend to offer him that option. And now, the President had instructed him to preside at this meeting of the Joint Chiefs of Staff at the Pentagon. Just thinking about it made him break out in a sweat. None of the protocols for a meeting of the Joint Chiefs had been observed. The Secretaries of the Armed Services had not been informed, let alone invited to attend. No adjutants or assistants were present. The only uninvolved witness was a female army major, who had top secret clearance and would serve as stenographer. The very building made him anxious. It was gray, airless, suffocating. The Pentagon had always been well protected but, since 9/11, the new aristocrats, the security experts, had been given free rein, and the Pentagon was one of their treasured domains. The reinforced glass and concrete, the steel doors, the impenetrable windows, the endless scrutiny – everything seemed calculated to make him feel he was being watched.

Latham looked around the small, claustrophobic conference room. The four men around the table were examining the black folders he had circulated to them, handling them gingerly; as if they might bite. General Terrell, Chief of Staff of the Army, the ranking officer present and Chairman of the Joint Chiefs, was scanning the confidentiality agreement, looking uncomfortable; Admiral McGarry, Chief of Naval Operations, was flicking through the several tabs quickly, giving nothing away; General Hessler, Commandant of the Marine Corps, looking every bit the career combat officer he was, wore his usual impenetrable scowl and showed no inclination to move beyond the Table of Contents. These were not Latham's people. He found them intimidating. But at least they were already aware of the Williamsburg Doctrine. General Raul Gutierrez, the first hispanic Chief of Staff of the Air Force, was the unknown factor. Gutierrez had just been appointed and was still adjusting to his new role. He had not yet been initiated. There had not been time.

'This is all new to you, General Gutierrez?'

'Yes, Sir. It is.'

Gutierrez had a relaxed manner, which concealed an intense dedication to the Air Force and to his career. He had first built his reputation as an outstanding fighter pilot. Later, when his eyes grew too old for combat flying, he had proved himself again as a commander. He was reputed to be sharp. Latham was particularly nervous about him.

'Well, let me summarize the political situation, and then I'll ask

8

General Terréll to talk to us about the Williamsburg Doctrine.'

Almost as if he were in high school, General Gutierrez raised a hand.

'Excuse me, Mr. Attorney-General, but before we get started – this is just because I'm the new kid on the block here and I have a lot to learn – I would like to make sure I understand the basis of this meeting.'

'Basis? What do you mean?'

Gutierrez shifted in his chair.

'Well, I guess what I'm asking is, which hat are we wearing? If I understand correctly, you're here today representing the President. Now, we report to the President as Commander-in-Chief, and we also report to the Secretaries of our Departments. But the Secretaries are not represented here. I was just wondering what the basis of the meeting was, exactly.'

Latham frowned. They were right about Gutierrez. He hoped to God it was not going to be a problem.

'We're here at the request of the President, General Gutierrez. There are certain matters the President believes would be better discussed in a small group. The Secretaries also report to the President, so I don't see any difficulty. Everything will become clear as we proceed. I must ask you to accept that for now.'

Gutierrez shrugged.

'Whatever you say,' he replied with a smile. 'Just wanted to know where I stand, that's all. Comes from responding to too many requests from the ground for air support during my flying days, I guess. Sometimes wires would get crossed, cause problems. I'm sorry if I spoke out of turn.'

'Not at all, General,' Latham said, as calmly as he could. 'We want everybody on the same page. Feel free to ask any questions you want.'

General Hessler snorted unpleasantly and looked at his watch. Latham nodded and coughed as he looked down at his notes. The room seemed to have become warmer.

'As you all know, Gentlemen, the impeachment has begun and, while it's early days yet, the indications are that things are not going too well for the President. The prosecutors need a two-thirds majority to convict, so if the Senate were to divide along party lines, the impeachment would fail. But some members of his party are leaning towards the prosecution. The President is doing all he can to encourage his supporters, but in light of the testimony developed by the House Intelligence Committee …'

Admiral McGarry gave Latham a grim smile.

9

PETER MURPHY

'In light of that testimony, the President is about to crash and burn,' he said. 'I think we all know that, Mr. Latham. The papers are saying they expect it to be over and done with next week.'

Suppressing his irritation, Latham ran a finger under the collar of his shirt, which was beginning to feel too tight.

'There is a possibility that the President may be convicted of high crimes and misdemeanors. It could happen as early as next week. Yes, that is correct.'

Latham took a sip of water.

'But we believe that our supporters in the Senate will pull back when the time comes ...'

'That's not what I'm hearing,' Hessler intervened.

'Me neither,' McGarry added.

'Be that as it may. The matter is by no means hopeless. Not yet. But, the point is, if the President is convicted, Article Two, Section Four, of the Constitution provides that he shall be removed from office. In that event, the Constitution further provides that the Vice President takes over as President.'

Latham bit his lip.

'Which... brings us to the Williamsburg Doctrine. General Terrell, for the benefit of General Gutierrez, would you please outline the history and basic principles of the Doctrine?'

Terrell exchanged a brief glance with McGarry. Gutierrez sat up in his seat, eyeing Terrell closely. The Army Chief seemed reluctant to begin.

'The Williamsburg Doctrine,' Terrell said eventually, 'is the name given to a resolution of the Joint Chiefs of Staff adopted at a meeting at Williamsburg, Virginia, in January 1965. It has no constitutional or legal effect ...'

'That's a matter for me, I think,' Latham broke in sharply.

Terrell shrugged.

'The Kennedy assassination made a lot of people start to think about what might have happened. Specifically, about the line of succession to the Presidency. As you know, General, we had a lot of foreign involvement under Kennedy – the Bay of Pigs, the Cuban missile crisis, Vietnam, not to mention the ongoing Cold War. There was some anxiety because of the unpredictability of the succession. There was a question about the commitment of the Vice President to our military policies.'

'I don't understand,' Gutierrez said quietly. 'I'm not aware the Military had any problem with Johnson.'

'It wasn't about Johnson,' Terrell said. 'But the fact that Johnson was in the White House was an unpredictable event. The Vice Presidency is always unpredictable. That's the basic principle of the Doctrine.'

'The Vice President is not an issue in an election,' McGarry broke in. 'He's an afterthought. Nobody cares who's Vice President. Everybody assumes he will never have anything to do with military matters, much less become Commander-in-Chief. We never paid much attention to the Vice President, or at least we didn't until Kennedy bought it.'

'Right,' Terrell agreed. 'So when the dust settled, the Joint Chiefs decided that there should be some kind of policy, just in case we lost a President in circumstances in which the Vice President might be ... well, unreliable.'

Gutierrez swallowed hard.

'Unreliable?'

'Yes. Unreliable. Maybe, at that time, they had little reason to think there would be a repetition. Since then, of course, we've lost Nixon, and we nearly lost Clinton. But in any case, they decided that there should be a policy. There was a top-secret meeting in Williamsburg, like the meeting we're having today. And certain guidelines were drawn up, which have since become known as the Williamsburg Doctrine. They have never been invoked - well, not until now, anyway.'

There was a silence.

'What exactly do these guidelines say?' Gutierrez asked, trying to sound composed. It took a major effort.

Terrell seemed equally ill at ease. He doodled absently on the yellow pad on the table in front of him for several seconds.

'Well, you understand, there are two possibilities. One, the President dies. In that case, the Vice President takes over immediately. And in that case, frankly, no one has speculated on how the Williamsburg Doctrine would apply. Two, the President is removed from office. In that case, we have time to think about it before it happens. The Doctrine is easier to work with. Essentially it provides that, if it should be the opinion of the Joint Chiefs that the Vice President is unreliable, and therefore not acceptable as Commander-in-Chief, then certain steps should be taken to ensure that the succession is delayed until the people have the opportunity to make a different choice.'

Gutierrez looked at the men seated around the table. Their faces offered no comfort.

'What?' he breathed.

'A number of circumstances were identified at the Williamsburg meeting that would make it possible to argue that the Vice President might be unreliable. The only one of any relevance today is that the Vice President might be considered overly left-wing or radical to be acceptable as Commander-in-Chief. To put it another way, that her patriotism might be open to question when it comes to military matters.'

For some seconds, Gutierrez stared blankly at Terrell. Then, abruptly, he laughed out loud.

'OK, OK . Now I get it. This is just my rite of passage? Right? 'Welcome to the Joint Chiefs'. Make the new guy look like an idiot. Well, I have to hand it to you. You did a great job. You really had me fooled.'

No one joined in the laughter.

'Oh, come on,' Gutierrez said.

PART I

OPENING

1

IN THE DIM light, Lucia could just make out their distant reflection in the mirror of the dressing-table against the opposite wall. They were a handsome couple, she thought. Perhaps not quite Abelard and Heloise, not quite Romeo and Juliet. But a handsome couple, nonetheless. Pity about the wife, but then again, no relationship was perfect. And it wasn't just business. Far from it. She liked him, perhaps even cared for him. There was no denying the physical attraction between them, something Lucia always appreciated. She looked at him fondly. Beautiful. Even if he were not the most powerful man in the world, he would still be quite a catch. Steven Marion Wade, Jr., President of the United States, looked younger than his fifty years, and his daily exercise routine, though a source of some amusement to the White House press corps, kept his weight in proportion to his six feet three inches of height. He had a full head of sandy hair and light brown eyes. He might easily have passed for forty, on his best days perhaps even thirty-five. His youthful looks never failed to surprise.

Neither did the fact that he was President. Before his election, most observers had written him off as a lightweight. In his home state in the south, he had served adequately as a district attorney, then as a state legislator, and finally as Governor, but he had made little impact on the national scene before entering the presidential primary race. No one saw him coming. Wade had a natural charm, a relaxed southern accent, and an astute mind, which he did not always fully reveal. He also had a shrewd understanding of the issues that mattered to the voters. Quietly, he began to build momentum, and by the time his opponents realized what was happening, it was too late. His election to a second term was achieved almost as a matter of course. The only real obstacle was persistent talk of a number of indiscretions, talk which his experienced campaign team was able to head off before it did any real damage. He was now halfway through his second term, and his popularity was at an all-time high. He was confident in himself, and it showed. The talk in Washington already was of a legacy, one of the better ones.

Lucia herself was quite a catch in anybody's book. In her mid-thirties, she was an exceptionally beautiful woman, only an inch or two shorter than the President, slim, with olive skin, long black hair, and bright dark eyes. Her accent was European, but difficult to pin down to a particular country. It was the result of being raised, she liked to say, as a gypsy. She was born in Italy to Lebanese parents who were immigrants, but not settlers. She lived with them in more homes than she could begin to count, as they moved constantly in an unending quest for a better life. But her education, if irregular, was broad and practical. She grew up speaking several languages fluently, and learned to deal naturally with people of all nationalities and backgrounds. When life eventually brought her to Washington, she felt strangely at home.

She first met the President at a White House dinner which she had attended as the escort of a male friend, a German diplomat. The friend was gay, and Lucia covered for him on occasions when he wanted to conceal that fact. The moment she was introduced to the President she felt his instant attraction to her, and she was not surprised when, later in the evening, a Secret Service agent discreetly asked for her telephone number. She first went to him a week later in the White House residence, while the First Lady was somewhere in Africa on a goodwill mission. There was no pretense between them. The moment the door was closed, she undressed, and began to show the President the full range of her skills. From that moment, he had been captivated.

The White House was not the best venue for a secret rendezvous. It was easier when he was on the road, in a hotel, as he was now in Chicago. Of course, she always had to deal with the Secret Service agents. At first they were very suspicious of her, searching her thoroughly before allowing her into the President's room, rifling through her purse, even making her take off her shoes to check for concealed weapons. But now they were more used to her, the searches had become more casual, and sometimes they even exchanged pleasantries with her. Except for the woman - Agent Linda Samuels. Nothing Lucia did or said made any difference there. Samuels made no effort to hide her dislike for Lucia, or her disapproval of Lucia's relationship with the President. Jealous, Lucia thought with a smile. She knew the type. She wondered if Samuels had a sex life of her own.

She raised her head from his chest.

'I hope that was to your satisfaction, Mr. President.'

'You know it was.'

'Better than the First Lady?'

The President kissed her, and she felt the passion stir again.

'You do things the First Lady hasn't even read about in books.'

Lucia kissed him happily in return, and settled her head back down on his chest.

The red telephone beside the bed rang. This was not the standard hotel phone. It had been specially installed by the President's staff before he moved into the room. Lucia groaned, as the President, making a face, stretched his arm across the bed to answer it.

'Let it ring,' she said.

'I wish I could, Honey. Hello?'

'Mr. President,' a male voice said, 'I have the Secretary of State on the secure line from Tel Aviv. May I patch him though?'

Wade winked at Lucia and blew her a kiss.

'Sure. Go ahead.'

He placed his hand over the receiver.

'I have to take this.'

Lucia, knowing the rules, kissed him on the cheek, climbed out of bed, and walked towards the bedroom door. Beyond the door lay the living room of the presidential suite, where their play had begun. By walking straight ahead, she would be able to collect her clothes from the floor where they lay discarded. She thought of it as removing the evidence from the crime scene, like erasing the fingerprints from the murder weapon, picking up the spent cartridges. Her black seamed stockings lay on the floor just beyond the bed. They had been overlooked during the urgent first session. Her black panties, bra, and MaxMara cocktail dress were in the living room, next to the President's shirt, pants and underwear. The empty bottle of Mumm Cordon Rouge and two glasses were on the small table beside the sofa. Lucia righted one of the glasses, which was on its side, and continued to the outer door of the suite, where she had abandoned her shoes as soon as she arrived.

She returned to the bedroom, carrying her clothes in a bundle. Wade was still talking with the Secretary of State, so she laid them on the bed and went to the bathroom to take a shower. The President was hanging up as she returned, holding a bath towel loosely around her. She smiled. He lay silently on the bed, watching appreciatively as Lucia dressed, brushed her hair, and applied her make-up and lipstick. Once she was ready to leave, Lucia sat on the edge of the bed to allow him to perform their final ritual. Kneeling in front of her, the President lifted each foot in turn, gently kissed each sole and placed her feet into her shoes. They walked arm-in-arm to the door of the suite, where they paused for a long good-bye kiss.

'Call me when I'm back in Washington?'

'Of course. Save all your energy for me. You'll need it.'

To Lucia's displeasure, Agent Samuels was still on duty, standing in the corridor opposite the President's door. Didn't that woman ever take a break? As usual, her expression was cold. Lucia thought Samuels must have been much the same age as she was herself, perhaps a shade older but not much. Samuels was one or two inches shorter, but muscular and well-built, and without any excess weight. Her looks were mid-western, her skin fresh, her hair and eyes light brown. Her accent matched.

'Good night, Agent Samuels.'

'Good night to you, Ma'am.'

Linda Samuels allowed her eyes to follow Lucia until she turned the corner towards the elevators. She caught herself fingering her side-arm, her favorite nine-millimeter Glock, and with an effort made herself stop.

'Bitch,' she added, under her breath.

2

'YOU'VE HAD a rough time,' Ted Lazenby had begun.

Almost two years had passed since the interview, but Kelly remembered those first words as if they had been spoken the day before. She remembered her first impression of his personal warmth, how she sensed instinctively that this was someone she could like and respect. It was usually when she was alone at night in her apartment that the memories returned. Memories not only of the interview, but also of the events which had brought her to Washington, to a job which made her the envy of many of her colleagues. If they knew what had gone before, if they knew the price she had paid, she thought, they might be less envious. She remembered her conversation with Lazenby clearly enough, but her impressions of the office she would later come to know so well were hazy. Of course, any young agent would have felt anxious on being summoned without warning into the presence of the Director of the FBI himself. But the events which had brought her there had damaged her self-confidence. She still felt as if she were feeling her way through a thick fog. Twenty-four hours before, she had been lying on the beach in Cancun. Now she was in the Director's office in the J. Edgar Hoover Building in Washington, and she was alone with the Director. Why she was there, she could only speculate. Her speculations were not encouraging.

'Yes, Sir,' she had replied, taking Lazenby's hand.

He had walked to the door of his office to meet her as his secretary ushered her in. In his other hand, he held a brown file folder, which she recognized at once as part of her confidential service record.

'Have a seat. Did Rose offer you some coffee?'

'Yes. I'm fine, thank you, Sir.'

'All right.'

Unhurriedly, Lazenby walked back to his desk and resumed his seat.

Kelly made herself as comfortable as she could in an armchair in front of the desk.

'You're Special Agent Kelly Smith, age thirty, single.'

It was technically a question, but Lazenby was reading from her file, and he made it sound more like a statement.

'Yes, Sir.'

'You're from Minnesota.'

'St. Paul, born and raised.'

'College at Notre Dame.'

'Yes, Sir.'

'Athletic scholarship. What did you do?'

'I ran track, middle distance, and I was on the tennis team.'

'Then back home to St. Paul to law school. William Mitchell College of Law. The school that produced Chief Justice Warren Burger, if I'm not mistaken.'

Kelly smiled and nodded.

'I'm impressed, Sir.'

Lazenby returned the smile.

'So are they, and I bet they never let you forget it.'

'No, Sir.'

'Why law school?'

'My parents are both lawyers. It was expected.'

'What kind of law?'

'General family practice, wills, trusts, estates, that kind of stuff.'

'But you didn't end up practicing law. Why not?'

Kelly shifted in her chair.

'I'd always wondered whether it was what I really wanted to do, or whether I was just drifting into it. But I didn't think about it seriously until my third year of law school. Up until then I had been too busy just keeping up with my school work. I hadn't really faced up to the reality of what it would be like once I got out of school. When I finally asked myself whether it was what I wanted, the answer I got was 'No'. If I had become a lawyer, I wouldn't have done the kind of stuff my parents do. I would have been a prosecutor.'

'Why?'

'It felt like I would be making a difference, dealing with things that really mattered. But it wasn't enough. I needed something more direct, more physical, I'm not sure quite how to put it.'

She paused.

'And I'm sure that's way more than you wanted to know.'

Lazenby put the file down on his desk and looked at her closely.

'So, you came to the Bureau instead of becoming a prosecutor?'

'I didn't have it all neatly worked out. To tell you the truth, it just so happened that the Bureau was interviewing on campus around the time I had my great revelation. I thought, 'what the hell, sounds interesting, can't do any harm to talk to them.' So I signed up for an interview, and suddenly, that was it. I was hooked. I knew it the moment I walked into the interview. I don't know how else to describe it …'

She hesitated.

'I understand,' Lazenby said. 'How did your parents react?'

'Actually, they were great. I know they were disappointed that I wasn't going to go into the family business, but they supported me totally.' She smiled. 'I was pleasantly surprised.'

'How do you feel about your decision today?'

Kelly closed her eyes, and sat back in her chair, silent for a while.

'I'm sorry,' Lazenby said. 'That wasn't a fair question. You've only been on leave for a few weeks.'

Kelly opened her eyes and wrapped her arms tightly around her body.

'Seven weeks.'

'Seven weeks. New York gave you four months without the option.'

'Yes, Sir.'

'Were the counselors helpful?'

Kelly hesitated.

'I guess so. But I'm one of those people who need people they know. I have a friend, an old friend from back home, Linda Samuels. I lean on her a lot. I don't know what I would have done without her.'

Lazenby nodded.

'So you feel you're making progress?'

She sat back up in the chair.

'I guess so. It took me the first two weeks just to stop shaking. The next two weeks, I couldn't stop thinking about Joe and Tina, and I cried the whole time. Since then, I've tried to think about other things, I've tried to remember who I am and what I'm supposed to be doing, but …'

Lazenby stood, walked around his desk, and leaned against it, just in front of Kelly's chair.

'Kelly, I've read the reports on *Operation Shakedown,* and I've spoken to New York about it. They should never have let you do what you did.

You were too inexperienced. I've made my views on that very clear to the agent in charge.'

'I volunteered.'

'I know. And I also know that what happened wasn't your fault. But they should never have let you do it.'

They were silent for a while.

'It was going fine at first,' Kelly said eventually, almost to herself. 'I got myself taken on at the factory.'

'Yes.'

'The whole place was just a front, a cover for the rackets the two Families were running in the Bronx. I was getting good information. My cover seemed to be secure, but something went wrong…'

'There are no guarantees when you're dealing with the Mob.'

'No, Sir.'

'There's no point in reliving it. Especially the shoot-out.'

Kelly closed her eyes again.

'I know I'll never be able to forget that. I still get nightmares about it. It's only been in the last week or two I've been able to sleep through the night.'

'I understand.'

'I don't really know why I'm still alive,' Kelly continued. 'I have no right to be. If Joe and Tina hadn't shown up, I would have been dead. That I do know. But the rest of it, well, it all happened so fast. Somehow, we were able to call for back-up. But we were outnumbered, and by the time they arrived…'

'Joe and Tina were dead,' Lazenby added quietly. 'Yes, I know. And I'm sorry. They were good agents.'

'They were my friends,' Kelly whispered. She made a desperate effort to suppress the tears, but it was no use. 'I keep thinking, there must have been something I could have done differently. I should have got out of there before they…'

'No,' Lazenby said. 'You did your job, and you did it well.'

He waited for some time until she recovered her composure.

'Look, Kelly, I didn't ask you to interrupt your leave and come all the way from Cancun to bring back such painful memories,' he said. 'I'm sure you had quite enough of that when they debriefed you. I brought you here to make you a proposition.'

Kelly looked up.

Lazenby walked slowly back to his seat.

'I don't know how you're feeling about the Bureau right now. It wouldn't surprise me if you feel bitter about it. If that's the case, I'm sorry. But I do know you're a good agent, and I don't want to lose you. I've looked at your service record. You were one of the best recruits we ever had at Quantico.'

He folded his hands in front of him on his desk.

'Keep this under wraps for now, but I'm losing my personal assistant, Fred Keenan. He's been seduced by the world of commerce. Better pay and regular hours. I can't say I blame him. In fact, I'm feeling a little jealous. But the point is, Kelly, I need a replacement. It's not an easy assignment. You'll be on call twenty-four hours a day. There's a lot of paperwork, and a lot of dealing with unreasonable people who don't know what's going on. That includes people at high levels of government, who damn well should know what's going on. It can be exhausting and frustrating, and there will be days when it will drive you insane.'

He paused, and his voice softened.

'But you'll be here in Washington, Kelly, you'll be out of the worst of the mayhem for a while, and maybe it will give you time to readjust. And if that happens, and we can keep you in the Bureau, it will be worth it. What do you say?'

Kelly was staring at Lazenby, her mouth open.

'Director, I'm… I'm overwhelmed. This was the last thing I expected. I thought…'

'You thought what? That we were going to let you go?'

Kelly nodded.

'I didn't know what else to think.'

Lazenby laughed.

'Well, we're not. Not without a fight. Your record speaks for itself. You're smart, you're courageous, you have initiative, and you want to make a difference. That's an unusual combination in any organization, the Bureau included, and I want you on my side.'

'I don't know what to say.'

'Well, how about 'Yes'?'

Kelly took a deep breath and released it sharply.

'Sir, are you sure about this? I've been around long enough to know that being your assistant is a senior assignment in the Bureau. Won't there be people who resent…?'

'That's my problem,' Lazenby replied firmly. 'All I need to hear from you is yes, or no. Look, if you want, you can go right back to Cancun. No one will hold it against you. But, if you still want to make a difference, I'm offering you the chance to do it.'

Kelly looked at Lazenby for a few seconds, then got to her feet abruptly.

'Actually, Director, I do need to go back to Cancun.'

'Oh…?'

'To collect the rest of my things.'

3

KELLY WAS LYING on her back on the sofa in the living room of her apartment, wearing an oversized sweatshirt, jeans and socks, and nursing a Coke. At five feet, nine inches, her slim figure took up almost the full length of the sofa. She had bright blue eyes, and jet black hair, cut stylishly short.

She stopped laughing long enough to interrupt the stream of complaints coming at her over the phone.

'But Linda, it's an honor to guard the President.'

'It is not an honor to hang around his hotel rooms and listen to him having orgasms,' Linda Samuels insisted.

She paused.

'Jesus, Kelly, I shouldn't be saying this on the phone. You're sure this line is secure, right?'

'I'm sure,' Kelly replied. 'Anyway, what difference does it make? Everyone knows he sleeps around. It's not exactly news.'

'That wouldn't help me if it leaked out because of me. I wouldn't tell anyone except you. It's all so demeaning, Kelly. And you ought to see this one. She's so fucking superior. She makes me want to throw up.'

'What's she like?'

'Foreign. Expensive clothes. Good-looking, I have to give her that. The Boss has good taste in that department. But she acts as if she owns him.'

'How does he keep her from the First Lady?'

'Oh, that's easy enough, with our cooperation. If the President wants to see someone, we know exactly how to arrange it discreetly. It's been part of our job since Kennedy's day, longer according to some. Senior agents take you to one side and explain it to you when you're first assigned to the Detail.'

'My God, what a use of the tax-payers' money,' Kelly said.

24

'Tell me about it.'

'Well, it's your own fault. You had to choose the Secret Service. You could have come with me to Quantico.'

'I'd already spent most of my life with you. We went all the way through school and college together.'

'So, you couldn't stand me any more? I thought we were to be life-long friends.'

'We are,' Linda insisted. 'You know how much you've always meant to me, Kelly. You remember me back in the old days, a kid from the wrong side of the tracks with alcoholics for parents. If it hadn't been for you and your parents, God only knows what…'

Kelly sat up.

'Don't start on that, Linda,' she said gently. 'You got yourself out of that, you made a life for yourself, and you did a damn good job of it.'

'I'm just saying you've been my friend. You stuck with me.'

'And you stuck with me.'

Linda sighed.

'Oh, I'm sorry, Kelly. I'm just upset, that's all. I'll get over it.'

'I don't blame you for being upset.'

'Maybe I should have gone with you to Quantico. I just didn't see myself as an FBI agent at the time. But maybe I'm having second thoughts. Maybe it's not too late. What do you think?'

'I think you had a bad day.'

'The job sucks sometimes.'

'Every job sucks sometimes.'

Linda laughed.

'Yeah, you're right, I know. Oh, the hell with it. We're back in Washington tomorrow, and the First Lady is in residence. Perhaps he'll give it a rest for a while. Let's change the subject. How's the love life?'

'It's fine when we have time,' Kelly said. 'It's just that Frank and I have such different schedules. It's getting harder and harder to spend enough time together.'

'He's still with Senator O'Brien, right?'

'Yes. Frank's Chief of Staff now. He's thinking of running for office himself eventually. But the trouble is, he would have to start back in Minneapolis. I don't relish the thought of a commuter relationship. How about you?'

'No better.'

'Have you heard from Bob?'

'No.'

'You still miss him?'

'Yes, the bastard.'

Kelly sighed into the phone.

'Some men don't know when they're well off,' she said. In the silence, the phone beeped.

'Damn,' Kelly said. 'That's the call I'm expecting, Linda. Got to go. Call me tomorrow, OK?'

'OK'

'Love you.'

'Love you,' Linda said, hanging up.

Kelly clicked in the incoming call.

'Phil?'

'Kelly?'

'Yes. Hey, there. How's it going out there in Oregon?'

'The Portland field office has never looked so beautiful,' Agent Phil Hammond replied.

Kelly laughed.

'Now, Phil, don't be bitter. It's just a temporary assignment.'

'Easy for you to say.'

'So what's up?'

'We've been keeping surveillance on Carlson and Rogers round the clock. They are the brains behind the Sons of the Land, Kelly, no doubt about it. They're both nasty pieces of work, too.'

'I know. I saw their rap sheets.'

'It goes a long way beyond that. At first, we had them down as your typical racist malcontents, preaching the usual gospel of reclaiming America for the White Man. But that's pretty routine out here. I have a feeling this goes much farther.'

Kelly pulled herself back up into a sitting position.

'Are they still holing up in that compound or whatever out in the country?'

'Yeah, most of the time. We can't get close to it. It's fenced in, and they have guards with some impressive fire power. So we're watching from a distance. Oh, and get this, Kelly. The last couple of days, they've had visitors in dark suits carrying briefcases. Definitely not your usual paramilitary types. Stood out a mile. And Carlson and Rogers seemed to be rolling out the red carpet for them.'

'So, what do you think? Mob?'

'I don't think so.'

'Why not?'

'They don't have that look. More like Wall Street. Anyway, I can't see what angle the Mob would have with these guys.'

'Who might show up at a paramilitary compound dressed for Wall Street?'

'I don't know. For some reason, I'm getting the impression that these people might not be Americans. We're trying to get some decent pictures. We have satellite coverage 24/7, but they're a bit camera-shy and we haven't had much luck with close-ups as yet. If we do, I'll send them to you. If you can't identify them, could we ask the Agency?'

'Sure. Are they using mobiles?'

'Not a lot. These guys are very aware, very discreet, but we have our analysts ready in case they do break cover.'

Hammond paused.

'What?' Kelly asked.

'I'm thinking, the only way to get to them may be to go in undercover.'

'Jesus, Phil,' Kelly said. 'You need to think about that. It could be very dangerous. And you would need authorization from the top.'

'I know. I have to report to the Director anyway. I'll probably fly back for a couple of days on Friday. At least that way I can enjoy a weekend of civilization.'

'You're just an East Coast chauvinist. There's nothing wrong with Portland.'

'Come out and savor it with me.'

'Gee, I wish I could, Phil,' Kelly grinned. 'I'm sick that my schedule's so full here.'

'Yeah, right. Look, I'll call in tomorrow.'

'OK. Take care, Phil.'

'You too, Kelly.'

Kelly hung up. She was almost ready to go to bed for the night. But something was troubling her and, try as she might, she could not work out what it was. She lay back down on the sofa, switched on the television, and finally fell asleep where she lay, watching a late-night talk show.

4

CONGRESSMAN GEORGE STANLEY, his face an angry red, was pacing furiously around John Mason's office. Stanley was short, and had trouble staying with the diets his wife continually planned for him.

'I don't know why we waste our money supporting this so-called think tank when you people can't ever think of anything,' he shouted.

Mason, sitting calmly behind his desk, was wearing a faint smile. In his mid-thirties, he had already built a successful legal career in Washington, representing the interests of the Party. For now, his reward was the directorship of the Wilson Foundation. Very few decisions at the highest Party levels were made without input from the Wilson Foundation, which meant that Mason was privy to most of the Party's secrets. He also knew where most of the bodies were buried, which meant that some influential people had good reason to be grateful for his discretion. For now, he was content to enjoy his large office, substantial salary, and almost limitless expense account. Somewhere down the road, at a time of his own choosing, he would call in the favors he was owed and walk into elective office. Mason was tall and effortlessly self-assured, his gray-blue eyes piercing. He was well past the point of being intimidated by average congressmen such as George Stanley.

'We do what we can, Congressman,' he replied smoothly. 'We are looking into every possible angle.'

'How many angles can there be?' Stanley protested. 'I only see one angle. The man can't keep his pants zipped up for more than a day. He's running around the whole damn time.'

'As is just about every other politician in Washington,' Mason replied maliciously.

He raised a placating hand as Stanley wheeled on him.

'Present company excepted, naturally. But the American people knew that before he was elected, and they elected him anyway. Twice. It's just not an issue right now, in light of his popularity.'

Stanley walked slowly over to Mason's desk. He leaned forward and placed both hands on its polished cherrywood surface, allowing his ample body to hang over it. His attempt to look intimidating amused Mason, but he diplomatically suppressed his smile.

'The Committee wants to make an issue of it.'

'And how does the Committee suggest we do that?' Mason asked.

'That's your job.'

Mason shook his head. He had a lot of work to do, and Stanley was wasting his time.

'As I told you, Congressman, we are doing what we can. We are monitoring the situation, and if we come up with anything promising, I assure you we will pass it on to the Committee.'

'The man is totally unfit to hold the office of President of the United States.'

'If you apply that standard, so were most of the men who have held it before.'

'We want him gone.'

Mason stood and looked directly into Stanley's eyes.

'You know, George, you might want to be careful what you say. Even here. Even to me. God forbid some crazy person should take a shot at the President after you go on record saying something like that.'

Congressman Stanley stepped back a couple of paces and suddenly sounded unsure of himself.

'Jesus, John, I didn't mean anything like that, for God's sake. It's the fact that the man was elected, that the people actually…'

'I agree,' Mason said. 'But the people have that right. I think it's in the Constitution somewhere. And, unfortunately, the people don't always agree with us, and we sometimes lose elections. It's part of the democratic process.'

'Perhaps if you people put more effort into showing the people the truth about their President, that might change.'

'Perhaps if the Committee put a little more effort into selecting a candidate people might actually want to vote for, we might do better next time.'

Congressman Stanley thought about continuing the argument, but Mason's manner made it abundantly clear that it would be a waste of time. He decided to retreat without further loss of face.

'I'll see what the Committee has to say. I'll talk to you later.'

'I'll look forward to it.'

Stanley turned abruptly and walked out of the office.

Mason remained standing, staring down at this desk, long enough to rein in his frustration and gather his thoughts. Much as he would have liked to, he could not afford simply to ignore Stanley's visit and the lurid interest it suggested on the part of the Committee. While he was not about to be intimidated by George Stanley, the Committee paid the bills, and, if he could not persuade the Committee to drop the thorny question of the President's indiscretions, he would eventually have to produce some usable material for them. On the subject of political wisdom, he could only advise. The Committee contained calmer and wiser heads than George Stanley's and, with any luck, they would prevail. But just in case, he needed a back-up plan. Resuming his seat, Mason called his secretary on the intercom.

'Helen, bring me some coffee. I don't want to be disturbed for the rest of the morning. And get Selvey on the phone.'

'Very good, Mr. Mason,' Helen replied in her native Oxford English accent, which the Committee found so charming.

He picked up a file from the stack on his desk, and was still reading it when Helen entered, tray in hand.

'Coffee,' she announced. 'And Selvey's on two.'

'Thanks.'

He picked up the telephone.

'Selvey?'

'Yo.' The voice was that of a middle-aged man with a thick New York accent.

'That woman we were talking about the other day? What was her name?'

'The one that's with the President?'

'Yeah.'

'Lucia Benoni.'

'Is it for real?'

'Oh, yeah.'

'Does the press know about it?'

Selvey gave a contemptuous snort. 'The press couldn't find Dolly Parton in a phone booth.'

'I take it that's a 'No'?'

'It's a 'No'. But it's also only a matter of time. Somebody will screw up.'

Mason took a deep breath.

'Don't do anything just yet, but be ready to move on it. I may want you to hand them the story.'

'What story? The President's banging some new broad? Big fucking deal. If it snows in Buffalo in January it would be more interesting.'

'I understand. But we may have to give it to them anyway.'

'Why?'

'Because I need the goddamned Committee off my back, that's why. I had to waste over an hour with that moron George Stanley this morning. I may need to throw them a bone, distract them for a while.'

'This story is not going to distract anybody. It's going nowhere, John. It's bullshit.'

'Maybe so. Get ready to do it anyway.'

Mason heard an exasperated sigh on the other end of the line.

'Whatever you say.'

'Thank you.'

Mason replaced the receiver, and pushed the intercom button.

'Helen, I need full press monitoring for a certain subject starting tomorrow until I tell you otherwise.'

'Yes, Sir. Who or what are we looking for?'

'Our friend Steve and a babe called Lucia Benoni.'

'Oh. Is it going to be interesting?'

'Not especially. But it will keep the client happy for a while.'

Though she would never have admitted it, this was the part of her job Helen enjoyed most.

'No problem, Mr. Mason,' she said brightly.

5

LINDA SAMUELS WAS on duty outside the Oval Office when Martha Graylor, the President's Press Secretary, arrived. Linda and Martha liked each other. They had hit it off instantly when Linda had first been assigned to the Detail. Martha had the gift of not taking herself too seriously. She was a cheerful forty-five year old, with the classic Irish combination of dark hair and sparkling blue eyes, an infectious smile, and a wicked sense of humor. Her energy made her appear taller than her five feet five inches of height, and made sure that her figure did no more than fill out her frame. She had worked with Steve Wade ever since he had been governor of his state, and had the reputation of being his most intimate confidante, of having his ear on the most sensitive questions. Martha was carrying a large stack of papers which seemed to be weighing her down.

'Good morning, Agent Samuels.'

'Good morning, Miss Graylor. Looks like they're still keeping you busy.'

'Oh, just a little light reading,' Martha smiled. 'In case I got bored over dinner last night. Are they ready for us in the press room?'

'Let me check for you.'

Linda put her radio on transmit, and turned the volume down to minimize the crackle.

'You guys ready down there?'

'Almost, Linda,' Agent Gary Mills responded. 'Give us five.'

'Five. Roger that,' Linda said. She turned back to Martha. 'They'll be ready by the time you get down there. Here, let me get the door for you.'

'Thanks,' Martha smiled. 'If I have to carry much more of this stuff around, I'm going to apply for some of that danger money you people get.'

Linda knocked on the door of the Oval Office, then opened it for Martha without waiting for a response.

Martha dispensed a smile around the room, and waited for her chance to speak. The President was with Ted Lazenby and his Vice President, Ellen Trevathan. Ellen was not a career politician. She had started out as a university professor. Her writings on public administration got her noticed, and she soon made the move from a tenured professorship at George Mason University to the first of a number of high-level government jobs. At just over six feet, she almost towered over the stocky Lazenby. Handsome and dignified, with short gray hair and blue eyes, she had a natural gift for dealing with people, with a charisma of her own just as appealing as the President's, many people said. Steve Wade trusted Ellen, and allowed her an unusual freedom of action. Taking full advantage of this, she had steadily built a reputation in Washington as someone who said little in public, but quietly got things done behind the scenes. Her trademark gray-black suits cut high at the neck, Nehru style, were a familiar sight in the corridors of power.

'Our people are keeping a close eye on them, Mr. President,' Lazenby was saying. 'But with all due respect, I don't think we can write them off as just another gang of crazies. Our intelligence suggests there may be more to it.'

'I can't say I'm losing too much sleep over them,' the President replied. 'What is it they call themselves again?'

'The Sons of the Land,' Ellen Trevathan grinned. 'Sounds more like a Boy Scout troop than a serious anarchist group.'

'Don't be misled by the name, Madam Vice President,' Lazenby replied. 'They're serious, all right. Our agents report that they have a well-organized operation and the satellite picked up some very useful hardware. We also believe they're working on some kind of common cause with other such groups in the Pacific Northwest. We've seen some familiar faces visit them in the last week or two. The general rule in the past has been that these kinds of groups hate each other more than they hate the Government.'

'I thought Obama kind of brought them together,' Wade said, with a thin smile.

'For a while,' Lazenby replied, 'but it didn't seem to last very long. So, up till now, we've been assuming these guys had reverted to their old ways as sworn enemies. But recently, the Sons of the Land have been rolling out the red carpet for the other groups. There's something going on out there.'

'Some kind of organization building?' Wade asked.

'That's the way it looks.'

'An organization of anarchists?' Ellen asked. 'Sounds like a contradiction in terms, doesn't it?'

Both men smiled.

'Yes, Ma'am,' Lazenby said. 'But they could turn into quite a force if they get their act together. Even now, I'm not sure there's any way to take them down. We couldn't go in there without risking a repeat of Waco.'

Steve Wade shuddered.

'Forget that. Any way of infiltrating them?'

'We're working on it. The field agents are due to report with an assessment this afternoon.'

Lazenby reached into an inside pocket of his jacket and took out a small brown envelope. 'The other thing that concerns me, Mr. President, is this.'

He handed the envelope to the President who, with Ellen looking over his shoulder, opened it and took out a single black-and-white photograph. It was a distant and not too clear shot of a man wearing a black suit, a dark gray tie over a white shirt, and shades, standing by the main gate of the Sons of the Land's Oregon compound. Despite the lack of focus, there was something about the man's appearance and dress that suggested he was not American.

'Who's this?'

Wade handed the photograph on to Ellen.

'I just found out myself. The picture was taken yesterday by Phil Hammond, one of the field agents we have in place. Phil sent it to us in the hope we could identify the guy, but the Bureau had nothing matching.'

'So, how did you…?'

'We ran it by the Agency and State. State nailed him.'

'The State Department? Are you telling us he's a diplomat?' Ellen asked, looking sharply at Steve Wade.

Lazenby nodded.

'His name is Hamid Marfrela. Assistant cultural attaché with the Lebanese delegation to Washington. Fairly junior, been in station about two years.'

'Suspected of irregular activities?' Steve Wade asked.

'Not till now. State had no particular concerns. Not until he showed up in Oregon.'

'I hope that got their attention.'

'It did. Oregon seems a strange place for a Lebanese cultural attaché to be plying his trade. Mr. Marfrela may have a little explaining to do.'

President Wade walked around the office, and eventually came to rest, leaning with his back against his desk.

'How sure are State about this? That's not a great picture, and he's wearing shades, for God's sake.'

'They were able to enhance it, Mr. President. You wouldn't believe the things they can do these days. They're sure.'

Wade nodded.

'You understand there are certain political considerations in the case of Lebanon?'

'Yes, Mr. President,' Lazenby replied at once.

'We must be careful about this. What are your people doing about it?'

'Keeping their heads down for now. State asked us to put a tail on him. Unless you have an objection, I'll have someone pick it up tomorrow. We're not sure whether he's back in town yet. But I don't want to give away the fact that we're on to him.'

Out of the corner of his eye, Steve Wade saw Martha Graylor move into his line of vision. 'Time to go,' she mouthed silently.

The President nodded.

'No objection. Just make sure the watchers are discreet. Keep me informed, Ted. I have to run to my press conference.'

'I will, Mr. President.'

* * *

'Talk to me on the way,' Wade said to Martha. He strode purposefully from the room for the short walk through the West Wing from the Oval Office to the press briefing room, with his Vice President and Press Secretary close behind, Martha struggling to keep up, still clutching her stack of papers. Linda Samuels fell in unobtrusively by his side.

'Good morning, Agent Samuels.'

'Good morning, Mr. President.'

'Am I safe?'

Linda smiled. It was the President's standard pleasantry with her.

'I believe you are, Sir.'

She deliberately increased her pace, walking a little ahead of the President so as to avoid appearing to overhear his conversation, and checked in with Gary Mills on her radio.

'What's new, Martha?' the President asked.

'Nothing much. Usual stuff. Lebanon, Israel, oil, unemployment. You read the briefs yesterday. If I may, Mr. President, I do need to remind you about your agreement with the British Prime Minister…'

'Keep quiet about our options if the oil supply is threatened. I remember.'

'I think that's about it.'

They paused outside the door of the press room. Linda Samuels walked briskly inside. Automatically, Martha scanned Steve Wade's appearance for any fault, however small. She adjusted his tie. Linda reappeared.

'All clear, Mr. President.'

'Looking good, Mr. President,' Martha said. 'Go get'em.'

The standing ovation and loud applause which greeted Steve Wade everywhere he went was one of the things he liked best about the job. It happened even in the White House press briefing room. The veteran news reporters who frequented it seemed to be swept up in the adulation almost as much as the general public. Wade relaxed as he reached the podium, and raised his hands to call for quiet. Gradually, the applause died away, the reporters retook their seats, and the questioning began. It was a routine press conference, and the President was not expected to make a prepared statement. He was, however, expected to answer questions on a wide range of topics. Steve Wade had the reputation of being the master of his briefs and of being adept at fielding even the toughest questions. Today seemed to be no exception. Effortlessly, he explained his policy in the Middle East and the oil question, and ventured a few sage remarks about where the experts thought the economy was heading. The press conference was nearly over, and Martha Graylor was leaning comfortably against the wall by the door through which the President had entered. A woman reporter raised her hand. The President smiled and pointed a finger.

'Mary.'

'Thank you, Mr. President. Mary Sullivan, *Washington Post*. Mr. President, I'm sure you're aware that your name is being linked in some quarters with a woman named Lucia Benoni. I wondered if you had any comment?'

Martha stood bolt upright. The President missed perhaps half a beat.

'Linked? I'm not sure what you mean.'

'Linked romantically, according to my source, Mr. President.'

'Oh, for Heaven's sake. What was this lady's name?'

'Lucia Benoni, Mr. President.'

The President bestowed his brightest smile.

'I'm sorry to disappoint you, Mary, but the name means nothing to me at all. And I'm not linked to anyone except the First Lady.'

Martha allowed her head to sink on to her chest.

'Fuck,' she muttered under her breath.

'With all due respect, Mr. President,' Mary Sullivan continued calmly, 'you have in the past admitted...'

'Mary, I'm surprised that *The Washington Post* would give any credence to a story like this. We went through all that during the election campaign. I did make mistakes in the past. I admitted that, I repented, and my wife forgave me. We have a good marriage today, and that's all I'm going to say on that subject.'

'So you deny any association with this woman, Lucia Benoni?'

'Categorically. I've never even heard of her. I don't know who she is, if she exists at all.'

Martha Graylor was gesturing to him frantically with her head.

'Now, I'm sorry, Ladies and Gentlemen. That's it for today. Martha will be with you tomorrow.'

Ignoring a loud chorus of shouted questions, Steve Wade walked out of the press room and led the way back to the Oval Office at a furious pace. When he walked at full speed, even Linda Samuels had trouble keeping up with him. Ellen Trevathan and Martha Graylor were trailing by quite a distance.

'Where the hell did that come from?' Wade shouted over his shoulder.

'From left field,' Martha replied. 'We had no inkling.'

The President paused outside the Office.

'Well, we need to damn well get an inkling. See what you can find out. I'm not going to let those bastards assassinate me again. If the *Post* is running a story like this, someone out there must have some information. Let's put the lid on this now.'

'All right,' Martha said. 'And you're sure you don't know...?'

'No.' Steve Wade held up his hands. 'No, I don't. I really don't know.'

With a brief glance in the Vice President's direction, Martha walked away towards her own office. Linda Samuels turned her back, pretending to be absorbed in her radio.

'Can I come in for a moment?' Ellen asked.

Wade nodded. They entered the Oval Office together.

Ellen waited until Steve Wade had seated himself at his desk. She drew herself up to her full height, and folded her arms across her chest.

'You promised me there would be no more of this crap.'

'There isn't, Ellen. I have no idea what's going on here, but I intend to find out.'

The Vice President looked straight into the President's eyes.

'Steve, you know how much this means to me. You know I'm thinking of running next time. I don't want this sort of stuff going on any more. It nearly screwed us in both campaigns.'

Wade stood, appearing agitated.

'What do you want me to say, Ellen? They come up with some name I've never even heard of, right out of the blue. What do you want me to say?'

'I want to hear you swear it's not true. If you lie to me about this…'

The President gritted his teeth.

'I swear to you. It's not true. Is that what you wanted? Can I carry on with what's left of my morning now?'

Ellen nodded briefly and headed for the door. She paused and turned back towards him on her way out.

'Thank you.'

Steve Wade sat back down, and prepared himself for another unpleasant confrontation. He picked up his internal phone to speak to his private secretary.

'Where's the First Lady?'

'Having her hair done, then lunch with the Capitol Hill Wives, Mr. President.'

'Ask her to see me as soon as she gets back.'

'Yes, Sir.'

'I mean as soon as she gets back.'

'Yes, Mr. President.'

'And get the Director of the FBI on the phone. On a secure line.'

* * *

In the privacy of her office, Martha Graylor was on the phone with Harold Philby, the editor of *The Washington Post* and one of the doyens of the Capital's press corps. The tone of Philby's voice as he wished her a good day suggested some amusement, which was almost as irritating to Martha as the questions his reporter had asked at the press conference.

'What can I do for you today, Martha?'

'You can start by giving me the head of Mary Sullivan on a silver platter. I can't believe you of all people would ambush us like that.'

'Mary followed the rules, Martha. We got the story at the last minute, but it has substance.'

'Says who?'

The editor remained silent.

'I won't forget this, Harold. You could have called me this morning.'

'We just wanted to get a reaction. I doubt we'll go any further with it unless the woman herself comes forward.'

'So she's not your source?'

Another silence. Then Philby gave a little.

'No, she's not.'

'Are you going to talk to her?'

'I'm not sure. We're having a conference this afternoon. We won't publish anything without giving you the chance to comment.'

'You've had all the comment you're going to get from us.'

'Oh, I wouldn't put money on that,' Philby replied quietly.

'For God's sake, Harold. You don't have to chase down every piece of tittle-tattle that crosses your desk. You could use a little discretion.'

'It's not personal, Martha,' Philby said. 'It's just a story. You, of all people, should know that by now.'

Martha hung up. She lowered her head into her hands.

'Jesus Christ,' she said to herself, out loud. 'Here we go again.'

6

KELLY AND FRANK had been asleep for only a short time when the telephone rang. Frank had just returned from a long road-trip with Senator O'Brien, and they had celebrated his return in Kelly's apartment with Chinese food and a bottle of Pinot Blanc. Kelly had sunk into a deep, dreamless sleep. When the jarring sound of the phone finally penetrated her senses, she was disoriented, feeling that she was hearing a sound from some other world which did not really concern her. The phone rang insistently several times before she slowly raised herself on to one shoulder, reached over to the small bedside table, and picked up. Frank appeared not to have heard the ringing; he was lying on his side with his back to Kelly, breathing rhythmically.

'Smith,' she said quietly into the receiver. Under her breath, she added: 'God, this better be good.'

'Kelly?' Lazenby said, 'I'm sorry to call at this hour.'

Slowly, Kelly sat up, rubbing her eyes.

'Director? I'm sorry. I was dead to the world. What hour is it?'

'It's a little after three,' Ted Lazenby said apologetically.

Kelly shook her head vigorously in an effort to force her brain into gear.

'OK, Sir. Go ahead.'

'I just got a call from Henry Bryson, the Chief of Police for the District. They have a murder in North West, and they think we should take a look at it. For some reason, the Chief didn't want to go into detail over the phone. I hate to do this to you, but I need you to go find out what's going on.'

'A murder in the District? What does that have to do with us? What jurisdiction do we have?'

Frank was waking up, and was looking at her sleepily, his head raised off the pillow a little. She kissed her first finger and placed it on his lips, shaking her head to tell him to go back to sleep.

'The same jurisdiction we always have in the District, joint jurisdiction with the D.C. Police. You know how it works.'

'Well, yes, Sir, but we would generally defer to them unless there's something…'

'As I said, Kelly, Chief Bryson didn't want to go into it on the phone. But jurisdiction isn't an issue as far as he's concerned. There's something there he needs us to take a look at, and at this point, I have to assume it's important.'

Kelly struggled to pull herself upright, and again tried to signal to Frank to go back to sleep.

'Sir, with all due respect, jurisdiction may not be a problem for the Chief, but I need to know it isn't a problem for us before I go trampling all over a D.C. Police crime scene.'

'It's not a problem for us. He's asking for our cooperation. He understands what's involved, and he assures me he'll take care of it. Get something to write with and I'll give you the address. I want you over there right away. You're not to discuss whatever this is with anyone except me. Call me at home as soon as you can get to a secure line.'

Kelly made a note of the details.

'Any questions?'

Frank was fully awake now, and his look was one of irritation. She turned her back to him and lowered her voice.

'Director, is there any chance you could send someone else? Frank just got back into town, and we…'

Her voice trailed away, and there was silence on the other end of the line.

'I'm on my way, Sir,' she said.

She turned back to Frank, replacing the receiver.

'I'm sorry, sweetheart.'

He was climbing angrily out of bed. She held out her hand towards him.

'No, Frank. You don't need to get up. I'll be back in a couple of hours. Go back to sleep.'

He was searching for his clothes.

'Maybe, one of these days, we can have some kind of life.'

Kelly tried to keep calm, but her own fatigue was kicking in, and she felt her voice become sharp.

'What are you talking about?'

'You heard me. God damn it, we can't even get a few hours of good sleep without the phone ringing off the hook.'

Kelly shook her head.

'Hey, I'm not the one who's at the beck and call of a senator twenty-four hours a day, and who goes out of town without saying goodbye. What are you making such a big deal about? I have a job too, you know. I'll be back by the time you wake up.'

'I've already woken up, in case you haven't noticed.'

'You know what I mean, Frank. Don't do this. Go back to sleep. I'll be back soon. It's probably nothing.'

But he was getting dressed as quickly as he could.

'No. I'll get out of your hair.'

Kelly sat down miserably on the side of the bed.

'I don't want you out of my hair. Frank…'

He was stepping into his shoes, and taking his car keys from the dressing-table.

'I don't want to discuss it,' he said.

'Fine,' she replied. 'Neither do I.'

Helplessly, Kelly watched as he opened the bedroom door.

'Frank, please don't go. Not like this.'

He turned back towards her, and for a moment, Kelly thought she saw a look of guilt cross his face.

'Call me later,' he said, closing the door behind him.

She wiped her eyes.

'Oh, sure,' she said.

* * *

Kelly drove quickly through the deserted early-morning streets of the District. It was cool and overcast, and a light drizzle was falling. She wore a thick sweater under her black FBI jacket. The address Lazenby had given her was an upmarket apartment building in North West, just off Wisconsin Avenue. She knew the building. It was one which had become fashionable with some members of Congress as a Washington base. She had visited it before, on occasions when she had found it necessary to ask a legislator one or two questions which called for a certain degree of discretion, questions which were better not asked at a public venue such as the FBI's Headquarters. She remembered the building's expensive taste in artwork, and had speculated that it was probably not a cheap place to live. And now somebody there was dead, and the Chief of Police for the District was anxious to share jurisdiction. As she approached the building, Kelly saw several D.C. police cars parked outside the front entrance to the building with their emergency call lights flashing. At the entrance, two uniformed officers were talking to the concierge. As she was driving her private car, Kelly parked in the next block, and walked towards the officers, holding up her badge. One of the officers inspected it and waved her inside.

'It's Number 462, Agent. The Chief asked that you go up as soon as you arrived. You are welcome to use the elevator. The scenes-of-crimes people are through with it now.'

'Thank you.'

Kelly walked across the foyer, a massive space with a proportionately high ceiling and marble floor, ornate crystal chandeliers and ponderous fixtures. Two confused-looking night janitors, hispanic women, were sitting on a red velvet sofa in the center of the foyer, talking quietly to each other in Spanish. Kelly smiled comfortingly and greeted them in the same language, then entered the elevator and punched the button for the fourth floor.

The fourth floor was swarming with police officers. One met her as she emerged from the elevator and inspected her badge carefully before directing her to apartment 462. Along the way, she noticed the doors of several other apartments slightly ajar, their occupants trying to get a look at whatever might be going on. The door of apartment 462 was open, but access was restricted by yellow crime-scene tape. Kelly's badge was inspected yet again before she was allowed to cross the threshold. The officer asked her to wait at the door. Moments later, he returned with Henry Bryson, Chief of Police for the District of Columbia. To Kelly's surprise, despite the antisocial hour, he was formally dressed in a suit and tie. Bryson motioned to her to follow him into the living room. One or two forensic officers were at work in one corner of the room, but there was apparently no reason to cordon off the rest of it.

'How can we help, Chief?' Kelly asked.

'We have a little problem here, Agent Smith. A murder.'

'Your people seem to have it covered, Sir. As you know, the Bureau has a very specific policy on jurisdiction, and the average murder in the District...'

'I'm aware of that, Agent Smith,' Bryson said sharply. 'I've already had that conversation with your Director, and I don't have time to go through it again.'

Kelly nodded patiently.

'Of course, Sir.'

Bryson took a deep breath.

'Believe me, if I thought this was an average murder, I would hardly have got the Director of the FBI out of bed in the middle of the night. I think we both know Ted Lazenby too well for that.'

Kelly grinned.

'Yes, Sir.'

'The only reason I'm out of bed myself is that one of my officers found something he thought needed my attention. I think he was right. I'll get to that in a moment. First, let me show you what we have in the bedroom.'

Bryson motioned Kelly to follow him. At the door of the bedroom, he stopped and turned to her.

'I take it you've seen this kind of thing before,' he said. 'It's not very nice in there.'

'Yes, I have, Sir,' Kelly said. 'But thank you.'

The Chief led the way into the bedroom and signaled to an officer in plain clothes, who appeared to be inspecting something on a dressing-table, to join them.

'Agent Smith, this is Lieutenant Jeff Morris, who works for me out of our Headquarters. Jeff, Agent Kelly Smith, FBI'

Kelly shook hands with Lieutenant Morris. His grip was firm. He was just a shade taller than Kelly, dressed in a dark gray sports jacket which suited him well. His black hair had some flecks of premature white, but this did not prevent him from looking young for his rank. He smiled at her.

'Jeff was the one who called me, Agent Smith, so I'm going to let him tell you all about it. Go ahead, Jeff.'

'Yes, Sir. Agent, we have a female, probably mid-thirties, shot once in the back of the head, execution style. Her hands were tied behind her back, and her feet were tied together.'

Morris pointed to the bed, where the naked body lay on its stomach, a pool of blood and brains splashed liberally over the bed and on the wall behind the head.

'The coroner says she's been dead about three hours, and she'd had recent sexual intercourse. There is semen on her body and on the sheets. That's all subject to the test results, of course, but there doesn't seem much doubt about it.'

'Do we know who she is?' Kelly asked.

Lieutenant Morris picked up a plastic evidence bag which contained a black purse.

'This was on the dresser. Inside we found two passports, one U.S. and one Lebanese. Both are in the name of a Lucia Benoni. The photos seem to match the body. She also had a New York driver's licence, which gives an address in Manhattan. NYPD is checking it out, but we haven't heard back from them yet.'

'Do you have anything on her?'

'No criminal record. But she was carrying a little over $5,000 in cash.'

'Anything else?'

'A set of keys.'

'Car keys?'

'No, for a building. Not this one. Could be her place in New York.'

'What else?'

'Just the usual make-up items, perfume, lipstick, a small pack of tissues, and some Advil.'

Kelly walked over and looked at the body for a few moments.

'Well, apparently it wasn't a robbery, since the money is still there. So, you figure, what? A Mob hit, a sexual affair that went bad, a drug deal?'

'Those would all be possibilities. The sex doesn't suggest a Mob deal to me, but you guys are the experts in that field. And if it was a drug deal, I wouldn't expect to find the money still there, either.'

'I agree,' Kelly said. 'Where are her clothes?'

'Neatly hung up in the closet. That suggested to me that the sex was consensual. Let me show you.'

Smiling, Morris led Kelly to the spacious walk-in closet.

'You're way more qualified to look at these than I am.'

'So this is why you had to get me out of bed at three in the morning?'

Kelly followed Morris into the closet. It was empty apart from Lucia Benoni's clothes. She turned to Morris questioningly.

'Yes, I noticed that too. There's nothing in the whole place. No evidence that anyone lives here at all. We're checking with the building management. What do you think of the clothes?'

'Have the scenes-of-crimes people finished with them?'

'Yes. They're all yours.'

Kelly examined the labels on the jacket of the black two-piece suit and the white blouse. A real pearl pendant was pinned to the lapel of the jacket.

'These are Gianni Versace,' she said, holding them up for Morris to inspect.

'Translation?'

'European,' she said. 'Originals. Very expensive. I didn't get a good look at the purse, but I would bet it's in the same league.'

She bent down on one knee, and picked up a black pump.

'The shoes are, too. Fendi. Top of the line. Black stockings, and an old-fashioned garter belt. That's something you don't see every day.'

'Sexy,' Morris said.

'I wouldn't know,' Kelly grinned. 'What brand of perfume was she carrying?'

'Chanel. Even I know that one.'

Kelly stood back up.

'Well, it all supports the identification in the passports. If she's not European, she certainly spent some time in Europe. Milan, most likely, judging by the clothes and accessories. What stamps does she have in the passports?'

'Quite a few between Italy and the States, some for Lebanon, one or two for other European countries, France mostly.'

They walked slowly back out of the closet, through the bedroom, and then into the living room, where Chief Bryson was waiting for them. Kelly thought he looked nervous.

'What do you think?' he asked.

'Well,' Kelly replied, 'obviously, we have a rather exotic murder here, but I still don't know what interest the Bureau has in it.'

Morris looked at Bryson questioningly.

'Go ahead, Jeff,' Bryson said.

'We also found this, tucked away in her purse.'

Morris reached into the inside pocket of his jacket, and produced a small evidence bag containing a plastic card. In the top left-hand corner was a head-shot of Lucia Benoni.

'We've printed it. It's OK to touch.'

Kelly took it, and examined it closely.

'Jesus Christ,' she breathed.

'Is this what I think it is?' Bryson asked.

'I think so,' Kelly said. 'We would have to ask the Secret Service, but it looks very much like a special pass.'

'Her own private key to the White House,' Bryson observed somberly.

Kelly nodded.

'That's what made me think of calling Chief Bryson,' Morris said. 'Of course, for all I know, thousands of people have them. Or it could be a forgery.'

'You did the right thing,' Kelly said. 'If it's a forgery, it's a real beauty. And, no, this isn't an ordinary pass. They're issued to very few people.'

'Issued by whom?' Morris asked.

'Someone high up,' Kelly said. 'Probably head of department level. As far as I know. It's not really my area. As I said, we'll have to check it out with the Secret Service. They would have been asked to clear it. And I think we should ask the State Department to see if they have anything on Miss Benoni. I can take care of all that. I'll have to run it by Director Lazenby, but I'm sure he won't have any objections.'

Suddenly, Kelly looked up at Morris.

'Jeff, did you say she's been dead for only three hours?'

'Approximately, yes. According to the coroner.'

'How did you find her? Did someone report hearing a shot?'

'No,' Morris replied. 'We received a call.'

'From whom?'

'Anonymous. Male with some sort of foreign accent, according to the dispatcher.'

'So someone wanted you to find her?'

'So it would seem.'

A uniformed officer poked his head around the corner. Lieutenant Morris put the pass away in his inside jacket pocket.

'Excuse me, Sir,' the officer said to Bryson, 'The building manager called back. Apartment 462 is leased out on a two-year lease to a company called Middle and Near East Holdings, Incorporated. The company's head office is in…'

The officer paused to consult a note.

'Wilmington, Delaware,' Kelly finished the sentence for him.

The officer looked up in surprise.

'Yes, Ma'am.'

'When was the apartment leased to them?'

'Three months ago. The manager is pulling their file. He thinks they supplied references.'

'Thank you, Officer. Good job. That will be all,' Bryson said.

'Yes, Sir.'

'The Middle and Near East Laundry Company,' Jeff Morris observed dryly.

'Yes. And the head office will be a plaque on the wall of some office building,' Kelly added. 'All the same, we should check it out tomorrow. They are required to have officers and directors. We need to know who they are and what they do.'

'I'll take care of it,' Morris said.

'Well, there's no more we can do tonight,' Kelly said. 'Have your forensic people call me tomorrow, and I'll arrange to have the evidence looked at.'

She walked to the door, and then turned back.

'Oh, one more thing. I don't think we need any publicity on this. Certainly not yet.'

'I wasn't going to mention the pass to anyone, naturally,' Bryson said. 'I guess we'll just tell them that a Lucia Benoni was murdered by persons unknown, we have no suspect as yet, we're following several leads.'

'Can you hold off giving them her identity for a few days?' Kelly asked.

Bryson hesitated.

'On what basis?'

'How about, we haven't been able to notify her relatives as yet?' Jeff Morris asked.

'We don't even know whether she has any relatives,' Bryson replied.

'Exactly my point, Sir.'

Kelly smiled her thanks.

'There are some potentially nasty issues here, Chief. I'd like to give Director Lazenby some time to work out a strategy.'

Bryson nodded.

'I guess I could hold off for a couple of days. After that, they're going to be crawling all over me.'

'I appreciate it,' Kelly said on her way out.

7

THROUGH THE DARK-TINTED window of his small office in the Sons of the Land compound, the self-styled Commandant of the movement, George Carlson, could see the two sentries who guarded the main gate. They were dressed in the same green fatigues he wore himself, and carried Kalashnikov sub-machine guns, a sample of the arsenal the Sons of the Land had patiently been accumulating for several years from sources in Eastern Europe and the Middle East. Carlson was a small man, wiry and thin, with impenetrable black eyes and the suggestion of a wispy moustache just below his nose.

After serving in the United States Army for some years and rising to the rank of Corporal, Carlson had resigned out of boredom, and had entered what he liked to call the sphere of private enterprise. He saw action as a mercenary in several of the hottest trouble-spots in Africa. This experience, and some disenchanted white comrades in arms from South Africa and Zimbabwe, convinced him that the white race throughout the world stood in mortal peril from the threat posed by aggressive minority groups, and that the liberal United States Government was giving in to that threat without a fight. What chance did white people have? George Carlson found that he was a man with a message.

Periodically, Carlson returned to the United States to spread this message, and acquired a criminal record for violence in three different states. In his mid-forties, feeling the need for a permanent base, he settled in Oregon and devoted his time to finding an outlet for his cause. It was at that point that he became aware of the Sons of the Land. When he first encountered them, the Sons of the Land were nothing, a small, motley collection of losers with no military expertise and no discipline - laughable, really. Carlson changed that. He gathered well-trained, like-minded men around him, mostly contacts from his mercenary days. The existing members of the Sons of the Land were subjected to military training and discipline, and were so impressed with the results that they soon accepted Carlson as their unquestioned leader. Money began to flow in from various sources, including drug deals and even the occasional bank robbery. The money was exchanged for arms and ammunition. Carlson established ranks, a chain of command. The Sons of the Land were beginning to have confidence in themselves. Soon, they would be ready.

Carlson also changed the pattern of relations with like-minded groups, of which there were many scattered around the north-west of the country, ranging from individual family concerns in small townships to large well-organized bands spread over one or more counties, such as the Sons of the Land had become. When he arrived on the scene, it reminded him of the Mafia families – no cooperation, constant arguments, and sometimes turf wars, culminating in gun battles over drugs or money. It was the height of stupidity. It made everyone more vulnerable to spying by the Government, and it stood in the way of what needed to be done. Carlson eradicated this type of behaviour from the Sons of the Land and made overtures to other groups. Reaction was mixed at first. Many were suspicious. And for several years after 9/11 there was little progress anyway. The destruction of the Twin Towers, and the subsequent military involvement in Afghanistan and Iraq, united patriotic Americans behind the Government and diverted attention from what that Government was really doing. Recruitment was down and each group concentrated on its own agenda. But then Barack Hussein Obama arrived. Obama, who may or may not have been born in Hawaii, and who may or may not have been a Muslim – who cared? – and overnight the landscape changed again. To Carlson, Obama was good news and bad news. On the one hand, his election was anathema, the groups' worst nightmare, and irrefutable proof of how far things had gone wrong in liberal America. On the other hand, recruitment went through the roof for a while, and Carlson had no difficulty in persuading the other groups that the time had come to unite against the common foe. There were those idiots who channeled their anger into the Tea Party and similar nonsense, of course. But the real patriots, the ones who were prepared to do something to reclaim America, quietly joined one of the groups and settled down to wait for their chance. By now Carlson's group was recognized as the biggest and best, and he was becoming a star on a bigger stage.

The compound comprised almost five acres, and was surrounded by a tall, barbed-wire fence. Carlson's office, like the other buildings on the compound, was a Quonset hut, painted both inside and out in a dull gray. The fluorescent lighting cast a yellow glow over the interior – the tinted windows excluded most natural light. The coffee mugs and the ash-tray on Carlson's desk were made of battered tin and on the wall behind Carlson's desk was a large map of the United States, on which were several brightly-colored pins with paper flags attached. The remaining wall space was taken up with computer print-outs, some beginning to yellow with age.

Carlson was scanning the day's newspapers and other on-line news sources while watching CNN. It was part of his daily routine to keep track of any political developments which might be useful in promoting his strategy of undermining the corrupt Federal Government of the United States. Any news items of particular note would join the existing collection on the walls. The half-hour news segment on CNN was coming to an end, and was due to be followed by sports news, in which he had little interest. He turned the volume down to concentrate on *The Washington Post's* report that the President was denying any knowledge of a woman called Lucia Benoni.

'And in a late-breaking story,' the female anchor was saying, 'Police in Washington D.C. made a grisly discovery early this morning, and are giving away very few details of what appears to have been the brutal execution-style slaying of a young woman. Lisa Jones reports from Washington. Lisa?'

Carlson looked up and turned the volume back up. The scene switched to an apartment block. A perfectly made-up young woman reporter holding a microphone was standing in front of the building, the entrance to which was guarded by a uniformed police officer.

'Jennifer, very few details are available at this time, but sources tell CNN News that the body of a woman was found in the early hours of this morning by D.C. police officers in an apartment in this city-centre building. The woman, whose identity is still unknown, had been shot once in the back of the head. Police are refusing to supply details of the shooting, and will say only that they are following several leads. But a source close to the investigation, who asked not to be named, told me that the murdered woman appeared to be either European or Middle Eastern. Jennifer, I should add that this apartment building is very well known in Washington, because a number of senators and congressmen live here while Congress is in session. No word yet, though, on who occupied the apartment in which the body was found.'

'Lisa, do the police have any motive in this killing?'

'Jennifer, if they do, they're not saying anything right now. Of course, there's a great deal of speculation going on here, but I repeat, nothing definite at this stage.'

'I see. OK, thanks, Lisa.'

'You're welcome.'

The scene switched back to the CNN studio.

'And we'll update you as soon as we have any more information on this breaking story,' the anchor said. 'That's the news this half-hour. Sports is next.'

Carlson turned the volume down again, and returned to *The Washington Post*. Having finished the article about the President, he stared out of the window for some time, then walked into the adjoining room, where his second-in-command, Dan Rogers, was reclining in an armchair, drinking a beer. Rogers was a little taller than Carlson, and powerfully built. The edge of a black dragon tattoo was visible under his left shirt sleeve. Like Carlson, he wore his hair cropped short. The two men had met during a particularly unpleasant campaign in Angola, and had been friends ever since. Rogers had a genius for technical and mechanical things which Carlson lacked, and he had been happy to put his skills at the service of the Commandant in return for some home-made insignia which proclaimed his high rank in the Sons of the Land.

'Where did our friend say he was going after he left here?' Carlson asked.

Rogers took a swig of his beer.

'Washington. He said there was some more information he was expecting from his source. Why?'

'It's probably nothing, but CNN just reported a murder in Washington, a woman, believed to be either European or Middle Eastern. The police wouldn't give out a name. Just a coincidence, probably.'

'Surely, you don't think…?'

'Who knows?'

Rogers frowned.

'That doesn't make sense. Why would he want to waste her?'

'No reason that I can think of. But, then again, we are talking about our friend, aren't we? He's not the most stable of characters. You remember that time you had to pull him off that woman in Portland?'

'Yeah, but he's got his head screwed on, George. I can't see him doing anything that stupid. In any case, if he has, that's his problem.'

Carlson shook his head.

'It's our problem as well, if he gets picked up by the police. He knows too much.'

Rogers stood, finished his beer, and set the bottle down on a small table which stood beside his armchair.

'What do you want me to do?'

'Have someone up there watch him for a few days. Maybe everything's fine and dandy, but if it's not, I want to know about it.'

'I'll give our people a call,' Dan Rogers said.

8

KELLY WAS BEGINNING to suffer from lack of sleep. In the light of what had been discovered, she decided not to speak about Lucia Benoni's murder to Ted Lazenby over the phone. She needed to meet with him in person. After a hurried breakfast at an all-night café, she rushed home to shower and change, tried without success to reach Frank by phone, then drove swiftly to the Hoover Building. When she arrived, a little before seven, she found the Director waiting for her impatiently in his office. He seemed as agitated as she felt herself. As calmly as she could, Kelly gave Lazenby a full account of her visit to the North West crime scene. He listened tight-lipped, without interrupting, sitting nervously at his desk. When she finished, Lazenby stood and paced up and down for some time.

'This is great, just great,' he observed grimly. 'Where's the supposed White House pass?'

'With the officer in charge, Lieutenant Morris. It's their evidence, Sir, and it's still their case. I had no basis for asking for it. I'm not sure there's anything to worry about. There's probably a simple explanation.'

Lazenby looked at her directly.

'Is there? You obviously haven't read the papers yet. What have you been doing since you got back?'

'Trying to salvage what's left of my love life.'

Lazenby managed a weak smile of sympathy, as he pushed his copy of *The Washington Post* to her across his desk.

'This should take your mind off that for a while.'

'What am I looking at?'

'Piece by Mary Sullivan, top right.'

Kelly leaned forward and began to read.

'Holy shit,' she said when she had finished the article.

'My sentiments exactly.'

Kelly pushed the newspaper back across the desk.

'What are you going to do, Sir?'

'I'm going to have to tell the President. I don't think he's going to be exactly ecstatic, do you? Kelly, is there any chance of a mis-identification here?'

'I don't think so. All the documents they found were consistent, and the photos matched the body. No, I would say our body is definitely Lucia Benoni. I asked Chief Bryson to keep a lid on it. He said he would. I hope he wasn't snowing me.'

'According to CNN, he's been a good boy so far. But, even so, that buys us a day or two at most,' Lazenby said. 'The press are going to be all over the *Post* article. It's not going to take them long to put two and two together.'

'I take it the President has an alibi?' Kelly grinned.

'Very funny.'

'Sir, if it's any comfort, there's a good chance we're dealing with an individual sexual motive here. Ms. Benoni may have just got into the bondage thing a little too deep for her own good. There's no evidence that it's anything more sinister than that.'

'I'm not sure the President will find that particularly comforting.'

'No, Sir.'

Lazenby sat back down behind his desk.

'What are they going to do with the evidence?'

'Their own people are going to go over it first, and I said our people would give them any technical support they might need. There are some things we can do more quickly than they could. I also suggested that we run the name of Lucia Benoni by State, since she seems to have been well up in the frequent flier stakes.'

'Yes, I suppose we should,' Lazenby agreed. 'The Agency, too, just in case.'

'Sir, what do you want to do about the special pass?' Kelly asked. 'Do you want to contact the Secret Service and ask? There is still a chance it's a forgery though, if so, it's a damn good one. They can scan it for us and tell us in a New York minute.'

Lazenby exhaled heavily.

'Not if there's any way to avoid it. Once we make a formal request, the cat's out of the bag. There has to be some way to check it out without going through the usual channels. There's not much time. But the last thing I want is to give the President a false alarm.'

Kelly considered the matter.

'I do have a very close friend on the President's Detail. If these passes are for real, she must see them all the time. I could ask her to take a look at it.'

Lazenby rose to his feet once more.

'Can she be trusted?'

'Absolutely, Sir. We go way back.'

Lazenby paced behind his desk for some time. Eventually, he made his decision.

'All right. But it has to be today some time. I can't wait to tell the President for more than twenty-four hours. He'll probably want to beat me over the head for waiting even that long.'

'I'll get on to it right away.'

'And Kelly, this has to be kept completely quiet until we're sure.'

'I understand, Director.'

Lazenby stopped pacing and exhaled heavily.

'What about this Lieutenant, what was his name, Morris?'

'He seems like a good guy. I don't think we have anything to worry about there. It was his idea to call Chief Bryson and have him call you. He seemed to be taking very good care of the pass.'

'God, I hope so. Let me know what your friend has to say.'

Kelly stood to leave.

'Oh, and Kelly…'

'Sir?'

'You are free to tell Frank it's all my fault, and what a heartless, demanding bastard I am.'

'I already did, Sir,' Kelly replied with a thin smile. 'Unfortunately, it didn't seem to help.'

9

MARTHA GRAYLOR HAD worked for Steve Wade, as Governor and as President, for over fifteen years, and she had spent a lot of time putting out fires for the First Family. But this was the worst she had ever known. The President was pacing relentlessly up and down in his shirt sleeves, clutching a cup of strong black coffee. The First Lady was sitting in a chair at the dining table as if she were glued to it, tense and drawn, her hands clenched tightly in front of her on the table. Julia Wade still had something of the fresh-faced homecoming queen look that had attracted Steve Wade to her when they were both much younger. The blonde hair was shorter now, the fresh complexion was marked by a few lines, and the pale blue eyes looked tired. But she was still a beautiful woman. Julia had retired from a successful career as an advertising executive when her husband had first been elected President. She had never really adapted to her new role. She had the reputation of being aloof and distant, and was known to the press and the White House staff, behind her back, as the Ice Queen. With their two children away at college, Julia found the isolation of the White House depressing. Most of her friends were in New York, and she seldom saw them. She accepted her public engagements without complaint, and traveled with the President whenever it was required, but she felt as though life were passing her by. Ever since the evidence of her husband's indiscretions had become too obvious to ignore, their marriage had been one in name only, and she had long since stopped believing his protestations of innocence. But he continued to expect her to support him in public, and pretend to believe his denials and excuses. Martha Graylor understood these dynamics very well, but they did not make her job any easier, especially today. She was sitting awkwardly in a straight-backed chair, trying her best to inject some calm into the situation.

'All I'm saying, Mr. President, is that I don't think it's a good idea for you to come to the press conference. Not today. I just don't think there's any need for it.'

The President stopped pacing, turned, and looked at her.

'Well, I do,' he replied. 'This has got to stop. If the *Post* is running the story now, everybody and his brother will be running it tomorrow. We have to kill it once and for all.'

'With all due respect, Sir, there's no way to kill it. With any luck it will die a natural death, but we can't help that process along.'

'I can issue a denial.'

'You've already done that.'

'It wasn't strong enough. I was ambushed. I didn't react as strongly as I should have.'

'Mr. President, I wish you would trust me on this. I was there. Everyone knew you were ambushed. Your reaction was completely natural. If you rush into another statement now, they may think you are trying to hide something. It's going to look as though we are worried about it.'

'We *are* worried about it,' Julia Wade said through clenched teeth.

Martha closed her eyes. She found handling the President difficult enough in these situations. When the First Lady weighed in as well, she felt trapped between two powerful forces.

'I understand, Ma'am. But we shouldn't be *seen* to be worried. I don't think it's advisable for the President to rush back out there now. In a day or two, they are going to find the Benoni woman and interview her, and we will have to give them a statement then. Let's hold off for now. Let's wait to see what she has to say. It may be nothing.'

'I can't believe the *Post* would even print this crap,' Steve Wade said, half shouting. 'Don't they have any standards over there any more?'

'I called Harold and chewed him out,' Martha said. 'He wouldn't tell me where they got the story, of course, but he did insist it was legitimate.'

'Legitimate, my ass,' Julia Wade said. 'It's obvious where they got the story. This bimbo is out to sell her story for whatever money she can screw out of the vultures, just like the rest of them.'

Martha took a deep breath before replying.

'That may prove to be true, Ma'am, but in all honesty, it's not looking that way right now.'

'What the hell do you mean?' the First Lady asked furiously.

'Well, in the first place, Harold did specifically tell me she wasn't the source.'

'And you swallowed that?'

'Yes, Ma'am, actually I did. Harold has as good an eye for a story as any newspaper man, but he's a straight shooter. He will protect his source, but he wouldn't tell me a deliberate lie. He could have just kept quiet.'

'And in the second place?' the President asked.

'In the second place, if she were a gold-digger we would have heard from her by now. She would have a lawyer, and they would be taking the lead, scheduling a press conference of their own. They wouldn't wait for the press to come to them. They certainly wouldn't lie low and let the *Post* put its own spin on the story. Not unless she's being very badly advised.'

'So, I'm being set up? The opposition is doing this?'

'That would be my guess, Sir.'

'God damn it.'

Martha hesitated and swallowed hard.

'Mr. President, if you don't feel inclined to just ride out the storm, there are some things we can do.'

'Let me hear it.'

'Well, Sir, we could do some digging of our own.'

'What kind of digging?' the First Lady asked sharply.

'We could have the Bureau run a check on her. Also the Secret Service. We could find out whether she's ever been to the White House.'

'Why the hell should she have been in the White House?' Julia asked, looking at her husband.

'Ma'am, thousands of people come to the White House in any given year, for functions and so on. It might help to know who she associates with. Maybe we can prove that she has connections with the opposition.'

Steve Wade turned his back on them, and finished his coffee.

'If you think it may get us somewhere, have someone take a look. Very discreetly, and for my eyes only.'

'I'll get right on it, Mr. President.'

'I'm still coming to the press conference.'

'Mr. President…'

'No, Martha, my mind is made up.'

Martha headed for the door.

'I'll alert them… if you're quite sure that's what you've decided?'

'He didn't decide,' Julia Wade said. 'I did.'

* * *

The President was just entering the White House press room when Ted Lazenby's call came in to his private secretary, Steffie Walinsky. After agonizing over it for some time, the Director had decided that he should tell Steve Wade what was going on, even though it had to be unofficially until the facts were confirmed. It was an uncomfortable decision. Whatever he did, the situation would do nothing to improve his relationship with the President. But Lazenby concluded that it was the best of the several unattractive options open to him. As soon as he made the decision, he called Steffie to arrange a meeting. He was a couple of minutes too late.

'This is important,' he said. 'Can't you interrupt him?'

'I'm afraid not, Director, not during a press conference. Not unless the United States is under attack. Standing orders from Miss Graylor. It could give the impression that there's some panic going on.'

Lazenby fought back an urge to tell her there was.

'I'll have him call you right back. We don't expect it to last very long. He's just making a cameo today. Miss Graylor's handling most of it.'

Lazenby went hot and cold in turn.

'A cameo? Why?'

'I'm not sure, Director. Will you be in your office?'

'Don't bother, Steffie. I'll call the President myself later.'

'All right, Director.'

Lazenby replaced the receiver.

'Oh, fuck,' he said out loud.

* * *

Steve Wade's arrival caused something of a stir in the press room. Martha had told the journalists only that the President would make a short statement and would take a few questions, and she had abruptly fended off further inquiries. No, she could not speculate about it, and no, there were no advance copies, there was no prepared text. The room was abuzz although, as Martha well knew, it was not because there was any doubt as to what the President intended to speak about. The applause as he took the podium was more restrained than usual. There were even a few cynical chuckles. Martha was relieved to see that Wade appeared quite composed. His manner betrayed no hint of unease.

'Good morning, Ladies and Gentlemen,' he began without undue haste. 'I have only one thing to say this morning. And I'm sure it will come as no surprise to you to learn that it has to do with the story which appeared this morning in *The Washington Post*.'

The male reporter who was sitting next to Mary Sullivan grinned at her and shook his head.

'Bad girl,' he scolded.

Mary gave him a kick on his shin, but could not stop herself returning the grin.

'I must admit,' the President continued, 'that when the subject was raised yesterday, I was rather taken aback. I may not have made myself as clear as I would wish. So I hope you will forgive me if I take a few moments of your time to do so today. For the record, I want to make it as clear as I possibly can that I know no one by the name of Lucia Benoni, I have had no relationship with any such person, and I find it disturbing that a newspaper as respected as *The Washington Post* would print a story like this without giving us a chance to comment on it. One might wonder, if there were any truth to the story at all, why this Miss Benoni has not come forward herself. I hope I have made myself clear, and I hope and expect that you will all consider this matter closed, and go back to reporting what really matters, which is the work the American people elected me to do.'

The President stopped. There was a brief silence while the reporters finished making notes, and made sure that he was not going to continue. All eyes turned to Mary Sullivan, but she remained silent, appearing to concentrate on her notes. The White House correspondent for CBS News picked up the ball.

'Mr. President, I wonder if you can comment on a report that was making the rounds this morning that Miss Benoni was an official guest at a White House function some time ago?'

'No, I can't, Bill. Several thousand people visit the White House every year for functions, yourself included, and I'm afraid I don't remember them all.'

'Following up, Mr. President, my network was told that Miss Benoni was the escort of a German diplomat at a function some months ago.'

'If that's the case, then that's the case,' Steve Wade replied testily. 'I don't personally supervise everything that goes on at the White House. And I repeat, I have no recollection of ever meeting this woman. Now, if you'll excuse me…'

A female reporter for *Elle* stood up.

'Mr. President, have you talked with the First Lady about this story? How does she feel about it?'

Steve Wade was already halfway to the door.

'How do you think she feels about it?' he replied angrily. 'She wishes you people would leave us alone. And so do I.'

Martha Graylor was seething as she made her way to the podium to resume what should have been a routine press conference. As soon as she was in place, almost every hand in the room was raised, and a chorus of voices erupted. She cut the first questioner off at the knees.

'Don't even go there,' she said. 'I have nothing to add to what the President has just said. And now, we're going to talk about the situation in the Middle East.'

* * *

As she left the President at the Oval Office, Linda Samuels was fighting off a desire to throw up. Listening to his lies disgusted her. She had even had the uncomfortable feeling that some of the reporters were looking at her, as if they thought she might have something to tell them. Surely that was just her imagination? She walked slowly back to the Presidential Detail office, poured herself a cup of coffee, flopped into a chair, and closed her eyes. Gary Mills opened the door.

'Oh, there you are, Linda. There was a call for you. Sounded urgent.'

He handed Linda a note.

'Thanks, Gary.'

'The Boss has quite a way with the press, doesn't he?'

'I don't want to talk about it.'

Gary grinned maliciously and left the office.

Linda recognized the number instantly. It was Kelly Smith's direct line at the Hoover Building. She dialed it absent-mindedly.

'Kelly?'

'Oh. Hi Linda, thanks for calling back so quickly.'

'Sure. What's up?'

There was a pause.

'Linda, I need you to take a look at a piece of evidence for me, and see if you can identify it.'

'Evidence? What kind of evidence?'

'I can't go into it over the phone.'

'What makes you think I can help?'

'I'm sorry, Linda. I wish I could tell you more.'

'This is on one of your cases?'

'Yes.'

'I didn't know I had any information on an FBI case.'

'You may not. But I need you to try.'

'OK,' Linda said slowly. 'Can't you at least give me a clue?'

'No. I'm sorry, Linda. It's something I have to keep the lid on for now. Also, I'm afraid it won't wait. When can you get away?'

'Today?' Linda asked in astonishment.

'Today or this evening.'

'I guess I could leave about six. Will that do?'

'I'll pick you up at your place at seven. Thanks, Linda.'

Kelly hung up.

'You're welcome, I'm sure,' Linda said into the dial tone. Her queasiness was getting worse, and she gulped the hot coffee, hoping it might somehow calm her down and make her feel better.

Then, just when she had concluded that her day could not get any worse, Bob called.

10

'HE ACTUALLY HAD the nerve to tell me I should wish him and his new bimbo well, let bygones be bygones. Jesus, where do men get that kind of crap? I mean, we're not even divorced yet, for Christ's sake.'

Linda was sprawling dejectedly in the passenger seat of Kelly's car, as they made their way through the tail end of the evening rush hour to the Headquarters of the Washington D.C. Police Department. Kelly had made an appointment with Lieutenant Jeff Morris and, feeling pretty sure that the situation was about to take a turn for the worse, she was in no mood for casual conversation. Linda had done most of the talking during the drive.

'It's almost as though we were never married at all,' she continued. 'Four years of my life just erased. He takes a fancy to some new woman and turns me off like a faucet. Why is this happening to me, Kelly? Am I a bad person? Do I have that kind of effect on people?'

Kelly made an effort.

'No, of course not. He's just behaving like your typical asshole. I thought he was talking about getting back together?'

'He was. He'll call and say 'let's talk', we'll have a drink, and I could swear he's ready to move back in. Then he'll call again, say he's not sure, could we think about it for a while. Then it's all off again. He's driving me nuts, Kelly. Every time he calls, I believe him. Even today, I thought it was just possible that he might... oh, what the hell.'

'It doesn't sound like he's too attached to the bimbo,' Kelly offered. 'Maybe he's not sure what he wants. If it's any comfort, I bet he will probably dump her before long.'

'I don't care. Oh God, yes I do. That's the trouble.'

Kelly reached out, took her friend's hand and squeezed hard.

'You deserve better. Just hang in there, Linda. The right guy is out there just waiting for you to find him.'

'He may have some time to wait. Bob may be able to change partners just like that, but I can't. I'm not available.'

'Well, if I were you,' Kelly said, 'I would work on becoming available.'

'I'll get started on it right now,' Linda replied.

They exchanged smiles. Linda turned to look out of the side window of the car, contemplating the people they passed in the street, and suddenly the thought of Bob passed, and she regained her bearings.

'This isn't the way to your office. We crossed Pennsylvania Avenue a couple of blocks back.'

'We're not going to my office,' Kelly said.

'Great. I knew the evidence thing was just a practical joke. You're taking me out for a wonderful dinner in some fancy restaurant to meet a rich, handsome doctor.'

Kelly laughed. 'I wish,' she said.

'So where are we going?'

'We're here,' Kelly announced, pulling up at a parking meter.

'This is the D.C. Police building.'

'Yes. This is where the evidence is.'

They climbed out of the car. Mechanically, her mind elsewhere, Kelly fed the meter, even though at that hour parking in the street was free.

'I thought you said it was one of your cases,' Linda said in the elevator.

'It is, in a manner of speaking. It's under the jurisdiction of the D.C. Police, but they've asked the Bureau to help out.'

'Why?'

'You'll see.'

They left the elevator on the third floor, where Jeff Morris had instructed them to meet him. He was waiting, and seemed tired and preoccupied. As she made the introductions, Kelly speculated that Chief Bryson was probably giving him little time to rest. This was a case nobody relished. Headaches all round. Morris led them to a small conference room.

'If you'll wait here,' he said, 'I'll go to the evidence room and get the exhibit. Help yourselves to coffee. Oh, and Kelly, if you have a moment afterwards, I did get some information about Middle and Near East Holdings, Incorporated.'

'I can't wait,' Kelly said.

She poured coffee for Linda and herself.

'Linda, I have to ask you to promise that you will keep what you're about to see to yourself for a day or two.'

'Can I do that?'

'Yes. I don't think it will embarrass you. It's only for a couple of days, anyway.'

'Now I'm really intrigued,' Linda said, sipping her coffee.

Jeff returned a minute or two later with the White House pass in its plastic evidence bag. The bag now had several identifying labels attached to it, signed by Morris and other officers who had handled it in connection with the various forensic tests which had been carried out on the pass. Kelly noted with appreciation that the D.C. Police Department was going strictly by the book. There was a label to account for every time the pass had been removed from, or returned to, the evidence room. Every minute of the exhibit's time was going to be strictly accounted for. When they had finished showing it to Linda, another label would be attached to the bag. Yet, even though all the handling was necessary and unavoidable, the thought that the pass was being exposed so much worried her. Every exposure was a potential leak, and a leak was the last thing they needed. She removed the pass from the bag and handed it to Linda.

'Do you know what this is?'

'Yes, it's…'.

As she took in the photograph and the name on the pass, Linda stopped abruptly. She turned pale, and sat down heavily in a chair.

'Where did you get this?'

'In a moment, Linda. I promise I'll tell you. But I need an answer first. Do you know what it is?'

'It's a special White House pass.'

'What do you mean 'special'?' Jeff Morris asked.

Linda's breathing was audible.

'Can I have some water?'

'Of course.'

A jug of iced water and some plastic cups had been left next to the coffee. Jeff poured a cup and Linda drank it slowly.

'No one gets into the White House without some kind of pass. There's a garden variety pass which is issued to employees and frequent business visitors, press people, congressional aides and what have you. Then you have occasional visitors, people who show up from time to time, but not that often. Mostly, they get a day pass. I don't mean the public, obviously, people taking the tour. I mean people who have some business in the White House and need to get into the non-public areas. But for certain people, who are thought to be important for one reason or another, they can issue one of these. We call them S-passes. It's a kind of VIP thing.'

'When you say 'they' can issue them, who do you mean by 'they'?' Kelly asked.

'The White House staff would actually issue them.'

'Well, yes,' Jeff said, 'but not on their own initiative, right?'

'No.'

'Well, then…?'

Linda grimaced.

'Something like this would be issued only at the specific request of someone at Cabinet or Department Head level.'

'Does the Secret Service run any security checks before one of these S-passes is issued?'

'Yes, of course. Always. We do it quietly, because we don't want to offend whoever has requested it. It doesn't happen very often. We try to discourage it.'

'Why?'

'For security reasons. Because the holder of the pass can pretty much walk in any time, and we have no paperwork beforehand. That kind of thing makes the Detail nervous.'

'Have you ever seen this particular pass before?' Kelly asked.

Linda looked at Kelly, then at Jeff Morris.

'Look, I…, I don't know…'

Kelly moved closer to Linda.

'Linda, anything you say here will be treated as confidential. But you may as well know that it's all going to be out in the open before very long. You asked where we got this. Jeff found it in Lucia Benoni's purse, not far from her body.'

Linda looked up in horror. Her voice was almost inaudible.

'What?'

'She was murdered. Execution style. Bullet in the back of the head. Probably by some guy she was sleeping with.'

Linda looked from Kelly Smith to Jeff Morris and back again in disbelief.

'This was the case that was in the papers, the woman whose identity hasn't been confirmed?'

'Yes,' Kelly said. 'But I'm afraid the reports are not quite accurate. We do know her identity, and eventually it's all going to be out there. All we did was buy a little time. My Director felt it was important that we find out what Lucia Benoni was doing with an S-pass before we go public with it. We thought it might even be a forgery.'

Linda stared at the pass for some time.

'No. It's not a forgery.'

'Do you need to scan it to be sure?'

Linda shook her head.

'You've seen it before?'

'Many times.'

'From which I take it she was a fairly regular visitor to the White House?'

'Yes.'

'Would there be any record of her visits?' Morris asked.

'Every one. Date, time, and place.'

Kelly bit her lip and turned away slightly.

'Linda, this is the woman you were telling me about the other night, isn't it? The one who was with him in Chicago?'

'Yes.'

'So, this pass would have been issued…'

'At the request of the President, yes.'

Abruptly, Linda Samuels stood and looked Kelly straight in the face. 'Kelly, how could your people do this?'

Kelly was taken aback by her vehemence.

'Do what, Linda? What are you talking about?'

'Set the President up like this.'

'Excuse me?'

'God damn it, Kelly, you know what I mean.'

'No, Linda,' Kelly replied with complete sincerity. 'I really don't.'

'You've known about this ever since the Benoni woman's body was found, and you let the President go into that news conference this morning and deny knowing her? And now the whole world will know he issued her an S-pass. For God's sake.'

Linda was almost shouting. Kelly put her arms on her shoulders and pushed her gently back into the chair.

'Linda, the Bureau has no control over what the President says at press conferences.'

'But if he had known she was dead…'

'Then what? He would have told the truth? Look, Linda, for whatever reason, the President chose to lie about knowing her. What difference does it make whether she's dead or alive? You just said there were records of her visits anyway. How long do you think it's going to take the press to find that out? They'll probably know before we tell them.'

Linda slumped in her seat, her head between her hands.

'Anyway,' Kelly added, 'Don't tell me you're suddenly starting to sympathize with him?'

'It's not a matter of sympathy,' Linda said quietly. 'It's a question of duty. My job is to protect the President.'

'From bullets, yes,' Kelly said. 'But from the consequences of his own actions? I don't think so, Linda.'

Linda stood and began to walk towards the door.

'I'll talk to you later,' she said.

With a glance at Jeff Morris, Kelly followed Linda out of the conference room and along the corridor, and waited with her for an elevator.

'I was going to take you home.'

'It's OK. I'll take a cab. Lieutenant Morris said he had more information for you. I'm done in. I need to get out of here.'

'Don't be silly. I'll be two minutes.'

Linda made no reply. Kelly pulled her unwillingly into a hug.

'You mad at me?'

'No. Yes. I don't know. I feel as though I've been hit over the head with a sledge hammer. I need time to think.'

'Well, call me.'

'I will.'

'Promise?'

'Promise.'

As the elevator doors were closing, Linda stopped them with her hands.

'He's cute.'

'Who is?' Kelly asked.

'Lieutenant Morris.'

Kelly smiled.

'You interested?'

'Me? No.'

The door closed and the elevator carried Linda down to the foyer.

11

KELLY WALKED SLOWLY back to the conference room. Jeff Morris was not there and, having helped herself to a cup of lukewarm coffee, she sat down and absent-mindedly contemplated the bare walls. The tiredness of a long day began to overtake her. A few minutes later, Jeff returned carrying some papers. Kelly stood.

'So, is that the information on the infamous Middle and Near East Holdings?'

He looked at her inquiringly.

'Is Linda OK?'

'I think so.'

'She seemed pretty upset.'

'She takes her job very seriously.'

'My boss, right or wrong?'

'Something like that.'

'How about you?'

Kelly forced herself to drain the last of her coffee, and tossed the empty plastic cup into the waste paper basket.

'What?'

'How are you doing?'

'Me? Oh, I'm fine,' she replied, a little too quickly. 'So, that's the info on Middle and Near East?'

Jeff looked at her closely for a moment or two.

'You want to get out of here?'

'Excuse me?'

'You look like you've had a hard day. Me too. I've been here since seven-thirty this morning, and all I had to eat was a sandwich from the café downstairs. If I don't eat something soon, I'm going to pass out. There's a little Italian place around the corner. It's not bad. We go there all the time. What do you think?'

Even the idea made Kelly feel better. She decided at once.

'Sure. Why not? If you think the sandwiches here are bad, you should try the grilled cheese *à la* FBI some time.'

They sat at a table for two near a window, and idly scanned the menu while the waiter poured glasses of Chianti from a carafe. The restaurant was full of Italian kitsch, the walls adorned with amateur murals depicting bucolic scenes from the Old Country. The accents of the waiters were authentic. It was a slow evening, with only a handful of other diners. Kelly found the quiet atmosphere and the subdued lighting calming and reassuring.

'The fettucini carbonara is to die for,' Jeff said from behind his menu.

'The heart attack special?' Kelly smiled. 'I don't think so. You go ahead. I think I'll go with the primavera.'

They placed the orders, and the waiter disappeared into the kitchen. Jeff seemed in no hurry to get to the subject of the Middle and Near East Holdings Company. He seemed content to sip his wine in silence for a while. To her surprise, Kelly found the silence quite comfortable.

'How long have you known Linda?' Jeff asked eventually.

'All my life. We've been best friends since almost before we could read.'

'Are you from around here?'

'No. St. Paul, Minnesota. Linda and I both grew up there. We went away to Notre Dame for college, but other than that we lived our whole lives there until it was time to find real jobs. My parents are both attorneys.'

'Both of them? You seem to have survived it pretty well.'

'I guess. I might not have, if I had followed in their footsteps. I did go to law school. That was the plan.'

'Their plan, or yours?'

'Theirs, really. I don't regret law school, but I don't think I would have made it practicing law.'

'But you had no family ties to law enforcement?'

'No. The Bureau was all my own idea. Actually, my folks were really good about it. They never gave me a hard time. How about you?'

Jeff re-filled their wine glasses.

'I'm from San Francisco,' he answered.

'No kidding?' Kelly smiled. 'I love San Francisco. I didn't think anyone was actually *from* there, though.'

'Oh, yeah. Born and raised. My dad was a patrol officer with SFPD all his life, never cared to become anything else. He's retired now. He and my mother live up in Marin County. He never suggested I should become a police officer. I think he probably wanted a different life for me, but he never said anything. I guess he thought I should figure it out for myself.'

'So, with your family connections, why aren't you with SFPD?'

'My mom insisted I go to college before making a decision. I came out here to George Washington, made a lot of friends, and never went back. Actually, it would have been hard in San Francisco. Everybody knew my dad. I would have spent my entire life trying to live up to his reputation.'

'I hear that,' Kelly replied.

There was a silence.

'Do you have a husband to wonder where you are?' Jeff asked eventually.

'No. I have a boyfriend, and I don't suppose he's given one thought to where I am.'

Jeff looked embarrassed.

'I'm sorry, Kelly. I didn't mean to pry. Let's change the subject.'

Kelly shook her head.

'No. It's all right. I'm not sensitive about it. I bore Linda to death with it all the time. It's not exactly an unusual situation. Like many men, he thinks that he's the only one with a serious job, and what I do is basically a hobby to tide me over until I get married and start to reproduce.'

Jeff laughed. 'Being an FBI agent as a hobby? That's something that would never have occurred to me.'

'Me neither.'

'What does he do, for Heaven's sake?'

'He's Senator O'Brien's chief of staff. Very glamorous. He travels around all the time and meets all kinds of movers and shakers.'

'And he says you're the one with the hobby?'

Kelly was lost in thought for some moments.

'It doesn't really matter. I can't see it lasting much longer.'

Jeff topped up their glasses.

'Do you want it to?'

Kelly considered.

'That's a good question. Until a few months ago, yes, absolutely, no doubt about it. But I'm not sure any more. I've come to the conclusion that I'm not going to give up my career for him, or anyone else. I have a feeling that's going to end it one way or the other, whether I want it to end or not.'

They exchanged smiles. She drank some of her wine.

'So, how about you? Is there a Mrs. Morris at home watching the clock?'

Jeff looked down at the table cloth. The waiter brought their salads, and Jeff waited for him to leave.

'No. Not any more.'

'Did she get tired of the long hours?'

Kelly started on her salad, but Jeff remained looking down.

'She had breast cancer. She was twenty-seven. Can you believe it?'

Involuntarily, Kelly put down her fork, reached across the table and put her hand on his.

'Oh, Jeff, I'm so sorry. I shouldn't have asked. I…'

'No. I'm the one who started this line of conversation. There's no reason not to talk about it. It runs in her family, but the other women who died of it were much older. She never really worried about it, and by the time she had a reason to be concerned, it was too late. It's strange. You always think you'll have enough time, don't you?'

They both became aware of Kelly's hand on his. Her first instinct was to withdraw it, but she decided to leave it where it was, and he did not try to pull away.

'How long has it been?'

'Almost three years.'

'Do you have children?'

'No. We hadn't gotten around to it.'

Kelly allowed their fingers to intertwine.

'You're right. You don't think about it happening to someone so young. I don't think about it happening to me. I think about getting shot in the line of duty, but not about something going wrong with my body.'

They said little for a while, but Kelly kept her hand lightly in place until the main course was served. They finished their pasta with light talk about families, colleges, and careers. The waiter brought cappuccinos, and a dessert menu, which they returned unopened.

'That was good,' Kelly smiled. 'I'd come here again any time.'

'Yes, it's not bad.'

'Well, we probably can't put it off any longer. You want to show me what you've got on Middle and Near East Holdings, Inc.?'

'Sure.'

Jeff reached into the slim leather briefcase he had brought with him from the D.C. Police Headquarters, and handed Kelly several pieces of paper.

'Don't get too excited. All this really tells us is that the company was incorporated in Delaware, which we knew already, and that five guys with foreign-sounding names claim to be the directors and officers. They have a P.O. Box mailing address and a phone line which is always answered by a machine.'

Kelly scanned the documents.

'Has the company filed any returns?'

'Not yet.'

'OK. Well, I guess we'll check these characters out, just in case we turn up anything interesting.'

'Yeah. What do you figure about the apartment?'

'Probably just a corporate hideaway for the directors to screw Lucia Benoni and others while taking a tax deduction. I should have known better than to expect too much.'

Jeff smiled and opened his briefcase again.

'Well, perhaps I should at least show you the pride of the collection.'

'There's more?'

'I saved the best for last. Actually, this came in as a fax while you were saying goodbye to Linda. I made you a copy. I haven't even had a chance to read it properly yet.'

He gave Linda a stack of photocopied pages with hand-written entries in a neat, feminine hand.

'What is this?'

'You remember we asked NYPD to turn over Lucia's apartment in Manhattan?'

'Sure.'

'Well, they took away a lot of stuff. They haven't made a full inventory of it yet, but they thought we should see this right away. It appears to be her address book. Names, addresses and phone numbers. I bet it's going to be worth following up.'

'No kidding.'

Kelly thumbed quickly through the first few pages.

'I'm seeing one or two fairly prominent Washington names in here.'

'Yes,' Jeff said. 'I noticed a couple myself when I scanned it. I'm sure we'll find more as we go through it.'

Kelly flicked rapidly through the pages, trying to find her way farther into the alphabet.

'Please, Jesus, let it not be the President or Senator O'Brien,' she said. Jeff grinned.

'Definitely not the President,' he reassured her. 'That I did check.'

To her relief, Kelly found no mention of Senator O'Brien under 'O'. She smiled.

'Perhaps we ought to be a little more systematic.'

They had been sitting opposite each other at the table, but now she moved to sit beside him so that they could read through the pages together. They read at a leisurely pace, finishing the coffee, sipping the wine, exchanging occasional glances when they came to an especially recognizable name. When they had worked their way to the end, Kelly laid the pages on the table between them, idly scanning the front page, which seemed to contain nothing but Lucia Benoni's own address and telephone number. Suddenly, she picked the page up.

'What are these markings here, at the foot of the page?'

Jeff held the page up to his eyes.

'Difficult to tell in this light. Maybe something very faint in the original which didn't copy.'

'Written in pencil, maybe. It looks like it could be a number of some kind. It may be nothing.'

'Or it may be something,' Jeff said.

He took his mobile phone from the briefcase and dialed a number.

'Detective Wernick, please… Lieutenant Morris with the D.C. Police. I spoke with him earlier in the evening… Thank you.'

He placed his hand over the mouthpiece to talk to Kelly.

'If he hasn't gone home and he hasn't logged the original into the evidence room yet, he may be able to give us a quick answer.'

'If not, I'll ask them to messenger it to me tomorrow,' Kelly said.

'Hello, Tom? Jeff Morris in D.C.… Yeah, listen could you do me a favor? Do you still have the address book in front of you? Good… Look on the front page, where her name is, and tell me whether you see anything written in the bottom right-hand corner. Could be in pencil. It didn't copy well.'

Jeff took a pen from his jacket and wrote on a napkin, which he showed to Kelly.

'Is that it? Great, Tom. I appreciate it. Talk to you later.'

Jeff had written a seven-digit number.

'Phone number, no area code,' Kelly said. 'If the area code was too familiar for her to bother writing it down, it's probably where she spent most of her time.'

'Either New York or Washington.'

'Right. You want to check it out?'

'Yeah. But not from the office, and not from here. Just in case...'

'Phone booth. I agree. Let's go.'

They paid the check and walked outside into the cool night air. A block away they found a phone booth outside a twenty-four hour launderette. They decided to try Washington D.C. first, a local call for which no area code was necessary. Jeff held the receiver between them so that they could both hear. A sequence of clicks on the line suggested that the call was being rerouted several times, but they finally heard a ringing tone. After three or four rings, a male voice answered with the single word 'Hello'. Jeff's eyes opened wide as he turned to Kelly. She placed her hand over his and forcibly returned the receiver to the hook, cutting off the call. The voice had been unmistakable to both of them.

They walked some distance towards Kelly's car without speaking.

'His private line,' Jeff said eventually. 'I just called the President of the United States on his private line.'

'His very private line, I'm sure. You can't call the White House and get straight through to the President. The official lines are answered by receptionists twenty-four hours a day.'

'So, now what?'

'I'll report to Director Lazenby first thing in the morning, and then it's up to him. I suggest you do the same with Chief Bryson. And then, let's get to work checking out the names in the address book.'

They had reached Kelly's car. After she had unlocked the door, he held it for her as she climbed in.

'I enjoyed this evening, Kelly,' he said, with a hint of shyness.

She gave him a warm smile.

'I had a good time too, Jeff. I'll call you tomorrow.'

At home, Kelly checked her messages. There was one from Linda Samuels asking her to call back, and one from Frank announcing that he was leaving for an unexpected road trip early the following morning. Kelly decided not to return either call that night.

12

THE WASHINGTON POST's White House correspondent, Mary Sullivan, did not like her source, Selvey. She found him vulgar and unnecessarily direct, qualities which her upbringing in a wealthy part of Boston had taught her to avoid. She did not like the way he always seemed to be amused at her. Nor did she care for the run-down cafés in which he insisted on meeting. But, like him or not, she had to admit that Selvey was good; in fact, all things considered, the best she'd ever had. His information was consistently of the highest quality, and his insights, if crudely expressed, right on target. For the life of her, Mary could not begin to imagine where he got it. Selvey did not seem the type to mingle with Washington's élite. She could picture him far more easily in a beer joint on the wrong side of town, or placing bets at a dog track. And he did offer her some pretty exotic material from time to time, the kind of thing that would be of more interest to *People* magazine than to the *Post*. Mary had developed the habit of listening patiently, knowing that when he came to the serious political material, he would be right on point. She could always pass on the stuff she couldn't use to contacts at other publications. But Selvey was an enigma. One thing Mary could never quite understand was that he never seemed interested in money. He never asked for it. When he did accept a gratuity, it was always with an amusement which seemed almost contemptuous. Nor did his material seem to be strongly biased in favor of either political party, even if it was often slanted against the President. Mary might have understood this better if she had known of Selvey's connection to John Mason and the Wilson Foundation. But Selvey had never spoken a word to her on this matter, and never would.

Usually, Mary took her time evaluating and checking Selvey's material before deciding what to write, or how to move a story forward. That was what she was known for. Her success at *The Washington Post* had not come easily. There were those who found her unimaginative, too prosaic for really top-flight political reporting. The Pulitzer Prize, of course, silenced her critics overnight. But she had won the Prize, not for her imagination, but for a painstaking trudge through thousands of pages of Freedom of Information Act material which many reporters would have found too daunting even to begin; a trudge that exposed a well-concealed political scandal, which took down several well-known public figures in its wake. Method was Mary's strong point. Always check, and never rush in.

But not this morning. After this particular early morning meeting, which Selvey had virtually ordered her to attend – the impertinence of the man – she ran to her car and drove as fast as she dared from the café to the *Post's* offices. On the way, she used her mobile phone to demand an appointment with her editor as soon as she arrived, and her seniority to refuse to take his secretary's 'No' for an answer. She parked crookedly in her assigned spot in the garage and took the elevator to Philby's office.

Harold Philby, a patrician by temperament, and a veteran newspaper man, was tall and thin, with distinguished looks including a fine head of silver hair. He looked ten years younger than his sixty-eight years. He enjoyed an enviable reputation for sound judgment and discretion and, over the course of his working life, had gained the trust of even the most skeptical of Washington insiders. The cluttered state of his usually neat desk bore witness to the prospect of an unusually hectic day. He looked up quizzically as a harried Mary Sullivan rushed into his office without even knocking.

'What's got you so fired up today, Mary?' he grinned at the sight of the normally composed reporter in such a state of excitement. 'I've never seen you like this. You look like the cub reporter who just caught the mayor with his hand in the cookie jar. Is the White House about to fall down about its foundations?'

Philby's secretary shot Mary a disapproving glance, and left them alone.

Mary took a seat, trying to catch her breath, trying to rearrange her hair, trying unsuccessfully to look like Mary Sullivan. She smiled.

'Quite possibly, Harold,' she said. 'Quite possibly.'

* * *

Kelly arrived at Ted Lazenby's office that morning with equal haste, but already frustrated. Her first call of the morning, to Frank, was too late to catch him before he left for the airport, and her second interrupted a tearful Linda Samuels during an argument with Bob. Linda had promised to call back, but had not done so before Kelly had to leave her apartment to drive to the Hoover Building. But Kelly did succeed in the most vital task she had set for herself. She made sure that she had the Director's undivided attention for an hour before he went into meetings which would take up the rest of his morning. As briefly as she could, she outlined for Lazenby the events of the previous evening, and handed him a copy of the pages of Lucia Benoni's address book. With some apprehension, she told him about the phone call she and Jeff Morris had made to the mysterious number, assuring the Director that they had not been mistaken in identifying the President's voice. Lazenby had turned away from her in his chair, staring at the wall as she spoke, but now turned slowly back towards her.

'No, you're correct,' he said heavily. 'That's the President's private line. It's for his own personal calls. A few of his close friends have access to it, myself included, but we would never use it except for social reasons, you know, to arrange a game of golf or a nightcap, off the record.'

'Well, it's a relief to know we were right,' Kelly said.

'You have a strange idea of relief,' Lazenby remarked.

'Yes, Sir,' Kelly grinned.

'Are there any interesting names in the address book?'

'At this stage, we don't know which are interesting and which aren't,' Kelly replied. 'There are quite a few you'll find familiar. We're running checks on all of them, of course, and at some point we'll interview them to see what they have to offer, including any alibis for the night of the murder. It's going to take some time, and it's going to be rather delicate, but I don't see any other way.'

Ted Lazenby flipped through the pages of the address book, smiling thinly from time to time on finding a name which registered with him, while Kelly sat concentrating on a spot on the wall above his desk, trying to force her mind not to stray into thinking about Frank and Jeff Morris. Abruptly, Lazenby sat upright in his chair and stared at the page in front of him in apparent disbelief. His reaction was so marked that Kelly sat up in her own chair in response.

'Jesus, Mary, and Joseph,' he muttered.

'Sir?'

Lazenby thrust the page across the desk to her, indicating a name with his forefinger. Kelly read it.

'It doesn't ring a bell.'

Lazenby stared at her for a moment, then nodded.

'That's right. Of course. I haven't had time to fill you in. You've been too busy with this mess. This guy showed up recently in another context.'

'This Hamid Marfrela guy?'

'Yes. Hamid Marfrela is a low-level member of the Lebanese diplomatic mission.'

'Makes sense,' Kelly said. 'Lucia Benoni had Lebanese family. Most of these foreign names we're running across in the address book are probably Lebanese.'

'Yes, but unfortunately, that's not all,' Lazenby replied. 'He is also the man Phil Hammond photographed going in and out of the Sons of the Land compound in Oregon. We had nothing on him, but State was able to make him. We haven't followed up on him yet.'

Kelly sat back and exhaled deeply.

'This is getting worse by the minute. What do you want me to do? Should we give Marfrela priority, interview him first?'

Lazenby looked intently at the ceiling, then back at Kelly.

'Interview him, my ass. We'd get nowhere. He's a diplomat, Kelly. We'd have the Lebanese ambassador all over us, not to mention the State Department, before he answered question one.'

'But, Sir, we can't just...'

'Get a warrant and turn his place over. Then we'll talk to him. And do it today.'

Kelly stared at the Director in disbelief.

'A search warrant?'

Lazenby turned his chair around to face her directly.

'Yes, a search warrant. Any questions?'

Kelly hesitated.

'Well, yes, Director. First, with all due respect, what would I be looking for?'

'Anything. Evidence linking him to the murder.'

'OK. Second, what do I use for probable cause? The fact that his name appears in her address book along with about sixty others? Any magistrate in the Washington area would laugh in my face.'

'You don't go through district court. You don't go through the normal channels at all. Not in this case. You go to the special court. They're a little more understanding about the realities of law enforcement over there.'

Kelly rubbed her eyes.

'Director, the special court is for cases involving national security. This is a domestic murder inquiry in which the Bureau may not even have jurisdiction.'

Lazenby made a visible effort to calm himself.

'Kelly, let me summarize the situation for you, as I see it. Just follow along, tell me if I get anything wrong, then tell me how you react to it.'

'OK.'

'The President of the United States is having an affair with a foreign national, Lucia Benoni, who has strong Lebanese connections. The United States is not exactly on the best of terms with Lebanon. Lucia Benoni turns up dead in Washington, the victim of a homicide, in an empty apartment rented by a Lebanese shell corporation which consists of nothing but an address in Delaware. When found, Lucia Benoni is in possession of a special pass which allows her pretty much free access into the White House, a pass issued to her, in all probability, at the personal request of the President. When her address book is examined, we find the name of Hamid Marfrela, a Lebanese diplomat. There is a serious possibility that Mr. Marfrela was sharing Ms. Benoni's sexual favors with the President. There is also a serious possibility that Mr. Marfrela killed Ms Benoni. Lastly, we find that Mr. Marfrela has been a regular visitor at the Headquarters of the Sons of the Land, an extreme White supremacist organization whose avowed goal is the overthrow of the United States Government. This is obviously not one of Mr. Marfrela's usual duties as a diplomat.'

Lazenby spread his arms out wide in front of him.

'Do you see where I'm going with this?'

With mounting anxiety, Kelly began to see all too clearly.

'Blackmail, or a conspiracy of some kind. Maybe even a direct breach of national security.'

'Right. Several possibilities come to mind, Kelly, and none of them is very appealing. We can't let the grass grow on this. The special court will back us up. I'll call the Agency and let Masterson know what's going on.'

'What about State?'

'We'll tell them too, of course – once it's too late for them to interfere.'

Kelly shook her head.

'There'll be hell to pay, Director.'

'There will be anyway,' Lazenby replied tersely. 'All we can do is make the most of the little time we have before the shit hits the fan. If Marfrela is there when you go in, place him under arrest. If there's nothing to arrest him for, we'll apologize later.'

'Jesus,' Kelly said.

'It's my responsibility, Kelly. I'll keep you out of trouble.'

'Yes, Sir.'

'Take Lieutenant Morris with you, since it's still his case. For the moment, anyway. I have a feeling that's about to change. And take a show of force with you. Marfrela is to be considered armed and dangerous. Understand?'

'I'll get right on it,' Kelly said, making for the door.

'Kelly…'

'Sir?'

'Have you fired a weapon since… since New York?'

She had her back to him. She closed her eyes for an instant, opened them again, then slowly turned back to face him.

'At the range, yeah. Several times. They signed off on me.'

Late at night and alone, the first time, she added silently. So nobody would see me. Just in case something went wrong. Nothing had. She hadn't cried. Her hands were steady. Her aim was as good as ever. But that was at the range, where the targets could not shoot back.

'Are you OK with this?'

'I'm fine, Sir,' she replied firmly.

Lazenby nodded, not taking his eyes off her.

'OK,' he said quietly.

'I'll call in as soon as I can,' she said, then turned away abruptly and left.

'And may the Lord have mercy on us all,' Lazenby said under his breath. He picked up his phone, called Steffie Walinsky at the White House, and asked for an urgent meeting with the President. The secretary told him he could see the President immediately after a staff meeting which was just due to begin.

At about the same time, Harold Philby telephoned Martha Graylor's office, and was told that he could speak to her immediately after the same meeting.

13

THE WORD SPREAD quickly through the White House that the President had called a meeting of his senior staff. Ever since the Lucia Benoni story had broken, there had been a sense of unease. The staff had been through similar things before, of course, and the surfacing of new allegations was not exactly a shock. But it was always a distraction, and never easy to deal with. The President and the First Lady would be tense, and it would be the staff's job to hold things together, and find ways to put the necessary spin on the situation. Martha Graylor, who bore the brunt of this responsibility, had convened the meeting, and was speaking with each staff member, as he or she arrived, ensuring that they understood the need for confidentiality. It would be a short meeting, she said. The President had to meet with the Director of the FBI as soon as possible. His only purpose was to reassure everybody that it was business as usual. Vice President Ellen Trevathan was the last to arrive. Avoiding Martha, she took a seat in a corner without a word to anyone.

Steve Wade entered the Oval Office with a cheerful smile. The First Lady was with him. She was not smiling. She was holding his hand in a grip which the President intended to suggest a gesture of solidarity, but actually looked more like a wrestling hold. The assembled staff stood as they entered. Wade signaled with his hand that they should all sit, pulled out a chair for the First Lady, and stood by her side.

'I want to thank you all for being here this morning,' he said. 'I know you all have a lot of work to do, and I won't keep you long. There is no way to tell you how much I appreciate your friendship and your loyalty. I could not do the job I was elected to do without you, and it is for this reason that I feel I must speak with you today. As you all know, the press has started in on us again. They are accusing me of having some kind of relationship with a woman called Lucia Benoni.'

A muted chorus of loyal boos ran around the room. The

President smiled gratefully.

'We've been through this kind of thing before, and we probably will again before our work in this office is done. At least this one has an interesting name.'

He paused to allow a ripple of polite laughter to die down.

'Now, I have denied these allegations categorically in the press. You all know that. But you deserve more than that. You deserve to hear it from me in person. I want to assure each one of you personally that there is no truth in the allegations at all, and I am confident that they will soon disappear. Hell, we don't even know if this Benoni woman exists. If she does, why hasn't she come forward? She may turn out to be the product of someone's imagination.'

A hand was held up at the back of the room.

'David?'

'Mr. President, if we're asked, is there any reason to think this is down to the opposition?'

'It's quite likely, in my opinion,' the President replied, to murmurs of outrage. 'We've been aware of this so-called 'Committee' the opposition has had for some time now. We believe they are operating under the cover of a so-called 'think tank', the Wilson Foundation. They are just a bunch of losers with no ideas of their own, their only agenda is to bring down those of us who are trying to get things done. They were probably responsible for some of the stories which were being spread during the election. These people can't stand the fact that we won, and that we are successful. They resent the fact that the American people know and appreciate the fine job we're doing. So it would not surprise me at all to find out that they had some involvement with this. And, if you feel it appropriate to express that opinion to someone who may ask, without attributing it to me, I certainly have no objection.'

'Thank you, Mr. President,' David said quietly.

The President waited for any more questions, but there was nothing but an uncomfortable silence.

'Well, again, thank you for coming. The First Lady and I appreciate it very much. I just want to add how grateful I am for Julia's love and loyalty. I'm sure you all understand how difficult it is for her. Without her standing by me, I just don't know what I would do.'

There was a final ripple of applause, and the staff began to file out. Julia Wade stood immediately and left the room quickly, without so much as a glance at her husband. The President's secretary came in from her office, and sought out Martha Graylor.

'Martha, your office called. There's an urgent message for you.'

'Thanks, Steffie. Mr. President, do you need me?'

'No. Go ahead.'

He turned to Steffie.'Is Director Lazenby here?'

'Not yet, Mr. President. He's been held up for a couple of minutes, but he's on his way.'

'Show him in as soon as he arrives.'

'Yes, Sir.'

As soon as they were alone, Steve Wade gestured to Ellen Trevathan to take a seat in one of the armchairs facing his desk.

'Well, I think that went pretty well, don't you? It's important to keep all our people involved, I think.'

'How is Julia doing?' the Vice President asked.

The President did not relish the question. He tried unsuccessfully to make light of it.

'Oh, you know Julia. She has to worry herself to death about everything.'

'Not without reason. The point of my question was to ask whether you can rely on her.'

Steve Wade laughed incredulously.

'What the hell do you mean? Of course I can rely on her.'

'It's going to look very bad if she...'

Ellen allowed the words to die away.

'If what? Come on, Ellen, you know better than that. I've already told you, we're working things out. I know she's had a rough time. I've apologized till I'm blue in the face, and I'm trying to make it up to her.'

'Fine,' Ellen said. 'I just ...'

Before she could continue, the intercom rang. The President pushed the speakerphone button.

'Martha's on her way over,' Steffie said. 'She says it's very urgent.'

Martha was as white as a sheet. She ignored Linda Samuels, who was just coming on duty, as the two passed in the corridor, causing Linda to turn and stare after her in surprise. She entered the President's office, and more or less collapsed into the armchair next to Ellen's in front of his desk. Ellen, who was just on the point of leaving, saw Martha's face and decided to remain unless Steve Wade asked her to go. He did not. He seemed almost unaware of Martha's agitation.

'What's up?' he inquired in a matter-of-fact tone. 'Steffie said you had something urgent.'

'Mr. President,' Martha stammered, getting the words out with difficulty, 'I just spoke with Harold at the *Post*...'

The President seemed irritated. 'Oh, for God's sake. What do they want now?'

'Harold asked whether we had any comment on a story they're going to run tomorrow. Do you remember, a few days ago, the Washington Police found the body of a young woman? She had been shot through the head.'

'No,' Wade replied. 'I guess I missed that one. Why would we have any comment on that?'

'I remember reading about it,' Ellen said. 'It was an execution-style murder over in North West. The police didn't know her identity.'

'Right,' Martha said. 'Well, they do now. According to the *Post*, the dead woman was Lucia Benoni.'

There was a long silence. Martha held her head in her hands. Steve Wade looked away sharply, and seemed to be fighting for breath. Ellen watched with fascination as he made a massive effort to control himself. He stood very slowly, and made his way from the office to his private bathroom. It was several minutes before he emerged again, the remains of the water he had splashed over his head still dripping down his face. The two women did not speak in his absence.

'Are they sure about this?' Wade asked.

'Harold said it was from a highly reliable source. The police were withholding the information until they could verify it, but they're expecting it to be released some time tomorrow. He also said the Bureau was involved.'

The President looked up.

'The Bureau? Why would they be involved?'

'I don't know, Sir.'

'Ted hasn't said anything to me.'

'I don't know, Sir.'

Martha seemed on the verge of tears. Wade stood and circled his desk once or twice. Watching him, Ellen noticed that his expression gradually became less grave. She could have sworn that, for just a second, he actually smiled to himself.

'OK, then, here we go,' the President said eventually. 'Of course, it's all very sad. We feel very sorry for Lucia Benoni, whoever she may have been, blah, blah, blah. But, at the same time, and obviously we shouldn't say this directly, but at the same time, we also feel some relief that this story is now going to go away. Perhaps we might even hint at the possible role of the press in this young woman's tragic situation, evils of irresponsible reporting, et cetera, et cetera. I leave that up to you.'

Ellen could hardly catch her breath. She looked at Martha, who was staring vacantly at the President.

'Why do I have the feeling it's not quite that simple?' Ellen asked.

'I have no idea,' Wade replied. 'It seems simple enough to me. I take it the *Post* isn't actually accusing me of killing her. Not that it would surprise me if they did. But in this case, I believe I probably have an alibi.'

Martha looked up.

'Mr. President, there's something else.'

Wade raised his arms inquiringly.

'The *Post* says the police found an S-pass in her purse.'

Ellen swore sharply under her breath. She turned her head away in a sudden fury, and jumped to her feet, ready to storm from the room. But as she did so, Steffie Walinsky entered the office, closely followed by Ted Lazenby. Steffie immediately noted the tension in the air, and regretted not having used the intercom before interrupting.

'I'm sorry, Mr. President. Do you need the Director to wait for a moment?'

'No,' Steve Wade replied, almost savagely. 'He's right on time. Come on in, Mr. Director.'

Lazenby realized at once that the President had already been told most of the news he had come to impart. As soon as Steffie had retreated to the safety of her office, the President turned on him violently.

'Why wasn't I told?'

'We are still in the process of verifying the facts, Mr. President. Please understand, this is not really our case. It's basically a D.C. Police matter. Chief Bryson called us in when they found… I take it you know about…?'

'The S-pass, yes,' the President shouted. 'Yes, I know about it as of about thirty seconds ago. Apparently, I'm the last fucking person in America to find out. Can you explain why the *Washington* fucking *Post* had this information before I did?'

Lazenby's jaw dropped.

'The *Post* knows about this?' he asked, genuinely shocked.

'They called a little while ago to see if we had any comment,' Martha replied quietly.

'Well, they didn't get it from us,' Lazenby said emphatically. 'We've kept it under wraps. The only person at the Bureau who knows all the facts is my personal assistant, Agent Kelly Smith. I guarantee you there's been no leak from the Bureau.'

Steve Wade exploded.

'I don't give a flying fuck where the leak came from. The fact is it happened. You've known about this all along. Why wasn't I consulted?'

Ted Lazenby stared at the President for some moments. Shocked as he was, he knew instinctively that the time had come to assert himself.

'Consulted? With all due respect, Mr. President, this is a criminal investigation. I don't know why I would consult with the White House about it. I came here today to inform you of certain facts as a matter of courtesy. But that's as far as I can go. This is not a consultation. I'm sure you understand that.'

The President suddenly picked up an ornamental paper-weight and slammed it down violently on the top of the desk. Ted Lazenby took a deep breath.

'I don't expect you to like this, Mr. President, but there is one further fact that I should bring to your attention. There may be nothing in it. We're checking it out right now.'

The Director felt every eye in the room fasten on him.

'The Benoni woman lived in New York. The D.C. Police had NYPD check out her apartment, and among other things, they found an address book.'

'So?'

'In this address book, there are two things of interest. The first was the name of Hamid Marfrela.'

'Who?'

Ellen Trevathan gave a deep sigh.

'He is the Lebanese diplomat suspected of being involved with those fascists in Oregon. Director Lazenby told us about him just a few days ago. Am I right, Mr. Director?'

'As always, Madam Vice President.'

Steve Wade was thunderstruck. He collapsed heavily into a chair.

'Well, what does that mean?'

'We don't know as yet, Mr. President. It may mean nothing at all. As I said, we're looking into it now.'

'What was the second thing?' Ellen asked.

'Mr. President, the other thing they found in Lucia Benoni's address book was the number of your private telephone line here at the White House.'

14

THE VAN WAS large, black, and nondescript. It had no windows. The radio and telephonic aerials were discreetly hidden away at the rear. The only occupant of the van, barely visible through the smoky windshield, was the driver, a casually-dressed man in his early thirties. Finding no empty parking space close enough to the building, the driver double-parked right in front of it without a second thought. His instructions were to get as close as he could. He would have preferred to be less conspicuous, but the rest of the team had to be able to leave the van without attracting attention. The van carried plates which would discourage the police from asking him to move, and the driver had a plan available to deal with any member of the public who might challenge him before a parking space opened up. He put the transmission in park, and turned towards the back of the vehicle, where the other occupants were sitting in silence, too close together for comfort.

'OK, folks, here we are, *chez* Hamid,' he said cheerfully. 'It looks pretty quiet out there. I'm not seeing anything to worry about. But I'll keep her running until you either come on back out or tell me you don't need it.'

'Thanks, Ed,' Kelly said, getting to her feet. 'OK, jackets on gentlemen, and remember, we're going to do this by the book. Let's not forget our suspect is armed and dangerous. Remember the drill, and be careful.'

One of the five male agents who had been sitting with her inserted a new magazine into his Glock and tested the action.

'Piece of cake.'

Kelly turned to help Jeff Morris into the black jacket she had brought for him. It had the initials FBI emblazoned on it in gold letters, back and front. All seven team members had donned bullet-proof vests before setting out from Headquarters, and an impressive array of weapons lay at their feet on the floor of the van.

'Put this on. We're making you an honorary FBI special agent for the day.'

'Great,' Jeff said. 'A man needs a hobby.'

Kelly swung a fake punch to his jaw.

'Wise guy. Everyone ready?'

The agents nodded. Kelly opened the back door of the van, and briefly surveyed the scene on the street. As Ed had said, it seemed quiet. But the last thing she wanted on this mission was to draw attention to it, so she took one more long look around. Once she was satisfied, Kelly led the way at a brisk pace to the door of the apartment building in which, at least according to Lucia Benoni, Hamid Marfrela resided. Three of the agents carried sub-machine guns. They would lead the way into the apartment and take the lead in dealing with any resistance. Kelly, Jeff, and the other two agents carried automatic pistols. The entrance to the building was locked. There was an intercom on the wall by the door, which listed the occupants of the building. Silently, Kelly indicated the name 'Marfrela' to the lead agents. As Lucia's address book had indicated, it seemed he did indeed live in apartment 315. One of the agents produced a small metal tool, and within a few seconds, the team entered the building unnoticed. In the van, Ed appeared to be happily engrossed in a sports magazine, without a care in the world.

Speaking in a whisper, Kelly indicated that she and two of the agents with sub-machine guns would take the elevator to the third floor. She directed Jeff to accompany the remaining agents on the staircase.

'This is just to minimize the risk of escape,' she said. 'No one goes in until we're all in place.'

The elevator was antiquated and slow, providing no advantage over the stairs, with the result that the two teams converged on apartment 315 at the same time. They stood outside, keyed up and ready to go. Kelly looked up and down the corridor. All was still. She nodded to one of the lead agents. He rapped hard on the door several times.

'FBI. We have a search warrant. Open up.'

The procedure was repeated once more. There was no reaction from within the apartment.

The lead agent looked inquiringly at Kelly. She nodded.

'Go.'

Within seconds, the agent had fixed a small explosive charge to the lock, and activated it. Jeff Morris had never witnessed the procedure before, and Kelly had to pull him back and make him face away from the door. The explosion, though minor, removed the lock instantly and completely. The lead agents pushed open the door and entered the apartment, their weapons trained ahead of them, ready for any resistance. There was none. Kelly and Jeff followed right behind them. Abruptly, the leaders stopped just inside the door, and Kelly heard one of them curse under his breath.

'What is it?' she asked quietly.

The agent stood aside, lowering his weapon to allow her to see for herself.

Sprawled on the floor, its back leaning against a sofa, was the lifeless body of a man. The body had several bullet wounds, and there was a lot of blood.

'Is that our friend?' Jeff asked, in a whisper.

Kelly took the photograph supplied by the State Department from inside her jacket and held it up.

'That's him,' she replied quietly. 'Check out the rest of the apartment. Assume the killer may still be here. Try not to contaminate the scene, but don't take any risks.'

Silently, the agents moved through the apartment, checking every room and closet for possible hiding places. It did not take long. The apartment was not a large one.

'Nothing,' an agent said to Kelly as they returned.

'Any other way out of the place?'

'No. Whoever did this came in through the same door we did, and left the same way.'

'All right. Harry, go down and alert Ed. Have him stay parked right outside the front door, and help him secure the entrance. No one leaves or gets in without showing ID and accounting for themselves. Any questions, you come up and get me.'

'Yes, Ma'am.'

'I'll get our forensic people organized,' Jeff said, taking out his mobile phone.

'Good,' Kelly said.

'So, what do we do now, Kelly?' an agent asked.

'We have a search warrant,' Kelly replied, 'and we are going to execute it as soon as we can. The problem now is that we can do nothing until the forensic guys get through with the place. I guess the good news is that there's no rush. We're not going to be interrupted.'

'What's the bad news?'

'The bad news is that I have to call the Director and tell him what's happening.'

'I bet it will make his day.'

'No kidding.'

'Anything I can do?'

Kelly considered.

'Sure. I noticed a coffee shop just down the street. We're going to be here for a while. We may as well make ourselves comfortable. Get whatever everybody wants, on me. Mine's a latté with an extra shot of espresso.'

'Can I leave the machine gun here? I don't want to alarm people unnecessarily.'

'Good thinking, Ben. I'll look after it for you.'

Kelly took out her mobile phone and called FBI Headquarters, asking to be patched through to the Director on a secure line. Ted Lazenby had only just returned from the White House, feeling bruised and battered, after a long and angry confrontation with the President, during which he had expressed himself strongly about what he saw as an attempt to interfere with an ongoing criminal investigation. It had even occurred to him to hand in his resignation and take an early retirement to his family home in Wisconsin. It was a possibility he had not yet completely rejected. His mood was not improved by Kelly's news.

'This is unbelievable,' he said, the shock obvious in his voice. 'Do you have any leads yet?'

'No, Sir. The D.C. forensic people are on their way. I don't want to contaminate the scene by getting too close but, from where I'm standing, it doesn't look like a professional hit. There are a number of wounds, but they're all over the place. I can't make a search till the forensic guys are through. I'm probably going to be here all day.'

'Do you need back-up?'

'Yes, Sir, lots of it. I'd appreciate it if you would call Chief Bryson and have him take over security at the main entrance here. It's his jurisdiction. We need enough manpower to start interviewing all the other occupants of the building, and at the same time, keep the press at a safe distance. They'll probably start showing up any minute now.'

'You got it.'

'I guess you'll be informing the Lebanese Embassy?'

'And the State Department. It's required in a case involving an accredited diplomat.'

Kelly hesitated.

'Is there any way you could hold off on that for a while?'

'Why, Kelly?'

'To give me time to look around. Once their people get here and start throwing their weight around, it's going to be a real circus.'

Lazenby sighed deeply.

'Oh, God, why not? I'm in deep enough as it is.'

'Sir?'

'I just had to chew the President out for trying to interfere in the investigation. This was just after he learned from *The Washington Post* that Lucia Benoni was the proud possessor of an S-pass.'

Kelly's jaw dropped.

'The *Post*? You're not serious.'

'I'm afraid I am very serious. Can you think of any way this could have leaked? Because right now, we're looking like we have egg all over our faces.'

'No, Sir, I can't. No one knew about it at our end except you and me. There were several D.C. people, obviously, Chief Bryson, Lieutenant Morris, and one or two other officers who would have been cataloguing the evidence. Do you want me to look into it?'

'No. I'll handle it myself with Chief Bryson. What about your friend in the Secret Service?'

'Linda? No way. She was mad at us just because of the possible damage to the President. She's very protective of him.'

'All right. Call in the moment you have anything new.'

'Yes, Sir.'

Frustrated, Kelly shut off the phone and walked over to Jeff Morris.

'Are your people on their way?'

'Yes. They'll be about half an hour.'

She took his arm and pulled him into a corner.

'Jeff, I need to ask you something, but it mustn't go any further.'

'Shoot.'

'I just spoke to Director Lazenby. He had just come from the White House. Someone tipped off *The Washington Post* about the fact that Lucia Benoni had an S-pass.'

Jeff's eyes opened wide.

'At our end?'

'That's his suspicion. Only he and I knew about it within the Bureau. I know it wasn't you, so…'

'Thank you.'

'It goes without saying, Jeff. But can you think of any possibilities?' Morris leaned against the wall.

'There are only two other officers officially involved with handling the evidence. As you know, as soon as I found it, I kept it hidden until I could talk to Chief Bryson. There were uniformed officers on the scene before I got there. They're not supposed to touch anything, and I have no reason to believe they did. But I guess you never know.'

'OK,' Kelly said. 'Lazenby has warned me off that aspect of the inquiry, anyway. He's going to talk to Bryson about it. But keep your ears and eyes open just in case. I don't like the way this is going.'

It was almost two hours later by the time the D.C. scenes-of-crimes officers had finished their work. Their quiet, methodical approach contrasted markedly with the chaotic scene outside the apartment building. The entire street had been taken over by the press and television camera crews. Several different crews were filming segments for the evening news at the same time. Cameras and lights had been set up in the street as well as on the sidewalk. The reporters' vigil was not particularly rewarding. Kelly had given instructions that no information should be released, except that a male had been found shot to death at an apartment within the building, and an investigation was ongoing. The reporters were clamoring for more. Ed had retired to a safe distance in the black van. The resources of the D.C. police officers were strained almost to breaking point as they held the reporters and sightseers at bay outside the cordon they had established around the apartment building, and tempers were becoming frayed. Detectives from the D.C. Police Department had begun a door-to-door inquiry.

The Medical Examiner stopped to speak to her on his way out.

'Male, about thirty, thirty-five, with six bullet wounds in different parts of the body. Probably from a good old-fashioned revolver. Kind of romantic. You don't see that very much any more. The shooter probably fired from just inside this door. I would say the victim's been dead between six and twelve hours. I know that's not very precise. I'll have more for you once I've done the autopsy.'

'Thank you, Doctor.'

As the body was being removed on a stretcher, Kelly and Jeff walked back into the living room, where two forensic scientists were finishing up their work.

'Any prints, Joe?' Morris asked.

'Everywhere. I have a feeling we may get lucky on this one.'

'You might want to try the door,' Morris said. 'The M.E. said the shooter may have fired from there. Maybe he didn't make it very far inside.'

'I'm afraid we weren't very helpful,' Kelly said ruefully. 'We took the lock out when we came in.'

Joe grinned cheerfully, and ambled towards the door.

'No problem. I've dealt with that one before. I'll pick up the pieces and take a look for you.'

For the next two hours, Kelly, Jeff, and a forensic specialist took Hamid Marfrela's home apart piece by piece. His personal effects were few and unremarkable. There were no secret hiding places, and the most important find was made in a drawer in the walk-in closet off the bedroom. No effort had been made to conceal it. Jeff Morris made the discovery, and called Kelly in to see.

'What have you got?'

Jeff indicated the drawer with a smile. Lying inside was a Ruger 357 Magnum and a box of ammunition.

'How about a possible murder weapon?'

'God, that would be nice, wouldn't it? Do you think this is standard diplomatic issue?'

'I don't know.'

Kelly stared at the weapon thoughtfully.

'I wonder if he was expecting trouble.'

'I don't think he was expecting it quite so soon,' Jeff replied. 'Otherwise, he might have kept his gun some place a little closer to hand, where he might have had a chance of using it.'

Kelly nodded.

'Well, we'll get it tested and see if he practiced with it on Lucia. What else?'

'Oh, you're going to love this. One brown folder containing a road map and what appear to be directions....'

'To get where?'

'Well, the map is a road map of the State of Oregon. And I would hazard a guess that the arrow here points to the friendly local Sons of the Land compound. I also think it might be fun to check out these phone numbers he scribbled on the back of the map.'

'Beautiful,' Kelly said. 'What else is in there?'

'A bunch of stuff I haven't even got to yet. I wanted to show you the good stuff first. Let's take a look.'

Kelly was suddenly apprehensive.

'Let's do that later, Jeff. I don't know how long Lazenby was able to hold off calling the Lebanese Embassy. With all the press activity, probably not very long. Let's get all this stuff bagged and out of here before they show up screaming diplomatic privilege. Did we find his passport?'

'Yes. They've bagged it already.'

'We're going to have to hand that over to them. Make a list of the stamps in it, and any other information.'

'OK.'

Jeff headed out of the bedroom towards the living room. Kelly took a last look around. She could not see anything out of the ordinary. Casually, she opened a drawer in the small bedside table. It contained a copy of *Hustler* magazine and photographs of two young women, no identification but, by their appearance, not American. Respectable looking. Perhaps family, girl friends, or marriage interests. One of the pages of the magazine was folded over slightly at the top right-hand corner. Kelly opened the magazine at the page. It featured a series of color photographs of a man performing various sexual acts on a naked woman who was tied, spread-eagled, to a bed, lying on her back. She appeared to be enjoying whatever he was doing.

'Probably not encouraged in Lebanon,' Kelly said to herself.

She smiled, replaced the magazine in the drawer, and began to walk away. But suddenly, she turned back, savagely yanked the drawer open, and flicked through the magazine until she came to the same page.

'Kelly Smith, God damn it, switch your brain on,' she told herself.

She ran into the living room, told the forensic officer to bag the *Hustler*, and called to Jeff Morris.

'Jeff, I need to speak to the M.E. Do you have a number?'

'He'll be back at the morgue with the body by now,' Jeff replied. 'Hold on. I have a mobile number.'

After a brief search, Jeff dictated a number.

'Thanks. Can you get all that stuff downstairs now, find Ed, and tell him to take it straight to Headquarters, and not let it out of his sight until we come for it?'

'Our Headquarters, or yours?'

They looked at each other.

'It should be yours, technically' Kelly said, 'but…'

'Yours,' Jeff said decisively. 'It will be OK. We can explain it. It was your search warrant.'

'Good,' Kelly said.

Morris called to the agents, who were waiting patiently by the door of the apartment.

'Guys, give me a hand with this stuff. It has to be out of here now.'

Kelly quickly dialed the medical examiner's mobile number. To her relief, he picked up.

'Dr. Edloe, this is Agent Kelly Smith. I've just thought of something I need you to do. I need you to take samples from the body for DNA testing.'

'I can do that,' the M.E. replied. 'What kind of tests did you have in mind?'

'I want them tested against samples taken from another body you have down there at the morgue, a woman called Lucia Benoni. There should be blood samples and a vaginal swab. Can you do that?'

'Sure. I remember Benoni. I was there when they brought her in. Is our guy a suspect in that one?'

'That's what I'm hoping you're going to tell us,' Kelly said.

A uniformed D.C. police officer came in, looking distinctly pleased with himself.

'Excuse me, Ma'am, …'

'Yes?'

'I just thought you ought to know, I just talked with a Mr. and Mrs. John Bacon. They live on the second floor.'

'And…?'

'Ma'am, they say they saw a man leaving the building by the staircase about three o'clock this morning. He was in a hurry, and he was carrying a canvas bag, the kind of thing you might carry your tennis gear in.'

'Description?'

'Yeah, kind of weird. They said real wild-looking, with a beard, plaid shirt, heavy boots, reminded them of some kind of mountain man. Young, about six feet tall. The staircase is pretty well lit, so they claim they had a good view.'

'What were the Bacons doing on the staircase at that hour?'

'They weren't actually on the staircase. They had been out of town, got a late start driving back, and they were just unloading their bags from the elevator. They heard someone running hell for leather downstairs, they looked and saw this guy going from three to two.'

'Did he see them?'

'Ma'am, they're not sure.'

'All right. Nice work, officer. Get a full statement, arrange for them to meet with a sketch artist as soon as possible, and tell them I'm going to arrange twenty-four hour security until we're sure there's no danger.'

'Yes, Ma'am,' the officer beamed, and ran out of the apartment.

As he did so, an official-looking delegation presented itself at the door, accompanied by Jeff Morris and a uniformed officer.

'Agent Kelly Smith?' the man who seemed to be the leader asked. He was tall and thin, with a short goatee beard, immaculately attired in a formal charcoal suit, white shirt, and red tie. His voice betrayed only the trace of an accent.

'Yes.'

'I am Kalik Amal, Deputy Head of Station, Embassy of the Republic of Lebanon.'

Amal produced his identification, and waved it briefly in front of her.

'I demand access to this apartment and possession of all diplomatic papers.'

Kelly stood aside, and gestured to Amal to enter.

'It's all yours, Your Excellency. Help yourself. This is Mr. Marfrela's passport. I'm not aware of any other diplomatic papers here, but if you should find any, you are welcome to remove them. On behalf of the Federal Bureau of Investigation, may I express my condolences on Mr. Marfrela's death. I assure you that we will spare no effort to bring whoever is responsible to justice.'

The diplomat seemed taken aback by her immediate agreement.

'Thank you, Agent Smith. What effects have been removed already?'

'Only evidence relating to the murder.'

'What is that evidence?'

'Your Excellency, I regret that I am not authorized to disclose that information. You would have to request it from my Director, and the Chief of Police for the District of Columbia.'

'You were here, Agent Smith. I demand that you tell me.'

'I'm sorry, Your Excellency. I would be happy to convey your request to Director Lazenby immediately.'

Amal was furious, but he realized that his options were limited. Kelly was within her rights. She breathed a sigh of relief that the evidence was safely in Ed's care and on its way by van to the Hoover Building, where it would be catalogued and then thoroughly tested in the FBI laboratory. Amal nodded to the three men with him, who began their own search of the apartment. Amal himself walked back casually into the living room, and sat in an armchair, studying the bloodstains with apparent fascination. Kelly took Jeff by the arm, and led him to the front door.

'I'm getting an urge to go look at the evidence before the Director has to decide whether we need to hand any of it over.'

'Fine with me,' Morris replied. 'Amal's not exactly a bundle of laughs.'

'Right,' Kelly said. 'Let's leave him to it.'

'Harry,' Kelly whispered to the agent who had just returned after carrying down the last box of evidence, 'Would you mind locking up after our guests leave? I need to get back to Headquarters.'

'I guess,' Harry replied. 'But what happens if he wants to take…?'

'He can take whatever he wants,' Kelly reassured him. 'We've got what we need, and we're pretty sure there's nothing left to interest Amal. Just get a receipt for anything he does take, and call me later.'

'Yes, Ma'am.'

With that, Kelly and Jeff left unnoticed.

15

'YOU LOOK AS exhausted as I feel,' Ted Lazenby said.

'I've had better days,' Kelly acknowledged. She had just entered his office, and was leaning weakly against the door frame. It was almost nine o'clock on a rainy Friday evening.

On arriving back at the Hoover Building, she had spent some time with the agents who had been assigned to conduct a preliminary examination of the evidence taken from Hamid Marfela's apartment. Mercifully, there was not much of it, and probably most of it would eventually be found to be irrelevant to the murder of Lucia Benoni. In ordinary circumstances, it would have been taken directly to the laboratory for testing, or to an evidence room for storage. But these were not ordinary circumstances. The Bureau had taken a number of significant risks in the way it had handled the case. It was essential to go by the book from this point on, especially where the Lebanese Embassy was concerned. If there were any papers or effects which should be turned over to the Ambassador, now was the time to find out. Kelly stayed long enough to be satisfied that the agents understood what was expected of them. She then left Jeff Morris with the agents as the representative of the D.C. Police Department, and made her way to the Director's office, where Lazenby was waiting for her.

Lazenby waved Kelly into a chair and used a small key to open the doors of a cabinet which formed the base of a book case behind his desk. The contents of the cabinet were more interesting than the volumes of the United States Code and the onyx book ends on the shelves above them. A bottle of single malt whisky, one of Lazenby's few indulgences. Without asking, he poured two glasses and handed one to Kelly. He pulled up a chair for himself across from her.

'This will get the blood circulating again.'

Kelly smiled.

'Thanks, Director.'

'How was it today – for you, I mean?'

'It was fine. I didn't have time to think about it.'

She sniffed her glass. 'Thank you for trusting me with this. It means a lot.'

'I had no doubts. All that mattered was how you felt. So, what does it look like down there? Anything we're going to have to turn over?'

Kelly took a grateful sip of the whisky and felt it warming and relaxing her whole body. She began to realize how much the day had taken out of her. She was drained.

'I don't think so, though some of it may be a judgment call.'

'Such as…?'

'Well, there's a clear paper trail from Marfrela to the Sons of the Land compound in Oregon. If we make the assumption that the Embassy was somehow involved with that…'

'That has to be a possibility.'

'Yes, but I doubt they would want to admit it. They're pretty much bound to take the line that whatever Marfrela was doing, he was doing on his own time.'

'Agreed. Why don't we just keep quiet and see whether they ask for it? If they do, we'll consider turning it over.'

'Right, Sir. Did you get my message that we found a handgun and ammunition?'

'Yes. I don't think we need to worry about that, at least as far as the Embassy is concerned. Hardly diplomatic material.'

'It could be Embassy property.'

'Whether it is or not, it's staying with us until it's been tested, and if there's any chance at all that it's the murder weapon in the Benoni case, it's staying with us indefinitely.'

Kelly allowed herself to stretch out her legs and sink into her chair.

'The truth is, Director, there's not much down there that's going to interest the Embassy. I'm not sure how much of it will interest us, really. We'll see what the tests turn up, and I'll run those phone numbers in Oregon by Phil Hammond. But I can't help thinking we would have gotten a lot more from a few minutes of conversation with Hamid Marfrela.'

'Yes. Very likely, whoever killed him had the same thought,' Lazenby mused.

'Yes, Sir. God, I just wish…'

'No, no, you know what they say about hindsight.'

Lazenby watched his personal assistant try unsuccessfully to suppress a yawn.

'Look, why don't you get out of here for the weekend and get some rest?' he suggested kindly. 'It's getting way too late.'

Kelly took a long drink of her whisky.

'I appreciate it, Director, but I think I'd better stay until they finish cataloguing the evidence. You never know what might crawl out of the woodwork.'

'No,' Lazenby replied firmly. 'It won't do the Lebanese Embassy any harm to stew for a couple of days. I can easily put them off until some time next week. State will back me up. They're not overjoyed that Marfrela was running around doing whatever he was doing without adult supervision, so the Ambassador's not exactly flavor of the month with State right now. The Lebanese Ambassador is not worth killing yourself for, Kelly. Just make sure it's all secure till Monday.'

'Thank you, Director,' Kelly smiled with relief. 'I have to admit I'm looking forward to getting home tonight.'

She finished her whisky and replaced the glass on the table at the side of her chair.

'And I hope you're going to take your own advice.'

Lazenby stood slowly.

'What?'

'You should get out of here too.'

'Oh, yes,' he muttered non-committally. 'I will. I have to make a stop on the way home, but I'm out of here.'

'OK Sir. Good night.'

'Good night, Kelly.'

After Kelly had left, the Director waited for a few seconds, then picked up his personal phone. He dialed a number, which was answered almost immediately.

'Steve, I'm sorry it's so late. Do you still want to...?'

'Hell, yes. I'm waiting for you. Come on over.'

'I'm on my way,' Lazenby replied.

16

'THE BASTARDS ARE out to assassinate me,' Steve Wade observed bitterly, handing Ted Lazenby a glass of whisky. The whisky was blended and undistinguished, so Lazenby had asked for water and a little ice, a form of pollution he would never have dreamed of inflicting on his own single malt.

'That's all it is. Assassination. Bastards.'

They were alone in a private den in the Residence on the second floor of the White House. Their friendship had begun years before in college, on the football field and in the fraternity house. The President still kept around ten friends from that time in his life, a kind of inner circle, who were close enough to be invited to spend time in this inner sanctum. Only three, including Lazenby, were now based in Washington, and of these only Lazenby had been offered a job within the Administration. Ever since Wade's election to his first term, Lazenby had visited him privately for a drink and casual conversation at least once a month. He had wondered whether that would change after his appointment as Director of the FBI, but it seemed that Wade continued to value their time together as friends, and saw no conflict in their meeting as before. They had a tacit, but clear understanding that these informal occasions were privileged, and that no matters of business would be discussed. It was a rare opportunity for the President to relax in the company of a trusted friend.

Lazenby waited for the President to take a seat in his armchair before doing the same, and shook his head to decline the offer of a cigar.

'Steve, I understand how it must look to you. You're the President. You're in the papers day-in, day-out, can't avoid it, and God knows they're always looking for a good story. But you don't have to see it as assassination.'

'I don't know what the hell else to call it.'

'You're a public figure. They think they own you.'

'So, that gives them the right to tell lies about me?'

'No. Not in my book.'

'Well, that's my point.'

Slowly, Lazenby drank some whisky.

'Is that what they're doing?' he asked.

Wade paused in the act of lighting a cigar and allowed the match to burn out.

'What the hell's that supposed to mean?'

'I'm just asking.'

'Jesus Christ.'

Wade struck another match, and there was silence while he lit his cigar and appreciatively blew out several smoke rings.

'Are you saying you don't believe me?'

'No.'

'That's what it sounds like. Christ, that's all I need.'

'I'm not saying anything, Steve. I'm asking you a question. You don't have to answer. But it's the same question the press are asking you.'

'Everyone's after me.'

'I doubt that.'

'You should live my life for a day. I can't get away from Lucia Benoni. If it's not the press, it's my wife or even my fucking Vice President, for Christ's sake. Why can't I get a break from it for five minutes? Would it kill you people to believe me and get on with your lives?'

'I'm not "you people",' Lazenby replied quietly. 'I'm your friend, and as your friend, I'm counseling you to face up to a few facts, to ask yourself why the press doesn't believe you.'

Wade flicked a small deposit of ash from his cigar.

'You mean the S-pass?'

'Yes.'

'A lot of people have S-passes, Ted. I can't keep track of all that. We have staff here in the White House who issue them. I can't understand what the big deal is. The Secret Service checks them all out. I don't get to just hand them out to anyone I want. Hell, if I ask for an S-pass to be issued, there must be at least twenty people who know about it. I couldn't keep it quiet if I wanted to. The President has no privacy, Ted. Jesus, living in the White House is like living in a fucking zoo. The whole world gets to peer into your cage.'

'Fine,' Lazenby said. 'Tell them that.'

'Do you really think that would make a difference? That Sullivan bitch has me in her sights, and she's loaded for bear. She has me in bed with the Benoni woman, and nothing's going to change that.'

'Mary Sullivan's not like that, Steve. Show her she's barking up the wrong tree and she'll back off faster than you can say '*Washington Post*.''

'The woman's a leech.'

'The woman's a Pulitzer Prize-winner with a reputation for sticking to the facts. Look, if this had come from *The Enquirer*, that's one thing. If it comes from the *Post*, that's another thing. And if it comes from Mary Sullivan, that's something else again.'

'You're saying they'll believe her rather than me?'

'I'm saying she has credibility. But if you tell the truth and she sees that you're telling the truth, she will go away, and so will the rest of them. It will die a natural death.'

Wade nodded, exhaling cigar smoke.

'The Benoni woman did have my phone number, didn't she?'

'Yes, she did,' Lazenby smiled. 'But then, so do I.'

'Right, and as far as I know, they're not on to the phone number yet. Or are they?'

'Not as far as I know.'

There was a silence.

'I'm not going to give in to them, Ted. Never. No matter what the bastards do.'

It was said with an intensity that took Lazenby aback. There was a look in the President's eyes which seemed unfamiliar; distant, preoccupied, even frightened. Lazenby allowed himself a long draught of his whisky before replying.

'I wouldn't expect anything else,' he said eventually.

Wade suddenly seemed to snap out of his reverie. He smiled and flicked more ash from his cigar before standing to refill both their glasses.

'So, are you going to any of the games?'

The abrupt change of subject took Lazenby by surprise.

'Harvard, for sure, and probably Dartmouth. I'm not sure about the others. Are you going to make one?'

'I'd like to,' Wade replied, handing Lazenby his glass. 'It brings back the old days, and they seem to like it if I put in an appearance every now and then.'

'I would say so,' Lazenby said, raising his glass as a toast. 'It can't hurt with the alumni to have the President show up for a game.'

'It could hurt with fifty percent of the alumni,' the President laughed.

Lazenby shook his head.

'Not in a million years. If you went to the same school as the President, you flaunt it, even if you didn't vote for him, and even if you don't agree with a word he says.'

'Well, you may be right.'

'I guarantee you that's what the president of the University thinks. The athletic director, too.'

Wade suddenly threw back his head and laughed uproariously.

'You remember when I went back there just after I got elected the first time?'

Lazenby joined in the laughter.

'Oh, God, yes. The thing with the dog…'

'Secret service dog. They were searching the athletic department offices for explosives, right? I was supposed to make a quick visit there before the game on my way up to the VIP box, say 'Hi' to the athletic director and the coaches. So they go in like they always do, sniffer dogs, the whole nine yards. And they take this one dog in there, very experienced dog, always been as good as gold. The dog takes one look at the head coach, gets bent out of shape for some reason, snarls at him, and takes a piece right out of his ass. This is an hour before the game. So now, the poor bastard has to find the team's doctor, get himself a tetanus shot, then stand on the sidelines the whole game with bandages over the tooth marks in his ass.'

'I remember,' Lazenby said. 'Whatever happened to the dog?'

'They were going to retire him,' Wade replied. 'But the athletic director said the coach should have had his ass chewed out long ago, and the dog was only doing what he should have done himself.'

'He got that right,' Lazenby laughed. 'We sucked that season.'

'Yeah, that dog knew exactly what he was doing, didn't he? Hell, if the Secret Service had retired him, I would have brought him to the White House and made him First Dog.'

Wade took a long drink of whisky.

'Oh, those were the days, Ted. They loved me back then.'

'They want to love you now, Steve,' Lazenby replied, 'if you would just let them.'

Wade was in the mood to talk. It was another hour, and many more reminiscences, before Lazenby, tired as he was, was able to take his leave. Wade stopped him at the door.

'Ted, I want to ask you something.'

'Sure.'

'Look, I'm not admitting anything, but…'

'Go ahead.'

Wade took a deep breath.

'Ted, you are going to get the bastard who killed her, who killed Lucia, aren't you? I'm relying on you. You are going to get him, aren't you?'

'It means that much to you?'

'You have no idea how much.'

Lazenby thought for a few moments about a 357 Magnum, a magazine with bondage photographs, a name in an address book, and a body with six bullet holes in it from a good old-fashioned revolver. He put his hand gently on the President's arm.

'Yes, we are, Steve,' he replied. 'We're going to get him. One way or the other. I promise you that.'

'Thanks, Buddy,' Wade said, with what appeared to be a sigh of relief. 'Take care driving home.'

17

KELLY WAS GRATEFUL for the respite of a leisurely weekend. Her week had been a long one, and the burst of energy she had gained from Ted Lazenby's whisky had been used up driving across town from the Hoover Building to her apartment. On arriving home, she made herself a cheese sandwich, took a long bubble bath accompanied by two glasses of white wine, fell into bed, and immediately sank into a deep sleep. She did not set her alarm clock, and when she finally woke, it was a little after two o'clock on Saturday, the following afternoon. She put coffee on to brew, threw on a sweat-shirt and jeans, and walked barefoot down to the foyer of her building to retrieve her mail. She ate a belated breakfast, and began to ponder what to do with the rest of her day.

At three-thirty Jeff Morris called.

'Hi, Kelly,' he said. 'Feeling any better?'

'Yes. I had a good sleep,' she replied. 'At least I don't feel like death warmed up any more. How about you?'

'I didn't sleep too well. I couldn't stop thinking about what happened yesterday. Or it could have been the pasta and red wine I had around midnight.'

Kelly laughed. 'That could have had something to do with it.'

'Yeah, maybe. Anyway, did you read today's *Post*?'

'No. I just woke up.'

'They broke the Benoni story. You want to hear the headline?'

'Sure.'

"Mystery Woman in Murder Case Linked to President."

'Jesus,' Kelly said. 'They're not mincing their words over this, are they?'

'It gets better,' Jeff said. "The mystery woman found shot to death in a North West apartment on Monday has been identified as Lucia Benoni, thirty-four, a resident of New York City, who has been romantically linked to President Steve Wade in stories reported by this correspondent. President Wade has denied the allegations. The motive for the execution-style slaying remains unclear, and authorities would say only that they are following a number of leads. The mystery deepened yesterday when a reliable source told this reporter that Miss Benoni, who is of Lebanese extraction, was in possession of a special pass, a so-called S-pass, which entitled her to gain entry to the White House without going through normal security channels. A spokesperson for the White House told the *Post* that such passes can be issued at the request of various officials, including the President. The spokesperson did not know who had issued the pass to Miss Benoni, or whether it had ever been used."

'A reliable source, huh?'

'Yeah.'

'Wonderful. Anything about our boy Hamid?'

'Oh, yes. Second mysterious murder in D.C. within a week, police tight-lipped, and so on. They got his identity, of course.'

'Of course. I'm sure the other residents were lining up to talk to them. Any mention of the Bacons?'

'No, thank goodness. And the Lebanese Ambassador declined to comment.'

'Yes, I bet he did,' Kelly said. 'I'm sure the last thing they want is for the press to start digging into Hamid's extracurricular activities.'

'Right,' Jeff agreed. 'I don't think we'll be hearing too much from the Lebanese.'

'But no one's made the link from Lucia Benoni to Hamid Marfrela yet?' Kelly mused.

'Not yet. But what do you want to bet we're reading about that on Monday morning?'

'Very likely, the way things are going.'

For some reason, Linda Samuels flashed through Kelly's mind.

'Jeff, did the White House have any other comment on the story?'

Jeff laughed.

'Oh, yeah, you're going to love this. I quote: 'Martha Graylor, the President's Press Secretary, this afternoon issued a categorical denial that the President was in any way involved in issuing an S-pass to Lucia Benoni. The President continues to deny knowing Miss Benoni, and further denies having any romantic relationship with her.' End quote.'

Kelly exhaled sharply into the telephone.

'This guy is too stupid to live. How long does he think it's going to take them to get the goods on this?'

'It's hard to believe, isn't it?'

They were silent for a while.

'So, what are you doing with the rest of your weekend off?' Jeff asked.

'I'm not sure I'm going to take the whole weekend,' Kelly replied. 'I should really go in and start ploughing through that evidence. Director Lazenby bought us a couple of days, but I really owe it to him to go in tomorrow and take a look.'

'Oh, don't do that, Kelly.'

'Why not?'

'It's my evidence too. If you go in, I have to go in as well.'

'No, you don't. I can call you if I find anything earth-shattering. I don't think I will. It will be mainly to check for anything we should turn over to the Embassy.'

'No. I couldn't let you do it alone. I would feel too guilty.'

'This is emotional blackmail,' Kelly smiled.

'Yes, it is. Is it working?'

'Maybe. What were you going to do tomorrow?'

'If the weather holds, I thought I might drive down to Virginia and take my friend's sail boat out. He hardly uses it, and he's been asking me to give it some exercise for a while now.'

Kelly responded without any conscious thought at all.

'Would you like someone to crew?' she heard herself ask.

'You sail?'

'Used to. It's been a while, but I used to spend my summers near Seattle when I was growing up. My folks had a place near the ocean. My dad loves to sail. He taught me. I'm sure I'm pretty rusty, but I wouldn't mind giving it a try. I guess the evidence will wait one more day.'

'Deal,' Jeff said. His tone was one of pleased surprise. 'I'll pick you up around eleven.'

Kelly smiled to herself as she hung up and prepared to take a shower.

'I can't believe I just did that,' she giggled to herself, as she stood under the welcome hot water.

As she stepped out of the shower, the phone rang again. Hastily wrapping a bath towel around her body, she ran into the living room, dripping water as she went. She picked up the phone.

'Kelly?'

'Yeah?'

'It's me, Frank.'

To her surprise, the sound of Frank's voice made Kelly feel anxious. Her stomach tied itself in a knot. She hesitated, not sure what to say.

'Sweetheart, are you there?'

'Yes. I'm sorry. I just got out of the shower.'

'Mm. I wish I was there. Tell me what you're wearing… if anything.'

'Where are you, Frank? You didn't call, and I…'

'Cleveland. The Senator has a fund-raiser here tomorrow. Actually, that's why I was calling.'

'Oh?'

'Yes. We're having a reception for some very wealthy people at one of the art museums. Formal wear, very swish. I need you to get on a plane and come on out to be there with me.'

Kelly sat down on the sofa, and rubbed the towel over her face. She was silent for some time.

'Kelly?'

'Frank, I can't. Not tomorrow.'

There was another silence, stony this time.

'Why not?'

'Because we've had two murders here this week, and I've hardly slept, and I have a stack of evidence to look through.'

She held the telephone away from her ear, hardly able to believe the lie she was telling.

'But sweetheart,' Frank was saying. She put the receiver back to her ear. 'I thought we agreed that my work with the Senator was more important to us. Once we get married, that's where our focus will be in terms of career. I know you're senior enough now to get a junior agent to fill in for you.'

'Not in this case,' Kelly said. 'I can't go into the details on the phone, but there's some heavy stuff going down. In fact, Ted Lazenby and I are the only people who are dealing with it.'

There was another silence.

'You're really letting me down here, Kelly.'

She raised her eyes to the ceiling. Before she could control it the anger flashed and removed any thought of guilt from her mind.

'What did you say?'

'I said you're really letting me down.'

Kelly took a deep breath.

'You just don't get it, do you? I have a career too, Frank, and it's important to me. You have no idea what I've had to deal with this week. But you call me up from Cleveland or wherever and tell me to jump, and I'm supposed to ask how high? I don't think so.'

'I think you ought to think more about us and our future, Kelly, that's all I'm saying.'

She shook her head, and made the decision almost without a thought.

'We don't have a future, Frank. You know what? I'm not going to look at evidence tomorrow. I'm going out with someone else.'

The silence was even longer.

'You're going out with another man?'

'That's right.'

'You lied to me?' Frank sounded incredulous.

'Yes. I'm sorry. Now I'm telling you the truth.'

'Fine,' he said. 'I hope he can offer you the future I could have offered you.'

'God damn it, Frank, I'm not thinking about a future. I'm going out sailing for the afternoon.'

'That's more important to you than our future?'

'Frank, I'm not ready for a future, not if it means giving up my work and being a wife who's nice to people at parties. I can't do that. I'm just thinking about what's right for me now. The future will just have to wait.'

'Well, you see, that's your whole problem right there,' Frank said.

Kelly gasped. 'I'm sorry. What is my problem – exactly?'

'That you don't want to think about our future. That you find it more important to go out and enjoy yourself, than do something for our future.'

'No, actually, that's now your problem,' she replied angrily. 'Find someone else to go to your fund-raiser. And find someone else to have a future with.'

'I might just do that.'

'Fuck you, Frank,' Kelly said.

She slammed down the phone, cutting off his call. She stood there for a full minute, her hand still resting on the receiver, before she started to shake, and had to sit down.

'Oh, fuck,' she said to herself.

She dialed another number.

'Linda?'

By now, Kelly was sobbing aloud.

'Hi, Kelly. Hey, you don't sound too good, girl. What's up?'

'Frank,' she managed to say through the tears. 'Frank is up.'

'Oh, Jesus. Don't tell me you finally did it?'

'Did what?'

'"Did what?" the girl asks. Ditched the bastard, that's what. It's about time.'

'Oh, Linda…'

'I'm sorry, I'm sorry. No. I'm not. He was making your life miserable. You're well out of it.'

'I need you, Linda. Could you come round this evening? Do you have anything planned?'

'Me? No. Free as a bird. Jesus, Kelly, of course I'll come round.'

'Bring a bottle and a movie. I'll get the pizza.'

'Oh, oh,' Linda laughed. 'Is it going to be one of those Patsy Cline evenings?'

'Looks like.'

'I'll be there. What kind of movie do you want?'

'Something to make me feel better.'

'OK. How about *Schindler's List*?'

'Linda…'

'Joke, Kelly, joke,' Linda said. 'It was a joke. OK?'

18

KELLY AND LINDA woke up the next morning at about nine thirty, both lying on top of Kelly's bed, more or less fully dressed, and seriously hung over. The lights in the bedroom were still burning, and the television had not been turned off. A large empty pizza box and an empty bottle of Don Julio Reposado lay abandoned on the floor at the foot of the bed. The dried-out remains of several limes lay on a plate nearby. Kelly groaned as she looked at her clock radio. Even the subdued red numerals hurt her eyes. She turned carefully on to her side and shook Linda gently by the shoulder.

'Time to get up.'

Linda rolled over on to her stomach and buried her head in her pillow.

'I can't. Just leave me here to die.'

Kelly patted Linda's shoulder several times, then slowly lifted herself into a sitting position on the side of the bed.

'I'll make coffee.'

Slowly, she walked into the kitchen and mechanically went through the motions of spooning coffee into the filter, filling the coffee machine with water, and setting it to brew. Sooner, and more brightly than Kelly had expected, Linda made it to the kitchen and sat on a stool at the counter. She grinned at Kelly.

'I'm too old for this Patsy Cline stuff, Kelly. I hope you feel better.'

'Definitely,' Kelly replied. 'Other than a splitting headache and wanting to throw up, I feel great.'

Linda nodded. 'Good. Mission accomplished, then?'

'Yes, I think so.'

'All right.'

'Do you feel terrible?' Kelly asked. 'I'm starting to feel guilty for putting you through this.'

'Oh, please,' Linda replied with a smile. 'I'll make it. I only hope this hot date of yours is worth it. I could have spent the rest of the day asleep on your bed.'

'So could I. You want orange juice, something to eat?'

'No,' Linda said. 'I just want to go home and see if I can sleep there instead. You want help with the debris in your bedroom? It doesn't look pretty in there.'

Kelly smiled. 'No, thanks. I'll do it.'

They drank coffee in silence for a while until Linda finally stood, hugged Kelly, and made her way out of the kitchen towards the door. Kelly held out her arms for another hug and squeezed her friend tightly.

'I don't know what I'd do without you.'

Linda squeezed back.

'You would do the same for me.'

'You know I would.'

'Love you.'

'Love you.'

Linda turned back just outside the door and smiled.

'And I want a full report on today.'

'Of course,' Kelly replied, closing the door.

* * *

Hoping she did not look as bad as she felt, Kelly got ready to go sailing. Her plan was to blame the queasiness she was experiencing on sea-sickness. It sounded plausible, but the plan depended on being able to hold the symptoms at bay until they were actually on the boat and underway. She assessed the chances of this at about fifty-fifty. Looking at herself in the mirror when she was ready to go, Kelly thought she looked rather pale, but otherwise fairly normal. When he picked her up punctually at eleven, Jeff Morris made no comment, but she could not help noticing that he was grinning from time to time, suggesting that he guessed what she had been up to the night before.

The rain had blown over during the night, so Jeff opened the roof on his convertible. As they drove towards Chesapeake Bay, Kelly began to feel better. Jeff said little, seeming content to leave her to her thoughts. She allowed the cool fresh air to blow away the cobwebs, taking deep breaths and stretching her neck and shoulders. Stealing a glance across at him while he was absorbed in his driving, Kelly was aware of a reassuring feeling that she had no need to hide anything from him, that she had no need to pretend. The embarrassment she had anticipated was simply not there. She felt safe, and the feeling surprised her. It was one, she realized suddenly, that she had not experienced for a long time.

Once aboard the superb forty-foot, wooden-hulled yacht which Jeff had borrowed for the day, she felt alive and energized again. It was obvious that Jeff Morris was an expert sailor, and even on this unfamiliar boat, Kelly amazed herself by the skills and knowledge she somehow remembered from her days of sailing off the Washington coast. It was as if she had never been away from the water, and Kelly settled easily into the technique of steering the craft out towards the ocean while Jeff adjusted the sails. The afternoon passed quietly and pleasantly. They spoke little, respecting each other's privacy and thoughts. It was almost sunset when they came about for the last time, and began to head back slowly in the dying wind to the marina. They stood together, relaxed, in the stern, and allowed the wind to carry them safely to shore at its own speed. As the dusk began to settle, Jeff switched on the navigation lights.

'I broke up with Frank yesterday,' Kelly said eventually. 'That's why I was in the condition I was this morning, which you were nice enough not to mention. Thank you for that.'

He laughed.

'I wondered if that was it.'

'Linda spent the night with me. We have a tradition of alcoholic consolations in such circumstances.'

'I've been known to do that myself. What triggered it, or shouldn't I ask?'

'He called me up out of the blue and insisted I fly out to Cleveland today on a moment's notice to be at some function his senator has scheduled. I said "No". He didn't want to take "No" for an answer. Hell, Jeff, he hadn't even called until then to let me know where he was.'

'Yes. I can see why that would have frosted you.'

Kelly leaned back against the stern of the boat.

'It did. But it wasn't just that. It's taken me a while to work it out, but I finally realized that I would never have been anything to him except the little woman at home. I'm not ready for that. I'm not sure I ever will be.'

'Did you tell him you had other plans for today?'

Kelly laughed.

'Yes. I fibbed about it at first, said I was going into the office. Then I thought 'what the hell?' and I told him I had a date.'

'Good for you. What did he say about that?'

'He said he hoped whoever it was could offer me the same kind

116

of future he could.'

'God. This guy sounds like he needs to get over himself.'

There was a silence, while Jeff made a slight adjustment in the tiller as the wind almost imperceptibly changed direction. She took his free hand in both of hers.

'It's not that I don't care about the future, Jeff. I guess it's just not the time for me yet, and I know now that Frank isn't the right person for me to share my future with.'

'That's good information to have,' Jeff said. 'You think we can make it in from here with the jib if I take the mainsail down?'

'It will be close,' Kelly replied. 'Of course, we could always cheat.'

'You mean use the engine?' Jeff asked with a grin.

'Just a thought.'

'Oh, I don't think we're in any danger of being becalmed yet,' Jeff replied. 'Let's see if we can do it the old-fashioned way.'

'Aye, aye, Captain. But I would give the mainsail another couple of minutes.'

'Good.' Jeff nodded approvingly. 'So would I. Your dad taught you well.'

Kelly suddenly squeezed his hand between hers.

'Jeff, thanks for listening. I don't know what you must think of me, laying all this crap on you. I don't mean to. I hope you know that. I came sailing with you to have a good time, and I'm certainly doing that.'

He slid his arm around her and pulled her close.

'I've never felt for a moment that you were laying anything on me, Kelly.'

'Thanks.'

'But I also want you to know that it wouldn't bother me if you did. I'm glad you feel you can talk to me. And I will make you one promise.'

'What?'

'I don't know where this is going with you and me, how it's all going to play out, but whatever happens, I will never ask you to give up doing what you want to do.'

She looked up into his eyes, and to their mutual surprise, they suddenly kissed. When it ended, they were silent for a while. The marina was getting closer. In a minute or two, the mainsail really would have to come down.

'Well, it seems we'll be working together for a while,' Jeff said eventually, handing over the tiller to Kelly and preparing to lower the sail.

'That should give us plenty of time and a good excuse for getting acquainted.'

Kelly shook her head thoughtfully. 'I don't think so, Jeff. I think we're going to be able to date socially, away from work, like normal people.'

'How so? What about our two murders?'

'I have a feeling we've done all we can on those, for now at least.'

'Oh?'

She looked away across the darkening water.

'I think we both know what happened. I think Hamid Marfrela killed Lucia Benoni. And I think a mountain man killed Hamid Marfrela. And I think the mountain man, by now, is holed up in a compound in Oregon.'

'Where we can't get him unless and until he chooses to come out,' Jeff said, lowering the mainsail the last few inches and tying off the line. 'Not without risking a holocaust.'

'Or until he becomes too much of a problem for them and they leave his body some place for us to find.'

'End of story either way.'

'Yes. We won't know for sure until we get the results of the forensic tests. But that's where my money is.'

Jeff shook his head. 'We still have unanswered questions.'

'Yes,' Kelly sighed.

'Do we have any kind of motive for these killings?' Jeff asked.

Kelly shrugged. 'For Benoni, maybe. It could have been as simple as a sexual frenzy. But for Marfrela, we just don't know.'

'Which means Benoni remains open as well,' Jeff concluded, rejoining her at the stern as she steered the boat gently towards the entrance of the marina.

'You mean, it's possible that someone had Benoni killed by Marfrela and then killed Marfrela to cover his tracks?'

'It's possible. Who knows? We may never find out, and it may not matter very much. After all, there's no one left to prosecute.'

Jeff was silent for a while. 'So the murders may be just history,' he said eventually.

'Apart from one thing,' Kelly objected.

'What?'

'The fact that in some way, these murders are connected to the President of the United States,' Kelly replied. 'Somehow, I don't think that fact is going to go away. The murders may be history, but I have a feeling the fall-out is just about to begin.'

PART II

MIDDLEGAME

19

THE HOTEL THAT Selvey had selected for his meeting was ideal. It was a small, run-down establishment in a dilapidated neighborhood, close to O'Hare International Airport in Chicago. The paint on the walls and doors was flaking, the furniture sagged, and the plumbing was in need of repair. The management insisted on cash in advance, the hotel had no amenities, and the neighborhood was not one to walk through without good reason. But comfort and safety were not what interested Selvey. He had no intention of staying long, and he was well able to look after himself. Secrecy was his main consideration and, for this, the venue was well chosen. The hotel was residential and had almost no casual trade. The residents were mainly preoccupied by the need to find their daily intake of liquor or drugs.

His visitor was expected just after the hour. Selvey lit a cigarette, checked his handgun and the envelope he had placed under a pillow, and made himself as comfortable as he could on the rickety bed.

Exactly on time, his visitor gave the prearranged four raps on the door. There was no peep-hole, so Selvey opened it cautiously to the extent permitted by the security chain he had put in place as soon as he entered the room.

'I'm Jeffers,' the man said. 'Is this the right room?' The voice was unsteady.

Without replying, Selvey released the security chain, opened the door, looked briefly in both directions along the corridor, then allowed the man to enter. He closed the door, replaced the chain, and secured the dead bolt. As a final act of caution, he walked to the window, drew back the drapes a little way, and looked down into the street. Some young men were playing a makeshift game of basketball in a vacant lot opposite the hotel. The transient who had been sitting on the sidewalk a little farther down the street was still in place, nursing the same brown paper bag. Selvey turned back to Jeffers.

'You came alone?'

'Yes. Just like you said.'

'Any chance you were followed?'

The question seemed to alarm Jeffers, or perhaps it was just that he wore an expression of perpetual anxiety He was a short man, late forties or early fifties, Selvey thought, a receding hairline, the beginnings of a beer gut, but wearing neat, well cared-for clothing. He was holding a black peaked cap which he had removed from his head on entering the room. Except for his occupation, Selvey knew nothing about him. But Selvey's instinct told him that Jeffers was not a threat.

'Why would I be followed?' he asked nervously. 'Look, what am I getting into here? You said…'

'It's OK,' Selvey replied. 'I've no reason to think you were. I'm just being careful. It's routine in this kind of work.'

'I'll take your word for it,' Jeffers said. 'I've never done anything like this before, and I'm not sure I should be doing it now. Where did you find this place, for God's sake? I didn't think I'd make it here alive. Those people on the street look as though they'd cut your throat as soon as look at you.'

Selvey smiled.

'Relax, Mr. Jeffers. You're in good hands. Have a seat. Drink?'

Jeffers sat reluctantly on one of the hard-backed chairs at the small table.

'Thanks. I don't mind if I do.'

Selvey took a bottle of Dewar's from a large briefcase he had left by the side of the table. He had already rinsed out the two glasses from the bathroom, which hadn't been particularly clean. He poured them both a drink.

'I'm sorry there's no ice. Room service here is not what it should be. It's a bit different from where you work.'

Jeffers relaxed slightly, and smiled as they touched glasses.

'Cigarette?' Selvey asked, lighting one for himself.

'No. I gave up.'

'Good for you.'

Selvey walked to the bed, lifted the pillow, and picked up the envelope. He placed it on the table in front of Jeffers.

'Go ahead, check it. It stays with me until we're done, but I want you to see I'm here to do the deal.'

As Jeffers opened the envelope and began to count the money, Selvey reached awkwardly into the briefcase, which had fallen forwards against the table, and took out a compact digital recorder. He sat down opposite Jeffers. Jeffers was still absorbed by the money. Selvey smiled inwardly at the look of sheer greed in the man's eyes.

'OK?'

'Yes, it's exactly right.'

'Good. We don't want any mistakes, do we?'

Jeffers had noticed the recorder.

'What's that for?'

'To make a record, Mr. Jeffers. We're going to be discussing some matters of great importance, and I don't want there to be any misunderstandings. I have people to report to, and when they're paying out the kind of money you're getting, they want to be sure the information is solid. You understand, I'm sure.'

Jeffers was still looking uncertain.

'You have nothing to worry about. The recording is not going to fall into the wrong hands.'

'Who is it you report to, exactly?'

'Certain gentlemen who have the national interest at heart. Very respectable people, I assure you. I'm afraid it is essential.'

Selvey pulled the envelope back to his own side of the table.

Jeffers nodded reluctantly.

'If you say so.'

Selvey nodded, and started the recording by stating the date and time, but not the place of the meeting.

'What is your name?' he asked.

'Harold Jeffers.'

'Age?'

'Fifty-two.'

'Where you do you live?'

'Central Chicago, just off Clark, born and raised.'

'Married?'

'No. Divorced. I have a son, who's grown. He's out in L.A. I don't see him much.'

'Occupation?'

'Head waiter.'

'Where?'

'Brown's Hotel, on the Mile, State Street.'

'How long?'

'Twenty-five years. I just got my silver pin.'

'Congratulations. I guess, after twenty-five years, they don't have you bussing tables any more?'

Jeffers smiled proudly.

'No, Sir. I get the best assignments in the hotel.'

'Meaning?'

'*Maître D*', if I'm in the restaurant, which I'm not very often any more. Usually, they put me in charge of service at functions. I make sure the kitchen and the waiters are doing their job, make sure the flowers are in place, liaise with the band if there is one, that kind of thing. If it's more like a business function, it's up to me to make sure the sound system works, make sure they have stuff to write with, a whiteboard, overhead projector, Power Point setup, whatever they need, podium, water pitchers. You know.'

'Your job is to make everything run smoothly?'

'Exactly.'

'Do you ever have VIPs or celebrities staying?'

Jeffers smiled knowingly. 'All the time.'

'What kind of people?'

'All kinds. Entertainers, politicians, visiting dignitaries from abroad. There's hardly a week goes by when we don't have somebody interesting.'

'I'm sure. What are your responsibilities when you have someone like that staying?'

'Basically, to find out what they need, and make sure they get it. Of course, it depends on how important the guest is. We make more effort in some cases than in others.'

Selvey smiled and nodded. 'How about when it's the President of the United States?'

Jeffers hesitated. He pulled a handkerchief from the pocket of his pants and mopped his brow, then took a drink of his whisky.

'Has that happened?' Selvey asked.

'Once or twice.'

'And, so that we're clear, we're talking about President Steve Wade?'

'Yes.'

'In his case, what do you do?'

'Well,' Jeffers began slowly, 'you have to understand that, with the President, and with certain other dignitaries, there are certain complications.'

'What kind of complications?'

'Well, you don't have unrestricted access. You have to deal with the Secret Service for everything.'

'OK.'

'They have certain requirements. The catering has to be done a certain way. Only certain people are allowed on to the floor where the President is staying. The security is beyond belief. I mean, they check everything out way before he actually arrives, Secret Service agents and sniffer dogs everywhere. They want a full life-history of any employee who is going to be anywhere near him. It just about brings the hotel to a standstill for a week or so beforehand.'

Selvey lit another cigarette and looked at the ceiling.

'All right. I'm not so interested in the food, and the flowers, and what have you. I'm sure you have your routine for all that. What concerns me more is what you might do unofficially, to provide the President with any more personal items or services he might require.'

'Could I change my mind about the cigarette?'

'Sure.'

Selvey gave Jeffers a cigarette and lit it for him.

'Let me be a little more specific,' Selvey said. 'Obviously, the President can't just go out on the town for the evening. And there must be times when he's off duty, and he might enjoy a certain kind of drink, or a cigar, or a movie, or whatever, aren't there? It's just human nature.'

'Yes.'

'Would you deal with that?'

'Yes.'

'So you're cleared to be on the President's floor?'

'I served him during both of his stays with us. Other presidents too, in the past.'

'What would you need to do?'

'It would depend. It would depend on what the President wants.'

'How would you find out what he wants?'

'It would be requested.'

'How?'

'The request would come from someone on the President's Detail. You know, an agent might come up and say 'the President would like a bottle of scotch', or whatever. My job then would be to get it to him discreetly.'

'Why discreetly?'

'Well, the press are all over the place, and it might be something the President doesn't want to draw attention to. Not that there would be anything wrong with it necessarily. But he might prefer to keep it to himself.'

'All right,' Selvey said, after a pause. 'Let's cut to the chase. What about women? Have you ever been asked to make arrangements for President Wade to see a woman?'

Jeffers finished his whisky in one gulp and drew heavily on the cigarette. Selvey placed his hand very obviously on the envelope containing the money.

'Once. The last time he was with us. Just a few weeks ago.'

'Tell me what happened.'

'I got word from one of the agents that a certain lady would be visiting the President one evening. The way he put it, she was an old friend of the President and the First Lady from their home state, who had helped in his campaigns for governor some time back. She was in town on business and wanted to touch base. It was all made to sound quite proper.'

'But it wasn't quite proper, was it?'

'No, of course not. They were just giving me a story. I know how these things go.'

'Go on.'

'She was supposed to arrive at about eight-thirty. The President had no official engagements. He had the night off. So he had arranged dinner for the two of them in his suite. I took care of that with the kitchen. Then my job was to look out for her at the main entrance of the hotel, and escort her to the President's floor.'

'Then what would happen?'

'The agents would check her out and take her to the President's suite, and then I would go back downstairs.'

'Was there anything else you would do?'

'Only if they wanted anything during the course of the evening. Other than that, I would be around to escort her back down again when she was ready to leave.'

'And did the President need anything else that particular evening?'

'Yes. Champagne. It must have been about half an hour after she arrived. The agent called and said the President needed a bottle of Mumm Cordon Rouge on ice, and two glasses. He has good taste.'

Selvey smirked. 'Yeah. So what did you do?'

'I went to the bar, got the champagne and took it up. The agent said it would be all right for me to take it in to him myself. They knew me by then, you see. So I knocked on the door, I waited for a few seconds, I didn't hear anything, so I went in.'

'And…?'

Jeffers exhaled heavily, nervous again.

'Go on,' Selvey said.

'Well, apparently, they hadn't heard me. I knocked loud enough, believe you me. But they must not have heard. I should have waited for a response before I went in. That's the way it should be done. But, you know, I never thought…'

'What did you see?'

'They were lying on the couch together.'

'On a couch? This wasn't in the bedroom?'

'No. When you go into the suite, the first place you come to is the living room. The bedrooms are farther in. It's the largest suite in the whole hotel. It has a kitchen and two bedrooms, everything.'

'All right.'

Jeffers hesitated. Selvey refilled his glass and waited for him to take a drink.

'I need the details, Mr. Jeffers. Don't be embarrassed. I've heard it all before.'

Jeffers nodded.

'Well, like I say, they were lying on the couch. Their shoes were on the floor. They were kissing and carrying on. It looked like they had their tongues in each other's mouths. His shirt was almost completely undone. Same with her blouse. He had his hand…'

'Go on.'

'Well, he had his hand on one of her tits, and she had hers on his cock.'

'She had it out?'

'No, through his pants. But it was pretty obvious, you understand.'

'OK. What happened?'

Suddenly, Jeffers laughed.

'It was funny, looking back on it. Nobody knew what to do. We just sort of stared at each other. I got my cool back before they did. I've been doing this a few years, and you never know what you're going to walk in on. I've seen it all. You get used to acting as if nothing unusual is going on. If it hadn't been the President, I wouldn't even have…'

'What did you do?' Selvey interrupted.

'Well, like I say, I recovered first. I walked a few feet into the room, left the tray on the table, and turned to leave. And, this was funny. Usually, in this kind of situation, the guy runs after me, and gives me a big tip, and tells me I never saw what I saw.'

'So?'

'Well, I guess the President doesn't carry money around. Sometimes the agents will give you a tip, though you can't rely on it. But not the President personally. So, the woman did it for him. She pretty much jumped up off the couch, told me to wait a minute, picked up her purse, and handed me three $100 bills. Then she put her finger up to her lips, as much as to say, 'it's our secret, don't tell anyone'. She got close enough to give me a good view of her tits too, as an added bonus. And I can understand why he was hard, let me tell you. She was a sight for sore eyes. Real high class. You see a lot of hookers in my line of work, and I'm here to tell you, this one was top of the line.'

Selvey reached into the briefcase once more, and produced a photograph, which he showed to Jeffers.

'This her?'

Jeffers responded immediately.

'That's her. That's the one. You don't forget someone like that.'

'Good,' Selvey said.

'Who is she?' Jeffers asked.

'You don't need to know. Don't get inquisitive,' Selvey replied brusquely. 'Who was the agent who told you she would be joining President Wade for the evening?'

Jeffers shook his head.

'I don't know. It was over the intercom, and I didn't recognize the voice.'

'Fuck,' Selvey whispered to himself, turning his head away from the recorder.

Jeffers smiled.

'But I do know the agent who was on duty when I took up the champagne. She was standing right outside the door. Her name was Linda Samuels.'

Selvey sat up in his seat, and wrote the name on a scrap of paper.

'You're sure?'

'Oh, yeah. She was the friendliest of the bunch. She would actually talk to you, treat you like a human being. Most of them are really into themselves. They think they're such hot shit, with their radios and designer shades and the rest of it. But Agent Samuels was different. She and I talked a few times. And I'll tell you something else as well. She didn't like what was going on one little bit.'

'How do you know that? Did she say so?'

'No,' Jeffers grinned. 'She was too professional for that. But you just had to look at her face. She knew exactly what the President was up to, and she didn't like it even one little bit.'

'What time did the President's visitor leave?'

Jeffers seemed hesitant.

'I don't know.'

'Why not? I thought you were supposed to see her out.'

'I was. But after what I'd seen…'

'You were worried about embarrassing the President even more than you already had?'

'Yes. I figured the Secret Service could escort her down, or at least make sure she left.'

Selvey nodded. 'I can't say I blame you. Is there anything else you remember?'

'No. I think that's about it.'

'All right.'

Selvey glanced at his watch, stated the time, then switched off the recorder. He pushed the envelope back across the table to Jeffers.

'Thank you, Mr. Jeffers. You did good. As we agreed, you will get the rest when we have confirmed the story, and provided you keep your mouth shut. Are we clear about that?'

'Yes, Sir.'

'Good. Because the gentlemen I report to are very insistent about that. I can't tell you how important that is to them. Be careful on the way home.'

Jeffers stood, finished his whisky, and replaced the peaked cap on his head.

'Thanks,' he said. 'If I need to, how do I…?'

'You don't,' Selvey said firmly. 'We will contact you.'

20

THE PRODUCER HELD up his left hand and, mouthing the numbers silently but clearly, counted down from five. Instead of zero, he gave the command 'go'. The camera was pointing straight into the face of the man behind the desk, and the producer, who had been through this kind of exercise many times before, intended that it would remain in that position throughout the short broadcast. It wasn't very creative, but it was what was needed.

The President coughed briefly, and gave the camera his most sincere look.

'Good evening,' he began. 'My fellow Americans, it is with a very heavy heart that I have felt obliged to ask for a few minutes of your time to speak to you this evening. Some time ago, questions were asked of me about a woman named Lucia Benoni. It was suggested that I had had some kind of improper relationship with that young woman. I denied any such relationship. Indeed, I denied having known Ms. Benoni at all. I was asked about the fact that, when she was found dead in such tragic circumstances, she was carrying with her a special pass which granted her access into the non-public areas of the White House. I denied any knowledge of this also.

'Tonight, I have to admit to you that I did not tell the entire truth about Lucia Benoni. I have to apologize for that. I have to tell you what really happened, and why I tried to conceal some of the truth. I can only hope for your forgiveness and understanding.

'I met Lucia Benoni about six months ago, when she attended an official function at the White House. I was attracted to her. I enjoyed the conversation I had with her. I arranged to meet her again so that we could converse further. We talked about books and music, things that interested both of us, things I have little time or opportunity to discuss these days. I requested that a special pass be issued for Ms. Benoni, so that she could come to the White House with less formality. I want to make it clear that, although I can request that such a pass be issued, I cannot insist on it. These special passes are issued only after a thorough security check. This is done by experienced White House staff, aided by the Secret Service. Miss Benoni's credentials were thoroughly checked before the pass was issued. Subsequently, she did visit the White House a number of times.

'When I was questioned about Miss Benoni and the special pass, I decided not to tell the whole truth about it, because I wanted to protect her privacy. I was concerned that she might be hounded by the press, which was eager to create a story which never existed. I knew Lucia Benoni as a very private person, and I knew how much such publicity would hurt her. Now that she is dead, none of that matters any more, and the American people deserve to hear the truth. I have already spoken to the First Lady and to my advisers. I have asked their forgiveness and understanding, and they have given it freely.

'Tonight, I have told the truth. I want to make it clear that that was the extent of our relationship. At no time did I have any kind of sexual relationship with Ms. Benoni. Now that she has died such a tragic death, the victim, apparently, of a deranged young man she had been seeing, I hope that we can all put this episode behind us. I have to focus on the work the American people elected me to do. Trouble is brewing in the Middle East which could threaten our oil supply. Too many people are out of work. I need to give my full attention to these urgent problems. I call on the press to allow Lucia Benoni to rest in peace, and to allow me to continue my job without these distractions. Finally, I want to thank my wife, the First Lady, Julia Wade, for the loving and forgiving way in which she has always stood by me.

'Thank you all for listening. I wish you a good evening. May God bless America.'

In her office in the White House, Vice President Ellen Trevathan closed her eyes.

'Yes, indeed,' she murmured to herself.

* * *

Inside the Sons of the Land Compound in Oregon, George Carlson switched off the television. He and Dan Rogers had watched the President's broadcast in Carlson's office over a beer. For some time, Carlson stood by the television set, shaking his head.

'Unbelievable,' he observed briefly.

Rogers stood and joined Carlson by the television.

'George, do you still think this is what we've been waiting for?' he asked. 'I mean, everybody knows there's more to this than Wade is admitting. Marfrela had it all set up, didn't he? We had Wade just where we wanted him, in bed with the Benoni woman. All we had to do was wait, and then jump when the time was right. Maybe we could still…'

'Yeah. But now she's dead, isn't she?' Carlson interrupted. 'Wade can just deny everything and get away with it. There'll be a scandal for a couple of days, and then the press will find something else to write about.'

'Right. God, George, Marfrela was a stupid asshole. If he hadn't panicked and taken the woman out… Jesus, why in the hell did he do that?'

'Janner said he was probably fucking her and something went wrong. You know Marfrela. Maybe she didn't think he was so hot in the sack and was stupid enough to say so.'

'I thought Janner was supposed to find out.'

'He was, but unfortunately he didn't. Apparently, he interpreted our instructions as being to blow Marfrela away once he admitted he was the one who iced her.'

'He should have brought him here for me to run a few volts through his balls. Then we would know all there is to know about it.'

'Well, it's too late for that now,' Carlson said.

'It may still be a good opportunity, George. A little civil unrest, the nation divided against itself. Time for us to strike. That's what you've always said.'

'I know. But we just need to choose our time carefully, Dan. The way things are now, it may not come to anything. Maybe this will be it, maybe not.'

Rogers breathed out heavily, shaking his head as the air escaped loudly between his teeth.

'You want another beer?'

'Sure.'

Rogers walked over to the refrigerator, selected two bottles of Corona Extra, and took the caps off both with two casual strokes of the bottle opener.

'George,' he said slowly. 'What about Janner, do you think? Are we going to keep him here indefinitely?'

Carlson took the beer from Rogers. He raised the bottle to his lips and swallowed almost half of it.

'I don't think we can. He will lead them to us. Goddamn it, he had to go and leave clues and witnesses behind.'

'It wasn't his fault those people were on the staircase, George.'

'It was his fault he left fingerprints. Without the prints, the people on the staircase wouldn't have been much use to the police, would they? There are a million people who look like Janner. And he would have been long gone. As it is now, they know exactly who they're looking for, and they have a pretty good idea where they might find him.'

'They're not going to risk busting in here. We've always agreed on that.'

'I don't think they are. But who knows what those crazy sons-of-bitches in Washington might do? They've done some crazy fucking things over the years. Who would have thought they would have pulled that stunt at Waco, or the one with that Cuban kid down in Florida? Anyway, it's not just a question of them breaking in. As long as Janner's here, they're never going to take their eyes off of us.'

'They don't now.'

'It's pretty low-key right now, Dan. It could get a lot worse.'

'So, you think, what? Cut him loose? On his own? Get him out in the middle of the night, use the back gate?'

Carlson looked Rogers in the eye.

'They're waiting for him out there, Dan. They'd find him within twenty-four hours. They've got him dead to rights for the Marfrela killing. He might be tempted to cooperate with them. They would pay a high price for information about you and me and what we're doing.'

'So, we have to keep him here?'

'No. The longer it goes on, the greater the risk. No. Janner goes out in a box, and we leave him somewhere where they can't help but find him.'

Rogers sat down heavily in a chair.

'Jesus Christ, George. Janner's been with us a long time. He was in Africa.'

'I know that, Dan. But he's a threat. This Marfrela business could get out of hand. We haven't worked all this time just to have some screw-up wreck everything. I feel bad about Janner, but he should have known better than to give himself away. We don't have a choice. Look, Dan, if you don't want to do it, that's OK. I understand. I'll find somebody else.'

Rogers finished his beer.

'No. I'll take care of it. You know I wouldn't ever let you down, George.'

Carlson put an arm around Rogers' shoulders and squeezed.

'You're a good man, Dan. I couldn't do any of this without you.'

21

IN THE CONFERENCE room of the Wilson Foundation, the Committee was silent as the broadcast ended. John Mason switched off the television and returned to his seat at the right hand of Congressman George Stanley. Stanley and the other six members of the Committee were seated in solid burgundy leather armchairs around the dark wood table. Mason's secretary, Helen, had provided tall glasses of iced water on coasters – other refreshments were arrayed on a discreet wet bar behind Congressman Stanley's seat at the head of the table.

Mason was not a member of the Committee. It was composed of two members of the House, one of whom was George Stanley, two senators, and three leading party strategists. Between them, they had an enviable amount of experience of campaigns – election campaigns, disinformation campaigns, and what the media was fond of calling 'dirty tricks campaigns'; within the Committee, the preferred term was 'tactical maneuvers'. Mason acted as the Committee's convener and secretary. His relationship with the Committee, which provided and controlled the finances of the Wilson Foundation, fluctuated with the quality of the information Mason supplied through his source. The Committee knew that the source existed, but knew better than to ask who he was, or how he got the information. In all their interests, Mason would keep that to himself. Tonight, his influence with the Committee was on an up-swing. Selvey was in the process of striking the mother-lode, and Mason would hand the nuggets to the Committee or the press as he saw fit. He felt in control.

Senator Joe O'Brien had just returned from pouring himself a generous scotch at the bar.

'Well, if I understand you correctly John, you don't place much credence on what we just heard. Is that right?'

'That's correct, Senator,' Mason said.

'You think the President is still lying about the Benoni woman?'

'I think that's pretty obvious, Joe,' said Alex Vonn. Vonn was a veteran campaign manager with a string of impressive victories to his credit. The only laurel missing from his brow was a successful presidential campaign, and he intended to put that laurel in its rightful place very soon.

'Well, I'm not sure what's obvious and what isn't,' O'Brien said. 'It all seems pretty murky to me. I'd like to get a better handle on it before we take any major decisions. John, leaving aside gossip and rumor, what exactly do we know here?'

Mason sat up in his chair, and made a pretense of looking through some notes, of which he had no need at all.

'The first thing we know is that Wade was involved sexually with the Benoni woman,' he began. 'He was sleeping with her in the White House, and a couple of different places on the road.'

'Are you sure of that? Can we prove it? The man just denied it on national television, for Christ's sake.'

'There's no question about it, Joe. We had been hearing about it for a while. It didn't seem to be a big deal, so we didn't pursue it. But after she was murdered, I had my source devote a certain amount of time and energy to it.'

'With what results?' Alex Vonn asked.

'With rather good results, I would say,' Mason replied, 'including a potential witness in Chicago.'

'Why Chicago?'

'That's where the trail led. My source went up there, interviewed the witness on tape, and got some interesting material.'

'How interesting?' Vonn asked.

Mason treated the Committee to a broad smile. He reached over to a small recorder he had placed on the table earlier, and pressed 'Play'.

'Listen for yourselves,' he answered.

The Committee listened with rapt attention, as the tape of Selvey's interview with Harold Jeffers was played to them. When the tape ended, there was a long silence.

'My God,' Senator O'Brien said, eventually.

'What do we know about this Jeffers character?' Congressman Stanley asked. 'How do we know he isn't just blowing smoke up our ass?'

'He checks out. My source was very careful about that. And his story is consistent. I don't think he has any reason to lie.'

Alex Vonn snorted.

'You mean, other than the money your source gave him? He's a whore. The press will eat him for lunch.'

'I don't think so, Alex,' Mason said, trying to conceal the irritation he always felt at Vonn's bluntness. 'He didn't approach us for money. He wasn't even going to come forward with the story. My source had to lean on him pretty hard to tell what he knew, and that involved making it worth his while. It's been done before. In any case, we don't have to hand him to the press. He gave us the name of the Secret Service Agent. We can hand them her. They'll believe her.'

'Well, let's put that aside for the moment,' Senator O'Brien said. 'What else do you have?'

'The other thing we know,' Mason said, 'is that the President was sharing Ms. Benoni's sexual favors with a man by the name of Hamid Marfrela.'

'For God's sake,' Senator O'Brien said. 'Who in the hell is that?'

'According to a reliable source within the D.C. Police Department, Hamid Marfrela was their number one suspect in Lucia Benoni's murder. And, by a curious coincidence, Marfrela himself was murdered by persons unknown shortly after he took out Lucia.'

There was a silence. The members of the Committee appeared dazed. Mason was enjoying himself.

'Now obviously, with Marfrela dead,' he continued, 'the police don't have much of an ongoing interest in the Benoni murder. But apparently someone did have enough interest in it to run some DNA tests. My source was told these tests prove that Marfrela had sexual intercourse with Lucia Benoni within a few hours of her death. Marfrela also had a thing for tying women up, which was how Benoni's body was found. Probable conclusion: Hamid Marfrela killed Lucia Benoni, and someone killed Hamid Marfrela to stop him talking about it.'

'Our friend Steve moves in interesting circles,' Alex Vonn observed.

'How in the hell do they know about the Marfrela guy tying up women?' Senator O'Brien asked.

'They found some literature in his apartment,' Mason replied. 'I don't know the details.'

'Unbelievable,' O'Brien said. 'Is that it?'

'Not quite,' Mason replied. 'Hamid Marfrela was an accredited diplomat in the Lebanese delegation.'

'Damn it, I thought the name sounded familiar,' Alex Vonn said. 'His murder was in the papers. The ambassador was making a big deal about how the United States should do a better job of protecting diplomats against the rampant crime in Washington. A real whiner.'

'Right,' Mason said. 'That's the guy. So, to summarize, what we have here is the President of the United States sharing a Lebanese mistress with a Lebanese diplomat. A mistress who could enter the White House pretty much any time using a special pass issued to her at the request of the President.'

'So,' Alex Vonn said, 'a reasonable question might be 'what kind of things might the President say to Lucia Benoni at the moment of climax or during the afterglow?''

'And a second reasonable question,' Mason added, 'is 'how much of what the President said did Lucia Benoni pass on to Hamid Marfrela?' But right now, it's nothing more than speculation.'

There was complete silence around the table for some time. Senator O'Brien felt the need to freshen his scotch.

'I don't believe that Steve Wade would betray his country, if that's what you were implying,' he said, walking slowly back from the bar to retake his seat. 'God knows I don't care for the man, but I can't believe he would do that. And that's the implication here, isn't it? That he divulged material during his pillow talk which might have compromised national security?'

'That is most definitely the implication,' Congressman Stanley said. 'And frankly, I don't care whether he did that or whether he didn't. The point is that it looks bad, and there's no excuse for it, and he's lying his ass off about it. That's enough for me.'

'Enough for what, George?' Vonn asked.

'To begin impeachment proceedings,' Stanley replied. 'What else?'

Every eye in the room was focused on Stanley.

Alex Vonn gave a contemptuous laugh.

'George, are you out of your ever-loving mind? Does the name William Jefferson Clinton mean anything to you?'

'This is a different case,' Stanley said.

'Yes, it is. Clinton lied his ass off to a Grand Jury and tried to lie and manipulate his way out of a federal lawsuit. And they still couldn't get him. So far, we have no evidence that Wade did anything other than screw the Benoni woman behind his wife's back. The only positive difference is that, with Steve Wade, we're probably not going to have to debate whether getting sucked off does or does not constitute having sexual relations.'

'He's right, George,' Mason said. 'Based on what we have now, impeachment wouldn't have a prayer. If anything, Wade is even more popular than Clinton was.'

'Then find me something else,' George Stanley said angrily. 'Let's find some evidence on the national security angle.'

'We're working on it,' Mason said, as evenly as he could. 'But we're not sure there's anything to find. If you're anxious to move it forward, we need to know what's been going on between the United States and Lebanon recently. If anyone wants to look into that for me up on the Hill while we're digging elsewhere, I could use the help.'

'It will be my pleasure,' George Stanley said. 'I'll get on it first thing in the morning.'

'Good,' Mason said. 'But discreetly, George. We don't want anyone jumping the gun here.'

'Don't worry about that,' Congressman Stanley said. 'The bastard will never know what hit him.'

* * *

'Did you see it?' Linda Samuels asked, when Kelly Smith eventually answered her phone.

'Yes, I did,' Kelly replied.

She reached over from where she lay on her sofa, and grabbed the remote. Pointing directly at the screen, she muted the dialogue of a British murder mystery which had just started on Public Television.

'What is with this guy?' she asked. 'Does he really think anyone believes him?'

Linda did not respond immediately.

'Is Jeff with you?' she asked eventually.

'No, he pulled duty tonight, a stake-out. Why?'

'I just wondered if we could talk for a while.'

'Well, of course. Why wouldn't we be able to talk?'

Linda hesitated. 'I don't want to get in the way.'

Kelly sat up.

'What kind of crap is that, Linda? Since when have men ever stopped us talking?'

'They haven't,' Linda admitted. 'It's just that this one is obviously special, and…'

'Yes, he is,' Kelly said. 'And so are you. Talk.'

Kelly heard her friend take a deep breath.

'Look, I probably shouldn't be asking you this. I don't mean to stick my nose in where it's not wanted. But are you guys still working on the Benoni-Marfrela thing?'

'Technically, yes. Since the results of the DNA tests came in, the Benoni case is more or less closed. There's no question it was Marfrela. The Marfrela case is open, but there's nothing we can do on it for now. Our only suspect is holed up in a compound, and there's no way we're going in to get him.'

Linda hesitated again. 'I'm scared, Kelly.'

'Why?'

'I'm a witness. I know what was going on. I know the President was having sex with Lucia Benoni.'

'Everybody knows that.'

'Yes, but I was actually there. Well, right outside the door, anyway.'

'So what? It will all blow over, Linda. Lucia wasn't the first, and she won't be the last. It's not your fault the President screws around.'

There was a silence.

'Kelly, haven't you ever been afraid without knowing why?'

'Sure,' Kelly admitted.

'Well, that's how I'm feeling.'

'Is there anything I can do?'

'Don't let my death go unavenged.'

Kelly laughed, but stopped abruptly. 'That was a joke, right?' she asked quietly.

'Yeah, I guess. But I just have the strangest feeling about it.'

'Linda, has something happened? Have you been threatened? Because, if so, I can get Lazenby involved. We can protect you.'

'No, Kelly. Nothing's happened. It's just inside my head.'

'You sure?'

'Yes.'

'Well, if it ever does…'

'You'll be the first to know.'

'Promise?'

'Promise.'

'So what else is going on?'

'Well… guess who I saw last night?'

'Tell me.'

'Bob.'

'Really?' Kelly said, smiling. 'What's the deal with him?'

'He called me up and said he wanted to meet. So we had dinner, and he told me that he wants us to think about getting back together.'

'I've seen this movie before, Linda,' Kelly said, not unkindly. 'What about the bimbo?'

'He says she's history. He really misses what we had together.'

Kelly shook her head. 'Yeah? And you let him stay the night, right?'

'Yes…'

'Linda…'

'I can't help it, Kelly. I want it to turn out right. What else could I do?'

'I don't know. I just don't think you can trust him.'

'When we're apart, I think that too. But, when we're together, he seems so sincere.'

'Oh, brother,' Kelly said. 'What are you planning?'

'Nothing definite. We're going to see each other again, take it one step at a time, see how it goes. Am I being stupid?'

'Would you listen if I told you?'

'No.'

'All right, then. Are we still on for Friday?'

'Yes. I'll pick you up at seven. Say' Hi' to Jeff for me. Love you.'

'Love you.'

Kelly hung up and watched the silent television screen for some time. She left it on 'mute' and called Jeff Morris's answering machine.

'Jeff, it's me. Listen, when you get this message, would you check with your department and see whether there's been anything new on Benoni and Marfrela? I'm interested in whether anyone has been asking questions, or trying to open the thing up again. Let's keep it between the two of us. I'll talk to you tomorrow. Good night.'

22

MARY SULLIVAN THOUGHT her desk might actually collapse under the mountain of paper Irene had left on it in response to her request. Irene was interning at *The Washington Post* during her senior year as a journalism major at George Washington University and, like all interns, she tended to get carried away with assignments given to her by celebrated reporters such as Mary Sullivan. When she returned to her office to find the results of Irene's search, Mary experienced a moment of irritation at the student's apparent lack of familiarity with the concept of relevance. But, remembering her own days as an intern, she had realized that Irene had made a sincere effort to impress her, and that much of the volume of paper was attributable to the wonders of electronic research.

Mary had asked for any details Irene could find about reports recently released by both political parties dealing with the major contributors to their campaigns. She read these reports carefully every year, not so much for the financial information, as for signs of shifting alignments among the major corporate donors. Over the years, these signs had enabled her to make some almost uncanny predictions about shifts in the balance of power. It was one of the things which had contributed most to her reputation as an observer of the Washington political scene.

Mary was now in her second day of ploughing through the morass of paper. She had tried to contact Selvey who, sometimes to her annoyance, often had insights which suggested access to materials she did not have. But Selvey was going through one of his irritating periods of not returning her calls. He could simply disappear from the radar screen for days or weeks on end, re-emerging when he saw fit. As there was nothing she could do about this, Mary resigned herself to working alone. One name she had found the day before was troubling her. It was one she did not know, which was unusual. She was familiar with all the older-established contributors, and the new ones usually showed up in news stories long before they became major players. But this one was an exception, and Irene's research had shed little light on it. The day before, Mary had filed the name away in her mind and moved on. It was probably of no real importance. The amount contributed was large, but no more than average in this list of major donors, and it probably meant nothing. But, for some reason, the name would not let her go, and on the second day, she returned to it.

The Western States Geophysical Research Institute was a not-for-profit organization based in Portland, Oregon, which advertised that it researched and wrote position papers for groups or individuals interested in the impact of industries such as mining and logging on the environment. These people probably took an anti-Government position on environmental issues. Why were they making such a large contribution to the President's party? Had someone promised something in return? Mary made herself a list of the senators and congressmen from the western States. There was no one she thought would have enough influence to make promises worth such a large contribution.

Who were these people? Mary played with her computer for a while and found a list of contributors to The Western States Geophysical Research Institute itself. The list was composed mainly of individuals whose names were unfamiliar to her. One of the few corporations listed was called Middle and Near East Holdings, Incorporated. That made sense. It sounded like an outfit which might have oil and gas interests. She turned to her computer again and soon printed out the company's corporate address in Wilmington, Delaware, and the names of the directors. Another reference source turned up a list of three branch offices, one of them in Washington D.C., North West. A bell rang in Mary's mind. She stared at the page blankly for some time, and then suddenly remembered.

'Jesus Christ,' she breathed softly.

For some time, she sat gazing out of her window, lost in thought. Then she picked up her phone, and dialed the number of an old friend who worked for one of the District's biggest real estate firms.

'Ruthie, it's Mary. How's the diet going?'

'Don't ask, Sweetie. You take off five pounds and put six back on. Go figure.'

'You don't need to be on a diet. You never did. I don't know why you do it.'

'You should look in my bedroom mirror some time. What's up?'

Mary bit her lip.

'Ruthie, could you do me a favor?'

'For you? Anything. What do you need?'

'I'm trying to track down a company called Middle and Near East Holdings, Incorporated. They have an address in North West, an apartment actually, and I'm interested in finding out the name on the lease. I know it's supposed to be confidential, but…'

'Baloney,' Ruthie said. 'What's the address?'

Mary told her.

'Hold a minute. Let me see if I have anything.'

Two minutes went by. When Ruthie spoke again, Mary could sense the smile on the other end of the line.

'You're in luck, Mary. It's one of ours. The named lessee is a guy called El-Rashid.'

'El-Rashid? Are you sure?'

'I'm looking right at it.'

'Damn,' Mary whispered to herself.

She thought for a moment.

'Is there any way to know whether he is the original lessee, or whether someone else may have been on the lease before?'

'Sure. Hold a moment. Yes, come to mention it, El-Rashid was substituted recently. The original guy who took the lease from us was called Marfrela, first name Hamid. You need me to spell that?'

'No, that's OK.'

'According to the file, this guy Marfrela died, and the El-Rashid guy took over from him. That's all I know. Does it help?'

Mary sat back happily in her chair.

'Oh, yes. Oh, yes. Ruthie, you just earned lunch at the venue of your choice.'

'Yeah, right, it will have to be the salad bar.'

Mary laughed.

'Whatever. You're a pal, Ruthie. Take care.'

'You too, Sweetie.'

Mary dialed a number on the intercom.

'Irene?'

'Oh, hi, Ms. Sullivan,' the intern said nervously. 'Was the work I did for you OK?'

'Irene, do you get a grade for your internship at George Washington?'

'Yes, Ma'am.'

'Well, so far, I would say you're looking at an 'A'. Would you like to go for the 'plus'?'

Mary could feel the young woman's pleasure on the other end of the line.

'Yes, Ma'am. I sure would. What do you need?'

'I want you to run down a guy by the name of Hamid Marfrela. Come by my office and I'll give you everything I've got on him.'

'I'll be right there. What do you need to know about him?'

'Let's start with everything his own mother knows,' Mary said. 'And we'll take it from there.'

Soon after Irene had practically hopped, skipped and jumped from Mary's office to start her new research project, Selvey called. Without any explanation of his failure to return her calls earlier, he instructed Mary in his usual peremptory way to meet him in his favorite dive in a bad part of town. Mary felt her temperature rising as she listened to him. As usual, Selvey was irritating her. But he seemed to sense that fact over the phone, because just as she was beginning an indignant protest, he interrupted her as brusquely as ever.

'Miss Sullivan, you really don't want to miss this one,' he said, with a suggestion of laughter in his voice. 'Trust me, you really do not want to miss this.'

With that, Selvey hung up. Tightening her lips and suppressing a desire to scream, Mary Sullivan picked up her purse and a yellow pad and made her way to her car.

* * *

'You don't think Linda's actually been threatened?' Jeff asked.

He was helping Kelly to wash up after a late supper in her apartment.

'No. I don't think so. But I worry about her anyway. She's under so much pressure.'

'Not helped by her asshole ex-husband.'

'Right. I feel so helpless with her sometimes.'

Jeff put the last plate back in the cupboard, closed it, turned and took Kelly in his arms.

'All you can do is spend time with her, which you do. I think she'll tell you if anything happens.'

'I hope so.'

He looked at his watch. 'It's getting late.'

He kissed her. Their eyes met and she knew the time had come.

'Jeff, you know you don't have to go.'

He pulled her gently into an embrace. They did not speak for some time.

'I haven't wanted to the last few times I've been here. I just wasn't sure…'

She kissed his cheek.

'I wanted it to be your decision.'

'I'd love to stay.'

She took his hand and led him into the bedroom. They sat together on the bed.

'There's just one thing,' Kelly said. 'I get nightmares sometimes. I want to tell you now, because I don't want you getting scared later if I wake up screaming.'

He nodded. 'New York?'

'Yes. Frank could never stand it,' she said. 'I think it's one of the reasons he went away so much.'

Jeff lay on his back, and gently arranged her on top of him with her head on his chest.

'I can deal with it,' he said. 'Do you want to talk about it?'

She shook her head, stroked him with her fingers.

'It can wait. I just wanted you to know. In case we fall asleep later and I forget.'

Much later, naked and at peace, they pulled the sheet and blanket up to cover them, and settled down, intertwined.

'We were investigating rackets two of the Mob Families were running out of the Bronx,' she said. 'They had this crappy factory as a front. It was supposedly making cheap dresses, but it was a place they used to store stolen goods, drugs, dirty money, God only knows what. I went in under cover as a clerk. I stayed too long. My cover was blown. I had to try to shoot my way out. Two of my support team, two agents called Joe Grant and Tina Mickelson, happened to be in the area, and picked up my distress call. They showed up in an unmarked car. The bad guys trapped us in a kind of storage area near the main gate, crates and boxes and all kinds of crap everywhere. We took cover, and there was a shoot-out. Joe had a radio, and he managed to call for back-up. But he exposed himself and took one in the head. Tina and I kept shooting, but we were outnumbered and outgunned. It was only a matter of time. Then they got Tina. She took three bullets, but they didn't kill her right away. She was lying by my side, crying, asking for her mother. She…'

He kissed her. 'It's OK.'

'Then by some miracle, our back-up came. The bad guys heard the sirens and took off. Two minutes later and it would have been over. I was amazed it wasn't over anyway. If they'd rushed us, we wouldn't have had a chance. By the time the back-up got inside the factory, Tina was gone. They sent me on leave for four months. I went down to Mexico, Cancun. Linda took some leave and came with me for the first two weeks. She slept with me every night, and every night I would wake up screaming. She just held me and held me, for hours. I wouldn't have made it without her. I still get the nightmares sometimes. It doesn't happen so often now, but you need to know that it will, once in a while.'

Jeff kissed her forehead.

'I blamed myself for not getting out of there sooner. We had all the evidence we needed to get the middle men. But I wanted to nail a couple of capos. Thought I could do it for sure if I had another week or so. Once I'd lain on the beach in Cancun for a couple of weeks and my mind came back, I was sure it was my fault Joe and Tina were dead. I was ready to quit. And then, for whatever reason, Lazenby called and rescued me.'

They were silent for several minutes.

'I get them too, sometimes,' Jeff said.

'About Susan?'

'Yeah. Being at the hospital when she died. I wake up in the early hours, panicking, feeling lost.'

She kissed him.

'I don't know whether I scream or not. There's never been anyone there to tell me.'

She held him as tight as she could.

'There is now,' she said.

23

FROM HIS VANTAGE point in the control tower, George Carlson took in the scene in the compound's training ground below with satisfaction. Using binoculars, he could see every detail of the action. They were getting better all the time. The assault drill had been carried out to near perfection, the results of his training, based on his experience in nameless military campaigns in Africa. Carlson considered himself an expert. But he could not do everything himself. He had hand-picked a small group of men to be his officers, and drove them hard until they had mastered the techniques of fast, mobile warfare. When they were ready, Carlson placed the officers in charge of the newer recruits. The practical training was continually reinforced by indoctrination sessions, offering the recruits a new vision. A new United States, free from corrupt liberal politicians interested only in feathering their own nests, a country relieved of the curse of racial degradation. A message to stir the blood of right-thinking men. And now it was beginning to pay off. Carlson had a fully-formed fighting force, a force ready to liberate America from its own corrupted institutions.

Dan Rogers was running up the last few steps of the rough metal staircase to join his commander in the control tower. His fatigues were covered with dust and his face was bathed in sweat. Despite his exertions, Rogers was breathing only slightly faster than usual. He was in good spirits. Carlson turned around and smiled appreciatively.

'Nice work, Dan. It was looking good down there.'

'It could still be faster. But it's coming along, George. The guys have been working their asses off. They're up for it. They're ready for the real thing. I can feel it.'

Carlson lit a cigarette.

'Good. So am I. Did the supplies arrive?'

'Yeah. Peters took care of them. All neatly stacked away.'

'How about the new guy, what's his name, Seager?'

Rogers accepted a light for a cigarette.

'The signals guy? Yeah, he's here. I was going to bring him up to see you, but we ran out of time. He arrived just as the drill was starting, so I sat him down to watch. He was pretty damned impressed.'

'He should be. Where is he now?'

'Down below. I told him to wait until I'd reported to you. You want to see him now or later?'

'Why don't you bring him up now. You're sure he checks out, Dan, right?'

'His references were good. Benson vouched for him.'

'All right. Let's take a look at him.'

Rogers picked up the field telephone and flicked the rotating dial. 'Henderson?'

'Sir,' a voice answered.

'Bring Captain Seager up to the tower right away.'

'Yes, Sir,' the voice answered smartly.

Rogers hung up. He and Carlson were silent, smoking, looking out over the tarmac where some of their soldiers were cleaning up after the assault drill and returning equipment to storage. After a few moments a man in his late thirties in clean fatigues joined them on the deck of the tower. He stood briefly to attention, gave a salute which ended almost as soon as it began, and finally stood at ease.

Carlson returned the salute.

'Captain Seager? I'm Commander George Carlson. You've met my XO, Commander Rogers.'

'Yes, Sir.'

Carlson extended his hand. 'You come highly recommended. I'm glad to have you aboard.'

'Thank you, Sir. I'm glad to be here.'

Carlson offered Seager a cigarette.

'No, thank you, Sir.'

'We're pretty informal here, Captain. We keep up salutes and ranks in front of the men, but amongst ourselves it can be first names.'

'OK,' Seager said.

Carlson exhaled from his cigarette.

'What did you think of our little show?'

'Very impressive.'

'You should know. You were in The Congo, I'm told.'

'Yeah.'

'Brazzaville?'

'Among other places.'

'Was that the Lightning Bolt Campaign?'

Seager seemed hesitant.

'Not many people know about that campaign. It was kept kind of quiet.'

'We're pretty well informed here, Jim. Among the people we associate with, it's something of a legend. From what I hear, it was downright ugly.'

Carlson and Rogers exchanged smiles.

'You don't want to believe everything you hear,' Seager said impassively. 'It was a good chance to improve my skills. I'm looking forward to putting them to use in a good cause. Commander... Dan... was telling me it may not be long.'

Carlson extinguished his cigarette.

'Who knows? I try not to talk about it around the men. They tend to get excited about it, and you can't keep them on the boil all the time. Are you familiar with your duties?'

'In general terms.'

Carlson lit another cigarette.

'Well, let's get a little more specific. First, we have a lot of men who have no experience of working with a signals officer. It will be your job to train them, show them what will be happening once we're in the field. You'll be a part of all our exercises from now on. Also, I need you to identify two or three men who you think can handle the job and teach them everything you know.'

'No problem,' Seager said. 'And second?'

'Second,' Carlson said, 'you'll take over communications with a number of sources.'

'Sources?'

'We depend a lot on information. Most of it is public record. We monitor press and TV reports, and a full range of websites, for all political and military content. But we also rely on some inside information, which we analyze and pass on to other groups we expect to join with us when the time comes. The volume of intelligence is constantly increasing, and I don't have time to deal with it all myself any more. Besides, this stuff is what you do. You'll be a lot faster than I am.'

'I assume you mean encryption?'

'Always. The sources are in vulnerable situations. We have to protect them. You'll have access to the code book, and you'll encrypt and decrypt. I don't want to see anything except the finished product. Except in one case.'

Seager looked at Carlson questioningly.

'We have one source in a very high place. His code name is Fox. He deals with me only. His terms. You give me the message encrypted and I read it myself. Same with outgoing. No one knows this except the three of us. We don't even use the name 'Fox' when anyone other than the three of us is present. No exceptions. Understood?'

Seager shrugged.

'Sure.'

'Good,' Carlson said. 'You got your schedule worked out?'

'Yeah.'

'And you've seen your office?'

'From a distance. The drill was about to start. I haven't been inside yet.'

'OK. Well, you better go get yourself settled in. Come by my office later. We'll have a beer and talk about old campaigns.'

'Thanks, I will.'

* * *

It was after midnight before Seager could excuse himself from Carlson's office and drive quietly out of the compound to his apartment in a shabby suburb of Portland, where he was known to the landlord by the name of Baker. He removed his fatigues, poured himself a glass of whisky, and placed a phone call. It was very late where he was calling, and it took Kelly Smith some time to disentangle herself sleepily from Jeff Morris' arms and pick up.

'Kelly, Phil Hammond,' he said.

Kelly was awake immediately.

'Phil, are you OK? How did it go?'

'So far, so good. Tell the Agency they did a nice job with my legend. It looks like I'm a Sons of the Land poster child.'

'Thank God for that,' Kelly replied. 'What's the situation?'

'Too early to tell. They're gearing up for action, that I can tell you. They ran a pretty slick assault drill to keep me amused this afternoon. But what they may be planning, where and when, it will probably take me a while to find out. They have a pretty hectic schedule planned for me. I won't be able to get away as often as I'd like to, so don't panic if you don't hear from me for a day or two.'

'OK,' Kelly said. 'Is there anything we can do for you right now?'

'Yes,' Hammond replied. 'There is one thing you can check out for me.'

'Hold on.'

Kelly jumped out of bed and grabbed a pen and notepad from her desk.

'OK. Shoot.'

'It seems the Sons of the Land have a pretty good network of information going. Carlson said they have sources that they need to protect. So they're using codes. The information is encrypted, ingoing and outgoing. They want me to handle communications with the sources, so they're going to give me access to almost all of the information. I'll fill you in as I go along.'

'That's a good break,' Kelly observed.

'Yeah. But there's one source who deals only with Carlson. Carlson says he's, quote, in a very high place, unquote. I assume that means Washington. Code name is Fox. I'm not going to see any of his stuff decrypted. I thought you might run a check with our people and the Agency and see if you can come up with a match for the name.'

'You got it,' Kelly said.

'Thanks, Kelly. I guess that's about it for now.'

'How's the place they found you to stay in?'

Hammond laughed.

'Let me put it this way. You guys owe me big time. Next assignment, I get to spend time in the big house with you and the boss.'

'I'll see what I can arrange,' Kelly promised, smiling.

Suddenly her smile disappeared. 'Phil?'

'Yeah?'

'Be careful, OK? Remember what the Director said. If there's any sign of trouble, any sign at all, get out of there. Don't walk, run.'

'Don't worry about it, I will,' Phil Hammond said. 'I'll call tomorrow if I can. Sleep tight.'

'You too, Phil… Oh, Phil?'

'Yeah.'

'Did Carlson tell you how long he has been dealing with Fox?'

'No. Would that help?'

'It might. It occurred to me that we might be able to link him to some other scenario, where we have more information.'

'OK, I'll see what I can do.'

24

'I APPRECIATE YOUR seeing me this morning, Gerry. I know you have a busy schedule,' Congressman George Stanley said, extending his hand as the secretary ushered him into the office.

Stanley looked around him. For all the times he had stood in the same place, he was still in awe of the sheer dimensions of the office. So much bigger than the Oval Office at the White House. So much more impressive in every way. The very length of the room, for one thing; enough space for two separate conference areas. The feeling of elegance, for another; the high vaulted ceiling, the handsome dark wood of the walls and door, the elegant mouldings atop the walls. It all served to emphasize the importance and power of the man whose office it was. The room would have been worthy of a national president. It was not the President's office, however, a fact which always reminded Stanley of the reality of where so much of the power resided.

'For you, George, any time, you know that. Come and take a seat.'

The House Majority Leader, jacketless, his tie loose around his neck, smiled amiably as he stood and accepted Stanley's handshake.

'Coffee?'

'That would be good.'

Gerry Parkinson nodded to his secretary, who had turned back inquiringly on her way out.

'Two, Jenny, please.'

George Stanley sat uncomfortably in a large armchair in front of Parkinson's desk. The Majority Leader's office was one of the very few places he found intimidating.

'Phyllis well?' Parkinson was asking, to make conversation as Jenny brought in the coffee.

'She's very well, Gerry, thank you. Up to her neck in good works as always.'

'She's going to visit us in Washington again soon, I hope.'

'She's planning on next month.'

'Good. You must both drop by for a drink.'

'Yes, of course.'

Stanley hesitated, feeling nervous.

'I was sorry to hear about Margaret,' he said awkwardly. 'I hope…'

Parkinson shrugged.

'Who knows?' he said quietly. 'They say the treatments are getting better, they're coming up with new remedies every day. We just don't know whether it will come in time. Still, you have to hand it to the doctors, don't you? They can perform miracles these days.'

'Yes, indeed,' Stanley said, sipping his coffee. 'Look, if there's ever anything Phyllis and I can do, Gerry, you only have to…'

His voice trailed away as Jenny left the room.

'Yes, thank you, George. Very kind. I'll be sure and bear it in mind.'

He resumed his business-like manner.

'Now, George, to the point. I've read your memo.'

Parkinson put on a pair of reading glasses, and rummaged through a pile of papers until he found what he was looking for.

'I must say it's very interesting,' he continued. 'It seems you've been hard at work in that committee of yours.'

'Yes,' Stanley replied nervously. 'Well, it's mostly Mason and his source, you know, who actually get the information. We leave that kind of thing to them. We just evaluate it and decide what to do with it. In this case, we thought it was serious enough to bring to your attention.'

Parkinson scanned the memorandum again.

'Well, you were right,' he said, after removing his glasses and staring at the wall to the right of his desk for some time. 'It is serious. Steve has been a naughty boy, hasn't he? No doubt about that.'

'Even more so than usual.'

Parkinson smiled.

'Yes. The question, of course, is what to do about it.'

He turned to face Stanley across the desk.

'I can't agree to your suggestion at the moment, George. However much I may agree with you that he deserves it.'

'Gerry…'

'No, let me finish. As things stand now, Alex Vonn is right. We would get nowhere with impeachment proceedings. We wouldn't get much more than a bare majority of our own people in the House. We'd be annihilated in the Senate. It would be a political train wreck.'

'I'm not so sure.'

'Remember Clinton, George. Even people who hated his guts and were disgusted by what he did thought impeachment was over the top. Not in the national interest. If anything, we would be in a weaker position here. I can't expose the Party to that kind of risk, not at the moment.'

Stanley shook his head and put his coffee cup down on the edge of the Leader's desk, as if about to protest. Parkinson raised a finger to cut him off.

'George, I'm not saying 'No'. I'm saying 'not at the moment'. We would have to build a case, a way better case than we have now. We'd have to get people thinking, not 'how can we impeach him?' but 'how can we not impeach him?' We'd have to have such a strong case that not even Wade's best friends would dare to defend him.'

Stanley seemed deflated.

'How would we do that?'

Parkinson smiled comfortably.

'Your Committee has the right idea. We have to prove that this is not just another instance of the presidential pants being unzipped. We have to prove that it hurts America, and I don't mean in the Clinton sense of a failure of moral leadership. I mean, something that has the potential to fuck the nation in a very tangible and visible way.'

'You mean the national security angle?'

'Exactly.'

Stanley frowned.

'That's where we're on the weakest ground, Gerry. It's a matter of proof.'

'Yes, I know,' Parkinson agreed. 'But, as it happens George, you came to the right man at the right time.'

'Oh?'

'It so happens that I have one piece of information which Mason's source didn't mention, which may help us quite a bit.'

Stanley looked up sharply.

'You mean we missed something?'

Parkinson smiled.

'No, not really. I doubt there's any way Mason's guy could have got to this, unless he's a lot better placed than I think he is. Your memo suggested that we should see if we could find any information on this

Hamid Marfrela character in relation to the Lebanon situation.'

'Yes.'

'Well, we did. Not only was Marfrela the number one suspect in the Benoni murder, as Mason's source discovered but, at that exact time, he was also under surveillance by the Bureau on behalf of the State Department.'

George Stanley's eyes opened wide.

'For God's sake. Why? Was it because of his connection to the Benoni woman? What interest did the State Department have in a murder investigation?'

Parkinson took a deep breath.

'George, you understand that this is…'

'Sensitive. Of course.'

'"Sensitive" would be an understatement. The information I'm about to give you originates in classified material supplied to a House Committee under the usual rules. Now, it can go to your Committee informally. You can tell them it came from this Office, but there are to be no further inquiries without my authorization. None. Understood?'

'Understood.'

'All right. Marfrela had contacts with an extreme White Supremacist group based in Oregon, called the Sons of the Land. According to the Bureau, these people are suspected of hatching some ambitious plans, which could involve the use of armed force against the Federal Government.'

Stanley's eyes had opened wide.

'My God.'

'Marfrela actually went out there to see them at least once. The Bureau was keeping an eye on the situation for obvious reasons but, at first, they had no idea who Marfrela was. Eventually, they were able to get a good photograph of him, which State was able to identify. Someone at State pitched a fit about it, and they decided to go into business with the Bureau. Up to a point, at least.'

Stanley sat back in his chair.

'God Almighty, Gerry,' he breathed. 'What's the connection?'

'We don't know for sure,' Parkinson said. 'The security people are working on the theory that these sons-of-bitches in Oregon might have enlisted the help of the Lebanese.'

'To do what?'

'Probably to supply them with some commodities, let's say arms, which they might have been having trouble getting elsewhere. The Lebanese interest being, we presume, in destabilizing the United States Government to relieve the pressure put on them by the President's Middle Eastern policy.'

George Stanley breathed heavily, stood, and walked a little way around the Majority Leader's desk.

'Well, Gerry, if that's true, it proves my point. It's even more serious than the Committee thought. We need to...'

'No, hold on a moment, George,' Parkinson interrupted firmly. 'First, we still don't have any definite connection to the White House beyond a possible one-night stand between Wade and Benoni in Chicago. Second, the whole thing is still very little more than speculation. We need more evidence.'

Stanley turned to look at the Majority Leader.

'What kind of evidence are you suggesting we look for?'

'It's not a matter of looking for it. Not any more. The bodies are buried in places where Mason's source can't go.'

'So, who can go there?'

'Nobody.'

'Well, then...?'

'No one person, I mean. It's going to take a congressional committee,' Parkinson said, rising to stand behind his desk. 'George, I can't give you impeachment proceedings – not yet. But here's what I can do. I have enough to begin hearings in some appropriate committee, and we'll have to think about which one, I'm thinking probably the House Intelligence Committee, on the issue of Marfrela's involvement with the White Supremacists. It has clear enough national security implications, even if you leave the President out of it. But we won't leave him out of it, of course.'

'So you would let the committee develop its own evidence?'

'Well, one thing the chair of that committee would have to do is gather all the available information about Marfrela's activities, including the Benoni situation.'

Stanley sat back down with a satisfied smile.

'Which would mean,' Parkinson continued, 'there would be an investigation of Ms. Benoni's activities, which in turn would mean that the committee would issue subpoenas for witnesses such as your Secret Service agent, what was her name, Samuels? Then, depending on the committee's findings, we may decide that further proceedings are justified. If so, we will have a much stronger basis for it than we do now. Either way, I can't see a down side.'

The Majority Leader smiled.

'Can you live with that?'

'I don't see why not,' Stanley replied.

'Good,' Parkinson said decisively, walking around his desk to offer his hand. 'Why don't you run it by your committee and see if they agree. If so, I will notify the Chair of the House Intelligence Committee, and we'll get the show on the road.'

25

THE YELL GARY Mills gave over the radio brought Linda Samuels up physically out of her chair. It was not yet time for her to walk over to the Oval Office, and she had been relaxing with a cappuccino and a doughnut in the Detail office. But in an instant, she recognized the moment for which every agent attached to the Detail spent his or her whole life preparing. There was danger. The President might be in danger. In such a situation, you reacted. Suddenly, your own life became dispensable. You might take a bullet, but the President must not. You never thought about that during the action. Afterwards, you thought about it a lot. Before, in times of quiet, sometimes. But not during the action. In a flash, Linda was racing out of the office, radio in hand, and running hell for leather along the corridor.

'Gary, where are you? Come back. Gary?'

With the radio on receive, Linda thought she heard Gary's voice, but it was indistinct, and there were other voices, other noises, in the background.

'Fuck,' she said desperately, to herself. 'Talk to me, Gary, damn it. Where are you?'

Linda realized that, not only did she not know where Gary Mills was, but she could not even remember where he was supposed to be. She glanced at her watch. Almost nine. Almost time for the President to be at work. She decided to make for the Oval Office. She switched the radio to transmit.

'Gary, come in. Gary. Where are you, Gary?'

As she neared the Oval Office, Linda almost collided with Agent Dennis Waite, a young African-American member of the Detail, who was running in the opposite direction. He had his gun drawn.

'Did you hear it too?' she asked.

'Yes.'

'Where's Gary?' Linda almost screamed.

'Not in the office. Must be in the Residence,' Dennis replied. He stood still for a moment, leaning against the wall, breathless.

'Oh, fuck,' Linda said. 'That's right. He was doing escort today.'

'Let's go,' Dennis said, forcing his back from the wall.

Linda held him back with an arm.

'No chances,' she said. 'We take no chances with this. Sound a code red, and meet me there.'

'A code red?'

'My responsibility, Dennis, do it.'

Dennis looked doubtful.

'Linda…'

But Linda Samuels was already in full flight.

'God damn it, Dennis, just fucking do it. And meet me up there.'

Dennis Waite exhaled heavily. What he was about to do would paralyze the White House for several hours, perhaps the whole day. Every exit would be sealed, the entire building would be closed and searched from top to bottom, and every armed agent would be at the scene of the suspected trouble within a minute or two. It would be total disruption. An unnecessary declaration of a code red would not be appreciated by the top brass of the Secret Service or by the White House staff. On the other hand, neither would a dead President.

'This is Agent Waite, for Agent Samuels,' he said into his radio. 'I'm declaring a code red. Unknown noises from the Residence, agent possibly in trouble. All armed units respond to the Residence immediately. Repeat, this is Agent Waite, declaring a code red. Waite out.'

As he began to run upstairs, Waite heard responses from several other agents. Help was on the way.

Linda paused briefly at the door of the presidential living quarters, a little out of breath after a desperate run up the two flights of stairs which had stood between her and the scene of the trouble. Inside she could hear shouting and, to her relief, the voice of Gary Mills. She quietly put down the radio, which she had silenced to conceal her approach, and drew her gun. At that moment, she heard a loud crash and a torrent of curses. She looked around. There was no one else in sight. Only one possible course of action. Without hesitation, she savagely kicked open the door, and looked around. Her training had left her in no doubt of what to do. If the President was even arguably in danger, she would shoot to kill. She was less than a second from squeezing off a fatal round.

But she did not pull the trigger. She stood just inside the door, and looked around her in disbelief. The President was standing on one side of the living room, holding a hand to the side of his head, which was bleeding from a nasty-looking wound. Fragments of what had been a blue ornamental Chinese vase lay at his feet. He was almost dressed for work, in his customary white shirt and a red tie. Only the jacket was missing. Across the room were the only other two occupants. Gary Mills was lying sprawled over the screaming and kicking body of a woman, who was barefoot and dressed only in a lace nightgown. Gary was attempting to subdue the woman, with only limited success. Seeing Linda enter, he held up a hand.

'It's OK, Linda. Put down the gun. It's under control.'

Linda did not put the gun down. Instead, she spoke, not loudly, but very seriously.

'Let me see, Gary. I can't see whether you're armed or whether she's armed,' Linda said. 'I need to see your hands now.'

Gary Mills nodded and rolled slowly off the woman, but made no move to stand up. The woman turned and looked at Linda. It was Julia Wade. Linda could see no weapon. Cautiously, she approached the First Lady.

'Ma'am, I'm going to have to ask you to stand and put your hands in the air.'

'Fuck you,' Julia Wade snarled.

'This is not a joke, Ma'am,' Linda insisted. 'Do it now. Please.'

The seriousness of Linda's manner had its effect. Very slowly, and with a bitter smile, the First Lady did as she was told. Linda breathed a sigh of relief. She could still see no weapon.

Gary Mills had climbed gingerly to his feet.

'You too, Gary,' Linda said quietly.

'Oh, for Christ's sake, Linda.'

'Do it,' Linda insisted.

With an expletive, Gary Mills turned and placed his hands in the air.

At that moment, all hell broke loose again, as a number of agents, armed with everything from sub-machine guns to standard automatics, burst into the room.

'It's OK,' Linda shouted. 'It's under control. Everyone relax. Mr. President, we have declared a code red, but I don't believe you are in any further danger.'

She turned momentarily to face behind her.

'Someone get medical attention for the President now.'

She turned back.

'Would you tell us what happened, please, Sir?'

The President turned to face the assembled agents, still holding a handkerchief to his head. The agents had lowered their guns, but they were still inching their way suspiciously into the room, towards the President, ready for any action which might even now be required.

'I regret to say,' the President said slowly, in a subdued tone of voice, his eyes lowered, 'that my wife and I had a disagreement. Agent Mills heard the disturbance from outside, and came in to see if anything was wrong. He tried to intervene, but I'm afraid things got out of hand. I wasn't in any danger. But he was right to be worried. As were you all. I'm sorry.'

The President looked sheepishly up at the battery of agents.

'Look, couldn't we cancel the code red? It obviously isn't necessary.'

Linda nodded to Gary Mills, who lowered his hands, retrieved his radio from the floor where it had fallen during the scuffle, and walked over to join the agents at the door.

'I'll speak to the senior officer about it, Mr. President,' Linda said.

She turned to the First Lady.

'Ma'am, you are free to put your hands down now. Do you require medical attention?'

Julia Wade shook her head sullenly, and sat down in the nearest chair, her face deathly white.

'Very well,' Linda said. 'I want the agents to make a formal search of the immediate area before I suggest canceling the code red. I'm sorry for the inconvenience, Mr. President. It's just procedure.'

The President nodded reluctantly, and also sat down as a nurse appeared at the door with a first aid kit.

With an immense sigh of relief, Linda Samuels put away her gun, walked outside into the corridor, and leaned heavily against the wall. Gary Mills joined her.

'Thanks a lot,' he said.

'What?'

'For assuming I… Did you really think I…?'

Linda turned to her colleague.

'Knock it off, Gary. I had a situation. It's the rule, remember? No chances with the President's life, ever, whatever the circumstances. You'd have done the same.'

'So if I hadn't shown you my hands, you… you would have shot me?'

'In a heartbeat,' Linda said.

Gary looked up at the ceiling. 'Fuck,' he breathed.

They stood together silently for a while.

'So, what the hell happened anyway?' Linda asked eventually.

Gary managed a weak smile. 'You obviously haven't read the newspapers.'

'Not yet. I've had a busy morning.'

'I'll show you when we get downstairs. You'll understand. I was on my way to see if the President was ready to come downstairs. When I got near the door of the living quarters, I could hear them screaming and carrying on. It got louder and louder, and then I heard furniture falling over. I wasn't sure what to do. I was embarrassed. But then I figured I'd be even more embarrassed if the President died on my watch, even if it was his wife who killed him. So I went in. Then she started screaming at me, and throwing things. I made one attempt to call for back-up. After that, I didn't get a chance. She was like a crazy woman, Linda. She attacked me too. I had to try to subdue her. I thought I had her just before you arrived. But she broke loose, picked up this big vase, and threw it straight at his head. It turns out she has pretty good aim. Then I jumped on top of her and hoped I could hold her till the Seventh Cavalry arrived.'

'Jesus Christ,' Linda said. 'It's not enough we have to worry about assassins? Now we have to worry about the President being a victim of domestic violence?'

'Tell me about it.'

'And I ordered a code red. Great way to start the day.'

Gary put an arm around Linda's shoulder.

'You're my hero. You were just like Clint Eastwood in… what was that movie?' he said with a grin.

Linda could not resist returning the grin.

'Yeah, fuck you too,' she replied.

They began to walk slowly downstairs together.

'You did that for me, right, not for the President?' he asked.

'Did what?'

'Order the code red.'

'Yeah, right.'

'And you wouldn't have missed me just a little bit…?'

'If I'd had to shoot you?'

'Yeah.'

Linda made a pretense of considering the question seriously.

'Actually, I might miss you.'

'You'd have to make your own coffee in the office.'

'That's true,' Linda said. 'I didn't think of that. I would miss you. Definitely.'

* * *

The Naval Physician Commander watched as the nurse finished setting in place the bandage around the President's head. He began to put the syringe and bottles of pills into his briefcase.

'Are you sure you understand your medication, Mr. President?'

The President nodded, and got up from the chair in which he had been sitting during the examination.

'Yes, thank you, Commander.'

The Commander appeared reluctant to leave.

'Mr. President, I'd still feel a lot happier if you would let us take you to Bethesda for twenty-four hours. I don't like leaving you when there's every likelihood you have a concussion, even if it is a mild one. I can easily find a reason which wouldn't cause any alarm…'

'I'll be just fine, Commander. I have a lot of people to look after me. They won't leave me alone all day, whether I want them to or not. I promise, if I feel any strange symptoms, or start falling asleep, I'll contact you straight away.'

'Very well, Mr. President.'

'Your concern is noted, Commander.'

'Yes, Sir.'

The Commander pursed his lips, walked to join the nurse at the door, and ushered her outside.

For some time, there was silence. Ellen Trevathan and Martha Graylor were sitting nearby. They had been called to the scene as the agents were leaving, and had watched silently as the President's physician performed his examination and treatment of the head wound.

'So, am I off the hook, as far as the Twenty-Fifth Amendment goes?' Ellen asked quietly. Her tone was not friendly.

'As far as I know, Ellen, I'm functioning just fine,' Wade replied. 'If I have some kind of seizure or start foaming at the mouth later in the day, I'm sure someone will notice and let you know, so you can take over. As of right now, I don't think I'm going to start World War Three by accident.'

The silence resumed.

'Mr. President,' Martha said eventually, 'I told everyone you had an accident without being very specific. But the fact is that a code red was declared, and that kind of thing can't be hidden, not on the morning of a press conference, anyway. Have you had a chance to think about what you want me to tell them?'

Wade shrugged, apparently carelessly.

'Tell them it was a misunderstanding. Someone got their wires crossed when they heard about my little mishap, and pushed the wrong button.'

Ellen shook her head vigorously.

'It won't fly,' she said authoritatively.

'Why in the hell not?' Wade asked.

The Vice President stood, picked up the copy of *The Washington Post* from the floor where Julia Wade had thrown it earlier, and began to walk around the presidential living room, reading aloud from Mary Sullivan's exclusive front page piece.

"President Steve Wade may have been sharing the sexual favors of a murdered Lebanese woman with a Lebanese diplomat who was also found murdered in Washington in still mysterious circumstances, sources have told *The Washington Post*. According to these sources, the President had a tryst with the woman, thirty-four year old Lucia Benoni, a resident of Manhattan, in a hotel in Chicago during his recent visit to that city. The alleged assignation is believed to have been attested to by at least one witness. Both Miss Benoni and Hamid Marfrela, a junior cultural attaché at the Lebanese Embassy, were shot to death in the North West district of Washington in separate incidents which still have police baffled. Even given the President's known history of extra-marital liaisons, the present circumstances are giving rise to concern in some quarters. The possible implications of his…"

Wade brought his fist down hard on the coffee table.

'I've read the article, Ellen,' he said forcefully. 'I don't need to have it read to me again.'

Ellen replaced the newspaper on the table.

'Really? For a moment, I thought you might not have taken it all in. For a moment, I thought I heard you suggest to Martha that she explain away your head injury and the declaration of a code red, on the same morning this article appears, as a series of coincidences.'

Wade seemed about to speak, but instead placed one hand over his mouth and was silent for some time.

'Do you have some other suggestion?' he asked eventually.

'It's going to sound a little radical.'

'Let's hear it anyway.'

'All right,' Ellen said. 'Why don't you try telling them the truth for once?'

Wade rounded on her.

'Now, you listen to me…'

'No.'

Ellen Trevathan was suddenly in the President's face, her voice just as insistent as his own.

'No, just for once, Steve, you listen to me. You swore to me that there was no truth in these allegations. You stood in the damned Oval Office and swore to me, after I told you how important it was to me. Well now all the world knows you're a liar – not just me, and not just *The Washington Post*. If you had told the truth then, what would have happened? You'd have been embarrassed for a day or two, you would have had a fight with Julia, and it would have been over. The subject would have been closed, forgotten. Now, look what's happened. You and a Lebanese diplomat screwing the same woman? Don't you see where Mary Sullivan's going with this?'

She picked up the newspaper again. '"the present circumstances are giving rise for concern in some quarters". You don't get it, Steve, do you? They're coming after you.'

'Coming after me?' the President asked. 'What do you mean?'

Ellen looked at him pityingly.

'Steve, you've handed them the opportunity they've been looking for. This administration has made enemies. Surely I don't have to tell you that. They're longing, just longing, for a chance to bring us down. And now you've given them that chance. You know what our relationship with Lebanon is like. And now you and this Lebanese Marfrela guy are sleeping with the same Lebanese woman? Are you seriously telling me you don't see the implications of that? Because, believe me, there are those who do.'

Wade sank slowly back into his chair. He seemed lost in thought for some time.

'But you can't think… no one could think… it's not true.'

'Whether or not it's true isn't the point,' the Vice President replied in exasperation. 'The point is that there's something to investigate. They can drag this out for the rest of your term, if they want to. So what if you're exonerated at the end of the day? By then, your reputation will have been destroyed. And, in the meantime, your authority to govern will be hopelessly compromised. You can forget about whatever agenda we had. It's history. You're not even going to get the support of your own party.'

The President had turned pale. 'You mean someone will call for congressional hearings?'

'That is exactly what I mean. Right, Martha?'

Martha sighed unhappily.

'That's what I would read into it.'

Wade exhaled heavily.

'So what should I say?'

'I've already given you my suggestion on that,' Ellen replied, walking towards the door. 'But let me just add this. Whatever you say better be good. In fact, it better be damn good. Otherwise, you're going down.'

She paused with one hand on the door handle and turned back towards him.

'And let me make this absolutely clear, Steve. I will not let you take me down with you. You should take me very seriously here. I will not let you take me down with you.'

Steve Wade and Martha Graylor just had time to notice the tears forming in her eyes before Ellen Trevathan turned abruptly and walked out of the room.

26

KELLY HAD ARRANGED for Phil Hammond's call to be patched through to the speakerphone in Ted Lazenby's office. The call was due just before Kelly was to leave to meet Jeff Morris and Linda Samuels for dinner in Georgetown. Linda had called earlier in the day, saying that she needed to talk. To Kelly's surprise, however, she had specifically suggested that Jeff join them for dinner. The conference with Phil was expected to be routine. Kelly had been monitoring Hammond's activities on a daily basis without supervision, and reported to Lazenby each day after speaking with him. So far, there seemed to be no cause for anxiety. But the Director was anxious nonetheless. Like everyone involved, he was acutely aware of the dangers of the operation, and sometimes needed to satisfy himself personally that all was well. Today, Lazenby needed to talk to Phil Hammond himself.

'Phil, I have Kelly with me in my office. How is it going?'

'Good, Director. Hi, Kelly.'

'Hi, Phil.'

'Are you guys keeping up with my messages?'

'Kelly is. I'll let her answer that one.'

'We're pretty much up to date, Phil. We've checked out everyone you've decrypted so far. They're mostly low-lifes, fellow-travelers, in it for the thrill of the secret society game, one or two Klan types. We don't see them as much of a threat. But the information is great. Keep it coming. It's giving us some real insight into their thinking. With any luck, we'll get some advance billing for any major productions they may have in mind.'

Kelly stopped, knowing this was not the answer Phil Hammond wanted to hear. There was a silence.

'What about Fox?' Hammond asked.

Kelly sighed.

'No news yet, Phil. It's a type of encryption our people are not familiar with. They're working on it.'

She hesitated.

'I don't suppose there's any chance they might trust you enough now to let you decrypt him yourself?'

'No way,' Hammond replied. 'Carlson keeps 'Fox' to himself. Even Rogers doesn't see the Fox material. Look, Director, it's very difficult getting the material out of the compound. I'm taking a huge chance every time. I'm not complaining, but…'

'I know, Phil,' Ted Lazenby said. 'Please believe me, we're doing our best.'

There was a silence. Hammond seemed exasperated.

'What's the problem?' he asked. 'I thought our people had the goods on every type of encryption there was.'

'That's what we thought, too,' Lazenby said. 'The analysts are pulling their hair out over it. They're putting in a lot of time. Something will give eventually. There's some speculation it may be some kind of older military code, perhaps something Carlson and his associates may have used during their mercenary days in Africa.'

Lazenby looked down at his desk.

'Actually, Phil, to be honest, they told me to tell you that it would really help to have more material from Fox. They don't have a lot to go on. They need more volume. I know it's dangerous for you…'

'It's not that, Director,' Hammond said. 'You already have everything that's come in. There's just not much volume from Fox. It's almost as if he doesn't speak unless there's a good reason for it. You get the feeling he, or she, is very conscious of the risks involved. And Carlson's replies are minimal.'

'Phil,' Kelly asked, 'are you close enough to Carlson to know whether he speaks any foreign languages? Maybe he and Fox don't communicate in English. It would really help to know whether we're dealing with encrypted English or encrypted something else.'

'I don't know,' Hammond replied. 'I'll try to think of a way to ask without arousing suspicion.'

'Don't take any chances,' Lazenby said firmly. 'Are you confident your cover is still intact?'

'Yes, Sir, as far as I know.'

'All right,' Lazenby said, nodding thoughtfully. 'Anything else?'

'Yes, Sir, actually there is. Yesterday, the Portland police recovered the body of a white male, mid-thirties, in a ditch a little way out of town. He had been shot to death, single bullet in the back of the head. Some guy's dog found it.'

'Anyone we're interested in?' Lazenby asked.

'I think I know,' Kelly said quietly.

'Yes, Sir. The body was not in good shape, so we can't do any kind of visual ID, but their forensic people got a pretty tight match of a print to the ones recovered from the scene of the Marfrela killing.'

Lazenby's eyes opened wide, as he looked at Kelly Smith.

'Our mountain man?'

'Yes, Sir. Looks like it.'

'No ID on the body, driver's licence, credit card, whatever?'

'Not a thing. We have a provisional make on him under the name of Janner. The Los Angeles police have him as a suspect for a bank robbery down there the year before last. We may or may not be able to confirm that in a couple of days.'

'Any hard evidence linking the body to the Sons of the Land?'

'No, Sir. The police think he was killed somewhere else and dumped there, so it could have been done at the compound. But if my associates did it, they didn't tell me about it. Do you want me to…?'

Lazenby looked at Kelly, shaking his head vigorously.

'No, Phil, no way,' Kelly said. 'No point. Those cases are closed. Don't take any risks for that. If you happen to hear something unsolicited, fine. Otherwise, don't go there.'

'OK,' Hammond said. 'I think that's about it. Talk to you tomorrow, Kelly. Good night, Director.'

* * *

'God, I wish that were true,' Lazenby said almost to himself, as he pressed the button to cut off Hammond's call.

Kelly looked up. 'Excuse me, Sir?'

Lazenby turned to look directly at her.

'What you said to Phil. That the Benoni and Marfrela cases were closed. I said I wish it were true.'

'Isn't it?'

'You tell me.'

'Well, there's no one left to prosecute,' Kelly smiled. 'Both suspects got rather rough justice, which I can't officially approve of, but it isn't going to make me lose any sleep. And it saved us from having to deal with a couple of really messy cases.'

Lazenby drummed his fingers on the top of his desk.

'I spoke to a friend on the Hill this morning,' he said. 'This is off the record right now, though it won't be for long. The House Intelligence Committee is going to hold hearings. There will be an announcement tomorrow.'

Kelly sat up in her chair. 'Hearings about what?'

'What do you think? About the relationship, if any, between Lucia Benoni, Hamid Marfrela, and the President. It seems we weren't the only ones worrying about the national security implications.'

Kelly bit her lip, and was silent for a time. '*The Washington Post* article,' she said.

'Yes.'

'Which means that you and I...'

'...are potential witnesses, yes.'

Lazenby ground his teeth in irritation. 'And we'll have to give them whatever we have. There's no way to protect it.'

'What about compromising an ongoing criminal investigation?' Kelly suggested.

'You said it yourself, Kelly. There's nothing ongoing any more.'

'We haven't formally closed the cases. We could make an argument.'

Lazenby shook his head.

'They'd see straight through it. Anyway, it wouldn't wash if there are national security issues involved. There's only so much I can say with a straight face to protect a murder inquiry with two dead suspects. It might even look as though this Office were trying to protect the President. I can't take that risk.'

'Oh, what the hell,' Kelly said, trying her best to sound off-hand. 'They probably already know more than we do.'

'Well, *The Washington Post* certainly does,' Lazenby said. There was frustration in his voice. 'How in the hell do they come up with this stuff?'

Kelly looked up, suddenly very concerned.

'Director, do you think they know about the Oregon connection?'

'The *Post*? I don't think so. I'm sure we would have read about it by now.'

'What about the House Intelligence Committee?'

'I don't know,' Lazenby said. 'It's possible.'

'Because, if they start getting into that...'

'It will blow our whole operation. I know, Kelly. I'm going to tell them something off the record myself. I have to have some kind of understanding with the Committee Chair that they will give us some warning before they go down that road. He can't give me that assurance if he doesn't know about it. We can't take the risk of it coming out accidentally. Obviously, if I tell them off the record, there's ultimately no way to prevent them from going into it on the record. All I can do is rely on their judgment.'

'What can I do, Sir?' Kelly asked after some time.

'For now, nothing. I'll let you know when I hear more.'

Ted Lazenby looked back at her and suddenly smiled. 'Oh, there is one more thing I should tell you.'

'Sir?'

'It seemed to me that Lieutenant Morris is in more or less the same position as we are. I mean as a likely witness. He's as good as been on our team for some time. So today I called Chief Bryson and asked him to release Morris to us on temporary assignment for the duration of this situation. The Chief agreed, but of course I wanted to run it by you. If you have any objection…'

Kelly somehow managed to keep a perfectly straight face.

'No objection at all, Sir, not if you think it best…'

She stood and made her way to the door of Ted Lazenby's office, turned, and looked at Lazenby very seriously.

'Director, if there should be any chance of the Marfrela-Oregon connection becoming public record…'

'I'll pull Phil out of there faster than you can say 'Hamid Marfrela'. I promise.'

The relief showed in Kelly's face as she turned to leave.

'Thank you, Director. Good night.'

* * *

Kelly drove absent-mindedly through the early evening traffic to the Indian restaurant where she was to meet Jeff and Linda for dinner. As ever, parking in Georgetown was a challenge but, after circling for a short while, she got lucky, and pulled gratefully into a space in a residential street not too far from the restaurant. As she entered, she saw Jeff sitting at a corner table. Miniature statues of Shiva and the elephant-god, Ganesh, stood in small alcoves built into the walls to each side of his chair, and a photograph of the Taj Mahal at sunrise hung above Jeff's head. The lighting was subdued, with flickering candles in burgundy glass holders on the tables, giving barely enough light to read the menu.

A woman's voice, accompanied on the sitar, filtered unobtrusively through the room, effortlessly finding the mysterious quarter notes so characteristic of eastern music, as it intoned a Hindu hymn. There was no sign of Linda. Kelly walked over to the table. Jeff stood and pulled out a chair for her as they kissed.

'Hi, sweetheart, been waiting long?' Kelly asked.

'No. Just arrived.'

Kelly took a drink from the glass of iced water in front of her. She grinned mischievously.

'Jeff, have you been keeping something back from me?'

'I don't think so.'

'So, you don't have any news to tell me?'

He laughed. 'Oh, you mean about turning my hobby into a paying gig?'

Kelly stuck her tongue out at him. He laughed.

'I only found out myself this afternoon. Chief Bryson told me. I tried calling you but you were already in your meeting with Lazenby. It was nice of him to arrange it.'

'Yeah,' Kelly said. 'Did Bryson tell you why?'

'Only that Lazenby thought I should be on the team until the Marfrela killing is finally resolved.'

Kelly shook her head.

'The Marfrela case is resolved, as of today,' she said. 'The assassin's body turned up in Oregon. No, this has nothing to do with the criminal aspects of the case. It's about the stuff *The Washington Post* published. The President's opponents are out to get him, and they see this as the perfect issue. There are going to be hearings in the House.'

'I see,' Jeff Morris said slowly. 'And I take it the House is going to be interested in what we know about the case?'

'That's what Lazenby is assuming,' Kelly replied. 'And I'm sure he's right. There's been no official announcement, by the way, so keep this to yourself.'

A waiter appeared silently behind Kelly. He placed a plate of poppadoms on the table, but did not withdraw.

'Excuse me, Mem'Sahib, you are Kelly Smith?'

'Yes,' Kelly said, turning towards him.

'A message has come for you, Miss Smith, it is coming by the telephone. It is coming from the party who was going to join you for dinner, Miss…'

'Miss Samuels?'

The waiter was reading hesitantly from a note.

'Yes, Mem'Sahib. Actually, Miss Samuels was calling and asking me to say she cannot join you as she had hoped. Actually, the case is, she is to be having to be working late, and she will be obliged if you will be calling her later.'

Kelly and Jeff looked at each other.

'You're sure that's what she said? She was working late?'

'Quite sure, Mem'Sahib. I am making the note of it myself, personally,' the waiter said, offering the piece of paper to her.

Kelly shook her head.

'Thank you,' she said. 'We'll be ready to order in a couple of minutes.'

'Very good, Mem'Sahib,' the waiter said.

He withdrew as silently as he had come.

Jeff picked up the plate of poppadoms, offered one to Kelly, took one himself, and broke a piece off.

'Maybe Julia Wade wants a rematch.'

Kelly smiled.

'I hope it's not to do with Bob,' she said quietly.

'I'd have thought she would have had it with him by now,' Jeff said, munching on his poppadom. 'Why hasn't she just told him once and for all to shove it?'

'You don't know Linda well enough yet,' Kelly replied. 'That would be far too simple.'

27

MARTHA GRAYLOR GRITTED her teeth.

'Come on, Conrad,' she said into the phone as assertively as she dared. 'You owe us one. The President gave you an exclusive in Paris last year. He handed you NATO's position on the Balkans, the whole nine yards, before the ink was even dry on the official communiqué. No one else had that.'

'That was in return for my being nice to him during the election,' Conrad Beckers smiled on the other end of the line.

The voice was deep, reassuring, self-confident. It belonged to a man whose hour-long news show on Public Television commanded more respect than any other television news program in the country. Beckers had spent years as a political columnist before a perceptive producer realized how good he would look and sound on television. He came with all the skills which had brought him success as a writer. He was a shrewd reader of people as well as politics. It was said that he could converse fluently in three languages besides English. It was whispered that he was consulted confidentially at the highest levels. His show was meticulously researched, and presented with a thoroughness and objectivity which was the envy of the sound-bite slaves who plied their trade on the networks. Anyone who was anyone in Washington aspired to be the next victim of Conrad Beckers' incisive cross-examination. Uncomfortable as it was to be publicly dissected, it was a sign that one mattered in politics, that one had arrived. When Martha Graylor called unexpectedly, Beckers was in make-up, preparing to tape an interview. He talked while an assistant unobtrusively applied foundation, and just a hint of black pencil around the temples.

'Nice to him, my ass,' Martha replied.

Beckers laughed.

'I was too. All right, Paris was a good story. I was grateful then, and

I'm grateful now. And I'm telling you, the President is welcome to come on the program as often as he likes. All I'm saying is, we need a little notice. We can't do it tomorrow. We have a major time-sensitive piece already recorded.'

'What about?'

'The likely consequences of the Fed raising the interest rate. And a background piece on market fluctuations.'

'Big deal.'

'It is a big deal. If we don't run it tomorrow, it's history.'

Martha snorted.

'History? You want to talk history? Conrad, I'm offering you the President's first word on his opponents' efforts to assassinate him. What more history do you want than that?'

'The partisan rhetoric doesn't play with me, Martha. You should know that by now.'

'All right, I'm sorry. But this is important, Conrad.'

Beckers reflected on the image of himself in the brightly-lit mirror in front of him, and gestured for a little more black pencil around one of his sideburns.

'What does he want to say?' he asked.

There was a silence. Beckers watched himself shake his head in the mirror.

'You can't play that game with me, Martha. If he's just going to repeat his story that he never banged Lucia Benoni, and anyone who says otherwise is a liar and a traitor, frankly that doesn't sound like history to me. He's said it before. So, what gives? What makes it so urgent that the President has to speak to the people tomorrow?'

'The House Intelligence Committee will be making an announcement about holding hearings,' Martha said, doing her best, but sounding unconvincing even to herself.

'I know that,' Beckers said. 'I read the papers. And in the usual way, we would expect the President to respond briefly through you and then more fully at a press conference a day or two later. I still don't get it.'

There was silence again. The assistant had finished her work. Conrad Beckers nodded appreciatively then, on impulse, suddenly gestured to her to leave him alone in the room. He waited until she had closed the door behind her.

'He's going to admit it, isn't he?' he asked. 'He wants to tell the people he's been lying to them.'

Martha hesitated a moment too long.

'There will be no advance statement, Conrad. But it will be worth your while. And the President will answer any questions you have.'

'That's the rule on my show,' Beckers said. 'Nothing is off limits. Whether it's the President or anyone else. That's the way I work.'

'Then it's not a problem, is it?' Martha said. 'So, will you do it, or do I have to ask CNN?'

This time it was Beckers who did not reply immediately.

'He *is* the President of the United States, Conrad.'

Beckers decided. 'All right. Where and when?'

'We'd prefer your studio. Any time before lunch.'

'Let's say ten-thirty.'

'Deal,' Martha said. 'My people will work with you on publicity, but there must be no advance statement of the subject-matter.'

'You think no one will figure it out?'

'All the same…'

'All right, Martha. All right. We'll gear up for it, and we'll shelve the story on interest rates for a day. My producer will kill me.'

'I think that's highly unlikely, Conrad,' Martha said, hanging up.

* * *

Martha looked at her watch. She was due to report to the President in a few minutes' time. She opened her purse and took out a small mirror and her lipstick. She was about to apply some lipstick when she paused, suddenly shocked by the lines on her face, the tightness around her mouth, the dark shadows around her eyes, the evidence of long hours and not enough sleep. She looked older. 'It's this damned job,' she thought. Angrily, she applied the make-up. She was in the process of replacing the lipstick and the mirror in her purse when there was a timid knock at the door. She looked at her watch again.

'Come.'

The door opened slowly. The young woman who walked uncertainly in looked pale, and her eyes were red. Martha put down her purse and stood.

'Agent Samuels? Come in. What's the matter? Is something wrong?'

Without a word, Linda Samuels almost ran over to Martha Graylor's desk, sat down in one of the armchairs in front of it, and held her head in her hands. Martha walked quickly around to the front of the desk, sat in the chair next to her, and put an arm around her shoulder. At her touch, Linda began to cry. Martha did not try to interrupt her, but simply let her arm rest gently in place on Linda's shoulder. After some time, Linda lifted her head, appearing to be embarrassed. She ran the back of a hand across her nose. Martha handed her a tissue from the blue, flower-covered holder on her desk.

'I'm sorry, Miss Graylor,' Linda said. 'Oh, God, I'm so sorry. I'm making a fool of myself. I shouldn't have disturbed you. I'll go… It's just that… I didn't know where else to turn. I just thought… I'm sorry…' She tried to get up, but Martha pressed down with her arm a little more firmly.

'Don't be silly. Stay right where you are. I'm glad you felt able to come to me. Why don't you tell me about it?'

Linda finished wiping her nose with the tissue, screwed it up into a tight ball and held on to it as tightly as she could. She looked vacantly across the room.

'I'm in trouble,' she said quietly.

Martha smiled.

'You mean, because of the code red? No, absolutely not. In fact…,' she took Linda's hand confidentially, 'look, I'm not really supposed to tell you this, so keep it to yourself, but if it will make you feel better, I happen to know that there's a commendation in your future. The President was pretty impressed, Agent Samuels. So were we all. We felt the President would have been well protected if it had been a real emergency. I promise you, you are not in any trouble. Quite the reverse.'

Linda shook her head vigorously.

'No, that's not what I mean,' she replied with a deep sigh.

Martha raised her eyebrows

'What, then? Boyfriend trouble? My God, have you ever come to the wrong person for that.'

Linda managed a weak smile, and turned to look Martha full in the face. She lowered her voice almost to a whisper.

'You know about the hearings they're going to have in the House?'

'The House Intelligence Committee? Yes,' Martha said. 'I wish I didn't, but I do.'

'I got a call yesterday from someone at the Committee Chairman's office. An aide of some kind. He said I was going to be subpoenaed as a witness. He said I was to pull together any written notes or records, and be ready to produce them. They want to interview me next week.'

Martha looked up sharply.

'You? Why would they want to talk to you?'

Linda wound the screwed-up tissue around her little finger as tightly as she could.

'I was with the President when he was in Chicago. I was on the Detail…'

Martha sat back in her chair for a moment, then stood and walked away towards the window of her office.

'I see,' she said eventually.

'I don't know very much, really,' Linda continued. 'I saw the Benoni woman arrive, and I saw her leave. In between… well, I was standing right outside the door, and I couldn't help but hear…'

Linda allowed her voice to trail away.

Martha Graylor seemed lost in thought for some time.

'We'll have to get you some legal representation,' she said decisively. 'I'll set up a meeting for you with a lawyer from the White House Counsel's office.'

'It won't do any good, Miss Graylor, will it?' Linda asked. 'They can order me to testify, can't they? There's no privilege. It was decided during the Clinton impeachment. They told us about it during our orientation when we joined the Detail.'

Martha turned back towards her, and nodded.

'Yes, you're right. You will have to testify. But the legal people can give you some good tips on how much you have to say, how to deal with the questions, how to act during your testimony. They're the professionals. They can help you a lot.'

Linda suddenly stood and leaned on the desk.

'I should tell the truth, shouldn't I?'

Martha's eyes opened wide.

'Yes, of course…,' she began automatically. She took a step back, and placed a hand over her mouth. She saw Linda close her eyes. A terrible thought came to her. She walked back to the desk and stood right next to Linda.

'Someone's got to you, haven't they?'

Linda shook her head desperately. Martha put her hands on Linda's arms and pulled her around to face her.

'Agent Samuels, you need to tell me what's going on. This is too big to fool around with. Who's been talking to you, and what did they say?'

Linda raised her head and looked straight into Martha's eyes. Her look was enough to confirm Martha's worst fears.

'The President?'

Linda swallowed hard.

'He called down to the Detail office yesterday, just before I went off duty. He said he wanted to see me for a moment. I assumed it was just about something that was to happen today. But when I got to the Oval Office, he was alone. He asked me if I'd heard anything from the House Committee, and…'

'Wait a minute,' Martha interrupted. 'Not too fast. This is important. I want you to be absolutely precise. Did you tell the President that you'd been contacted by the Committee, or did the President ask you? How did the subject come up?'

'He asked me directly, Ma'am. I didn't volunteer anything, believe me. He asked me, had I heard from them. It was as though he knew it was going to happen, but he didn't know when. So, I told him the truth, I said I had, that I had received word they wanted me to testify.'

Linda hesitated.

'Go on,' Martha said gently.

'Well, that's when he said he expected me to be loyal, to stand by him.'

Martha collapsed into the armchair. Aghast, she stared at Linda, her mouth open.

'Lord have mercy,' she whispered. 'Are you sure that's what he…'

'Yes, Ma'am, quite sure,' Linda interrupted bitterly. 'He didn't put it in so many words, but I knew exactly what he meant. He was asking me to lie for him.'

'And what did you say?'

'I honestly don't remember, Miss Graylor. I was shocked. As far as I remember, I made some excuse, and got out of there as soon as I could. But since then… well, I've had all night and all day to think about it, and…'

'You're right to be shocked,' Martha said, as calmly as she could. 'Look, I'm sure the President didn't mean anything by it. You must understand, he is under a great deal of stress, and…'

Linda shook her head decisively.

'I'm sorry, Miss Graylor, but he meant every word. I know he did.'

She stood, turned and walked away a step or two towards the door. 'In any case, he's right. I should be loyal to him.'

Martha Graylor was not sure she had heard correctly. 'Excuse me? What did you say?'

'I should be loyal to him,' Linda repeated, less certainly.

'I don't believe this,' Martha said after some time. 'Agent Samuels, for

God's sake. He has no right… Think about what you're saying…'

'No,' Linda said. 'No. I'm not talking about committing perjury. I know that would be wrong. I wouldn't do that.'

'What, then?' Martha asked.

'Just not testifying, refusing to cooperate with them.'

'But you said it yourself, you have no choice. There's no privilege. They can make you.'

'They can put me in jail,' Linda replied, a determined edge creeping into her voice. 'But that's all they can do. They can't make me testify.'

Martha walked over to Linda, put both arms around her, brought her back gently to the armchair, and sat her down. She knelt on the floor in front of her.

'Linda, listen to me. If you do that, your career will be over. You will spend a long time in jail, because there is no way these people will give up. Believe me, I know them. They will not just give up.'

'I know that.'

'And you would still do it?'

'It's my duty.'

Shaking her head, Martha climbed slowly to her feet. She glanced at her watch. She was about to be late for her meeting with the President.

'Would you at least talk it over with someone else, someone who knows a lot more about this than I do? I feel the President had no right to do this to you. I feel you're being led astray. But I have a feeling you need to hear it from someone other than me? Will you do that?'

'Yes, Miss Graylor, of course. I didn't mean to imply…'

'That's all right.'

Martha walked quickly back around her desk, picked up the phone and dialed an internal extension.

'Vice President's Office,' a female voice said.

'Julie, is the Vice President there? I really need her.'

'Just a moment, Miss Graylor,' the secretary replied. There was a short silence. 'You're in luck. She was just about to leave. Putting you through.'

'Martha?' Ellen Trevathan said brightly. 'What's up?'

'Ellen,' Martha said, 'I really need you over here for a couple of minutes. Can you come?'

There was the briefest of pauses, as the Vice President weighed the edge in Martha's voice.

'I'm on my way,' Ellen said.

28

MARY SULLIVAN AND Irene had been waiting impatiently in *The Washington Post*'s conference room for over an hour by the time Harold Philby was finally able to extricate himself from a production meeting to join them. While waiting, they had assembled a small mountain of paper. Irene was seated at the table, thumbing through a file, trying to make sure she had mastered her brief before having to confront the Editor, a prospect which made her even more nervous than submitting her work to Mary Sullivan. Harold Philby was a legend and, despite the prospect of an A-plus, she was worrying that her internship might be about to spiral out of control. Mary was pacing up and down in front of the window, apparently distracted, clutching a cup of coffee. Philby grinned at the sight, as he entered and took his seat.

'Sorry to keep you, Mary,' he said. 'Those damned production meetings can be like old-time revival meetings. Sometimes you think they'll never end.'

'Good afternoon, Mr. Philby,' Irene stammered, standing awkwardly as her chair stubbornly resisted her efforts to push it backwards away from the table. 'I don't know whether you remember me, but I'm…'

'Irene,' Philby replied. 'You're our intern from George Washington. Of course I remember. I may be getting older, but reports of my senility have been greatly exaggerated. Isn't that so, Mary?'

'If you say so, Harold,' Mary smiled thinly, joining him at the table. She gestured to Irene to sit also.

'Well, thank you for that vote of confidence,' Philby replied, taking a spectacle case from an inside pocket of his jacket. 'Let me see if I can force my mind to concentrate for a few minutes.'

He waved the spectacle case in Mary's direction. 'You were right, by the way, or rather your source was.'

Mary looked up. 'About what?'

'About the President appearing on the Conrad Beckers show this evening.'

'Really?' Mary mused. 'I wonder what the occasion is. My source said they were keeping a very tight lid on it at the station.'

'I couldn't get anything out of Martha Graylor either,' Philby said. 'All she would say was that it's not unusual for the President to appear on Beckers.'

'It's unusual for them to bump a show just for the pleasure of his company. I can't recall them ever doing that except for a national crisis of some kind,' Mary pointed out.

'I put that to Martha. She insisted it was a normal courtesy to the President, or some baloney to that effect. Obviously, the intention is that we all find out at the same time. I've set up a viewing, of course. Are you free?'

'I'll be there. But can we get the pizza from our usual place this time? The stuff we had last time, during the budget fight, was terrible.'

'I'll make a special note to arrange it personally, Mary,' Philby replied. 'I'm just the Editor, after all. I have almost nothing else to do.'

Irene bit her lip in an unsuccessful attempt not to giggle.

'Now,' Philby continued, 'you said something about needing a decision. What have you got here?'

Mary Sullivan folded her arms in front of her on the table.

'Some time ago, I asked Irene to put together materials on the major players making contributions to both political parties. It's something I do every year.'

Philby nodded.

'This year, Irene came across an outfit which was new to me, calling itself the Western States Geophysical Research Institute. Does that mean anything to you?'

'Not a thing. What do they do?'

'Ah, well, that's a good question,' Mary replied. 'According to their website, they research and write position papers for groups interested in supporting the environment against special interests like logging, mining, oil exploration.'

'But…?'

'But they don't. Or at least, they haven't yet.'

She looked at Irene.

'I did a complete check, Mr. Philby,' Irene said hesitantly. 'All the web sources, the journals that would run pieces on something like this.

I even called the clients they list. Nothing.'

'Well, maybe they're just getting started,' Philby ventured.

'No, Sir, the company's been around for several years,' Irene replied.

'And, what's more to the point,' Mary added, 'is that they've been extremely well funded during those several years.'

She slid several documents, clipped together, across the table.

'Feast your eyes on this.'

Philby removed his reading glasses from their case, put them on, and scanned the documents carefully.

'Yes, I see what you mean,' he said, replacing the documents on the table. 'If I were funding them on that kind of scale, I might want to see some return for my money.'

'My feelings exactly,' Mary continued. 'Now, you'll notice a contributor mentioned in there called Middle and Near East Holdings, Incorporated. That's a company incorporated in Delaware. It's essentially a shell, formed by a group of Lebanese nationals. Other than contributing to Western States, they don't appear to do anything, and they seem to be shy about divulging information about themselves, especially in the form of filings.'

'Assets?' Philby asked.

'Nothing we can find,' Mary answered.

'They must have some money,' Philby pointed out. 'They gave quite a chunk to Western States.'

'We don't know it was their own money they gave,' Mary rejoined. 'In fact, it probably wasn't.'

'You mean, they were laundering it?'

'Possibly. Or at least providing cover for the real donor.'

Philby nodded. 'Interesting.'

'It gets better,' Mary smiled. 'It turns out, Middle and Near East also have the lease on that apartment in North West, where the President's friend, Lucia Benoni, was found murdered.'

'Well, for God's sake,' Philby muttered, moving across to pour himself a cup of coffee.

'Not in their own name, naturally, but their idea of cover isn't very subtle. The original named lessee was one of their own people, a guy called Hamid Marfrela.'

'That rings a distant bell,' the Editor said wryly.

'I thought it might.'

Philby paused, coffee pot in hand.

'Is there a paper trail to the money?'

'Oh, yes,' Mary replied. 'Middle and Near East is a generous underwriter of Western States, which in turn is a generous contributor to the President's party, even though the President's policy on environmental issues is generally bad news for the type of causes Western States is supposed to represent.'

Philby walked back to resume his seat.

'So, you think there's something else going on?'

'There has to be,' Mary said. 'It's too much money to be just a sop to keep the local congressmen and senators happy. In any case, they could do that by making contributions to their individual campaigns, which they haven't done.'

'And the local incumbents aren't much more interested in the environment than the President,' Irene added tentatively. 'There's no obvious reason for Western States to support them.'

'Right,' Mary agreed. 'So I asked Irene to dig deeper into Hamid Marfrela and see what she could come up with. Go ahead, Irene.'

Irene opened her file.

'Nothing very unusual in his past on the face of it, Mr. Philby. School in Beirut, followed by a spell in the Lebanese army, mandatory for two years under their law. Then he works for a family business, exporting rugs to Europe and the States for a while, does a fair amount of traveling. He seems to have made some money. He disappears from sight for a year or two. Finally, he shows up in Washington as a diplomat. He speaks fluent English and French, and he seems to be a favorite on the cocktail circuit. But he also makes some strange friends, some of whom later become contributors to Western States. He makes several extended trips out to Oregon.'

'To visit his strange friends at Western States?'

'Presumably, Sir. Well, let's put it this way, he had no legitimate diplomatic reason for being in Oregon.'

'How did you find that out, for God's sake?'

'I have a classmate who's interning at the State Department,' Irene grinned sheepishly.

'Good work,' Philby nodded encouragingly. 'What else?'

'Well, Sir, the people associated with Western States also have close ties to other individuals, who are involved with some of the white supremacist groups they have out there. I checked with Archives. Quite a few of them show up in articles we've run on those groups in the past. And…, Miss Sullivan…?'

'And,' Mary added, 'my source says the police are pretty much convinced Marfrela was murdered by a hit man working for one such group, a bunch of nasty specimens calling themselves The Sons of the Land, who run a military-style compound near Portland.'

Philby drank his coffee thoughtfully.

'I think I see where you're going with this,' he said quietly. 'No wonder the House wants to hold hearings. I'm sure the Intelligence Committee has been down the same road you have.'

'The way it looks to us, Harold,' Mary said, 'is that we have a money trail leading from Lebanon to the President, or at least to his party, filtered through some rather nasty people, by way of two companies which have no apparent activities except as part of the laundering process, if you want to call it that.'

'Motive?' Philby asked.

'That's what Irene and I kept asking ourselves. There are only three conclusions that make sense. One is the Lebanese Government or some Lebanese interests are providing financial support to white supremacist groups, presumably with the intention of destabilizing the United States Government, and the President's involvement with Lucia Benoni is coincidental.'

'Let me hear two and three.'

'Two is the President is playing footsie with the Lebanese Government or some Lebanese interests, and is getting paid off by means of illegal foreign contributions in return for favor or favors unknown in the foreign policy field. An unpleasant thought.'

'Very,' Philby agreed. 'Three?'

'Three is the Government of Lebanon or some Lebanese interests are interested in compromising the President by creating an appearance of motive two.'

Philby nodded grimly.

'Conclusions two and three also being supported by the presumed fact that Marfrela set the President up with Lucia Benoni as a sweetener.'

'And as a possible source of information. But for some reason, Lucia became too dangerous, and couldn't be trusted any more. Perhaps she got too fond of the President and they were afraid she might blow the whistle.'

'So they told Marfrela to get rid of her, which he did, but then they decided they couldn't trust Marfrela to keep his mouth shut, either, so he had to go, too.'

'Looks that way. But the other thing, Harold, is that everything they've done seems calculated to be discovered. They reported the Benoni murder to the police. The Marfrela killing was bound to be discovered as soon as he didn't show up for work at the Embassy. They left his body in his apartment for the police to find. And the money trail is so amateurish it's almost comical. All you had to do to find it was fall over it. I can't think of any reason why they would play it that way, except to set the President up.'

'That points to three,' Philby said.

'I agree.'

'Well, then, I suppose the question is,' the Editor said ponderously, 'whether they are setting him up for something he did or something he didn't do.'

There was a long silence.

'So, can I write the story?' Mary asked.

Philby looked at her across the table.

'That depends,' he answered quietly. 'Which story are you going to write?'

'I'm not sure. Why not put them all out there? Let the chips fall where they may.'

Philby shook his head decisively.

'No, not on something like this. Write me a draft with alternative endings, like one of those wretched audience-participation dinner theater who-done-its my wife is always dragging me to. We'll publish once we see which way the wind is blowing.'

'Harold…'

'You know it's the only way, Mary. Let's see what the President says on the Beckers Show, and let's listen to the opening statements in the Committee hearings. After that…'

'After that it won't be a story.'

'Yes it will,' Philby said definitively. 'It's going to be a story for quite a while. And we're way out in front. Nice job, both of you. Write the draft. I'll organize the pizza. From our usual place.'

* * *

In Philby's office they had watched the President's appearance on the Conrad Beckers News show in silence.

'So, why exactly was it so important for him to get on the show tonight?' Mary Sullivan asked. 'Irene, wind the tape back to where Beckers asked him about Chicago.'

The intern leapt to her feet and started to cue the tape to the desired point, using notes of digital numbers from the tape counter she had carefully compiled during the recording. Harold Philby thoughtfully brushed a few morsels of pizza from his lips on to a paper napkin.

'Beats me,' Philby said. 'It sounded like the same old tune to me. I bet Conrad is royally pissed off.'

'Here we go,' Irene said.

The camera was trained on Conrad Beckers who, as was his custom, was sitting in his film director's chair, an expensive pen in his hand and a pad full of notes on his lap.

'Mr. President,' he was saying, 'I'm sure you know that there have been allegations that you entertained Lucia Benoni in your hotel room in Chicago during a recent visit. Yet, you have maintained that your contact with her was minimal and quite innocent. What do you say to those charges?'

The camera shifted to Steve Wade, who was seated opposite Beckers in an armchair.

'Look at that,' Philby said in a low voice. 'I've never seen the man look so uncomfortable.'

'He'd rather be having a root canal,' Mary agreed.

The President had taken several seconds to reply.

'Conrad, I will tell you that I did see Ms.Benoni one evening during my Chicago trip,' Wade said. 'Let me say first that it was entirely innocent. She happened to be in town, and wanted to discuss some matters of mutual interest. It also happened that I was free for the evening, and I invited her to come by for a drink. She did. She stayed for a while. I have no recollection of exactly how long. It was entirely innocent. You must remember that the President of the United States is never left completely alone, especially when he's away from the White House. I had a Secret Service Agent right outside the door. Even if I were tempted to stray, Conrad, please don't underestimate how difficult it would be.'

Beckers twirled the pen between his well-manicured fingers for a few moments.

'So, Mr. President, are we to understand that there was never any kind of sexual relationship between Ms. Benoni and yourself?'

'That's correct. I've made that clear from the beginning, and I'm glad to have the chance to make it clear again on your show.'

'Then, Mr. President, why didn't you tell the American people this, about your meeting with Ms. Benoni, when the matter first arose?'

'Because I didn't think it would be of any interest to anyone. I still don't.'

'But you are aware that it seems to be of great interest to certain members of Congress?'

Steve Wade pulled himself up forcefully in his chair, his eyes looked piercingly at his interviewer.

'That's more like it,' Philby muttered.

'Conrad, that's why I was so anxious to be on your show this evening, and make my views known to the American people. What's going on here has nothing to do with my acquaintanceship with Lucia Benoni. What's going on here is an attempt at political assassination by those who oppose the work the American people elected me to do, and who resent the success my Administration has had in doing that work. I want to tell the misguided people who are responsible that this attack will not deflect me from my work. I will defend myself with every resource at my disposal and, after I have repulsed the attack, let there be no mistake, I will be coming after those people. Let them heed my words and beware.'

The camera turned to Conrad Beckers, who seemed transfixed by his guest's eyes. It took him some time to refocus awkwardly on his notes and come up with another question.

'When you say you will be 'coming after those people', Mr. President, exactly what should we understand you to mean?'

'Just what I said, Conrad,' Wade replied with the faintest of smiles. 'It's not prudent warfare to give away one's plans in advance, so I'm not going to say any more on that subject. But I sincerely hope they take me seriously.'

'OK, Irene,' Mary Sullivan said. 'Hold it there. What was it he said later about Marfrela? Did you get a note of that?'

'Yes, Miss Sullivan, I sure did,' Irene replied. She consulted her yellow pad. 'Never met him, never heard of him, don't have any idea who that is, anyone who says otherwise is the Antichrist. Do you want me to run it?'

Mary shook her head, turning to look at Harold Philby.

'How in the hell can Martha Graylor let him do this?' she asked quietly. Philby shook his head in reply.

'She wouldn't. No way. It's out of her hands. I'd put money on it. Wade's calling the shots himself. This has all the indications of an administration about to career out of control.'

'What does that do to our story?' Mary asked.

'I would say it's taken us one step closer to publication. Let's gear up. I'll talk to the owners and our attorneys tomorrow. Start polishing your draft.'

29

POLLY CHAIKEN FLASHED the Secret Service Agent outside the door of her apartment her most insincere smile, and virtually slammed the door in the man's face. Turning round to face her guest, she raised her eyes and hands to the ceiling in a gesture of frustration.

'What is with these people?' she asked. 'It's not enough they trample all over my apartment and then follow me around town all day? They have to lie in wait for me outside my own front door?'

Julia Wade smiled sympathetically.

'I'm sorry, Polly. It comes with the territory. At least you only get it for a day. I have to live with it.'

'I hear that,' Polly said. 'Well, it could have been worse. He could have insisted on following us inside again to make sure I don't slit your throat with my letter opener.'

She exhaled heavily and made an effort to relax her body.

'Oh, what the hell? Forget about him. We've had a hard day pounding the streets of Manhattan. You did good, kid. You haven't lost your touch as a shopper. I think we're entitled to a drink. What will it be? You still a gin and tonic girl?'

'Thanks, that would be great.'

The First Lady also began to relax in the privacy of her old friend's apartment. The out-of-town shopping and lunch expedition she had arranged at short notice had irritated her Detail, which had been forced to produce a security plan to protect her in a crowd without much time to reflect on it. The expedition had also left her breathless. She was no longer used to the pace of New York City, or to being almost alone and fighting her way through large crowds of people. But the day had also exhilarated her. It had reminded her that there was life outside the White House, and that she had once reveled in that life.

'Do you mind if I take my shoes off?'

'Take off whatever you want,' Polly replied. 'I'm going to do the same. I can barely feel my toes any more.'

Leaving her shoes by the drinks cabinet, Polly brought their cocktails over to the sofa, and joined Julia. They toasted silently and sat back on the sofa, savoring the refreshing first swallow. Polly suddenly giggled.

'Can you believe that saleswoman who wanted your autograph? What was it she kept shouting? 'Look, everyone, it's her, it's the First Lady, it's the First Lady!'.'

Julia joined in the giggle.

'I know. It was like she wanted everyone in New York to know I was in Bloomingdales. I kept trying, but I couldn't shut her up. I autographed everything I could lay my hands on, but it didn't seem to calm her down one little bit.'

'I thought your agent was going to have a heart attack. You could see him thinking, "Oh, my God, there are too many people, how do I protect her? Maybe we should go to Defcon 4", or whatever.'

They both laughed uproariously, then allowed the laughter to die away. Polly turned to face Julia.

'This was like old times. It's been so long, Julia. I miss you.'

'I miss you too.'

'Can I ask you something?'

'Sure.'

'Other than the autograph thing, how do you really like being the First Lady? From what I'm reading in the papers, it doesn't sound all that great at the moment.'

Julia looked away, then turned back towards Polly with tears forming in her eyes.

'This is the most I've laughed in a long time,' she said quietly.

'You're kidding. That's not like you. You used to be the life and soul of the party. I never saw you without a smile on your face.'

'Not any more, Polly. Oh, I smile for the camera, of course, for strangers, for the American public. That gets to be automatic. You learn to do it without even noticing. But as far as real smiles go, smiles for people close to me? No, I don't have those any more. You know what they call me at the White House?'

Polly shook her head.

'The Ice Queen. Maybe that's who I am now. I don't know any more.'

Polly drained her glass and, without asking, held out her hand to take Julia's. She stood and walked back to the drinks cabinet to pour refills.

'That doesn't sound like such a good deal to me,' she said, with concern.

Julia pushed herself to her feet, took her refilled glass, and walked a little way around the spacious living room, as if admiring the several original paintings her friend had hanging on the walls. Polly sat back down and did not intrude.

'The whole world knows he's fucking around on me,' Julia said eventually. 'And the funny thing is, Polly, I'd almost got used to it, you know, finding out about the latest woman, listening to his stupid lies, having to keep up appearances in front of everybody, Mrs. Unflappable First Lady, doing the stand-by-your-man routine. And now this latest thing. He's getting himself in so deep, I'm not even sure there's a way out.'

'Why would you even care after all that's happened?'

Julia took a long drink, and sat back down on the sofa.

'That's the strange thing. I really thought I was past it. I was thinking, 'who cares? I can last till the end of his term, then I'm out of here'. And then this Benoni thing came up, and I came unglued again. Polly, the other morning, I got into such a fight with Steve that an agent came into our private living quarters to break it up, thinking I might kill him.'

'Damn,' Polly whispered.

'I threw a vase at Steve and cut his head open. I was actually wrestling with the agent on the floor when his back-up arrived. At one point, I was actually standing there in front of half of the Secret Service in my nightgown and bare feet, with my hands in the air and guns being pointed at me. Pretty First Lady-like, huh?'

Julia broke down, and Polly put her arms around her, holding her until her tears had subsided a little.

'You want some advice from an old friend?'

Julia wiped away the tears on the sleeve of her sweater. 'Yes.'

'I think you need to resume your life.'

'My life?'

'Yes, Julia, your life. Here in New York. And don't tell me you don't miss it. I could see it in your eyes today. You wanted it back so much you almost couldn't stand it.'

Julia leaned back against the sofa clutching her drink.

'What would I do in New York now, Polly? It's been so long.'

Polly Chaiken snorted. 'What would you do in New York? Excuse me? Earth to Julia, hello.'

Julia's eyes opened wide. 'You mean… are you talking about the firm? You think they might…?'

'Might? Are you serious?'

Polly put down her drink and took her friend by both arms.

'Julia, they would kill to have you back. You were there at the beginning. You're one of the best, and you're one of us, always were, always will be. Plus, now, you're the First Lady. Julia, we do advertising, remember? It would be a dream come true.'

Julia sighed. 'Just because I'm the First Lady?'

Polly reached out and pushed a strand of hair away from Julia's forehead.

'No. Not just because you're the First Lady. Mostly because we love you. You must know that, Julia. Nothing's changed. Hell, we were together when Steve fucking Wade wasn't even a blip on the national radar screen. No one dreamed you would be First anything back then, except maybe First Advertiser, which you could have been, and still could. You were just Julia. You still are.'

There was a long silence.

'Don't tell me you haven't thought about leaving,' Polly added eventually.

'I think about it every day.'

'So?'

'Polly, I'm the First Lady. I'm married to the President. I live in the White House.'

'So that entitles him to cheat on you, and you have to just lie back and take it?'

'Not for ever. But I couldn't leave before the end of his term.'

'Why in the hell not?'

'Polly…'

'Hillary Clinton did. And she came to New York.'

'The Clintons bought a house in New York together.'

'Oh, yeah, right. Look, you can always invite Steve to join you if you want. Cross that bridge when you come to it.'

She paused. 'Hillary's not a bad precedent, Julia. Besides, if you stay, you might just bring his term to a premature end. The Secret Service Agent might not get there so fast next time.'

Julia smiled thinly.

'And he probably deserves it,' Polly continued, 'but it wouldn't be good, Julia. It might be safer for both of you if you leave now.'

'I don't know… I… God, Polly, it would look like I was just giving up…'

'There's not a man, woman or child in America who wouldn't stand up and cheer for you.'

'Yes, there is,' Julia replied grimly. 'My husband is a very popular man. Don't ever underestimate that.'

Polly picked up her drink again, and sat back.

'Be that as it may. He doesn't own you, and he doesn't have the right to treat you the way he does. Think about that, Julia. And when you finally wake up and realize I'm right, call me. We'll all be here for you.'

30

THE MARSHAL'S KNOCK on the door, announcing that the House
Intelligence Committee was ready for its next witness, came as a relief to
Ted Lazenby. The conference room in which he had been waiting was
small and stuffy, and the coffee was terrible. Lazenby had been there for
an hour-long final preparation session, trying his best to breathe and
concentrate at the same time, and he was developing a significant
headache. It seemed to Lazenby that he and his legal adviser, Senior FBI
Counsel Jerome Wills, had been going over and over the same ground,
time after time, for days on end. Kelly Smith and Jeff Morris, who had
also been subpoenaed and were scheduled to testify next in order after
Lazenby, were seated with him at the table, and seemed to have similar
symptoms. What was worse, Lazenby had a guilty conscience. He had
withheld an important part of the truth from his attorney, he had
supplied him with a carefully-edited selection of documents, he was
about to treat a congressional committee in the same manner, and he
had instructed Kelly and Jeff to do the same. Together, they had
carefully concealed, even from Wills, any mention of the Oregon
connection and the Bureau's activities there. Off the record, in a
confidential meeting, Lazenby had outlined the circumstances to the
Committee Chair, Congressman Vernon Moberley. He had received an
assurance that the subject would not be broached in open hearings. But
they both understood that the assurance was not absolute, that neither
of them could control a random question from some other member of
the Committee or a leak from some over-zealous staffer. In that event,
the most Lazenby could count on would be a recess to consider how to
respond, followed by the offer of a hearing behind closed doors. And if
that happened, the justifiable anger of Jerome Wills would be the least
of his problems.

Lazenby followed Wills and the marshal the short distance from the conference room to the Committee's hearing room, gratefully breathing the cooler air in the corridor. The marshal led the way, pushing his way respectfully but firmly through the throng of reporters, as two of his colleagues held the doors open for them. The photographers' flashlights exploded in Lazenby's face. One or two reporters shouted questions. Lazenby ignored them.

The hearing room, though large, was hot, crowded, and claustrophobic. The Committee members sat on a raised dais in a semi-circle at the front of the room, their staffers sitting behind them as best they could. The table and chairs reserved for the witness and his counsel faced the dais. Stenographers sat nearby, poised for action. Every inch of the room not occupied by the furniture seemed to be taken up with reporters, photographers, and camera operators jostling for position. The atmosphere was frenetic. Lazenby experienced an uncomfortable flashback to his Senate confirmation hearing. Wills was motioning to him to stand at the table. A book was held up for him. He placed his hand on it and, swallowing hard, took an oath to tell the truth, the whole truth and nothing but the truth. Silence fell. The Committee Chair Vernon Moberley, an elderly member of the House, of the party opposed to the President, carefully arranged his papers in front of him.

'Would you state your full name for the record, Sir?'

'Edward James Lazenby, the Third.'

'You are the Director of the Federal Bureau of Investigation?'

'Yes, Sir.'

'For how long have you held that position?'

'I was confirmed early in President Wade's first term of office, and I have held the position ever since.'

'You are a personal friend of President Wade, are you not, Sir?'

Jerome Wills leaned forward to his microphone. 'With all due respect, Mr. Chairman…' But Lazenby restrained him with a light touch of his hand.

'Yes, I am. We were classmates at Princeton.'

'Thank you, Sir. Now, I believe, Mr. Director, you are aware of the testimony which has been given to this Committee so far?'

'In general terms, yes.'

'You know that Chief Henry Bryson of the Washington D.C. Police Department has testified to us at some length about the murders of Lucia Benoni and Hamid Marfrela, the Lebanese diplomat?'

'Yes, Sir.'

'The Chief told us, in fact, that your agents had cooperated with his officers in the investigation of those murders. Is that correct?'

'On my instructions, Mr. Chairman, yes, they did.'

'Are those murders still the subject of ongoing investigations?'

'Technically speaking, yes, they are.'

'What do you mean by 'technically speaking'?'

'Well, Mr. Chairman, I am satisfied on the evidence, as I believe Chief Bryson is also, that Hamid Marfrela murdered Lucia Benoni. But Marfrela himself was killed shortly afterwards, and we have not reached any conclusions about the reasons for that murder. It may be that whoever killed Marfrela was also involved in the Benoni killing. But we don't know for sure. So the files remain open but, frankly, I must tell the Committee that I hold out little hope that we will ever finally solve these murders.'

'Is it your testimony to this Committee that you have no evidence as to the identity of the killer of Hamid Marfrela?'

Lazenby bit his lip.

'That is partly correct, Mr. Chairman. We did get a description of a person who may well have been the killer, and there were various fingerprints in the apartment, but we haven't been able to tie the evidence to a particular suspect.'

There was a silence while the Chairman rearranged his papers. Lazenby took a sip of the water in front of him, and hoped he did not look as nervous as he felt. The eyes of the members of the Committee seemed to be focused directly on him. The camera lights were blindingly bright.

'Mr. Director, are you aware of the evidence that Ms. Benoni was found to be in possession of a special pass, enabling her to enter the White House without going through the usual screening procedures for each visit?'

'The S-Pass? Yes, Sir, I am aware of that.'

'And are you further aware that this Committee has heard testimony that this S-Pass was issued to Ms. Benoni at the personal request of the President?'

'I'm aware that that has been alleged.'

'How did you become aware of it? From following our proceedings?'

Lazenby leaned forward in his chair.

'No, Mr. Chairman. I believe I read about it in *The Washington Post.*'

A loud outburst of laughter ran around the room. The Chairman seemed vexed, but smiled in an effort to appear gracious.

'As Director of the FBI, is it your normal practice to get information about your ongoing investigations from *The Washington Post*?'

Wills was touching Lazenby's arm with his hand. Lazenby nodded almost imperceptibly.

'Mr.Chairman, this information had nothing to do with the investigation into Ms. Benoni's death, so whether I got it from the *Post* or anywhere else is not really very relevant.'

The laughter was replaced by a gasp of surprise. A staffer rose from her seat behind the Chairman and handed him a handwritten note.

'It was not relevant that the victim of this crime had an S-Pass? Why not?'

'Because the President had an alibi, Mr. Chairman. He wasn't a suspect.'

The laughter was even louder. Out of the corner of his eye, Lazenby noticed that even Wills had managed a smile.

The laughter subsided and there was a long and uncomfortable silence. The Chairman seemed frustrated.

'The Chair yields two minutes to the Honorable Lady from Maine.'

Lazenby and Wills exchanged glances. Helen de Vries was a former prosecutor, with an incisive mind and a fiery partisan temperament. She did not like Steve Wade, and had already made clear in the press her intention of linking him to some wrongdoing, if it was at all possible. Unlike the Chairman, Helen de Vries needed no notes.

'Mr. Director, what investigation did you do into the activities of Hamid Marfrela?'

'His activities? I'm not sure what you mean.'

Helen de Vries pursed her lips and nodded briefly. 'Well, follow along with me if you can. Marfrela was a Lebanese diplomat, correct?'

'Correct.'

'The evidence suggested that he and Lucia Benoni were lovers?'

'The evidence suggested that they had sex on the night she was killed.'

'His name was in her address book, correct?'

'Yes, it was. Along with a large number of others.'

'And you were aware that the President also had a relationship with Lucia Benoni, correct?'

This time, Wills leaned right across in front of Lazenby. 'Excuse me, Congresswoman, what kind of relationship are you referring to?'

'What kind of relationship does the witness know about?'

'From his own personal knowledge? I assume you're not asking him to speculate.'

Helen de Vries hesitated.

'From his own personal knowledge, or information gathered during the investigation.'

Wills nodded. 'You may answer on that basis, Director.'

'Congresswoman,' Lazenby said, 'the only relationship suggested by the evidence is one of personal friendship, which I believe the President has already conceded. Again, I don't believe this had any bearing on the investigations.'

'Director, is the Committee to assume that you see no cause for alarm in the fact that both the President and the man Marfrela were having a relationship with Lucia Benoni?'

Lazenby bristled.

'As I've already tried to make clear, Congresswoman, the evidence suggests that Marfrela had sex with Lucia Benoni on one occasion, while her hands were tied behind her back, after which he shot her in the head. I don't know about you, but to me, that doesn't qualify as a relationship.'

There was more laughter. Helen de Vries seemed vexed. The Congressman sitting next to her whispered something to her. She drummed her fingers on the table.

'I yield back my remaining time to the Chair,' she muttered venomously.

Vernon Moberley made a great play of looking at a gold pocket watch on a heavy link chain, which he had removed from the vest pocket of his suit.

'It is approaching the time for recess,' he observed. 'We have had a full day. I think the wisest course would be to resume tomorrow. Mr. Director, I would request that you not discuss your testimony with anyone other than your attorney overnight.'

'Very well, Mr. Chairman,' Lazenby said.

As the members of the Committee filed out, Lazenby stood wearily. His headache had now taken a full grip.

'Well, I thought that went pretty well,' Jerome Wills ventured. 'How do you feel about it?'

'I don't know. Where do you think de Vries was headed with those questions?'

'They're out to nail the President any way they can,' Wills replied. 'I'm sure she was hoping you had some smoking gun to hand her. But you don't.'

'I have a feeling she thinks she has one already,' Lazenby said. 'Look, Jerome, since I'm in quarantine, why don't you go and do whatever you have to with Kelly and Jeff, and tell them I can't talk to them now? I'll see you in the morning.'

'All right, Director. Have a good evening.'

'I'll do my best,' Lazenby said.

At the door of the committee room, he signaled to the marshal, who stood ready to escort him to the car waiting for him outside.

'Home, Director?' the driver asked cheerfully.

'No, the Bureau. I have some calls to make.'

* * *

'So, eventually,' Linda said despondently, 'Miss Graylor asked the Vice President to come and talk to me. The Vice President in person. Imagine that.'

'What did she say?' Kelly asked.

She and Jeff had listened to Linda talk almost without interruption through a makeshift dinner at Kelly's apartment. They were all very tired. After a long day, they had settled down to watch lengthy television coverage of Ted Lazenby's testimony before the Committee. When the direction of the questioning became clear, Linda had become very agitated. She was scheduled to testify immediately after Kelly and Jeff. Kelly settled her friend down with a glass of wine, and that had been the point at which Linda had broken down, sobbing out the story of what had happened to her during the previous two days. Kelly and Jeff listened incredulously.

'She told me that the President had no right to say what he said, and she would speak to him about it. She said I had to testify, and I should tell the truth.'

'She's absolutely right,' Kelly said.

She stood and walked noiselessly on bare feet from the small living room to the adjoining kitchen to fetch the wine bottle, from which she refilled the glasses.

'Remember, Linda, you don't actually know what went on in the hotel room…'

'Oh, come on, Kelly…'

'No, you don't. All right, you saw the woman go in, you heard some noises…'

'The kind of noises I remember from the days when I used to have sex.'

'Whatever. If that's all they have, it won't stand up. They need some other evidence Linda, evidence you can't give. When all is said and done, you really don't know what happened.'

'I know what happened.'

'That's not evidence. It's not for you to draw conclusions. You know that. That's up to the Committee. If the Committee chooses to draw some conclusion the President doesn't like, that's his fault for putting himself in a bad situation and then lying about it. Your job is to state the facts. The facts are, you saw the woman go in, you heard noises, you saw the woman come out. If they ask you what the noises were, you say you don't know and you can't speculate.'

'I've already heard that from the lawyer they got me.'

'Well, she's right,' Kelly said firmly. 'Listen to her.'

'In addition to which,' Jeff said, 'the right thing is to tell the truth. No one's above the law, Linda, not even the President.'

'I know, I know,' Linda sighed. 'I just don't want to be the one who sinks him.'

'He's doing that all on his own,' Jeff replied. 'There is absolutely no reason for you to go down with him. Hell, Linda, even the Vice President doesn't want you to do that. Martha Graylor told you, your lawyer told you. What more do you need?'

There was a silence.

'And if you refuse to testify,' Kelly said, 'not only will they throw you in jail, but it will look just as bad, maybe even worse, for the President than if you testified.'

'How do you figure that?'

'Simple. It will be obvious you're trying to protect him, and if you're prepared to go to jail to do it, they will probably think whatever you're hiding must be even worse than it is.'

Kelly took Linda's hand between her own and squeezed gently.

'In any case, Linda, you have your own future to think about. I'm not going to sit back and watch you throw away your career over this.'

Linda sat silently for a long time.

'It's getting late,' she said eventually. 'I'd better be on my way. They want me there first thing tomorrow morning. Apparently, they don't think they'll be long with you guys.'

'I'm sure Director Lazenby has told them everything we could,' Kelly said.

They all stood.

'Do you want to stay the night?'

'I can sleep on the sofa if you want to be with Kelly,' Jeff volunteered.

'No, thank you,' Linda said. 'I should go. Dinner was great. Thanks.'
She kissed Jeff and Kelly in turn.

'Oh, by the way,' she added on her way out, 'just to make it a perfect day, Bob called to say he was shacking up with the bimbo again. If you know anyone else who wants to join in 'Fuck Linda Week', tell them all they have to do is take a number.'

Kelly made it to the door just in time to catch Linda as she broke down, weeping desperately, uncontrollably. For several long minutes, she stood by the door holding her friend tight, as her convulsions followed each other in quick succession. Slowly, she maneuvered Linda towards the bedroom.

'You don't mind?' she asked Jeff.

'No, no problem. Take her to bed. I'll clear up here. I'll drive her home early tomorrow morning.'

Jeff quickly cleared away the dishes, ran the dishwasher, turned out the lights, and tried to settle down on the sofa in the darkness. But the persistent sobbing coming from the bedroom would not let him rest. An hour went by, and then another. Tired as he was, he gave up the idea of sleep and switched on the television. Eventually, when his eyes refused to stay open any longer, he drifted into a shallow sleep. Just before five o'clock, leaving Kelly also exhausted and asleep, Linda quietly climbed out of bed, dressed, and left the apartment without a word.

31

THE COMMITTEE BEGAN Linda's testimony just after lunch. They had shown little interest in what Kelly and Jeff had to say. Ted Lazenby had already covered the same ground, and as the Lebanese diplomatic corps had invoked its collective diplomatic immunity, it seemed that little progress could be made on the subject of Lucia Benoni and Hamid Marfrela. Frustrated, the Committee was ready to turn its attention to Chicago. Kelly and Jeff, anxious since waking up to find that Linda had left Kelly's apartment so early in the morning without telling them, decided to remain in the Committee's hearing room to listen. They were not alone in their interest in Linda's testimony. The House Majority Leader, Gerry Parkinson, was sitting unobtrusively at the back of the room with Congressman George Stanley and John Mason. Known only to Mason, Selvey was also sitting nearby, ostensibly no more than a curious member of the public.

After Linda had taken the oath, the Chairman asked only a few token questions about her background and current assignment before handing over to Congresswoman de Vries. After being thwarted by Ted Lazenby the previous day, the former prosecutor was not in a charitable mood.

'Agent Samuels, I understand you were on duty as a member of the President's Detail during his trip to Chicago, is that correct?'

'Yes, Ma'am.'

'What were your duties?'

'To make sure the President was secure.'

'And how did you do that?'

'I checked everyone who came to his suite at the hotel.'

'Checked…?'

'For weapons.'

'I see. And do you recall a woman by the name of Lucia Benoni coming to see the President in his suite one evening?'

'Yes, I do.'

'Did you know who this woman was?'

'Only what I was told.'

'And what were you told?'

Linda looked briefly at Sue Williams, the assistant White House Counsel assigned to represent her, who nodded.

'That she was an old friend of the President from his home state.'

There was some laughter in the room, which the Chairman suppressed with two or three strokes of his gavel.

'What was the purpose of this old friend visiting the President?' Congresswoman de Vries continued.

'I'm sure I have no idea,' Linda replied.

A little more laughter, which died away quickly.

'But, Agent Samuels, you were there to guard the President. Is it your testimony to this Committee that you made no inquiries about who she was, what she might want?'

'With all due respect, Congresswoman, that wasn't my job. I…'

'Well, what was your job exactly?'

'To check whether she was carrying any weapons, which I did. It was none of my business why she wanted to see the President, or why he wanted to see her.'

Helen de Vries paused momentarily to consult some notes.

'So, having checked Miss Benoni out, you admitted her to the President's suite?'

'No. She knocked on the door, and the President admitted her.'

'All right. And then what happened?'

'After three or four hours, she left.'

'Where were you during this period of three or four hours?'

Linda hesitated. 'Outside the door of the suite, most of the time.'

'Most of the time?'

'I took a bathroom break once or twice, and another agent replaced me for a few minutes.'

'All right. Did anyone else enter or leave the President's suite while Miss Benoni was there?'

'No…, oh, yes, I'm sorry, a waiter did come with some refreshments. That was not long after Miss Benoni arrived.'

'The waiter was someone you knew?'

'Yes. He had been cleared, and he was in charge of whatever the President might need from the kitchen.'

'Do you remember the waiter's name?'

'No, Ma'am.'

'What kind of refreshments did the waiter bring?'

'Mr. Chairman, I can't see how that has any relevance,' Sue Williams interrupted.

Vernon Moberley shrugged.

'Maybe it does, and maybe it doesn't,' he replied. 'Let's find out. Answer the question, please, Agent Samuels.'

'The waiter brought a bottle of champagne.'

'Really? Good champagne?'

'I would hope so, Congresswoman. It's not my drink.'

There was a short burst of sympathetic laughter, in which Helen de Vries joined.

'*Touchée*, Agent Samuels. How many glasses did the waiter bring?'

Linda hesitated. 'Two,' she answered reluctantly.

'All right. Now, at any time when the President was alone with Miss Benoni in his suite, did you hear any sounds or noises that might have indicated what was going on?'

Linda bit her lip and looked at Sue Williams. But Sue seemed preoccupied with her pen and gave her no response.

'I'm not sure what you mean, Congresswoman. What kind of noises?'

'I don't know. That's what I'm asking you. What did you hear?'

'You can't hear too much through the door. I heard their voices.'

'Talking?'

'Yes.'

'Laughing?'

'Yes, once or twice.'

'Nothing else?'

Linda felt herself turning red. Her stomach was churning.

'May I have a moment to confer with counsel?'

Helen de Vries raised her eyebrows and glanced at the Chairman.

'By all means,' Moberley said.

Linda turned to Sue, whispering.

'Miss Williams, I can't do this.'

'Linda, we've been over this,' Sue answered. 'You have to answer.'

'I can't. It's disloyal.'

'No, it's not, Linda. You have no choice.'

There was a silence.

'Whenever you're ready,' Moberley said impatiently.

'I'm sorry,' Linda whispered to Sue. She turned back to face Helen de Vries. 'Congresswoman, anything I might say would be no more than speculation. I did not go into the President's suite that evening. I don't know what was going on inside.'

'That's not what I'm asking,' de Vries said smoothly. 'I'm not asking you to speculate. I'm asking you to describe what you heard as best you can. I'm sure the Committee will be quite capable of drawing its own conclusions. I'm merely asking you to tell us what you heard.'

'I'm sorry,' Linda said. 'I must decline to answer.'

The noise which broke out after the initial shocked silence took Chairman Moberley over a minute to suppress. Everyone was talking at once. The reporters were in top gear, pencils flying hurriedly over pages. Several left to alert the media that a major story might be about to break. When order had at last been restored, Helen de Vries deferred to the Chair to deal with the situation.

'Agent Samuels,' he said slowly, 'You are represented by counsel, and I'm sure you have been advised that there is no privilege attached to your testimony here today. Would you like to confer with your counsel again?'

'No, Sir,' Linda replied evenly. 'I understand the position.'

'In that case, would you care to explain to the Committee the basis on which you decline to answer?'

'Loyalty,' Linda replied simply. 'I will not put the President in the position of being condemned because of what I might or might not have heard. As I've already said, I wasn't in his suite, and I don't know what was going on or not going on inside.'

To complete silence, the Chairman weighed the position, and turned briefly to confer with an aide. Sue Williams tried to get Linda's attention, but was dismissed with a curt shake of the head. At the back of the room, Kelly and Jeff exchanged horrified looks. John Mason looked surreptitiously across at Selvey, who seemed amused by the proceedings.

'Well, Agent Samuels,' Moberley said at last, 'loyalty is an admirable virtue, but I think a little misplaced in this situation. I'm going to have to ask you again to answer my colleague's question. If you wish, you may confer with counsel again. But if you refuse to answer, I will have to call for a vote of the Committee as to whether you should be held in contempt. Do you understand?'

'Yes, Sir.'

'Good. Are you prepared to answer the question?'

'No, Sir,' Linda said, swallowing hard.

Sue grabbed her arm. 'Linda, for Christ's sake,' she only half whispered.

Linda threw off Sue's grip on her arm.

At the back of the room, Kelly put her hands up to her face.

'Linda, don't do this,' she breathed.

Vernon Moberley pulled himself up in his chair.

'I call for a vote on the question of whether the witness should be held in contempt,' he said.

The vote was taken, and by a vote split on party lines, Linda Samuels was held to be in contempt of the House Intelligence Committee.

'Before taking any further action,' the Chairman said, 'I will give you one last chance. Will you answer the question?'

Linda had turned white, but seemed outwardly calm.

'No, Sir. I will not,' she said.

Moberley nodded.

'Very well,' he said. 'The House Officer will take the witness into custody until such time as she is prepared to comply with the Committee's orders.'

Pandemonium broke loose in the hearing room, which the Chairman's gavel was powerless to control. Sue Williams leapt to her feet, her protests lost, however, in the general din, as Linda was led from the room. Kelly put her head on Jeff's shoulder and sighed. The Chairman was trying to declare that the proceedings were recessed pending the restoration of order, but no one was taking much notice of him. The Committee members remained where they were.

John Mason sprang to his feet and walked quickly across the room to Selvey. 'Is our friend ready?' he asked.

'Are you sure you want to do this?' Selvey countered.

'You brought him into this. You tell me.'

'Mr. Jeffers is standing by, ready to go,' Selvey said brusquely.

'OK, I'll give the Committee's counsel the nod.'

Mason turned away, and then suddenly back to Selvey again.

'But he has been prepared, hasn't he, Selvey? I mean, he knows what answers are expected to certain questions?'

Selvey smiled. 'Don't worry about it, Mr. Mason. Our Harold will be as good as gold.'

'I certainly hope so,' Mason said grimly to himself, as he made his way towards the front of the room.

After a short conversation with Mason, the Committee's counsel approached the dais and whispered briefly to the Chairman. The noise was dying down by now, and the Chairman was eventually able to restore order.

'It was my intention to recess the proceedings,' Moberley said, 'but it has been brought to my attention that another witness is available. We will take testimony from this witness, after which the Committee will be in recess for the weekend, and will resume proceedings on Monday morning. We will now hear from Harold Jeffers.'

Angela Moran, the leader of the President's party's minority on the Committee, searched her papers in vain, and exchanged whispered remarks with her colleagues, who were none the wiser.

'On a point of order, Mr. Chairman,' she said. 'I don't find this witness among those listed in the documents supplied to me by your office. I thought we had an understanding that we would be notified in advance of the witnesses to be called, so that we might have an opportunity to prepare. This is rather irregular, to say the least.'

'I share the Honorable Lady's surprise,' the Chairman said suavely. 'Counsel for the Committee has just notified me of the availability of this witness, and has confirmed that the witness has some information which may be relevant. I see no reason not to proceed. Of course, I will allow the minority the weekend to prepare any questions they may wish to ask, having heard his testimony.'

The minority leader looked questioningly at her colleagues, wondering whether to call for a vote on the point of order. Seeing no advantage in losing a further vote on party lines, they shook their heads, and Angela Moran accepted their judgment.

The Chair had delegated the primary examination of Harold Jeffers to Helen de Vries. It was a wise move. De Vries had many years of experience in dealing with witnesses like Jeffers, and would not be put off by his nervousness or his tendency to ramble. Jeffers certainly looked the part. Selvey had seen to that personally. He was smartly dressed in a gray suit, white shirt and red tie, his black shoes shined. De Vries began with details of his name, family, and occupation, using her most polished professional style to paint a sympathetic portrait of a devoted long-time employee. The press was eating up every word. Before turning to the main subject of her examination, Helen de Vries signposted it with a lengthy pause.

'Mr. Jeffers, you have described in general terms your duties at the hotel during the President's visit. But now, I want to ask you about a particular occasion. Did there come a time when the President requested you to bring something up to his suite?'

'Yes, Ma'am.'

'What time was this?'

'During the evening. About eight, eight-thirty.'

'And what did the President request?'

'A bottle of champagne and two glasses.'

'Did you take those items to the President's suite?'

'I did.'

'How did you gain admittance to the suite?'

'I checked in with the Secret Service Agent on duty, and…'

'Before you get to that, do you know that agent's name?'

'Yes. It was Agent Linda Samuels.'

'Thank you. Continue.'

'I knocked on the door of the suite. There was no reply, so I decided to enter. I probably should have waited, but there seemed no need.'

'I'm sure you didn't want to keep the President waiting?'

'No, Ma'am.'

'So you went in. What did you see?'

The moment had arrived. Jeffers was feeling hot under the lights, and his shirt collar was sticking to his neck. Selvey had warned him that his appearance before the Committee would not be a comfortable experience, but it was worse than he expected. He was beginning to sweat profusely. Forcing himself to concentrate, he summoned up Selvey's instructions. Remain serious, be strictly factual, and avoid obscene euphemisms. He hoped he would remember the correct vocabulary for what he had to describe.

'I saw the President and Miss Benoni lying together on the couch in the living room.'

There were audible gasps from the audience. Vernon Moberley was so fascinated by the story which was unfolding that it took him some seconds before he rapped his gavel for order.

'What was their state of dress?' Helen de Vries asked calmly.

'Ma'am, they had both taken off their shoes. The President's shirt was partly undone, as was Miss Benoni's blouse.'

'I see. And were you able to observe anything they might have been doing?'

'Yes, Ma'am. I was able to observe that the President had his hand on the general area of Miss Benoni's left breast, and that she had her hand in the general area of the President's genitals.'

The audience snickered. Vernon Moberley ignored it, and waited for the noise to subside, before gesturing to Helen de Vries to continue.

'And then what happened?' Helen asked, with undisguised contempt.

'I was very embarrassed. I put the champagne and the glasses on the table as quickly as I could and started to leave.'

'And as you were leaving, did anything else happen?'

'Yes, Ma'am.'

'Please tell the Committee what it was.'

'Ma'am, as I was leaving, Miss Benoni got up, ran after me and gave me some money.'

'How much money?'

'Three hundred dollars.'

'Three hundred dollars in cash?'

'Yes.'

'How did that compare with the kind of tip you would normally expect to receive from guests at your hotel?'

'It was very generous.'

There was a gale of laughter. Helen de Vries joined in, playing to the gallery and the cameras.

'I'm sure. Did Miss Benoni offer any explanation for this unexpected largesse?'

'She said I was supposed to keep quiet about what I had seen.'

'And where was the President when Miss Benoni gave you this money?'

'He was still on the couch.'

'In the same room?'

'Yes.'

'Just a few feet away?'

'Yes, Ma'am.'

'Thank you, Mr. Jeffers,' Helen de Vries said. She turned to Vernon Moberley. 'Mr. Chairman, may I suggest that we recess now, so that both I and my honorable friends can consider what further questions we may have for Mr. Jeffers on Monday?'

Moberley looked across at Angela Moran.

'Mr. Chairman, may I have a moment to confer with my colleagues?' Angela asked.

'By all means.'

Angela turned to Dick Stinson, a young up-and-coming congressman from California who had made a name for himself as a trial lawyer before being elected to the House. They spoke in whispered tones.

'Does this seem strange to you?' Angela asked.

'It's beyond strange. How come de Vries was able to do that perfect direct examination without prior warning?'

'Right. What should we do? Get out of here and figure out what to do over the weekend?'

'Let me get a couple of digs in now,' Stinson suggested, 'just to let the press know we're still in the game. Just to give them something to think about.'

Angela nodded.

'Mr. Chairman, I ask to yield one minute of my time to the Honorable Gentleman from California, after which I would be content to recess for the weekend.'

'So ordered,' Moberley said obligingly.

'Thank you, Mr. Chairman,' Stinson began. 'Mr. Jeffers, you say you accepted three hundred dollars from Miss Benoni, is that right?'

'Yes, Sir.'

'And in return for that three hundred dollars, you were to keep quiet about what you say you saw. Is that also right?'

'Yes.'

'Well, you must not feel too good about yourself today?'

Jeffers hesitated. The sweat on his forehead was building up. His entire shirt was sticking to his body. Had Selvey told him how to answer this question? It sounded familiar, but somehow he could not quite remember.

'I don't understand the question,' he ventured lamely.

'Well,' Stinson continued, 'you haven't kept quiet about it, have you?'

'No. I suppose not.'

'What persuaded you to speak out, Mr. Jeffers?'

The sweat was now dripping into his eyes, making it difficult to focus. He took out a handkerchief and wiped his eyes and brow.

'I suppose I thought it was the right thing to do.'

'Really?' Stinson said. 'I don't suppose, by any chance, that you were offered something, perhaps more than three hundred dollars, to change your mind?'

Jeffers almost choked. The room had gone completely silent.

'No. Of course not. I just thought it was…'

His voice trailed away.

Stinson made sure the whole room saw his look of disgust.

'Well, let me just ask you this, Mr. Jeffers, just so the record is clear. Is it your testimony under oath before this House Intelligence Committee that you have not accepted any money or consideration associated with your testimony, other than the three hundred dollars you received from Miss Benoni? Is that your testimony?'

'Yes,' Jeffers replied, almost inaudibly.

'I can't hear, Mr. Jeffers,' Vernon Moberley intervened. 'What was your answer?'

Jeffers swallowed hard. 'I said 'yes',' he replied, only a little more loudly.

Stinson nodded briefly and sat back in his chair.

'I yield back any balance of my time to the minority Chair,' he said.

Helen de Vries contemplated asking the Chair for a little more time to have the last word, but Jeffers' manner persuaded her not to do so. Everything was fine, she told herself. The testimony of Harold Jeffers had been heard, and would be headline news on every television channel and every radio station that night, and in every newspaper the following morning.

However, having been affected more than she would have cared to admit by the earlier events of the day, she also suggested to the Chairman that, in the light of Jeffers' testimony, there would be little purpose in any further questioning of Linda Samuels. She made a motion that Agent Samuels be released from custody, without prejudice to the finding that she was in contempt of the Committee. A vote was taken, and the motion was agreed to unanimously. Then the Committee recessed for the weekend.

32

BY THE TIME Harold Philby and Mary Sullivan had watched the highlights of the House Intelligence Committee's proceedings, which Irene had recorded for them during the day, it was after two o'clock in the morning. They were both very tired. Cold remains of a pepperoni pizza and plastic cups of cold black coffee competed for space on the conference room table with the stacks of paper which now comprised Mary's research on Hamid Marfrela. Irene had eagerly offered to sit up with them but, to her disappointment, Harold Philby had thanked her for her work and sent her home. There were matters he had to discuss with Mary Sullivan which were not for Irene's ears.

'It's hard to believe the Committee hasn't cottoned on to the Oregon angle,' Philby remarked. 'Do you think they really don't know about it?'

'Apparently,' Mary replied. 'I would have expected some questions to Lazenby about it if they did.'

'So would I,' Philby agreed.

'Maybe they have a surprise witness next week.'

'Maybe. It's still strange that they didn't raise it with Lazenby. And they had that other agent who worked on the Marfrela murder, what was her name?'

Mary consulted her notes. 'Kelly Smith.'

'Smith, right. It just doesn't add up.'

'Well, add up or not, I'm falling asleep,' Mary admitted, leaning back in her chair. 'Let's go home for the weekend and think about it. I'll have my phone on if you want to give me a call.'

Philby shook his head.

'We need to stay a few minutes longer, Mary,' he said. 'We have to decide what to do with this.'

Mary yawned. 'I thought we already decided,' she said. 'I thought the only question was how we write it.'

Philby nodded.

'The Committee has decided that for us, hasn't it? We started out with three possible stories, remember? But now, we know what the story is. Or at least, we think we do. But we have some facts the Committee apparently doesn't have, facts which could take this thing in a new direction. So we're back to square one. The question is, do we publish?'

'That's a no-brainer, Harold,' Mary replied emphatically. 'Of course we publish. But I want to take the weekend to think through how to actually write it.'

'The owners and the lawyers have something to say about this,' Philby said. 'So far, you're the only one to make the connection between Hamid Marfrela and Oregon. That's something the Committee might want to investigate if we tip them off about it.'

Mary turned to face the Editor.

'I don't know why we wouldn't publish. It's a legitimate story.'

'It is.' Philby agreed. 'And, as far as I can see, the President is buried up to his neck in this mess. Still, it's quite a rock to throw at him.'

'We're not throwing rocks.' Mary protested. 'And, if we don't publish, it's only a matter of time before someone else does. The competition can't be more than a couple of steps behind us. I want to be first, Harold. This is my story.'

'I understand that, Mary,' Philby said, walking over to the window and looking out at the sodium lights which illuminated night-time Washington. 'And I enjoy a scoop as much as anyone else in our business. But this is going to cause major shock waves. Who knows what might happen? In its own way, it may turn out to be as momentous as Watergate.'

He turned back towards Mary.

'I was the office boy when that broke,' he said with a smile. 'I'd been with the *Post* less than a month. It was an incredible introduction to journalism, Mary. Woodward and Bernstein burning up the front pages, bringing down the Administration, and risking bringing the *Post* down with it. Everyone, from Katharine Graham down, running around, holding conspiratorial meetings behind closed doors all day and all night.'

Mary was smiling broadly.

'It must have been fantastic,' she said.

'It was. Of course, I wasn't in on the big secrets. I was just a kid. I made the coffee and tried to listen through doors. But I do remember the atmosphere in this place, all the coming and going, the air of conspiracy. And I remember a lot of talk at that time about what would happen if the story didn't fly. The conventional wisdom was that it would be the end of the *Post*.'

Mary nodded thoughtfully.

'I could see that happening with this story. But this time, it would be on my watch. If we're wrong, Wade will eat us for lunch.'

Mary got up and walked over to join Philby at the window without her shoes, which she had abandoned some hours before.

'Harold, Wade isn't in any position to eat anyone for lunch. The Committee has him nailed. The only question is what they decide to do with the information. All we're doing is putting one of the last pieces of the puzzle in place, a piece which the Committee apparently isn't aware of.'

'They'll be aware of it when we publish. And you may be their next star witness.'

'Fine with me. The story is solid, Harold. We have paperwork to back it up every inch of the way.'

'What about your source?'

'I'll protect him, of course. But I don't see that as a problem. He needn't come into it. We can make our case with the research we've done ourselves.'

Philby nodded thoughtfully and turned back to the window.

'What about Irene?'

'I'm going to credit her with an assist,' Mary smiled, 'in addition to her A-plus.'

'You're putting her on the byline? That's generous.' Philby observed.

'It's deserved. She found the Western Geophysical material, and she worked her tail off on Marfrela. I think we ought to take a serious look at her when she gets out of school.'

'I have no problem with that. But I'm concerned. Are you sure she's not vulnerable... she's not...?'

'My source? No way, Harold. She has no idea who he is. Come on, you know me better than that.'

'I'm sorry, but in this situation I'm paranoid. I admit it. We can't leave any hostages to fortune here, Mary.'

'Agreed,' Mary said, 'and we're not going to.'

For some time, they both stared out of the window in silence.

'So, have you thought what you're going to recommend?' Mary asked.

'Have you ever been to Portugal?' Philby asked in turn.

'Portugal? No. Never. Why?'

'It's where Becky and I plan to retire. Beautiful country. The people are wonderful, the food is out of this world. Paradise on earth. A simpler way of life.'

Mary smiled. 'I didn't know you were planning to retire.'

Philby returned the smile. 'I may have to. We publish on Monday.'

Mary's jaw dropped open. For a moment she could not speak.

'Monday? But…'

'But what? I thought you wanted to go ahead.'

'Well… yes… yes, I do. But… Harold, you old fox, you've already done it, haven't you? You've already run this by the owners without telling me?'

Philby could not resist a broad smile.

'Guilty, Your Honor.'

'You swine,' Mary grinned. 'Why didn't you say something?'

'I'm sorry,' Philby replied. 'It was their preference. They wanted to keep quiet about it. But only until tonight. They wanted to wait and see what emerged in the Committee today. But they said it was up to me. If the Oregon story didn't come out, I should feel free to bring it out. It's to be my decision, they said. By which they meant, of course, that my head is on the chopping block if it goes south.'

Mary sat back down at the conference table, trying to catch her breath.

'Harold, we have to give the White House time to respond.'

Philby's eyes had hardened.

'I'll call Martha tomorrow,' he said with a shrug. 'It won't do them any harm to put in a little overtime over the weekend. We know what they're going to say in any case.'

Mary raised her eyebrows.

'Mary, the White House has been screwing around with us ever since this thing started. And not just with us, but with the American people. One lie after another. It's inexcusable. I don't blame Martha. I think this is coming directly from His Majesty. But enough is enough. We're going to bring this out into the open, and let the chips fall where they may. Polish your story, Mary. Now, let's get out of here before I change my mind.'

33

WITHOUT MAKE-UP, her hair all over the place, Kelly ran at full speed from the elevator into Ted Lazenby's office. She had driven desperately from her home to the Hoover Building in what should have been an impossibly short time, ignoring red lights and speed limits, but mercifully attracting no attention from the traffic cops. It was six o'clock on a cold, rainy Monday morning, and Lazenby was already at his desk, the telephone in his hand. His jacket was off, and his tie was hanging loosely around his neck. He was on hold.

'Did you see…?' Kelly began.

'Yes. I saw it. I'm on the line to the Portland field office now. They're trying to track Phil down. They're not sure where he is.'

'Sir, what happened?'

'That bastard, Moberley. That fucking bastard. He gave me his fucking word. I'm going to crucify the son-of-a-bitch.'

Lazenby shook his head violently, and held out the phone.

'Take over this line for me. It's our people in Oregon. I have another call to make.'

Kelly studied the Director's face. She had never seen him so angry. He was pale and tense and, when he spoke, he almost spat out the words. Throwing her briefcase to the floor, she took the telephone from his hand and sat down at his desk, while Lazenby strode to a table and picked up another phone. He consulted a private directory and quickly dialed a number. Someone answered.

'Mrs. Moberley? This is Ted Lazenby… Lazenby… I'm the Director of the FBI… I'm fine, thank you. Is your husband there?… Well, would you get him for me, please?… He's doing what?… Ma'am, I frankly don't give a damn what he's doing. This is an emergency. Please get him now… Thank you.'

Half a minute elapsed. Kelly's line remained quiet.

'Vernon? What in the hell do you think you're doing? Do you have any idea what this could mean?…'

An agent from the Portland field office came on the line, and Kelly heard no more of Lazenby's verbal assault on the Chairman of the House Intelligence Committee.

'Director…?'

'Mike? It's me, Kelly. The Director's on another call. What gives?'

Mike sighed into the telephone.

'No luck, Kelly. We've been trying to reach Phil to warn him about the *Post* breaking the story. But it seems he spent the weekend inside the compound, and he hasn't come out. Before he went in, he told us he was scheduled to be there through Thursday, and there's no way to reach him while he's inside.'

'Fuck,' Kelly said.

'We're hoping Phil will pick up the story himself. He says they're pretty dedicated to keeping up with the news in there. He has access to all the net sources, plus CNN and the main papers. Of course, so does everyone else in there. Hopefully, Phil will realize what's going on and find a way to get himself out of there before they have time to figure it out.'

'God, I hope you're right,' Kelly replied.

'Kelly, how did this happen? I thought the Oregon connection was supposed to be under wraps.'

'So did we. We don't know yet, Mike. The Director's talking to the Chairman now. Look, keep trying, and let me know the moment you hear anything, OK?'

'Will do.'

Mike hung up. Kelly turned her attention back to Lazenby, who was still in full flow.

'Well, the first thing you can do is drag Mary Sullivan's ass in front of your Committee in closed session and make her tell you where she got the story… What?… I don't give a rat's ass about protecting her sources. You didn't have any problem throwing a Secret Service Agent in jail. Do the same with her… I don't want to hear it, Vernon. If any harm comes of this, heads will roll. You have no idea what I might do. Trust me.'

Without another word, Lazenby slammed down the receiver and cut off the call. He drew both hands through his hair, and looked questioningly at Kelly. She shook her head.

'Nothing. He's in the compound, and they have no way to talk to him while he's in. Unless he realizes the danger, he'll be there until Thursday.'

'Thursday? Jesus Christ. That gives them four days to…'

'Phil's a smart agent. And we've always told him to run if there was any sign of his cover being blown. He just has to find a way out.'

'Jesus Christ.'

'What did the Chairman say?'

Lazenby pursed his lips, the fury still consuming him.

'He says the leak didn't come from the Committee, but he'll look into it, just in case.'

'And you don't believe him?'

'Well, where the fuck else could it have come from?' Lazenby demanded.

'I don't know. But I can't see what reason there would be for anyone on the Committee to leak it. Who else knew about it?'

Lazenby made a huge effort to calm himself. He walked over to his coffee machine and poured two cups. They both sat down at his desk and Lazenby thought for a while.

'According to Vernon, only his senior aide plus, of course, the entire intelligence community. It's my fault, Kelly. I should have pulled Phil out. I should have known there was no way to keep the lid on it.'

Kelly shook her head.

'Director, there was no way to anticipate this. The intelligence people have no interest in blowing our cover. We had every reason to think they would give us notice if anyone was going to get into it.'

'Then, where did it come from, Kelly?'

'I don't know. It doesn't mention our involvement. All it does is…'

'All it does is cut a trail a mile wide from Hamid Marfrela to Middle and Near East, to the Sons of the Land, to the President.'

'Yes, Sir. All I'm saying is that Mary Sullivan probably sees this as an official corruption story. There's no reason to think she has any angle involving the Bureau. If she does, she hasn't said anything. She hasn't asked us to comment.'

'I've a good mind to pull her in for questioning.'

'I can't advise that, Director.'

For the first time that morning, Lazenby gave the hint of a smile.

'I guess you're right.'

'Not that it wouldn't be satisfying,' Kelly said. 'Do you want me to fly out to Oregon? Maybe there's something I can do…'

'No. The office there can do whatever there is to do. I need you here. Stay by the phone, Kelly. Let's hope for some good news.'

34

'I don't want to go through it again,' the President shouted. 'I've already told you I don't know anything about these people or what they do. I don't know anything about any goddamned Hamid whatever-his-name-is.'

Martha Graylor reached into her purse and extracted her fifth and sixth aspirin tablets of the morning. Mutely, she looked across at Ellen Trevathan for help. They were the only three people in the Oval Office. The President had cancelled his press conference and his other engagements for the morning. Martha was trying to put together a press release, but her efforts to find out what the President wanted to say had achieved little except to provoke him to anger. Sensing Martha's desperation, Ellen nodded her understanding, and decided to try her own hand.

'Steve, I know this is frustrating for you. But we have to give them some kind of answer. This story has gone way beyond whether or not you had an affair with Lucia Benoni, which is all the Committee has really proved so far. This story links you directly to some Lebanese involvement with the Sons of the Land. The implications are that you were doing some kind of deal under the counter on the foreign policy front in return for contributions, or being set up with Lucia, or God knows what. Maybe worse than that, maybe fooling around with national security. We can't just say we don't know anything.'

'Those bastards at the *Post* ambushed me. Ambushed me in broad daylight. They call Martha at home on a Saturday morning, for God's sake. What sort of response are we supposed to make to that?'

'I agree,' the Vice President replied. 'It was an ambush. And no one can criticize you for putting up the shutters over the weekend. But now, we have to do more.'

Wade shook his head, and continued pacing up and down behind his desk.

Martha picked up the *Post*. Her hand was shaking.

'Let's try and make sense of this, Mr. President,' she suggested tentatively. 'First of all, are you sure you have never heard of these Western Geophysical people?'

'No,' Wade said. 'I have not.'

'Because, apparently, they've been making some pretty hefty contributions to the Party.'

'Many people make hefty contributions to the Party, Martha. That's not my department. I am the President of the United States. I don't personally solicit every contribution that comes in to every campaign. Especially not from the White House. In case you didn't know, that would be illegal.'

'Take it easy, Steve,' Ellen said quietly.

'I'm trying. But this is driving me crazy… All right, Martha, I'm sorry. Next question.'

Martha ran her hand across her brow. Her head was still pounding. She could hardly focus on the newspaper any more.

'What about the Middle and Near East Company, Mr. President? They seem to be one of the main supporters of Western Geophysical. They are also the link to Hamid Marfrela. He was one of their directors.'

'No. Nothing there either.'

Martha shook her head.

'Let me try,' Ellen said, after a few moments of silence. 'Steve, when you and Lucia talked, would she ever speak about Lebanon, or anything political, for that matter?'

Wade paused in his pacing.

'Look, I can't…'

'Steve, please, that's water under the bridge. The whole world knows you were sleeping with her. Frankly, that hardly matters any more. So, just cast your mind back and tell me what you used to talk about.'

For a long time, the President gazed, apparently absently, out of the window. Finally, he turned back towards Ellen.

'I never talked about politics with her. Never. I never discussed my work. She always seemed more interested in talking about the plays she saw in New York, or the people she met at parties, or where she went shopping in Paris or Milan. It was always just light conversation. That's why it was fun to be with her. I live politics every hour of every day. It was good to get away from it for a while.'

'Did she ever talk about herself, where she came from, her family, anything like that?'

Wade considered the question.

'Yes. She did talk about her life growing up, how hard it was constantly moving around, never settling down. She used to say she was a gypsy at heart.'

'But she didn't go on to say how hard life might be for people in Lebanon generally? She wasn't trying to get your sympathy for them, maybe?'

'Not as far as I could tell. If she was, she didn't do a very good job of it.'

'And she never, even indirectly, tried to talk about your foreign policy. Think, Steve, please.'

Wade exhaled audibly.

'No. I never recall anything like that coming up.'

'OK. How did you first meet?'

Wade walked back to his desk and sat down heavily.

'Oh, God. It was at some function here. I don't even remember what function. She was obviously trying to get me to notice her. I got her number and invited her here while Julia was away some place.'

'What was her attitude at that time?'

The President laughed.

'We both knew what it was about. I think she was naked within five minutes of walking in the door. It was about sex, from first to last. All this other stuff… I have no idea where that came from.'

Ellen sat back in her chair. 'Bottom line, you were set up,' she said.

Wade nodded. 'Looks like. But by whom, for God's sake? All along, we've been blaming the opposition.'

'Yes,' Ellen replied. 'And there's no question they're fanning the flames. But I don't think they're behind it. Somehow, they found out about it, and they are making capital out of it. But they couldn't have put all this in place themselves.'

'So, what do you think?'

'My money's on some kind of clandestine operation by the Lebanese.'

'They used Lucia to get to me?'

'That's the way it looks to me. That way, there would be no need for you to know anything about Marfrela or those other people, or what was going on in Oregon. They were probably hoping you would compromise yourself at some point, and then they would move in for the kill.

Blackmail, threats, who knows? Whatever it took to get you off their back, soften your policy a little, approve some aid, whatever.'

Wade sat silently, nodding, for some time.

'All right, that makes sense. But why kill her, for God's sake? I don't understand. Why did they have to do that?'

Wade's voice faltered, and for the first time, Ellen thought she saw a hint of regret and pain in the President's eyes. She nodded.

'It does seem strange. My guess would be that Lucia wasn't willing to play ball any more. Or maybe she thought she was in too deep and got scared and wanted to quit. Or maybe she had actually come to like you. Who knows? Stranger things have happened.'

Wade smiled thinly. 'Thanks a lot.'

'All we do know is that, for some reason, they couldn't trust her any more.'

It was some time before anyone spoke again.

'I'm sorry, Martha,' Ellen said eventually, 'I'm not sure I've been much help. I'm sure the President doesn't want to go on record as being the victim of a Lebanese plot. At least, not yet.'

'What do you mean, "not yet"?' Wade asked.

'I mean, not until it becomes the best of several bad alternatives. Unfortunately, by the time the Committee has finished its work, that may be the case. Obviously, they will be running down this rabbit trail as fast as their little legs will carry them, as of this morning.'

Wade nodded. 'I'm sure Helen de Vries is eating raw steak for breakfast to get herself in the mood,' he observed sourly.

'Count on it,' Ellen said.

The intercom buzzed. The President hit a button.

'I'm sorry to interrupt, Mr. President,' Steffie Walinsky said. 'I have one of your agents in my office, Gary Mills. He wants to see you. He says it's important.'

'Steffie, I said I didn't want to be disturbed this morning.'

'I told him that, Mr. President. He says it's really important.'

'What do you think?'

'I think you should see him.'

Steve Wade shrugged wearily. 'All right. Send him in.'

Gary Mills looked tense and nervous, as he walked slowly into the Oval Office. He nodded to Martha.

'Good morning, Mr. President, Madam Vice President.'

'This better be good, Agent Mills,' Wade said. 'It's a very busy morning. Do we have some security problem? Not another code red, I hope.'

'No, Mr. President,' Gary said hesitantly. He seemed unwilling to continue.

'Well, come on. I haven't got all day.'

'Actually, Sir, it's about the First Lady…'

All three of the other occupants of the room leapt to their feet.

'What about the First Lady?' Ellen demanded. 'Has something happened?'

'No, Ma'am,' Gary replied, holding up his arms defensively. 'I'm sorry. I didn't mean to alarm you. It's just that… well, the fact is, Mr. President, we felt you ought to know that she's not in residence…'

Ellen sat back down abruptly, glancing at Martha, who was standing rigidly at attention with her eyes and mouth wide open. Steve Wade was the last to catch on.

'Not in residence? What do you mean? Her next trip isn't till next month. She's going out to California. I don't know of anything else until then.'

Gary Mills looked down at his shoes.

'Mr. President, what I'm trying to say is that… that the First Lady left this morning with a full complement of clothes and personal effects. She told her assigned agents she was going to New York, and declined their protection.'

'Oh, God,' Ellen breathed.

'Declined… what do you mean, declined? They're supposed to…'

'The First Lady insisted, Sir. They didn't… well, the agents didn't feel they could physically restrain her, Sir. They didn't know what to do. So they followed her. At least, that is, until she got to National Airport…'

'The airport…?'

'Yes sir. At that point, they contacted the office in New York and asked them to continue surveillance. They didn't know what else to do, Sir.'

Steve Wade felt that all the breath had been pumped from his body. He resumed his seat, and fought for control.

'I'm not sure I follow,' he said quietly. 'How was the First Lady able to leave the White House without the cooperation of her Detail? I mean, physically, by what means?'

Gary had folded his hands in front of him, and was rocking backwards and forwards slightly on his feet.

'I was told she called a limo service, Mr. President. It was a limo the agents followed to the airport.'

'Agent Mills,' Ellen asked, 'has there been a report from the New York office?'

'Yes, Ma'am. Her Detail obtained information that she had booked a flight from National to La Guardia. They passed this information to New York, and New York had people waiting in the baggage claim area when she deplaned. A female met her there, and the First Lady seemed to know her, seemed to be expecting her. The female is described as white, well dressed, about the same age and height as the First Lady. They left together.'

'Then what?' the President demanded.

'They took a cab from La Guardia in the direction of Manhattan, Mr. President. The agents had a surveillance team in place near the cab stand and followed. That's the latest information I have. New York is due to report in again soon. But they said to tell you there's no reason to think she's in any danger, Mr. President. Apparently, no one even recognized her at La Guardia.'

'Did the First Lady leave any message for the President, or anyone else?' Ellen asked.

'Ma'am, I was told by a member of her Detail that there was a letter for the President in the residence,' Gary replied. 'And she said she would call later today.'

'Send someone to bring the letter,' Ellen said, 'with your permission, of course, Mr. President.'

Wade nodded in silence.

'Other than saying she would call later today, did the First Lady indicate how long she was likely to be in New York?' the Vice President asked.

'She has friends in New York,' Steve Wade said. 'Maybe she felt like an unscheduled break.'

'I couldn't say, Mr. President,' Gary replied. 'But her Detail said she had enough personal effects with her for a long stay.'

'I'm sorry, Sir,' he added gently. 'I'll let you know as soon as I hear back from the New York office. If you're worried, we could bring her back. But of course, that would mean…'

'No,' Wade said quickly. 'I'm sure that's not necessary. I'm sure all will become clear later in the day. Thank you, Agent Mills.'

'Yes, Sir.'

'She's gone, isn't she?' Wade asked, after Gary Mills had left the room. 'Yes,' Ellen replied. 'I'm afraid she is.'

* * *

It was almost four o'clock the next morning when the phone next to Ellen's bed rang. She had been tossing and turning for several hours, finding it difficult to sleep, and was at least half awake when the shrill tone made her roll over to pick up the phone.

'It's Commander Laing, Ma'am', a familiar voice said. 'I'm going to need you 'on' for about twelve hours.'

Ellen sat bolt upright. Being 'on' meant that the President would not be in a position to perform his duties for some time. It might mean just making herself available, or it might mean actually taking command under the Twenty-Fifth Amendment. It might mean anything. It was the first time in her six years on the job that she had received this call.

'What's happened?' she asked, her pulse racing.

'The President isn't feeling too well,' Laing replied calmly. 'I thought it best to give him some medication which will make him a little drowsy. It's probably best that you make yourself available, just in case. He ought to be back to normal early evening, but I want to keep the situation under review. Does that cause you any problems?'

'No, Commander,' Ellen said, 'No problems.' She paused. 'Can you be any more specific?'

'He had an episode,' Laing replied. 'I'm sure it's nothing, but he got a bit excited about things, well… you know about the First Lady… and I thought it best to give him something to calm his nerves a bit.'

Ellen waited, saying nothing, for some moments. Eventually, Laing gave a deep sigh into the phone.

'All right,' he said. 'Off the record, he had a full-blown panic attack. Steffie Walinsky called me. He was hysterical, crying and incoherent. I gave him a shot of Diazepam and I've given him some sleeping pills. He's going to be out for between six and eight hours, and then he's going to be pretty groggy for the next three or four.'

'Thank you,' Ellen said. 'Who else knows about this?'

'No one was around at the time except Steffie. She said she would take care of things. She's expecting your call once I hang up.'

'Thank you, Commander,' Ellen said. 'I'm on it.'

35

THE HOUSE MAJORITY Leader could not help smiling as Vernon Moberley was shown into his office. Moberley was short of breath, and he was trying, without being too obvious, to return the knot of his tie to its proper place above the top button of this shirt. Gerry Parkinson was seated at his desk in his shirtsleeves, the jacket of his suit draped unceremoniously over the back of his chair. Congressman George Stanley, wearing his jacket, was sitting in an armchair to the left of the Leader's desk. Moberley stood still just inside the door, trying to catch his breath, shaking his head. Parkinson gestured to a chair in front of his desk.

'Take a load off, Vern. Press give you a hard time, did they?'

Moberley collapsed into the chair.

'You're not kidding. It was like running the damn gauntlet. Jesus. I didn't think I was going to make it. Wouldn't have without a couple of marshals pushing and shoving them out of the way ahead of me. They would have ripped the shirt off my back. I'm too old for this kind of thing, Gerry.'

'I'm sorry about all the fuss, Vern,' Parkinson said placatingly. 'How about some coffee?'

'No, thanks.'

'OK. What can I do for you this morning?'

'You could tell me what's going on. That would be a good start.'

Parkinson stood and leaned against his desk, looking thoughtful.

'You haven't made any statement to the press, right?'

'What would I say? I'm in the dark here. All I know is, I show up for work, I get a call from the House Majority Leader who asks, as a courtesy, would I recess my Committee's hearings indefinitely for reasons he can't go into on the phone. I tell the Committee, who are not exactly overjoyed about it, and within minutes my phone's ringing off the hook and all hell is breaking loose. And this is after I have to jump out of the shower in my own house this morning to take a load of abuse from the Director of the FBI. It's been quite a day.'

He paused to consult his watch.

'And it isn't even lunchtime.'

Parkinson frowned.

'Lazenby called you at home? What about?'

Moberley shook his head in frustration.

'It's unbelievable. He thought the story in the *Post* had been leaked from inside my Committee. He has some kind of undercover operation going on in Oregon that he thought might have been compromised. He was as mad as hell about it. Cussed me out every which way. Like I could do anything about it.'

'Did the leak come from inside your Committee?'

Moberley crossed his legs impatiently. 'No,' he replied defensively.

'How do you know that?' Parkinson asked.

'Oh, for crying out loud, why would they? Look, Lazenby came to me before we started and asked if we intended to talk about Oregon. I didn't know what he was talking about. He asked me to let him know in advance if it looked like we would mention anything about Oregon. He said he just needed some time, because he had an operation which could be compromised if Oregon was mentioned publicly. He didn't tell me what the operation was, and I didn't ask. All I needed to know was that there was some material involved which wasn't for public consumption. I didn't have any problem agreeing to what he wanted. End of conversation. Then today, he's dragging me out of my own shower, loaded for bear, blaming me for some story in the *Post*. Hell, Gerry, we had no idea about that stuff. Who knows where they got it from? Who knows if it's even true?'

'Oh, it's true, all right,' Parkinson said, with a sideways glance at George Stanley. 'George's Committee started to take the lid off this can of worms some time back, but I told them they couldn't go any further until you guys had taken some testimony and built up something of a record. Now that you have, and now that the *Post* has beaten George's people to the punch, we have to consider what to do about it. And we have to consider very carefully. That's why I called you. I'm concerned that your Committee might feel they need to pursue the *Post's* story.'

'We haven't had time to catch our breath, never mind figure out what we need to do about the story.'

'Well, before you do, I think we ought to talk the matter over. There are some decisions we need to take which we should consider very, very carefully.'

Moberley looked doubtful.

'I'm not sure I understand, Gerry. I hope you're not suggesting we back off. I don't mind giving Lazenby some time, but I'm not about to tell my Committee they can't go after this. Hell, Helen de Vries would hand me my balls on a platter just for suggesting it.'

Parkinson smiled up at the ceiling, and allowed himself the pleasure of visualizing that eventuality.

'No. That's not what I mean, Vern. This has nothing to do with Lazenby, and I don't think Helen will have any problem with what I'm going to propose.'

He leaned forward confidentially.

'But what I'm about to tell you doesn't leave this room for a few days…'

'A few… oh, for God's sake, Gerry. What am I supposed to tell my Committee? What am I supposed to say to get the press off my back?'

'As little as possible. Go into hiding if you want to. Say you'll hold a press conference as soon as you can. Blame it on this office if you want. Just don't repeat what you're about to hear.'

Moberley closed his eyes. 'All right. Go ahead.'

Parkinson paused again and glanced at George Stanley.

'You're not the only one whose phone has been ringing off the hook this morning. I've got two extra secretaries back there trying to cope with it.'

Moberley opened his eyes again.

'Just about all of our people are calling, and quite a few from across the aisle. They seem to feel that this whole thing has gone too far for just a House Committee. Some of us think we now have evidence of what the Constitution calls 'high crimes and misdemeanors'.'

Parkinson paused for effect. The Committee Chairman's eyes were now open very wide. He looked at George Stanley, who was smiling maliciously.

'You're not serious.'

Parkinson stood and picked up a booklet from his side table.

'I'm very serious.'

He opened the volume.

'Allow me to read from our governing document. It's Article Two,

227

Section Four. I quote: 'The President, Vice President and all civil Officers of the United States shall be removed from Office on Impeachment for, and Conviction of, Treason, Bribery, or other high Crimes and Misdemeanors'. Now, I don't know whether what Wade has done amounts to treason or bribery, but I'm pretty sure it's going to come under the heading of high crimes and misdemeanors.'

It was some time before Moberley responded.

'I don't know, Gerry. That would be a big step.'

'I know. That's why I showed George the red light when he first came to me with the Lucia Benoni story. I thought we needed more. Now we have it.'

'Based on this story in the *Post*? You think Wade has been consorting with the enemy?'

'He's been consorting with somebody. And I think, once we look into it a little deeper, turn over a few more rocks, we're going to uncover some pretty ugly stuff.'

Moberely shook his head.

'Is Alex Vonn on board with this? He has the best head on his shoulders, politically, of any man in the Party. We should take his advice on this.'

'He's on George's Committee, Vern,' Parkinson pointed out.

'Alex is on board,' George Stanley said.

Moberley still seemed unsettled.

'It's a hell of a leap, Gerry, a hell of a leap. And you do remember that we would need a two-thirds majority in the Senate? Or is it enough for us to embarrass him, and we don't care about the ultimate result?'

'No. We care a great deal about the ultimate result, and I think we can get it. Joe O'Brien has been working on this in the Senate. I spoke to him just before you arrived this morning. We're not there yet by a long way. But the word is that the President's friends in the Senate are not too happy with him. Joe's expecting a good number of them to jump ship. He's had some conversations with his leader and the minority leader, in complete confidence, of course. That's why we need to keep it quiet for a few days. We have to give them time. They want to make sure they're on solid ground before they move.'

Parkinson walked around the front of his desk and perched on the edge.

'So you see why I need your help?'

Moberley sat back thoughtfully in his chair.

'You can't keep this quiet, Gerry. Word is bound to leak out. It's going to get back to the White House.'

'Not if we're careful,' Parkinson said. 'And in a few days, it will all come out anyway. But you do see why I need you to be discreet until then?'

'Yes,' Moberley said quietly. 'All right, Gerry. I'll hold off for a couple of days. As long as I can say it's at your request, and refer all inquiries to this office.'

'Be my guest. I'll take on another secretary if I have to. What difference would one more make?'

Moberley rose to his feet. 'And you will keep me fully informed?'

'Of course. I'm counting on your support.'

The House Leader extended his hand with a smile. 'Do you need an escort back to your office?'

Moberley returned the smile, rather ruefully.

'No. I expect my marshals are right outside the door. We'll take the scenic route. I'll talk to you later.' He nodded to Stanley. 'George.'

George Stanley stood and shook hands with Moberley, then watched with satisfaction as he left the room.

'So, George, you're all set, then?' Parkinson asked.

'Absolutely. You and I will be the main case managers. I'll have the names of the other case managers to you by close of business today.'

'Make sure you include Helen de Vries.'

'Of course. John Mason will be working behind the scenes with our counsel. We'll be ready to move within a week.'

'Good,' Parkinson said. 'Let's just make sure we cover all the bases.'

'Don't worry about it,' Stanley replied. 'I've been waiting for this for years.'

36

TRYING TO DISGUISE the fact that his hands were beginning to shake, Phil Hammond drove slowly across the rough, unfinished grounds of the compound from the signals office to the main gate, where two armed sentries stood on guard. He had rehearsed the story he was going to tell them over and over since reading *The Washington Post*'s story, and had realized that his position had become insecure. The story was all he had. It would have been too risky to try calling the field office, even using an unlisted number. For security reasons, all outgoing calls were monitored. And even if he did, he knew that the office could do nothing to help him. He was on his own, and he had to find his own way out.

The electronic gates were locked firmly shut. One of the two sentries casually stepped in front of the car, his sub-machine gun tucked under his arm, and motioned to him to stop. Hammond pulled up, leaving the transmission in drive, and rolled down the driver's side window.

'Captain Seager, can I help you, Sir?'

'Yes. I'm going to have to leave for a few hours. I'll be back this evening.'

'Just a moment, Sir.'

The sentry returned to the small gatehouse, went inside, and started to look through a pile of papers on his desk. His colleague stood at the gate, facing Hammond and looking carefully at the car. Hammond tightened his grip on the steering wheel, then reluctantly forced himself to put the transmission in park. After looking through the papers, the sentry picked up a red telephone and made a brief call. He then began to walk back to the car. Hammond felt his stomach start to churn.

'Open the fucking gate,' he muttered to himself.

The sentry approached and leaned in slightly through the driver's window.

'I'm sorry, Captain Seager,' he said. 'I don't seem to have any paperwork for you. You are booked in through Thursday. You have to have a special pass to leave, Sir.'

'Yes, I know,' Hammond replied, hoping his voice would not betray his anxiety. 'But I got a message just a short while ago. It's my mother. She's… well, she's very sick. Heart condition. I've been expecting it for some time. I nearly cancelled my time here. I knew I might have to leave suddenly. I did mention it to the office when I arrived.'

Hammond tried staring the sentry down. He seemed unimpressed.

'I'm sorry to hear about your mother, Captain Seager. But I have my orders, Sir. I can't let you leave without an exit pass. May I suggest you go by the office and get one, Sir? After you meet with the Commander.'

'After what…?' Hammond asked quietly. 'After I meet….'

'With Commander Carlson, Sir. I called the office myself to check on any paperwork. They didn't have any, but they did have a message for you. It seems you're required in Commander Carlson's office. Urgently. I'm sure the office can take care of your pass while you're in your meeting.'

Hammond nodded grimly, and put the car in reverse for the short drive to Carlson's office.

'Thank you, Sir,' the sentry said. He returned to his post.

As he approached the office, Hammond saw that two armed guards had been posted, one on each side of the door. He recognized the men. One of them was beginning his signals training. Hammond nodded to them casually. One of the guards knocked on the door of the office, opened it, and gestured to Hammond to enter. George Carlson was standing by the window, smoking a cigarette. Dan Rogers was to his right, leaning against a table. It was all Hammond could do not to run for his life in desperation. He was feeling faint.

'Jim,' Carlson said. 'Sit down.'

'What's up, George?' Hammond said, in what he hoped was a light tone.

Slowly, Carlson seated himself at his desk.

'Well, I don't know, Jim. I'm not sure what's up. I was thinking maybe you could tell us.'

He picked up a newspaper which had been lying on his desk.

'You know all about the publicity we've been getting, of course?'

'Yes. I saw it. Where the hell did they come up with that story? I'm assuming there's no truth to it?'

Carlson smiled at Rogers.

'What do you think, Dan? Should we enlighten our signals officer? Should we tell him whether there's any truth to it?'

Rogers shrugged.

'I don't see how it could do any harm, George. Not now.'

Carlson nodded. 'I agree.'

He looked closely at Hammond.

'Is there any truth to it, the man asks? Well, Jim, yes, there is some truth to it. It's not the whole story, obviously. It never is, is it? You know what they say, never believe everything you read in the papers. But they've got the basic outline right, I would say.'

Carlson stood again, replaced the newspaper on his desk, and stood behind his desk, looking out of the window.

'The idea came from Fox you see, Jim. Fox is pretty well connected, travels a lot, meets important people. Well, one day, in the course of his travels, he happened to meet our late and unlamented friend, Hamid Marfrela. Fox recognized him for the weasel he was, of course, but he thought he could be bought. Not just for money, Jim. That wasn't Hamid's deal. You couldn't just hand him cash and send him away. No, Hamid was high maintenance. He liked to feel important, see, Jim. He liked the glamorous life, women, booze, drugs, being on the circuit, you name it. He loved being in America, Jim. I don't think they have so much of the good life in Lebanon. What do you think, Dan?'

'I would guess not,' Rogers agreed with a grin.

'Yeah. So what better way for Hamid to keep his employers happy with him and keep himself in America than to make some useful contacts and get some deals going? Makes sense from his point of view, doesn't it? So Fox led him down the primrose path, indulged his appetites a bit, and when he had him by the short and curlies, so to speak, something to do with photographs taken at a party, you understand, he referred him to us. So one day, out of the blue, there's Hamid standing at the gate, asking what he can do to help. So I ask Hamid, 'Well what do you have to offer us?' You with me so far, Jim?'

Hammond nodded. 'Sure.'

'Good. So Hamid thinks for a while, and then he says he knows this babe, Lucia Benoni. Turns out to be very well connected. Better than Hamid, anyway. Not that that's saying much. And unlike Hamid, she is into the money. Really into it. She likes the European fashions, expensive perfume and so on, and she likes to go buy it all personally. And Hamid thinks she might be useful. I think, maybe he's right. So I contact Fox and I say this seems promising to me, but it's going to cost some money, and I ask does he think it's worth it. And, damn me, Fox comes back and says, 'Yes, go ahead, it's definitely worth it', because it just so happens that this babe has a direct line to the President's cock. Of course, then again, what woman doesn't?'

Rogers sniggered.

'It seemed like a good opportunity, Jim. Know what I mean? If we could get the President in deep enough, it might be worth something down the road. How often do you get a chance like that? Plus, Hamid said his employers would probably make a contribution, money, arms, whatever, because it was in their interests as well as ours to stick it to our philandering President. So, long story short, the deal was done, and now we're reading about it in *The Washington Post*. Not the ending I'd hoped for actually, Jim. If we could have kept it going a bit longer, who knows? But at least it worked, up to a point.'

Hammond swallowed hard.

'So, what happened to the Benoni woman? Why was she killed?'

Carlson shook his head with a look of disgust.

'Fucking Hamid Marfrela happened to her. Fucking pervert. Part of the deal was that he got her for whatever he was into, which I don't even want to speculate about. Dan will tell you. He took care of him when we let him go into Portland. There were a couple of incidents which weren't very pretty, let me just put it that way.'

'So… so, you took care of Marfrela?'

'You bet your ass we did. Too much of a risk letting him roam around and maybe shoot his mouth off. Trash. Good riddance.'

Carlson resumed his seat.

'Anyway, Jim, that's all water under the bridge, as they say. The point of our meeting today is, I'm curious about how *The Washington Post* got their story. How did this Sullivan woman make the connection to us?'

He looked at Hammond directly.

'Any ideas, Jim? Any thoughts at all?'

Hammond felt his pulse racing. He shook his head.

'No idea, George. Maybe she has a source in law enforcement. It doesn't sound like Marfrela would be too difficult to keep track of.'

Carlson nodded.

'Yes, that's what I thought. At first. But then, I got a message from Fox. Just this morning. Just finished decrypting it, as a matter of fact. Guess what Fox thinks?'

Hammond attempted a casual shrug.

'I don't know. What does Fox think?'

'Fox thinks we have a mole in our midst, Jim. Mole, as in small animal that burrows underground. That's what Fox thinks. He has friends in high places, you see. He hears about this kind of stuff. The word is our friends in the FBI have placed a spy in our midst. What do you think of that theory, Jim?'

'Sounds a little far-fetched to me,' Hammond offered. 'Why would they take the trouble?'

'Oh, they'd take the trouble,' Carlson replied. 'If they thought we were up to no good, and especially if they thought we were after the President. I think Fox is right. I think we have a mole, Jim.'

'Who would that be?' Hammond asked quietly.

'Good question,' Carlson replied. 'Who indeed?'

He paused.

'It wouldn't be you, by any chance, would it, Jim?'

'No, of course not. Why would you think…?'

With a smile, Carlson stood again.

'Well, let me put it this way. This morning, Dan and I spent some time reviewing the credentials of all the people who joined us within the last six months. Trying to figure this thing out, you see, Jim. We have no way of knowing when the mole came on board, of course, but we figured it would have to be within the last few months. And we happened to ask ourselves a few questions about the information you gave us.'

'What about it? Benson vouched for me.'

'He did,' Carlson said. 'He did indeed. But you see, Jim, Benson wasn't quite up to date. I didn't realize it at the time. But Benson had to retire from the Congo campaign a few weeks before it ended. He took a bullet in the leg, you see.'

'Ye … I remember,' Hammond said.

'Do you? Well, you see, the interesting thing was, as the question had been raised, I made a couple of phone calls. I talked to one or two of the boys who made it the whole way through the Lightning Bolt campaign, and asked them if they remembered Jim Seager, and they said, 'Sure, Jim Seager, best damn signals man we ever worked with'.'

'OK.'

'And you know what else they said?'

'No.'

'The other thing they said was that Jim Seager stepped on a land mine just a couple of days before they pulled out. Nothing left of him but bits and pieces. Benson wouldn't have known about that, you see, Jim. They flew him out after he got shot. When Seager stepped on the land mine, Benson was in the hospital in Dar-Es-Salaam.'

Carlson raised his eyebrows inquiringly.

'Any comment on any of that, Jim? Any light you can shed on it?'

Hammond's head sank on to his chest.

'I'm sorry about your mother, Jim,' Carlson added.

He nodded to Rogers, who opened the door of the office, and gestured to the guards to enter. One of the guards approached Hammond from behind and a struck him a single hard blow to the back of the head with the butt of his weapon. Hammond slumped forward in his chair, unconscious.

Carlson looked at him in silence for a moment or two, then turned to Rogers.

'Dan, take our friend here to the interrogation room and attach the wires to his balls. Find out who he is, what he's been doing, and everything he knows. When you're sure you know everything, and not before then, dispose of him.'

Rogers motioned to the two guards, who picked Hammond up and carried him out of the office.

'You got it, George.'

'And,' Carlson added just before Rogers left the room, 'when I say 'dispose' of him, I mean I don't want any part of him found. Ever. Got that?'

'Got it, George.'

'Oh, and Dan…'

'Yeah?'

'As soon as you get through, come back up here. Fox says it's going to be time soon.'

'Fucking A,' Rogers replied.

37

'I NEED TO see everything,' Ed Monahan said. 'Everything you've got. On Lebanon, on the Sons of the Land, on Hamid Marfrela, on Lucia Benoni. Everything. Is that a problem?'

Monahan looked across at the President, who was sitting dejectedly at his desk. In the silence which followed his request, Monahan permitted himself to reflect briefly on the vagaries of his life. How in the hell had he ever come this far? What was he doing in this place? He was the youngest of six children of a poor Irish family in South Boston. A talent for boxing, developed on the street, won him a scholarship to Boston College, where he got interested in the law. After law school he became a federal prosecutor, and developed a reputation as a tough, resourceful trial lawyer. Ed might well have remained a prosecutor his whole career, if it had not been for Jimmy Walker. Walker was a high-profile white-collar criminal defense lawyer. He and Ed crossed swords in the courtroom a number of times, and Jimmy was very impressed by what he saw and heard. Once or twice, in fact, he had his ass comprehensively kicked by the prosecutor, an experience which was not a common one in Jimmy Walker's professional life. The time came when Jimmy asked Ed to dinner at Fuglio's. He had been consulted by Senator Frank Lawton, who was about to be indicted for extortion and racketeering. Jimmy's health wasn't what it was, and he needed help. With the aid of a significant quantity of Bushmills, and an attractive financial offer, Jimmy persuaded Ed that he would not go straight to hell if he crossed over to the other side. Shortly before the Lawton trial began, Jimmy Walker's prostate cancer got him, and it was to Ed Monahan that Senator Lawton owed his continued liberty and position in public life. The name of Ed Monahan began to be whispered in high places. Other political clients followed, and he represented them with consistent success. And then the President called. And now here he was, sitting in the Oval Office. With the President of the United States.

'I don't see any problem,' Steve Wade replied. 'There may be some stuff we will need special clearance for, but I'm sure it won't be a problem. Everything important we've been doing in Lebanon has been in the *Post*, as far as I know. There's nothing to hide.'

Monahan nodded.

'My main concern is to cover all the bases. The problem with this procedure, Mr. President, is that there are very few rules. Impeachment is a political witch-hunt rather than a legal trial. So we have to be prepared for just about anything.'

Wade sighed heavily. 'Well, for my benefit, why don't you go through what we do know. I know Ellen and Martha would like to hear it too, since they're going to be working with me on it closely.'

Monahan nodded to Ellen Trevathan and Martha Graylor, who had been sitting quietly in armchairs close to his own.

'We would like you to brief the staff later,' Wade added. 'But the first thing is to make sure we understand this ourselves.'

'Yes, Mr. President,' Monahan replied. He went through the motions of spreading a few documents and notes on the coffee table in front of him, though it was mostly to inspire confidence. Clients liked to see documents and notes. They suggested that work was being done, that help was on the way, that it was all under control. This was, of course, an illusion. The truth was that the real work was invisible. Monahan could by now have lectured on the subject of impeachment for two hours in his sleep. Nonetheless, he made a deliberate show of referring to the notes.

'The grounds for impeachment are stated in the Constitution,' he began. 'Article Two, section Four, says any officer of the United States, which would include the President, can be impeached for certain offences, namely treason, bribery, and what it calls 'high crimes and misdemeanors'. That's kind of vague, obviously, and I'll get back to that in a moment. The procedure of impeachment requires two things: first, a formal act of impeachment, an indictment if you will, by the House; and, second, a trial in the Senate. In most cases of impeachment, the Vice President presides at the trial, but for obvious reasons, in the case of impeachment of the President, the Vice President has a conflict, so the Chief Justice of the United States presides in her place. So you're off the hook for this one, Madam Vice President.'

Ellen smiled thinly. 'Thank God for that. I thought I was going to have to preside for a federal judge last year. I wasn't looking forward to it.'

'I remember,' Monahan replied. 'I thought I was going to have to defend him. I'm sure we're both glad that one went away.'

'Amen to that,' Ellen said.

'The impeachment cannot succeed without a two-thirds vote of the Senate, so they need sixty-seven votes. I'm sure you knew that, Mr. President, but it's important to emphasize it because, realistically, it's your strongest point. They can't impeach you without significant support from senators from your own party. I'm sure you've already given some thought to that.'

'Absolutely,' Wade replied. 'I have people manning the phones already, making preliminary calls. I'll follow up later myself, unless you think that would be unwise, you know, that it wouldn't look good. Frankly, I think I need to call on them all personally.'

'I agree,' Monahan said. 'I would encourage it. Don't think of this as a normal trial, Mr. President. You're not dealing with a jury here. There's nothing wrong with trying to influence the outcome. In fact, that's the whole idea. This is a political process, and it's expected that both sides will use whatever political influence they have. You can bet your bottom dollar the House managers will be doing whatever they can to get the votes against you. You need to do whatever it takes to line up the votes on your side.'

'I hear you,' Wade replied.

'Ed, how long is this going to take?' Ellen Trevathan asked.

'Hard to say,' Monahan replied.

'I guess that would depend on the number of witnesses they call, and the number of witnesses we call,' Wade said.

'They may not call witnesses,' Monahan said. 'In the Clinton impeachment, there was a vote on that question, and the Senate decided not to call them.'

'Yes, that's right,' Ellen said. 'They relied on records from other sources, the Grand Jury proceedings, and so on.'

'Right,' Monahan said. 'They got a little squeamish about hearing all about the stained blue dress and the cigars in the little corridor ...'

He paused, slightly embarrassed.

'That's right,' Wade grinned. 'It's just through there. That's where history was made. We're thinking of adding it to the tour. And, for the record, I have never taken a woman in there, or done anything with a cigar.'

Monahan returned the grin.

'I'm relieved to hear that, Mr. President. Anyway, the point is, they could do the same here, dispense with witnesses and rely on the record of the hearings in the House Intelligence Committee. But in the Clinton case, they did set time limits. They gave both sides twenty-four hours to present a case, which came out as three working days each side. Plus, the senators had sixteen hours to ask questions and participate any way they wished. So we're not talking about a long time.'

'Well, we want to call witnesses, don't we?' Wade asked.

Monahan shook his head.

'It's too early to say, Mr. President. First, we need to look at the articles of impeachment, see what they say. Then we need to review the House Intelligence Committee record. I've started on that, but it's going to take me a while longer. If you have any ideas on potential witnesses, please let me know. So far, I haven't had any inspiration.'

'Let's get back to this question of what constitutes a high crime or misdemeanor,' Ellen Trevathan said. 'Look, the treason thing is dead in the water, isn't it?'

'Yes,' Monahan said. 'They don't have more than a handful of votes in the House for treason. George Stanley has been pushing it, but nobody's really buying it. So, as far I can see, all they have is one article charging a high crime or misdemeanor. It seems to have come down to a single article of impeachment. When I left my office to come over here, they were still debating the final wording, but it seemed like they were pretty close. I'm sure they've voted on it by now.'

'And a high crime means...?'

'It means whatever the Senate wants it to mean,' Monahan said. 'It has to be some kind of serious misconduct while in office, or an abuse of power. In Clinton's case, it all came down to allegations of perjury before the Grand Jury and obstruction of justice. Obviously, these would have been crimes that could have been tried in the courts, but the House seized on them as high crimes and misdemeanors. I'm not sure they even have to show that the President's conduct was criminal in the sense we understand that term in the courts. That's part of the problem. It's all so vague. Everything means what the Senate wants it to mean.'

Wade stood and thumped the top of his desk angrily.

'It's outrageous,' he shouted. 'What happened to the rule of law?

How can they just assassinate me like this. No proof beyond reasonable doubt, no rules of evidence. Jesus Christ, it's like some kind of kangaroo court.'

'Steve, you've got the Australian Ambassador coming to dinner this evening, among others,' Ellen said. 'You might want to find a different way of saying that.'

Wade smiled reluctantly, and resumed his seat, a little calmer.

'And,' Ellen continued, 'there is one comforting fact. So far, we've never had a President who has been successfully impeached. They didn't come close with Clinton, did they?'

'No, they didn't, Madam Vice President,' Ed Monahan replied. 'The closest they came was with Andrew Johnson. They only missed him by one vote. But that was back in 1868, and the issues were very different. I didn't find anything useful there. Clinton is a better example. They charged him with some pretty serious stuff, but they still couldn't lay a glove on him.'

'Clinton was a popular President,' Steve Wade said. 'So am I. That's our best point. Our good friends in the Senate are answerable to their constituents. I don't think the people will let them impeach me.'

No one replied to this remark. During the ensuing silence, Steffie Walinsky knocked and entered the Oval Office.

'It's time, Mr. President,' she said, and withdrew immediately.

Monahan looked up inquiringly.

'I asked Steffie to let us know when they delivered the articles of impeachment to the Senate,' Wade explained. 'Apparently, you were right. They've made up their minds. Needless to say, the whole thing is being carried live on the networks for the edification of the American people. I thought we should watch the show.'

Martha Graylor stood, walked over to a television set which had been wheeled in on a trolley for the occasion, and switched it on. They were just in time. To the soft tones of Conrad Beckers' commentary, the camera followed the House case managers, led by Gerry Parkinson, as they processed into the entrance to the Senate. They were received by the Sergeant-at-Arms, who was standing in front of a battery of cameras and microphones. With a show of pomp, Parkinson solemnly handed the Officer the black file he had been carrying, as George Stanley, Helen de Vries, and the other case managers looked on self-importantly.

'I have the honor, Sir,' Parkinson said, 'on behalf of the House of Representatives, to present to the Senate an article of impeachment against Steven Marion Wade, Junior, President of the United States. The article charges that he, Steven Marion Wade, Junior, while President of the United States, corruptly accepted inducements from a hostile foreign power in return for exercising the foreign policy of the United States in a manner which directly compromised the national security of the United States.'

The Sergeant-at-Arms accepted the file without comment. The two men shook hands, and the case managers made their way back towards the House of Representatives.

Conrad Beckers appeared on camera, microphone in hand.

'So there you have it,' Beckers intoned solemnly. 'A rare moment in our country's history. The article of impeachment has been duly delivered to the Senate, which must now set a date for the trial, in a proceeding of the gravest possible kind, a mercifully rare event, which has only happened twice before in our history. We understand that the House case managers are about to give a press conference, probably outside, on the steps of the Capitol, and of course, we will bring you that conference live as it happens. At six this evening, on the news program, I will have a panel of experts in the studio to comment on the legal issues surrounding the impeachment. But, for now, I am going to make my way to the Capitol steps.'

Beckers turned, and walked away from the camera.

Wade gestured to Martha Graylor, who turned the television off.

'How's the press release coming?' he asked her.

'I was just waiting for confirmation of the text,' she replied. 'Parkinson's office promised to messenger over a complete copy of the file once it had been delivered to the Senate. We'll have it ready to go soon.'

'Thank you, Martha,' Wade said.

'So, if you'll excuse me…'

'Of course.'

Martha left hurriedly.

Wade turned back to Ed Monahan.

'So, what in the hell does that mean?'

Monahan shrugged.

'It sounds like they decided to go with Mary Sullivan's theory. Nameless Lebanese influence, some right-wing group in Oregon, you being held to ransom because of your involvement with Lucia Benoni, threat to national security. I'm not sure it makes much sense, but we'll

241

just have to see what they've got. As I said before, Mr. President, the vital thing is to make sure of your political support in the Senate. My role is to go back to my office and get myself ready for trial. Try not to worry too much. I know that's easy for me to say, but...'

Wade smiled. A smile which Ellen Trevathan would never forget, a smile which struck her at the time, for reasons she could not have begun to explain, as one of the most sinister she had ever seen.

'I won't worry too much, Ed,' Wade said. 'You see, I'm very popular with the people. Very popular indeed. There's nothing to worry about. There's always a way out. You just have to know the escape routes.'

He laughed to himself, before standing and leaving the room.

PART III

ENDGAME

38

'WE'RE VERY serious,' Dick Latham insisted.

General Raul Gutierrez shook his head in disbelief. Had he just heard the Chairman of the Joint Chiefs talk about something called the Williamsburg Doctrine, according to which the Military could interfere with the succession to the Presidency of the United States? Had he just heard the Attorney-General confirm that it was not a joke? Surely he was having a dream, or a nightmare – or an hallucination?

'So, you're saying the Joint Chiefs get to decide who becomes President?'

'That's not necessarily the case,' Latham said. 'The Doctrine suggests only that some action could be taken in one of the circumstances identified at the 1965 meeting, in which the Vice President might be considered unreliable.'

'Right. And what 'circumstances' did they identify back in 1965, Mr. Latham?'

'As General Terrell said, the only circumstance which remains relevant to the discussion today is whether the Vice President is unduly left-wing or radical,' Latham replied stiffly.

Gutierrez shook his head. 'They said the President couldn't be a woman, didn't they? That's what this is about.'

'It is not about that,' Latham insisted.

'Did they or did they not say that in 1965?' Gutierrez persisted.

'Yes, they did,' Latham admitted. 'But…'

'I knew it.'

Latham thumped the table in frustration. 'Nobody thinks that way now. How could you, for God's sake? With women like Hillary Clinton and Condoleezza Rice in positions of power the way they have been?'

'That doesn't mean a damn thing, and you know it,' Gutierrez said. 'What else did they say in 1965? Did they also say the Vice President couldn't be a person of color? Would that make the Vice President unreliable?'

Latham turned his head away from Gutierrez with a muttered expletive. General Terrell held up a calming hand.

'Well, we've had a black president,' he said. 'Barack Obama served as our President, and I never heard any senior military personnel question his fitness to be Commander-in-Chief. Please remember, General Gutierrez, that this was 1965. There was a lot of paranoia involved due to the Cold War and, frankly, due to some social attitudes that many of us thought belonged in the Dark Ages. They did and said a lot of things we wouldn't do or say today.'

'Then why are we having a meeting today?' Gutierrez asked. 'If we wouldn't do it today, why is any of this relevant? It's because the Vice President is a woman, isn't it? Isn't that what you're talking about? Jesus Christ. I don't believe I'm hearing this.'

General Hessler had been shifting in his seat, listening to the discussion with growing impatience. 'Ellen Trevathan is not only a woman,' he broke in, almost savagely. 'She's a radical left-winger. That's why it's relevant.'

Gutierrez laughed incredulously. 'Ellen Trevathan, radical? Left-wing? You must be joking.'

'You don't think so?'

'Next to Genghis Khan, she's left-wing, maybe. Not in any real-world scenario.'

'Well, that's your opinion,' Hessler muttered.

Latham held up his hands. 'May I suggest we look at the evidence?' he pleaded. 'You'll find the text of the original Williamsburg Resolution behind tab two in your folders, but we don't need to review that right now. Can I ask you to turn to tab three?'

Those around the table complied with little apparent enthusiasm. Latham began to run through the materials he had carefully selected for inclusion in the folders.

'Ellen Louise Trevathan, born 7 February 1949, Erie, Pennsylvania. Father was Edwin Trevathan, a lifelong railroad man and union organizer who became Treasurer of the Amalgamated Brotherhood of Railroad Engineers. Suspected of communist sympathies, brief involvement with the House Unamerican Activities Committee, which came to nothing…' Seeing Gutierrez about to react, he continued quickly. 'Again, that may have been of interest in 1965, maybe not today.

Mother was Annie Gibb Trevathan, high-school teacher, political sympathies, if any, unknown.'

He paused for a sip of water. 'Over the page, please. Ellen's résumé. She is educated locally, wins a scholarship to Penn State, double major in political science and history. Brilliant grades. On to a masters followed by a doctorate in political science at Yale. Assistant professor of political science, George Mason University, appointed 1977, rises rapidly through the ranks to full professor. Later enters political life, which we can pass over for the moment. Tab four, please. Now we come to the point.'

'About time,' Gutierrez said quietly.

'May 1964,' Latham continued, pointedly ignoring the Air Force Chief. 'A conference is held in Belgrade, Yugoslavia. The Conference of Heads of State and Governments of Non-Aligned Countries. The conference concludes with a Declaration calling for more effective cooperation on international problems with a view to contributing to international peace and security and peaceful relations between peoples. Marshall Tito, Head of the State of Yugoslavia at the time, is trying to promote his image as an international statesman, and invites some young people of school and college age from different countries to attend the conference as observers. The proceedings have an annex with a list of names. The sole American representative is named as a fifteen-year-old Ellen Louise Trevathan, of Erie, Pennsylvania.'

Gutierrez shrugged. 'So?'

'In case you forgot, General,' Hessler said. 'Yugoslavia was behind the Iron Curtain.'

'Ancient history,' Gutierrez replied. 'And I assume the State Department must have approved her application for a visa at the time. In any case, Tito was no communist, and he never bought into Soviet doctrine. He was far more interested in playing us and the Russians against each other and hitting us both up for money.'

'Possibly so,' Latham conceded. 'But the declaration issued by the conference is of concern. Take a moment to read the summary provided by my staff, please. Not only does it call for total disarmament in the field of nuclear, biological and chemical weapons. It also calls for the abolition of weapons and military capabilities generally. In short, it's a call for pacifism.'

Latham waited for those around the table to digest the summary.

'She was fifteen.' Gutierrez said.

'Turn the page, she's all over the Vietnam War protests,' Latham said. 'Surveillance shows her at various marches and demonstrations, though she seems to have avoided arrest. Over the page again, please. Fast-forward to September 1967. International Youth Conference for Peace and Disarmament, held in Florence, Italy. Guess what was on the agenda there? Once again, among the delegates was one Ellen Louise Trevathan, now a little over eighteen years of age. You will note one or two other conferences of a similar kind. I could go on, but I'm sure you get the point.'

Latham looked around in an effort to confirm his assumption, but his audience seemed absorbed in flicking through the documents.

'Tab five, please. This is extracted from her résumé. A list of academic writings by the Vice President in various journals over the years, published both here and abroad. My staff have been through them in detail, and you will find summaries of each article. I think it's fair to say they show a consistent pattern of anti-militarism, and criticism of American foreign policy as being, in effect, colonial and based on the use of unequal force. I'm going to give you a few minutes to look through this material.'

Latham stood and walked slowly to what passed for a window in this ghastly cell-like room, thick chunky squares of opaque glass which reminded him of a prison. It was an image he preferred to suppress. He loosened his tie and tried to breathe normally. The air seemed hot and suffocating. After several minutes, the Chiefs decided they had read enough and he returned to his seat.

'These are just a few articles out of many in a long career,' Gutierrez said. 'If you look at the list of her writings, most of it is about politics and government, the relationship between the states and the federal government, that kind of stuff, nothing to do with the military at all. I notice your staff didn't summarize any of that. But that's the stuff she was known for.'

'There was limited time,' Latham insisted. 'My staff summarized what seemed important. Some of these papers were prepared for and delivered at conferences behind the Iron Curtain, two or three in Belgrade, for which she seems to have developed a special fondness, one in Prague, one in Warsaw.'

Gutierrez shook his head. 'Next, you'll be telling me she speaks French.'

'And finally, tab six. Position papers written by Ellen Trevathan for several so-called think tanks, detailing grounds for opposing military involvement in both Afghanistan and Iraq, and advocating the closure of Guantanamo Bay and the end of what she calls torture and extraordinary rendition. She believes that the United States should not act alone militarily, but that we should cooperate fully with the United Nations in taking military action as a member of the, quote, international community, end quote. She also advocates strict compliance with the Geneva Conventions, regardless of the amount of information about terrorism we would have to forego by doing so. You have summaries of these also. Please take some time to review them.'

The process took more than twenty minutes. Latham's staff had gone to town on these papers, which they obviously regarded as the pride of the collection, and in some cases the summaries were not a great deal shorter than the papers themselves.

'Any questions?' Latham asked.

Gutierrez pushed his folder away across the table. 'Obama voted against the Iraq war when he was in the Senate. A lot of people agreed with Trevathan about all those things.'

'A lot of people were ready to sell America out.' Hessler said. 'That's the way I'd put it. I don't want to make one of them President.'

'Bullshit,' Gutierrez said. 'And this is all because of some Cold War fantasy game they played in 1965 to persuade themselves they were keeping the world safe for democracy? The best thing we can do with tab two, and any other copies of this crap, is to make a bonfire of it all outside.'

'Let's not get carried away, General,' Latham said. 'I understand that this has probably come as something of a shock to you. I assure you that you would have been initiated into the Williamsburg Doctrine in due course. Because you were appointed so recently, there wasn't time for that. I'm sorry it's had to be put to you in this way. But there isn't much time, and we have to make a decision.'

'A decision?'

'Yes. We have to decide whether, in the event the President is impeached, the Military will let the succession proceed, or whether certain corrective steps will be taken. It's entirely up to all of you. It's your policy. All the President is doing here is asking for your input. He needs to know where he stands if he's impeached.'

Gutierrez rose from his chair.

'I'll tell you where he stands, Mr. Attorney-General. He stands on the front lawn of the White House waving goodbye before he boards his helicopter out of there.'

'That's not your decision, General,' McGarry said.

'That's exactly right, Admiral. It's not. That decision was made by the framers of the Constitution.'

'The framers of the Constitution didn't have to address this issue,' McGarry said. 'Women weren't allowed to vote, let alone be Vice President.'

'Neither were black slaves. So what?'

'So, we have to interpret the Constitution for our own times, in the light of our own circumstances.'

'It's not a question of interpretation,' Gutierrez shouted. He was now leaning against the back wall of the conference room. 'It's a question of reading what it says. The Constitution provides that the President shall be removed from office.'

'Yes, it does,' Latham said. 'But that presupposes that it is possible to remove him, or perhaps it raises the question of who would remove him.'

'He removes himself,' Gutierrez said. 'How could he not? What else could he do?'

Latham looked at the ceiling.

'Well, he could stay put, and await the judgment of the people. Ultimately, all power derives from the people. If the President's judgment were to be wrong, the people would remove him very quickly, wouldn't they? But if the people agreed with the Joint Chiefs... well, that would be a different question. In this case, President Wade is a very popular man. Most polls seem to say the people don't want him to be impeached.'

'That is totally beside the point,' Gutierrez replied. 'The decision is in the hands of the Senate. If the people don't like it, they can voice their displeasure the next time they get to vote for their senators.'

'Yes. But by that time, the Vice President would be President. The President is not sure that would be in the national interest. That's why he is asking the Joint Chiefs to consider the matter.'

'He apparently had no problem with campaigning with her through two elections,' Gutierrez pointed out. 'I don't see anything in these papers to cause alarm.'

'That's not the same as the question facing us now,' Latham replied. 'Campaigns are designed to give the people an attractive package to vote for. They don't always reflect reality.'

'The point,' Hessler said, 'is that we could not rely on her if the United States were to be attacked, or if we had to take action abroad to protect our national interests. She's a pacifist who advocates the abolition of the military. She is too dangerous.'

There was a frustrated silence around the table.

'The Williamsburg guidelines call for a vote to be taken,' Hessler continued sourly. 'I don't see any point in wasting the whole day talking about it. The President has asked us to consider it. Let's consider it. Let's take a vote.'

'You don't see any point in talking about it?' Gutierrez laughed out loud. 'It's such a simple matter for you to commit treason?'

Hessler threw back his chair and stood bolt upright. He began to walk towards Gutierrez.

'What did you say?' he asked. 'What the fuck did you just say?'

Gutierrez did not flinch.

'You heard what I said, General. This talk is treasonable.'

'You little…'

Gutierrez did not flinch as Hessler sprang at him. He raised both arms and pushed Hessler violently away. Before the Marine Commandant could renew his assault, Terrell and McGarry leapt to their feet to restrain him. Hessler reluctantly allowed himself to be escorted back to his chair.

'I'm not through with you,' he muttered venomously.

'Any time you want a piece of me, you know where I am,' Gutierrez replied quietly.

Latham banged his water glass down on the table. He shook his head in the direction of the stenographer, who was asking with her raised eyebrows whether the details of the last exchange should be recorded.

'Order,' Latham said firmly. 'I must ask you all to behave in a manner appropriate to this meeting.'

Gutierrez resumed his seat.

'What manner would that be exactly, Mr. Attorney-General?'

Latham ignored the question.

'The matter we have to resolve is this. The President has raised the issue of whether the Vice President, having regard to her long history of support for left-wing and radical causes, falls within the terms of the Williamsburg Doctrine. He expects the individual opinion of each of you. Please understand that the President has made no decision. It would be premature for him to do so before the outcome in the Senate is known. At this point, he seeks only your opinions. Depending on events, and on what those opinions might be, he may later request further action.'

Latham surveyed those around the table again. 'General Hessler is correct in saying that a vote is appropriate under the guidelines. If there is to be no further discussion, I suggest we proceed.'

A furious silence hung over the room.

'Very well. I will proceed in reverse order of seniority. General Gutierrez?'

Gutierrez exhaled heavily and shook his head. 'It's very simple. There's no problem with Ellen Trevathan in my mind. But that's not even the point. We all took an oath to uphold the Constitution. If the President is impeached, he is to be removed. If he doesn't remove himself voluntarily, our duty is to do it for him.'

'General Hessler?'

'Trevathan is a left-winger, a radical, and a pacifist. She's right within the guidelines. We keep the President in office or protect him until suitable arrangements can be made.'

'Admiral McGarry?'

'I'm with General Hessler.'

'General Terrell?'

Terrell shook his head.

'I don't know what exactly was in the minds of those people back in 1965, but I don't believe it has any place today. There's no Cold War any more. I don't care for Trevathan that much, but neither do I have any real problem with her. Even if I did, I don't see any legal basis for what's being suggested. I'm with General Gutierrez.'

Latham breathed deeply and looked down at the table.

'So, we have a hung jury. Is that what I'm to report to the President?'

'You report to the President whatever you want to report,' Gutierrez replied. He seized his hat from the chair next to him, rose, and began to walk to the door. 'I'm having nothing to do with this. I'm out of here.'

'One moment, General Gutierrez,' Latham said. 'Please remember that you signed the confidentiality agreement. We are entitled to expect that the proceedings of this meeting will remain secret.'

Gutierrez wheeled around.

'The President is entitled to that,' Terrell agreed.

'That depends,' Gutierrez said. 'There are some things which take precedence over a confidentiality agreement. The Constitution, for example.'

'I must advise you, General Gutierrez,' Latham said heavily, 'that the President places the utmost trust in your discretion. It would be very unfortunate if that discretion were lacking. Very unfortunate indeed.'

Gutierrez looked briefly into the implacable faces around the room and left without another word.

39

ELLEN TREVATHAN LOOKED at her watch again, and rose angrily to her feet. She had been waiting for over an hour for the meeting she had scheduled with the President. She had made several calls to Steffie Walinsky, only to receive the reply that the President was still in a meeting with the Attorney-General. It was not the first time she had been treated like this recently. The message was becoming clear. She was being excluded from the President's inner circle. He had not asked her for advice, and he had not asked her to make any calls to senators to solicit votes. Used to being one of the President's most trusted advisers, Ellen was chafing at the bit. That was far from being the worst problem. The impeachment proceedings were not going well. There was every chance that Steve Wade was about to be removed from the Presidency. Ellen might be on the point of taking over from him, and yet she could not even see him to talk about the transition. She was being put on hold because the President was engaged in 'important business'. What could be more important than the business she had to discuss with him? Didn't the President read the papers any more? Didn't he know what was going on in the Senate? Ellen walked hurriedly from her office in the West Wing back to Steffie's office. Steffie was nervous. Ellen Trevathan was not the person she wanted to see.

'I'm sorry, Madam Vice President, the President is still…'

'I don't care what the President is still doing, Steffie,' Ellen interrupted. 'Call him, and tell him I'm here in your office, and I want to see him now. Either he's going to go ahead with our meeting, or he's going to explain to me personally why he's not available.'

Steffie looked into the Vice President's eyes, hoping that she might change her mind. She did not.

'Yes, Ma'am.'

Steffie picked up her phone and punched the intercom button. She turned away from Ellen and spoke in a half-whisper. She replaced the receiver.

'Someone will be right out,' she said.

'Someone…?'

Steffie threw up her hands.

'That's what they told me. Look, I'm sorry, I really am. But it's not up to me…'

Ellen began to recover her composure.

'I know, Steffie. I'm sorry.'

The door to the President's office opened, and Martha Graylor came out. She walked up to Ellen and took her by the arm.

'Come with me,' she said quietly.

'Come with you where, Martha? I'm here to see the President.'

'My office. Please, Ellen. I'll explain everything, I swear. But not here.'

Ellen studied Martha's face carefully. She looked pale and tense. And her face was covered in lines that Ellen felt sure had not been there when she had last looked. Martha and Steffie both looked as if they were on the verge of a nervous breakdown. Something told Ellen to do as Martha had suggested.

They walked in silence and entered Martha's office. Martha slowly seated herself behind her desk. Ellen took an armchair in front of the desk and waited patiently.

'The President can't see you today, Ellen. He has to meet with the Attorney-General and some other people, and…'

Martha's voice trailed away.

Ellen placed her hands on the desk and leaned towards her.

'Isn't he following what's going on in the Senate?'

'He is following it, Ellen. Believe me.'

'Well, what are you telling me? He's not going to deal with it? He's setting up some Hitler-style bunker in there, except Eva Braun got out while there was still time? What's going on, for God's sake?'

Martha looked away.

'I can't talk about it. I…'

Ellen took a deep breath.

'Martha, look, I understand that the President has some important decisions to make about his defense. But he has to understand that we need to have some kind of plan in case things go against him. I intend to keep his team in place, those members of it who are willing to serve under me, anyway. But it's still going to be a nightmare. I need to be able to reassure the country and our allies abroad that the administration will continue as smoothly as possible. I know Steve doesn't want to face that prospect, but he owes it to the country, Martha. I need his attention, and I need it now. When is he going to see me?'

'I'm not sure.'

Martha was avoiding her eyes. Suddenly, Ellen's stomach seemed to tie itself in knots. For a second or two, she had difficulty drawing breath. When her mind focused again, she realized that Martha knew much more than she was saying. Martha was trying to stall her. There would be no meeting with Steve Wade, at least not any time soon. But why? She had to find out. Ellen became conscious of the silence. Nothing was to be gained by arguing with Martha in this frame of mind. She had to try a different tack. She managed a tentative smile.

'Forgive me for saying this, Martha, but you look like shit. Is all this getting to you?'

Tears formed in Martha's eyes.

'I feel like I'm falling to pieces.'

'You look like you're falling to pieces. You want to tell me why?'

Martha shook her head.

'Look, I know it's tough for you. You've been with Steve a long time. I understand that. But there's nothing you can do about this, Martha. There's no point in making yourself sick over it. Whatever happens in the Senate happens. There's nothing either you or I can do to stop it.'

Ellen paused.

'I assume you're still trying to pull some votes among our friends up there. How is it going?'

'It's not going,' Martha replied bitterly. 'Rats leaving a sinking ship.'

'So, it's going to turn out the way the press is predicting? He's going down?'

'Barring a miracle,' Martha replied. 'I can't believe it. The President has denied any relationship with Marfrela or anyone else until he's blue in the face. There's been no evidence of damage to national security. It's just speculation. You'd think at least some of them would give him the benefit of the doubt.'

Ellen shrugged her shoulders.

'After his record of lying about Lucia Benoni? It's hardly surprising. I admit I didn't expect such a negative reaction from our party, but it's not as though they don't have their reasons. And if you're blaming yourself for not being able to make them leap to his defense, forget about it. There was never a way to save him.'

'It got a lot worse after it finally came out that Julia had left him,' Martha added. 'Not that it had much to do with the impeachment really. But Steve insisted we stall for so long, with that crap that she was just visiting friends to explore resuming her career, that by the time we told the truth, even that was held against us.'

Martha suddenly looked directly into Ellen's eyes.

'You want to know why I look like shit, Ellen? I'm tired of telling lies, telling lies to the press, telling lies to myself. Ellen, there are times when I come out of a press conference and go straight into the john and puke my guts up. I'm not sure how long I can go on.'

Ellen reached across the desk and took Martha's hand.

'I'd really like to see you hang in there, Martha. If I have to take over, it would mean a lot to me to have you there beside me. The continuity is important. And you're so good at what you do. I have no idea who else I would ask. Are you taking anything?'

Martha nodded. 'Everything I can lay my hands on. My doctor's using up whole prescription pads on me.'

For the first time, Martha smiled thinly. Ellen returned the smile.

'What can I do to help?'

Martha swallowed hard. 'You really want to know?'

'Sure.'

'Get out of here. Don't press for a meeting right now. Go back to your official residence and wait it out.'

Something in Martha's eyes disturbed Ellen. She gently withdrew her hand.

'For God's sake, Martha… why? I don't understand.'

Martha leaned forward across the desk.

'Haven't you been watching the news on TV? Have you been seeing what's going on across the country?'

Ellen laughed. 'You mean the thing in Portland, those people protesting? Yes, I've seen it. It's nothing to worry about.'

'You don't think so?'

'No, I don't.'

'It's not just Portland though, is it, Ellen? It's Seattle, Denver, Phoenix, Dallas. It's a new city every night, Ellen, haven't you noticed that? There are people in the streets, and these are very angry people.'

Ellen sniffed dismissively. 'It's just a few people jumping on the bandwagon. If the media would quit paying so much attention to it, it would die out in a day or two.'

'I don't think so.'

'Well, so what, anyway? It's not exactly a surprise that people are reacting. Steve's a popular guy. The fact that he's being impeached hasn't changed that. It didn't in Clinton's case. Besides, they're on our side, Martha. Have you considered that it might be good news, that it might just tip one or two senators over the edge into supporting us? These people are on our side.'

Martha bit her lip.

'No, they're not, Ellen,' she replied softly. 'They're on Steve's side.'

Abruptly, the knots returned to Ellen's stomach.

'What are you saying…? I…'

Martha took Ellen's hand again.

'I can't say any more. Please believe me. I wish I could. But I can't. Now, in the name of God, Ellen, take my advice. Go home and wait this out.'

Slowly, Ellen stood and walked to the door. As desperately as she wanted to ask more questions, to shed light on a situation that was making less and less sense every minute, she knew now that Martha Graylor was not going to help her. Somehow, she had to figure it out for herself.

'Take care of yourself, Martha,' she said, on her way out.

'You too,' Martha replied.

After Ellen had gone, Martha remained seated at her desk for some time, until she reminded herself that she would be missed in the President's office. Slowly, she stood and walked back along the corridor and into the anteroom, where she ignored Steffie Walinsky's inquiring look. She opened the door of the office without knocking and entered. The meeting had broken up. Only the President and the Attorney-General remained. Steve Wade looked up as she resumed her seat.

'How did it go?' he asked tersely.

'She left,' Martha replied. 'But, Mr. President, with all respect, you can't go on ignoring her. It's only a matter of time before…'

'I know, I know,' Wade said. 'I'll get to her. But it's a matter of putting first things first. While you were gone, we decided that I should speak to the American people the day after tomorrow. I need you to arrange coverage. I want all the networks. I'm going to do it from the Oval Office.'

'Mr. President, I don't know what you're going to say. If I'm asked…'

'If you're asked, you tell them that, given the state of the proceedings in the Senate, my advisers believe I should reserve that information for the speech itself. They'll get copies from your office just before I go on the air. They should be able to live with that. It's happened before.'

'In times of crisis, yes, but…'

'This *is* a crisis, Martha, or hadn't you noticed that? The Senate may be about to impeach me, based on no evidence at all. We're involved in all manner of important foreign policy negotiations, some of them very sensitive. This charade, this political game, is not in the best interests of the country. I need to stay in office to make sure these important matters are handled correctly. The country needs to come together on this.'

'Come together? … I'm not sure I understand.'

'You will.'

'Mr. President, I'm your Press Secretary. If you can't take me into your confidence, I don't know what I can do to help. If you'd prefer to get someone else… if you'd like me to resign, I…'

Steve Wade stood, walked around his desk, and perched on the edge of it near Martha's chair. He smiled.

'Resign? For God's sake, Martha, how long have we worked together?'

'A long time, Sir.'

'A very long time. And during that very long time, how many crises have we gone through together?'

Despite herself, Martha smiled. 'More than I can count.'

'Exactly. And that's all that's happening here, Martha, another crisis. One that we'll live through, just like we have all the others.'

'But Mr. President…'

'Don't worry about it. All will become clear. I fully expect that it may not be necessary to give the speech at all. We're still working on people on the Hill. Some of them are regretting having come out against me, now that such large numbers of their constituents are out on the streets, telling them they want me to serve out my term. I'm a very popular President, Martha. The people aren't going to let me go. They want to keep me, and they'll find a way to do it. I'm betting we will have nothing to worry about.'

'But, Sir, what if you're wrong?'

'I'm not wrong. Even if the Senate does something stupid, the American people will know the right thing to do. So I will speak to the

American people, and we'll go from there.'

Martha swallowed hard. 'But you won't tell me what you're going to say?'

'My advisers think it would be better if I kept that under wraps for a short time. Even from you. Isn't that right, Dick?'

Martha glanced at the Attorney-General. He looked almost as tense as she was herself.

'Yes, Mr. President.'

Martha stood. 'I'll go make the arrangements.'

'Thank you. Oh, and Martha, just so you know, I have a meeting with the Joint Chiefs tomorrow afternoon. We're not notifying anyone, so it's unlikely you'll get any questions, but if you do, you know nothing about it.'

Martha looked up abruptly. 'The Joint Chiefs? I don't have that on my calendar. Have I missed something? Do we have a situation going on abroad some place? What about a briefing?'

Wade stood.

'You know nothing about it,' he repeated firmly. 'But if it will put your mind at rest, no, we do not have a situation going on. Now, you'll have to excuse me, Martha. Dick and I still have one or two things to discuss. Let me know when everything's arranged for my broadcast.'

40

TED LAZENBY WALKED briskly into the large situation room which had been set up several days before at FBI Headquarters to monitor the rising tide of demonstrations across the country protesting against the impeachment of President Steve Wade. Initially, he had regarded the demonstrations as a matter of concern only to local police departments, but phone calls from a number of police chiefs had convinced him that there was more to it. The demonstrations were not massive, but there was evidence that they were being coordinated across state lines, and the chiefs thought it was something the Bureau should be keeping an eye on. Lazenby instructed every FBI field office across the country to work with the local police, and to send as much information as possible to Headquarters as soon as it came in. He placed Kelly Smith in charge of receiving and evaluating the information, and assigned Jeff Morris to assist her. Technically, Jeff should have returned to his duties with the District of Columbia Police Department, but Lazenby had been impressed by his cool, clear head. He also realized that Jeff's presence was keeping his personal assistant in a positive frame of mind, and given the workload Kelly was carrying, that was another strong reason for not letting him go. He talked Chief Bryson into letting him stay until the crisis had passed.

Kelly and Jeff were seated near the door at the large table which occupied most of the situation room. The table was packed with computers, telephones and masses of paper, and some twenty agents were working on the task of coordinating and analyzing the rapidly increasing volume of information about the protests. Large flat screen televisions on the walls were tuned to all the major news channels.

'Anything new?' Lazenby asked.

Kelly looked up as if to reply, but the red telephone by her side rang before she could speak. She held up one hand and picked up the phone with the other.

'Not a lot, Director,' Jeff replied. 'But it's not going away. Everyone seems to be expecting more demonstrations this evening. It's reaching as far as Minneapolis, St. Paul, in the north, and there's word that Miami may be involved by tomorrow.'

Lazenby frowned. 'It's spreading right across the country, isn't it?'

'Looks that way.'

'Jesus Christ, how did we miss this?'

'I'm not sure we did,' Jeff replied. 'We just don't know why it's got so far so fast. There's no pattern to it yet. Once we find out who's behind it, we should have a better idea of what's going on.'

'I hope so,' Lazenby said.

Kelly placed a hand over the mouthpiece of her telephone and turned to Lazenby. She seemed hesitant.

'Director, there's someone down at reception to see you. You're not going to like it, but I'm going to advise you to see her anyway.'

Lazenby raised his eyebrows.

'Who?'

'Mary Sullivan, from the *Post.*'

Lazenby turned his head away in disgust. 'Forget it. The woman costs us one of our best agents, and now she has the balls to ask for an interview. Tell her to go screw herself.'

Kelly bit her lip. 'I understand how you feel. But she's not asking for an interview. She says she has information. She's here in person, and off the record. That's highly unusual, to say the least. I think you ought to listen to what she has to say.'

Lazenby raised his eyes to the ceiling. 'God in heaven. Why did I ever take this job?… All right, have them bring her to my office. You come with me. Jeff, you too.'

Kelly looked at Lazenby in surprise. 'You think you might need witnesses?'

Lazenby was striding through the door. 'No. I might need a couple of strong people to pull me off her if I decide I have to kill her.'

Mary Sullivan was subdued as she shook hands formally with Lazenby and his two assistants. She declined coffee and sat down in front of the Director's desk.

'Thank you for seeing me, Director Lazenby,' she began hesitantly. 'I know this is irregular. And I guess the first thing I want to say is how sorry I am about your agent in Oregon. I'm probably not supposed to know about it even now…'

'That's correct,' Lazenby said.

'I heard about your operation through the grapevine, obviously, after the event. I knew nothing at the time. I checked with all my sources. None of them knew anything. I know there's nothing I can say that will make it better. But I want you to know that I would never knowingly have placed him in danger. I haven't been able to sleep since it happened. Nothing like this has ever happened to me before. I don't know what to say, Director. But I want you to know I'm truly sorry.'

Lazenby bowed his head. Kelly watched him closely. It was some time before he replied.

'I appreciate what you've said, Miss Sullivan.'

'Thank you,' Mary said.

'As a matter of fact, we don't officially know whether we have lost him or not. We just haven't heard from him for a long time. He's officially listed as missing. But, if he were still alive and in good health, we would probably have heard something from him by now. Anyway, Miss Sullivan, I'm assuming you didn't come here just to talk about that.'

'No, I didn't. I'm here because of something else I picked up from a source out of town. It may be that you have similar information, but just to be on the safe side, I thought I should pass it on to you. It may have something to do with the demonstrations, but it has a different angle.'

'Go ahead.'

'I have a local source in Albuquerque, New Mexico, who is convinced that a number of white supremacist groups from out west, including the Sons of the Land, are beginning a quiet but organized movement of personnel towards Washington.'

Lazenby glanced across at Kelly, his eyebrows raised. 'Personnel?'

'That was the word my source used. He says they're moving in groups which should be too small to invite suspicion, but there may be a lot of them. And they may be armed.'

Lazenby opened his eyes wide. He turned towards Kelly and Jeff, who were staring at Mary Sullivan in amazement.

'What evidence does your source have of this?'

'My source was approached by a woman who supplies him with information from time to time. Local stuff. Nothing to interest me, or even him, most of the time. This woman is… well, she's a member of a profession which doesn't usually command the highest credibility…'

Kelly bit her lip to suppress a grin. 'She's a call girl?'

'Yes.'

'Oh, for God's sake,' Lazenby said.

'No, Director, hear me out,' Mary said. 'Please. It may be important.'

Lazenby raised his hands. 'Go ahead.'

'Thank you. Evidently, this lady had been requested to attend at a certain motel to provide personal services for two gentlemen who were passing through on their way east. She said they had been drinking heavily, and they were rather careless about what they were saying. They told her they were part of some kind of plan to take over power in Washington, and that there were a lot of other people headed the same way for the same purpose.'

'And the woman took this couple of drunks seriously?' Kelly asked.

'Not at first. But they had so much to drink that they fell asleep after she had serviced them. She says that when she arrived, she noticed a big metal chest against the wall by the television. As she was getting dressed to leave, it occurred to her to take a closer look. Maybe she thought there might be some additional compensation in it, who knows? So she lifts the lid of the chest, and what does she find but an assortment of weapons; handguns, rifles, semi-automatics, you name it, even a couple of things she thought were hand-grenades.'

Jeff Morris whistled quietly.

'And she reported this to your source?'

'Yes. My source would have paid her something. And the option of going to the police wouldn't have seemed very attractive, given the circumstances.'

Lazenby drummed his fingers on his desk.

'How reliable is your source?'

'Very. He freelances for several local newspapers, does some television reporting. He's honest, and he has his ear to the ground.'

Lazenby nodded.

'All right. It may be nothing, or it may be something, but we'll look into it.'

He stood and extended his hand.

'Thank you for coming, Miss Sullivan. I appreciate it.'

'You're welcome.'

Mary paused uneasily.

'I don't quite know how to put this,' she said quietly. 'But Harold Philby told me to tell you that he spoke with the owners of the *Post*. If there's anything the agent's family needs, you know, we would like to…'

Her voice trailed away. Lazenby nodded.

'Thank you,' he said. 'I'll make sure that gets passed on to the appropriate people.'

Mary Sullivan stood and shook hands with Lazenby, Kelly and Jeff. She made her way to the door.

'Miss Sullivan,' Lazenby asked, 'why exactly did you come to me with this? You could have added yet another scoop to your tally, and let us find out about it by reading it in the *Post*. That seems to be the way we get most of our information these days.'

Mary smiled. 'The information indicated a possible violation of federal law, transporting arms across state lines. As a citizen, I have a duty to report it to the appropriate authorities.'

'I was asking for the real reason.'

Mary paused with her hand on the door handle.

'I hoped it might make me sleep better,' she said. 'Besides, I'll still have my scoop. But I'm going to hold off on it for a couple of days, so you can do some investigation without having the suspects tipped off in advance. I guess it's just another way to say I'm sorry.'

'Classy,' Kelly smiled at Lazenby after Mary Sullivan had left.

'I hate to have to agree,' Lazenby replied, 'but you're right. And it may explain the information we got from the Portland field office a few days ago.'

'That small convoy of trucks heading out of the Sons of the Land compound,' Kelly said.

'Right. What's the story on that?'

'They started out heading east. Seemed like they were in no particular hurry. We've been keeping track of them as a routine matter. But until now it was just a small part of the overall picture. We haven't given it priority.'

'Well, that just changed,' Lazenby said. 'As of now, it has top priority, at least until we know more about what's going on.'

'So what do we do?' Jeff asked. 'Have our agents find them and pull them over?'

'Or have the local police do it,' Kelly said. 'Less obvious. Do we have probable cause for a search?'

'We'll find probable cause,' Lazenby replied through gritted teeth. 'But get satellite coverage first. Let's see if we can find a pattern. Let's not move too soon. Once we pull them over, we tip off whoever else may be involved. Sullivan has bought us some time. Let's use it. Alert all police departments that we are interested in any traffic stops that seem in any way unusual. Let's see if we can cross-check vehicles stopped with criminal records and known members of those extremist groups.'

'I'll need more people, Director,' Kelly said. 'That's a big task.'

'I'll take care of it. Go to work.'

Kelly and Jeff returned to the situation room and gave the necessary instructions. They both sat down wearily at the table, and surveyed the ever-growing piles of emails and faxes. Kelly let her head sink down on top of the table.

'I feel like I've been on duty for weeks without a break. Is this ever going to end?'

'Not any time soon. Are you still on to meet Linda for dinner?'

Kelly sat up abruptly.

'Oh, God, yes. I'd forgotten. What time is it?'

'Six-thirty.'

'All right, I still have time. Are you sure you don't mind if I disappear for a while?'

'No. I had lunch, remember, and I'm sure we'll be making the daily pizza call before long. Go for it.'

'OK. Love you. I won't be long.'

Jeff Morris blew Kelly a kiss as she left the situation room. A female agent seated at the far end of the room called his name. He made his way around the table to where the agent sat, her fingers gliding rapidly over her computer keyboard.

'What have you got, Jenny?'

'We've been tracking the Portland convoy. But guess what? They're not really a convoy any more. The field office thinks they figured out we were watching, and split up. They're still moving in the same direction, but now they're just individual vehicles.'

'But still moving east?'

'Yeah.'

'All of them? Are you sure?'

'Yeah.'

'God damn it,' Jeff said. 'That means, if there are any more of them out there, they will all be doing the same thing.'

'Yes, Sir,' Jenny replied. 'Our job just got a lot harder. Satellite coverage may not tell us much now. The only reason we're in touch with the Portland trucks is because the field office is familiar with the individual vehicles.'

'Where are they now?'

'Somewhere east of Chicago. It's too soon to be sure, but Washington is certainly a possible destination.'

Jeff leaned against the table and looked towards a large map of the United States which was on the far wall of the situation room. The map was dotted with brightly-colored pins.

'If there's a large-scale movement on Washington, we have no way to control it, do we?'

'Realistically, no. Not unless you want to set up checkpoints along the entire length of the eastern standard time zone meridian. And that's before we talk about the airports and the railroads.'

Jeff nodded.

'Let me know if anything else develops. I need to go see Director Lazenby.'

'I'm sure he'll be thrilled.'

'I'm sure,' Jeff called back on his way out.

* * *

Linda Samuels stood up and embraced Kelly as she approached the table.

'Well, hi there. I was beginning to think you were going to stand me up.'

Kelly kissed Linda on the cheek and sat down.

'I'm sorry, Linda. It's been crazy. I've been running around non-stop all day, and I've left Jeff in charge, so I can't take too long. It's good to see you. I've missed you. What do you recommend?'

'For the hungry law enforcement chief who only has minutes to spare, I would suggest a burger and fries.'

'Good call. And I'm going to begin with some of that garlic bread.'

Linda smiled as she passed the bread basket to her friend.

'So what's so crazy over at the Bureau? Can you talk about it?'

Kelly hungrily broke off a big chunk of garlic bread and began to chew on it. A young waiter arrived and took their orders with an obvious lack of interest.

'We're trying to figure out where all these protests are coming from,' she replied through the bread, 'and why they're spreading on the scale they are. The Director is beginning to think they're being orchestrated. They seem a bit over the top for spontaneous demonstrations by small groups of the President's supporters. Is there any word on this at the White House?'

'Well, actually, Kelly, ever since I was hauled before the House

Intelligence Committee, the President doesn't confide in me as intimately as he used to. If he has an opinion, he hasn't shared it with me.'

Kelly smiled. 'Hey, you went to jail for him. I would have thought you would be his closest confidante by now.'

'Maybe he's not sure I would do that a second time. And maybe he's right.'

They both laughed.

'I'm sure he's not too unhappy about having all those people on the streets,' Kelly ventured after a silence. 'There must be a few senators sitting up and taking notice.'

'As they damn well should,' Linda replied. 'He's being railroaded. There's no evidence he had any dealings with Hamid Marfrela, or anyone else, for that matter. Hell, Kelly, do you know how damn near impossible that would be? The President is almost never left alone. I don't even know how he would go about it if he wanted to. There was no way he could keep Lucia Benoni from us. How could he be doing business with Hamid Marfrela?'

'Well, you knew about Lucia, but you don't know what they may have talked about while he was getting his rocks off with her,' Kelly pointed out. 'Maybe she was the go-between.'

'I know Steve Wade hasn't betrayed his country,' Linda insisted.

Before Kelly could reply, the waiter returned with their food. Kelly decided to let the matter drop.

'Did the President or anyone on his staff ever say anything about what you did at the House Intelligence Committee hearing? Were they appreciative?'

'He thanked me personally. No word yet on whether I get the Medal of Honor.'

Kelly devoured part of her burger and wiped her lips with a napkin.

'So, how will you feel if you're protecting President Trevathan next week?'

'That's not going to happen,' Linda replied firmly. 'Steve Wade is going to serve out his term.'

Kelly looked at her friend, a french fry suspended in mid-air on the way to her mouth.

'You sound very sure of that.'

Linda shrugged.

'Why shouldn't I be? He's done nothing wrong, and the people want him to stay. You were talking about how the protests are spreading. Don't you think that's what it's all about? The people are telling the Senate to lay off of him.'

'It's not up to the people, Linda. It's up to the Senate. Are you saying the protesters should be able to dictate to the Senate what to do? Look, I understand you are very loyal to Wade. You've proved that time after time. But…'

'We'll just have to see, won't we?'

'Yes. I guess so.'

Kelly resumed work on her burger, but watched Linda carefully. Linda seemed to have lost interest in her meal, and was staring vacantly to one side.

'Let's change the subject,' Kelly offered.

Linda looked briefly around the restaurant, and then turned back towards her.

'Kelly, we've always been able to talk, haven't we? Off the record, I mean?'

Kelly put down the remains of her burger and looked up.

'Sure.'

Linda leaned forward confidentially.

'Kelly, you talk about the Bureau being crazy. Believe me, it's nothing compared to the White House. Everyone's running around like chickens with their heads cut off. The senior staff members seem like they're in a daze. Martha Graylor, you know, the Press Secretary, is having a nervous breakdown right in front of our eyes. But nobody seems to have any idea what's going on. We hardly ever see the President any more. It's as though they've all lost it.'

'That's understandable,' Kelly replied. 'They must be under incredible stress. That's not going to change while the impeachment is going on.'

'Yes. But it's not the only thing.'

Linda hesitated, looking around again.

'Do we need to go some other place to talk?' Kelly asked.

Linda shook her head. 'No. I haven't got time. I need to get back.'

'OK.'

'Kelly, the really strange thing is the military presence we have with us.'

Kelly sat up with a start. 'Military presence? What do you mean?'

'There's been a procession of military people in and out of the building. Marines mostly. And I'm not talking about the Chiefs of Staff, or even generals. They've been around, but so have a bunch of other people, lower-rank officers. Armed. There are even some patrolling the grounds, almost as though they're looking for something.'

Kelly's eyes opened wide. 'Is there some kind of foreign crisis? I haven't seen anything like that on the news.'

'Nothing anyone knows about. Or, if they do, they're not saying anything. The President has pretty much closed the building to the press.'

'I heard that,' Kelly said. 'The entire press corps has been bitching about it. All they're getting is the occasional statement from the Press Secretary.'

'Which says almost nothing. And if we ask, we're told in no uncertain terms to mind our own business.'

Thoughtfully, Kelly rested her chin on her hands. 'So, you really have no idea what's going on?'

'No. The speculation on the Detail is that there's some big-time covert operation going on that they don't want to talk about.'

'If that's true, they picked a hell of a time for it.'

'Yes, they did.'

'On the other hand, maybe they're making *Wag the Dog Two*, something to take people's minds off the impeachment.'

'I don't think so, Kelly. They don't have time. The impeachment isn't going to last much longer.'

There was a silence.

'Linda, look, I really have to run. Is there anything I can do? I mean, you obviously thought it was important to tell me this. Do I need to pass this on to the Director?'

'Why would you?'

'I don't know. But you're obviously concerned about this, otherwise why would you have told me?'

'I told you because we're friends. I'm not asking you to do anything. You understand, I'm still loyal to the President.'

'I understand.'

'But I still wanted to tell you about it. As friends.'

Suppressing the urge to discuss the matter further, Kelly stood and gave Linda a hug.

'Tell Jeff I sent my love.'

'I will. And Linda… if you want to talk some more…'

'I'll call.'

'Promise?'

'Promise.'

'Love you.'

'Love you.'

Kelly stood outside the restaurant long enough to watch Linda pull out of the parking lot and turn into the traffic for her drive back to the White House. Slowly, she walked to her car, and sat silently in it for some minutes without starting the engine. When she did leave the restaurant parking lot, instead of driving directly back to FBI Headquarters, she took a detour through the darkening streets of Washington, and parked as close as she could get to the White House. For several minutes, she walked up and down in front of the building, scanning the grounds as carefully as she could. She saw nothing out of the ordinary. One or two police officers were on routine patrol on the streets outside, and only one or two token tourists seemed to be taking any interest in the President's residence. Inside the fence, she could see no movement. Eventually, she turned away, returned to her car, and drove back to work.

41

LATE INTO THE evening, Ted Lazenby, flanked by Kelly and Jeff, watched CNN's nightly coverage of the pro-Wade demonstrations, which had now spread to several major cities in the east. In Chicago, against a backdrop of burning cars, a chanting mob, and squads of police officers in full riot gear, a nervous reporter was saying that thousands of protesters, some carrying clubs or throwing rocks, had tried to storm civic buildings in Daley Plaza, and that police had only just managed to repel them. Other reporters had similar stories from Atlanta and Miami. Governors in several states had put the National Guard on standby and cancelled all Guard and police leave. Only now, as midnight approached, was some semblance of order being restored in the streets. The senior CNN White House correspondent added that the President had made no comment on the situation. As Lazenby reached for the remote to mute the spin of the political commentators who were to make an appearance next, there was a knock on the door. A young female agent entered.

'I'm sorry to disturb you, Director. We have a situation down at main reception. The duty agent requests that you come down right away.'

'A situation?' Lazenby asked.

Kelly's right hand drifted automatically towards her side-arm, and came to rest on her holster. The agent noticed.

'It's under control, Agent Smith. Sir, we have two visitors, accompanied by two men who say they are Secret Service agents. They have no appointment, but they say they have something very urgent they have to see you about personally. Security won't release them from reception without your personal authorization. It's getting a little tense. I really need you down there, Director.'

'Let's go,' Lazenby said, authoritatively.

With Kelly, Jeff and the female agent in hot pursuit, the Director

271

virtually ran to the elevators, and within a few seconds, all four were making their way along the main foyer of the building towards the security desk. A number of intense-looking FBI agents were surrounding the three men and a woman who had arrived so unexpectedly, and were paying particularly close attention to two men in dark suits, white shirts and ties. On seeing the Director approach, one of the FBI agents stepped forward.

'Agent Kimble, are you in charge here?'

'Yes, Sir.'

'Report.'

'Director, this lady and three gentlemen arrived at the main door in a private vehicle, which then left. Two of the gentlemen, the two wearing suits, immediately identified themselves as Secret Service agents, and stated that they are carrying side-arms. The lady and the other gentleman claim to be... well, I'll let them explain for themselves, Sir. The two of them are unarmed. I let them into the building under close supervision, and asked that you be sent for Sir.'

Lazenby held up his hand. 'One moment, Agent Kimble.'

Lazenby's gaze took in the woman, with large spectacles and long, loose hair, wrapped in a cheap coat which was much too big for her; and the man in blue jeans, casual shirt, and a red windbreaker with a hood. For a moment, the Director seemed nonplussed, but suddenly his face broke into a grin.

'Well, I'll be damned.'

The female visitor also broke into a smile.

'Agent Kimble, you say you have not been able to establish the identity of our guests?' Lazenby asked.

'No, Sir.'

'Then allow me to introduce you. Agent Kimble, meet the Vice President of the United States, Ellen Trevathan, and General Raul Gutierrez, Chief of Staff of the United States Air Force.'

Agent Kimble blinked several times in rapid succession as Lazenby shook hands with his visitors and introduced them to Kelly and Jeff. He came stiffly to attention.

'Ma'am, I apologize if I was discourteous, or if I have caused you any inconvenience. You too, Sir. I was...'

'You were doing your job, Agent Kimble,' Ellen Trevathan said graciously. 'There is nothing to apologize for. Do you think you could find my agents a cup of coffee while I confer with the Director?'

'Yes, Ma'am,' Agent Kimble smiled weakly. 'Consider it done.'

Lazenby took Ellen Trevathan's arm. 'Ellen, I'm sensing that officially, this visit is not taking place?'

'I would appreciate if it stayed that way, Ted.'

Lazenby turned to the assembled agents. 'Did everybody hear the Vice President?'

'Yes, Sir.'

'Good. Make sure there's no record of this unless and until I authorize it.'

'You know, Ellen,' Lazenby said once they were in the elevator, 'all you had to do was call ahead. I would have been glad to arrange a proper welcome.'

'If I could have called ahead,' the Vice President replied, 'there wouldn't have been any need for us to dress up like street people, would there?'

'Hey, what are you talking about?' Raul Gutierrez said. 'This is the way I always dress.'

Not another word was spoken until the Vice President and General Gutierrez had joined Lazenby, Kelly and Jeff in the Director's office, and a pot of fresh coffee had been brewed.

'I'm going to let Raul do the talking, Ted,' Ellen said. 'He's the one who saw and heard what you need to know, and he's putting his career, and possibly his life, on the line by being here.'

'That's fine,' Lazenby said. 'Look, General, I'm assuming that this is connected with what we might loosely call the present situation in the country. Kelly and Jeff are my right-hand people on this, but if you need them to wait outside, if it's something too confidential to...'

Gutierrez shook his head. 'No. That's OK. As long as we all understand that this is all off the record for now.'

'Agreed,' Lazenby replied.

Gutierrez took a deep breath.

'Director, have you ever heard of the Williamsburg Doctrine?'

'No. I can't say I have.'

'Neither had I. Until recently. A few days ago, the Attorney-General summoned me to a top-secret meeting of the Joint Chiefs at the Pentagon...'

'Dick Latham?' Lazenby interrupted. 'What does he have to do with...?'

'I'll come to that,' Gutierrez promised. 'When I arrive at the meeting, it's just the Chiefs and a stenographer, plus Latham. No one from the Secretary of the Air Force. No one from anywhere. Completely outside the usual protocol. And everything's hush-hush, not a word to anyone. Then Latham and Terrell explain to me that, back in the 1960s, after the Kennedy assassination, the Joint Chiefs had this conference at Williamsburg to discuss what to do in the event they had a Vice President they didn't like, who suddenly had to take power.'

'You mean, if a future President were to be assassinated?' Lazenby asked.

'If a future President had to leave office for any reason,' Gutierrez replied, nodding. 'Apparently, the conclusion they reached was that, if the Joint Chiefs had some reason not to trust the Vice President as Commander in Chief, they would take action to prevent him, or her, from becoming President. This idea became known as the Williamsburg Doctrine.'

'God in Heaven,' Lazenby muttered. 'Take action, how?'

'They weren't specific about that. But I assume it would involve some kind of military response.'

'I don't believe it.'

'Neither did I. At first. But Latham told me that the President had ordered him to convene this meeting, so that the Joint Chiefs could consider whether the Doctrine should be invoked in Ellen's case.'

Lazenby exhaled heavily. 'I assume the Joint Chiefs told Latham he could go fuck himself?'

'Not exactly. I did, almost in so many words. General Terrell seems to agree with me, but Admiral McGarry and General Hessler voted the other way.'

There was a prolonged silence.

'Two members of the Joint Chiefs went for this crap?'

'That's right.'

'But what could they have against Ellen, for God's sake,' Lazenby asked.

'She's too left-wing,' Gutierrez replied quietly.

'I knew I shouldn't have put that Che Guevara poster up in my office in the West Wing,' Ellen observed with a grim smile.

'This is fantastic. I feel like I've disappeared through the looking glass with Alice.'

Lazenby sat back in his chair, looking over at Kelly and Jeff, who were visibly shaken.

'So, you see,' Gutierrez concluded, 'why I felt I had to do something. I felt I owed it to Ellen to tell her in confidence what's going on. Quite apart from the fact that we've been friends for years. Incredible as it seems, there is some possibility that these people are going to try to stop her taking over the presidency if Wade is impeached, and the fact that the Attorney-General is involved suggests to me that the White House is up to its neck in it. I wasn't even sure Ellen would be safe once the vote in the Senate comes down tomorrow. So I went to see her, and we talked it over, and she mentioned that you two go back a long way, and that she trusted you, and we decided to pull this stunt. Maybe we're out of line but, to be honest, Director, I'm out of my league here. I've only been on the Joint Chiefs a short time, and I've never been a politician. All I know is that the Constitution says one thing, and some of my colleagues are planning something different.'

'We're all out of our league here, General,' Lazenby said.

There was a long silence.

'Director,' Kelly ventured tentatively. 'May I say something?'

Lazenby nodded.

'I had dinner this evening with a friend who's on the President's Detail. You remember, she helped us identify the S-Pass in the Benoni investigation?'

'You mean Agent Samuels?' The Vice President asked.

'Yes, Ma'am. She seemed worried about what was going on in the White House. She didn't know anything specific, but she said everybody was going crazy, and there was an unusual military presence in the grounds for no obvious reason. Nobody was aware of any operation going on, but there were armed officers all over the place. General, do you know of any operation taking place which might explain that?'

'None that I know of,' Gutierrez said. 'Did she say which branch?'

'Marines, mostly.'

'That bastard, Hessler,' Gutierrez snarled. 'He's up to something.'

With a massive effort, Lazenby pulled himself up in his chair.

'All right. Raul, you said that Hessler and McGarry voted in favor of the doctrine, and Terrell voted with you. Is that right?'

'Yes. But I wouldn't bet on Terrell holding firm. I think he might bend under pressure. God only knows what Dick Latham told the President.'

'How in God's name did Steve Wade even get into the position of calling such a meeting?' Lazenby asked. 'It's beyond belief. Has the man totally lost it?'

'I don't know,' Ellen replied. 'But I could tell something was up when I was over there yesterday. I was supposed to meet with him to discuss a transition plan. It's getting urgent. The meeting had already been rescheduled several times. I couldn't get in to see him. I couldn't get past Martha Graylor and Steffie Walinsky. There's something going on, that's for sure. And, whatever it is, they're not going to let me in on it.'

'They, being who?' Lazenby asked.

'I was told Steve was meeting with Dick Latham, that's all I know. Martha advised me to go home and wait it out. Ted, you know Dick better than I do. Would you think he would involve himself in an intrigue like this?'

Lazenby shook his head. 'Not in a million years.'

'And you haven't heard anything about this before now?'

'Not a word, Ellen, I swear to you.'

'So, now what?' the Vice President asked.

Lazenby shrugged.

'Well, let's see. We have a President who's about to be impeached, and we have at least two of the Joint Chiefs saying he shouldn't be removed from office, and maybe it's their job to make sure he isn't removed. We also have carefully-orchestrated riots going on in support of the President across the country, and a large number of concerned citizens making their way to Washington to voice their opinion on the matter. What we have here is the makings of a monumental fuck-up.'

'What we have here, Director,' Raul Gutierrez said quietly, 'is the makings of the second American Civil War.'

42

JOHN MASON SMILED at his visitor.

'You look like you could use a drink,' he said graciously. 'Come and sit down.'

The Wilson Foundation was officially closed for the evening, and its director was alone in the boardroom. He had no intention of going home, at least not yet. The Senate was getting close to voting on the impeachment of President Steve Wade, and Mason wanted to know what the tally was going to be. He had Selvey on standby to leak the information to Mary Sullivan without delay, so that any statement by Steve Wade would be pre-empted by whatever spin he, John Mason, chose to put on it. It was a moment he had been anticipating for some weeks, and at last it had arrived.

'Thank you. I don't mind if I do. It's been a long day,' Senator Joe O'Brien said, seating himself in one of the comfortable leather chairs around the conference table.

Mason poured the senator a stiff scotch whisky, exactly as he liked it. He placed the drink in front of O'Brien, walked around the table and sat opposite.

'From what you said on the phone, it sounds like we're in business.'

O'Brien gratefully took a deep drink of the scotch, nodding.

'It was touch and go until today, despite what they've been saying in the papers. The White House has been fighting tooth and nail. Dick Latham has been telephoning their people non-stop, trying to buy them, even threatening them in some cases, so I hear. But it hasn't been enough, John. Too many of their people are thoroughly disgusted with Wade. They've decided it's time for him to go. I made a final check this evening. We're six or seven votes over the two-thirds we need. Wade is history.'

Mason nodded with satisfaction.

'In that case,' he said, 'I believe I'll join you.'

He returned to the wet bar and poured himself a generous bourbon over ice.

'I have arrangements in hand to make sure we have the attention of the press, just so they give the thing proper coverage,' he said contentedly on his way back to his seat. 'Just as we discussed. No attribution, of course. All from sources who spoke on condition of anonymity.'

O'Brien drank again. 'Good. I just hope to God we can keep George Stanley quiet until your people have had the chance to put everything in place.'

'I think we can. I had a long talk with him this morning. I think he understands how important it is. Joe, when do you expect the actual vote? On the Six O'Clock News they were saying tomorrow morning.'

'Afternoon, more like. We still have a couple of Wade die-hards to listen to, but I'm pretty sure it will be over by mid-afternoon.'

'And you're sure it's solid?'

'It's solid. I wouldn't have told you so otherwise.'

'Outstanding,' Mason replied. 'Then I'll try to stop worrying.'

O'Brien put down his drink.

'Well, I hope that's not premature,' he said slowly. 'Actually, John, I wanted to ask you something. Perhaps it's nothing, but it concerns me.'

'Of course, Senator. Shoot.'

O'Brien seemed hesitant.

'Do we have any… does your source know anything about all these riots that have been going on?'

Mason smiled.

'What's the matter, Joe? Getting nervous about your constituency? Look, it's a tempest in a tea cup. Once Wade is out of the picture, we will be waging war on Ellen Trevathan. Trying to find out how much she knew about all this, and when she knew it. That should be more than enough to take the pressure off you guys. By the time the next election comes around, they will have forgotten that Steve Wade ever existed. The public has a short attention-span, Joe. The timing of all this couldn't be better.'

The Senator put his hands on the table in front of him.

'John, I'm worried. When I left the Senate office building earlier this evening, there was a crowd starting to build outside. My driver had to go pretty slow to get through them. They were pretty rough-looking types, too. I felt threatened.'

Mason sipped his bourbon thoughtfully.

'How many?' he asked.

'Difficult to say. I didn't see any more than a hundred or so, I would guess, but I didn't go the whole way round the building.'

'What were they doing?'

'Just standing around, nothing in particular, you know. Looking at everyone coming out of the building, or going in.'

'What about the police?'

'There were a few on horseback, one or two cars, about the same as usual. That was it.'

'Well, if they thought there was a real problem, they would be out in force, I'm sure. Look, if you're worried about it, why don't you have your office call Chief Bryson tomorrow?'

'What can Bryson do about it? I didn't see anyone doing anything against the law. They're entitled to be there, as far as I know.'

'They can protect the legislature from harassment. Bryson could clear them out if he wanted to. Perhaps he doesn't think they have anything to do with the riots. Have your people keep an eye on them over the next day or two. Assuming they're still around. They will probably have gone home by the time you show up tomorrow.'

Senator O'Brien walked towards the wet bar to freshen his drink, without being asked.

'Well, that's the thing, actually, John. I don't believe they will be gone. I'm not sure why. But they just had the look of people who might be around for a while.'

He paused, before walking back to his seat. 'John, look, what I wanted to ask is, this has nothing to do with us, right?'

'No,' Mason said firmly. 'But I'll find out if my source knows anything.'

* * *

From the top of the Capitol steps, George Carlson and Dan Rogers kept track of the arrival of the crowd. Using mobile phones, they contacted colleagues stationed along the Mall and around the Monuments, with the object of covering as large an area as possible while attracting the minimum attention from the growing number of police officers. Incoming calls kept them advised about the influx of protesters into Washington from across the country. This was being closely coordinated, and the protesters were being ordered to spread out as far as possible along the various routes into the city. Soon, they would occupy almost all the space around the centers of the United States Government. It would be like the anti-war demonstrations of the 1960s, or the Million Man March. Although he despised those particular demonstrations, Carlson had no doubt of the power such a concentration of people could wield. Unlike those earlier demonstrators, his people would be armed. And it was almost too late for the authorities to stop them. The beauty of it was that they were not arriving in huge numbers, just a slow, steady trickle of people, spreading themselves out over a large area, almost too gradually for anyone to notice. That was the plan, anyway. He needed just a few more hours.

'Make sure you tell them to keep all weapons out of sight,' Carlson reminded Rogers. 'The police are on to us. There are more of the bastards every time I look.'

'Yeah? Well, they're too late, aren't they, George?' Rogers replied. 'We're here now. Enough of us.'

'Almost. And there'll be a lot more by tomorrow. Fox wants to make sure they're all in place by the time the vote is taken. We go into action as soon as it's announced.'

'And Fox is sure the vote is going to be tomorrow?'

'That's what he said.'

'Well, I just hope he's right, that's all. The last thing we need is a fight with the law before we're ready.'

'That's why we need our people to keep calm, Dan. Not do anything to cause trouble. Especially, no weapons on show.'

Rogers surveyed the crowd anxiously.

'It's not our people I'm worried about, George. We know they're disciplined. The same goes for units from the other groups, as far as I know. But a lot of these people...'

'May not be attached to the groups, yeah, I know,' Carlson said. 'It's a bigger crowd than I'd been expecting.'

'Who knows who the hell they are, where the hell they come from?' Rogers asked. 'They could be Fox's people, or they could just be trouble-makers, who thought it would be fun to bring the riots to Washington.'

'I know.'

'When is Fox going to call again?'

'Soon.'

Unseen by Carlson and Rogers, a man wearing a black, leather jacket standing nearby turned his back to them and made a telephone call of his own. He was a member of the FBI team which had followed the leaders of the Oregon compound all the way to Washington.

* * *

Frank Worley, Chief of Staff to Senator Joe O'Brien, spent several anxious minutes tossing his mobile phone nervously from hand to hand before he decided to make the call. He was sitting in the Senator's limousine outside the Wilson Foundation, waiting for his boss to return. They were due to have dinner with a group of lobbyists from back home in Minnesota to discuss the possibility of finding funding for some lucrative projects in the Senator's home State. Not Frank's idea of a fun evening, but it was all part of the job. Frank had sent the Senator's driver for coffee while he thought it over. He was troubled by the thought that what he was about to do might somehow be disloyal, but he had never been comfortable with what went on inside the Committee. Politics was one thing, but playing the kind of games he suspected the Committee of playing was another. Not that he would ever set foot in the Wilson Foundation himself. Even as Chief of Staff, he was excluded from meetings at that level. But he had access to enough information to put two and two together, and what he knew disturbed him. He was also disturbed by what he had seen as they had driven from the Russell Senate Office building. He suspected that Senator O'Brien was troubled too, though he had been typically guarded and had made only a passing comment about layabouts who had nothing better to do. Frank had to decide. The Senator or his driver would be back at any moment. He placed the call.

'Smith', a familiar voice said.

'Kelly... it's Frank.'

Kelly took the call during a period of silence in Ted Lazenby's office, one of several such periods when no one seemed to know what to say next. She was still profoundly shaken by what Raul Gutierrez had revealed about the Williamsburg Doctrine and, in her state of disorientation, Frank was the last person she was expecting to hear from. Her initial reaction was one of irritation.

'Frank...?'

'Yes, I need to talk, Kelly.'

Kelly shook her head. 'I can't talk now.'

'Kelly, please. It's important.'

She turned to Lazenby. 'I'm sorry. I'll be right back.'

She saw Jeff look inquiringly at her and walked quickly out of the room. She leaned against the wall.

'Frank, this isn't the time. I have too much going on…'

'Kelly, it has nothing to do with us. There's something I need to tell you.'

'About what?'

He hesitated. 'It's about the riots.'

Kelly's mind suddenly focused. 'What about the riots?'

'Look, I'm not sure, and I only have a minute or two. I'm waiting for Senator O'Brien, and I don't know when he will be back. But when we left the Russell Building tonight, it looked like there was a crowd beginning to build. Even the Senator was nervous about it. I think it has something to do with the impeachment. I thought you ought to know.'

Kelly bit her lip, uncertain of how much to say.

'Frank, look, I appreciate your calling, but…'

'Kelly, that's not all…'

He bit his lip. This was it. It was now or never.

'I think there's more to it than meets the eye. Have you heard of the Committee?'

'The Committee?'

'It's a kind of think-tank the Party has, very high-powered. They plan Party strategy. Senator O'Brien is a member. I think they may have something to do with it…'

'Something to do with what? I'm not following you, Frank. What are you trying to tell me?'

'I…'

'Frank?'

'He's coming back. I have to go.'

The phone went dead. Kelly closed her eyes. She stood lost in thought for a minute or two before rejoining the meeting in Ted Lazenby's office. Jeff raised his eyebrows. She smiled, and silently mouthed 'It's OK.' Then she turned towards Ellen Trevathan.

'Madam Vice President, have you ever heard of something called the Committee? It could be something to do with the other side, the people who are behind the impeachment?'

43

At dawn, Jeff Morris was handing out cups of coffee to the occupants of Ted Lazenby's office. Ellen Trevathan was lying on Lazenby's sofa, covered by a blanket, her head propped up on a cushion. Raúl Gutierrez and Kelly Smith were sprawled in armchairs. Lazenby himself alternated between sitting at his desk and walking slowly around his office. It had been some time since anyone had spoken. Slowly, the coffee began to revive them.

'They're going to miss me soon,' Ellen said, giving way to a yawn. 'I need to be going. The press will be camping outside my house today waiting for the big story to break. It's not going to look so good when I try sneaking in through the back door at this hour of the morning.'

'We'll get you home, Ma'am,' Kelly volunteered. 'They'll never know.'

'That's all right, Kelly. My agents should still be around somewhere. I'd better go wake them up.'

'No disrespect to your agents, Madam Vice President, but they'll find their own way home. We can do a better job of getting you in the back door.'

'She's right, Ellen,' Lazenby said. 'The press will spot your car and agents a mile away. Let us put you in something a little more nondescript, something to match your disguise.'

'I didn't know you guys kept a fleet of Yugos,' Ellen said.

'Only for special occasions,' Lazenby smiled.

'Sounds like a good idea,' the Vice President replied. 'Thanks.'

'Ellen, I know you have to get back, but we haven't reached a decision about what to do,' Gutierrez said. 'We can't do this again. Sneak in here in disguise, I mean. We need to have something worked out.'

Lazenby paused in his walking. 'My view hasn't changed. We have to get you out of Washington. It isn't safe. Once that vote comes down tomorrow, there's no telling what these people might get up to.'

The Vice President shook her head. 'I told you, Ted. I'm not going abroad.'

'Ellen, England is just a plane ride. We have friends there. The Prime Minister has never cared for Wade, and he's certainly not about to help him stage a coup. You'll get a warm welcome, and you'll be safe. In the meanwhile, we can do what we can to take care of things here without having to worry about you. Time is on our side. Wade has to go eventually. We wait it out, then we bring you back.'

Ellen sat up, holding the blanket around her shoulders. 'I'm not going abroad.'

'Ellen...'

'Ted, if Wade is impeached a few hours from now, I become the President of the United States. Do you understand that? I become the Commander-in-Chief, for God's sake. I can't run away.'

'It's not running away. It's a tactical retreat.'

'Call it whatever you want. What kind of message would that send to the people? That I hide in England while you guys fight for me? That I'm a President in exile? No. I can't do that. I won't do it. You can't protect me like that.'

Lazenby shook his head and glanced towards the Air Force Chief.

'She's right, Ted,' Gutierrez said quietly. 'And she would be too far away to take decisions, military or otherwise. It wouldn't work.'

Lazenby sat down at this desk.

'All right, then. How would you feel about staying in the States, but setting up a temporary government outside Washington?' he asked.

'Where outside Washington?'

'We'll get to that. But, as a matter of principle? If you could establish a temporary base of operations somewhere else? Somewhere those loyal to you could defend? Just until the problem in Washington is resolved?'

The Vice President hesitated.

'Ellen,' Lazenby continued, leaning towards her over his desk, 'you're not the only person who's in danger here. Anyone who supports you, anyone who believes enough in the Constitution to stand up to Wade, is a potential target. You said it yourself. You're going to be the President. So you need to act like the President. You need to put together a functioning administration which has some legitimacy. You need to be able to gather the necessary people around you, and you owe it to them to offer them protection. What about the judges, for example? The

Courts may be crucial in convincing the people of the legitimacy of your Presidency.'

Ellen stood, still clutching the blanket around her.

'If I did that, it could only be for a very short time. Just enough to let the crisis die down and force Wade out. It still seems an awful lot like running away. Besides, there would be no way to run the government like that on a long-term basis. I couldn't take enough people with me. The country would fall to pieces.'

'I agree,' Lazenby said. 'It would be a short-term measure. But, in my opinion, we need to get you out, and we need to do it the moment Wade is impeached.'

The Vice President looked across at General Gutierrez.

'Raul?'

He nodded.

'I can go along with that. I can get you anywhere you need to go. The arrangements can be in place by this afternoon. Ted is right. You do need to protect yourself and those around you. Frankly, I'm more worried about Hessler and McGarry than Wade. I honestly don't know how far they might go, and I'm not sure I want to find out.'

'Well, OK, let's assume you're right,' Ellen said. 'Where would I go, for God's sake? I can't just pick some city, drop in at the local airport, and say, 'Hi, I'm your new President. I'd like to stay over for a few days and run the country. Can you fix me up with somewhere to do it?' And I don't think it ought to be Richmond, Virginia, do you? That would give the wrong message altogether.'

The others smiled through their tiredness.

'How would you feel about Houston?' Lazenby asked, after a pause.

Ellen turned her head to look at him. 'Why Houston?'

Lazenby stood again. 'A close friend of mine from Princeton is a law school dean there. I went down there and spoke at their graduation last year. Ken is a very big fan of yours.'

'Well, that's very nice, Ted, but I don't see…'

'Wait, let me finish. The school is called South Texas College of Law. They have a great building that takes up an entire block of downtown Houston. It's the best-equipped law school I've ever seen. They have state-of-the-art technology. They could have the building ready for you to occupy in a matter of hours. There's a parking lot right next to the building, where you could land a chopper if you had to. The Court could even sit in the moot courtroom. And there's a Four Seasons Hotel two blocks away, for the residential side. Most importantly, Ken would do it if I asked. Without hesitation. He's a constitutional law specialist. All I have to do is pick up the phone.'

Ellen sighed and looked up at the ceiling.

'How would you feel about Houston from a military point of view, Raul?' Lazenby asked.

'Houston has good air accessibility, military and civilian,' Gutierrez replied. 'I like that. And it's not too far away. It's within reasonable range of Washington, and it's central. We could move in enough forces to defend the city within a day or two.'

'General, forgive me if I'm speaking out of turn,' Jeff broke in. 'Obviously, I'm no expert on these matters. But isn't Houston a bit close to the ocean? If we can't rely on the Navy, aren't we offering the opposition an easy target?'

Gutierrez nodded.

'You're right, Jeff. But if any one of the branches goes entirely against us, we're in a pretty hopeless situation, wherever we decide to go. What I believe, and what we have to hope for, is that all the branches will do no worse than split. If there's a reasonable balance of power, then I believe the Director is correct. I believe that most military officers will support Ellen once they have time to think about it, whatever some of their commanders may be telling them. Time is on our side. All we have to do is hold firm, and Houston seems like a pretty good place to do that.'

'So, you agree with Ted?' Ellen asked.

'It seems the wisest course to me,' Gutierrez replied.

'All right,' Ellen said. 'I'll leave as soon as it becomes clear that I need to.'

'That time has already arrived,' Lazenby said. 'You should be in Houston by the time the vote is announced.'

'Agreed,' Raul Gutierrez said.

'Oh, come on, Ted. Look, I have no legitimate reason to be in Houston today. What happens if Wade isn't impeached?'

'That's academic.'

'OK. What happens if he is impeached and goes quietly? Why am I in Houston when all this is happening? Shouldn't I be in Washington waiting to take over?'

Lazenby shrugged.

'Ellen, if that ends up being the only problem we have out of all this,

I'll be doing an Irish jig all over the office. If we need to invent a story for you being in Houston, we'll do it. No one's going to care. Besides, I think we all know Wade isn't going to go quietly.'

'I think he might,' Ellen said.

'What about the Williamsburg Doctrine?' Gutierrez asked. 'What about the crowds of people camping out around the Capitol? It doesn't look to me like he's going quietly.'

The Vice President shook her head.

'It's one thing to fantasize in the privacy of the White House or the Pentagon, Raul. It's another thing to take the fantasy on to the streets or national television and ask people to go along with it. It's so blatantly illegal. How can they think they would get away with it?'

She paused.

'I think if I could get Steve alone for half an hour, I could talk him out of it. I think perhaps that's what I should be trying to do.'

Lazenby and Gutierrez shook their heads emphatically.

'Forget it,' Gutierrez said.

'Why not, Raul? He trusts me. He's always listened to me.'

'Not this time,' Gutierrez replied.

'Ellen, have you forgotten that you already tried to see him, and you couldn't get past his secretary?' Lazenby asked. 'He's not going to see you. And even if he did, it's gone way too far for him to pull back now. Later today, you will be the President of the United States. The time to act is now.'

They were interrupted by a knock on the door. Lazenby's secretary opened it and entered. She stopped abruptly, momentarily taken aback, but then, as a veteran of many unusual situations, made an instant and complete recovery.

'I'm sorry, Director. I just got in. I had no idea you were already here. Good morning, Madam Vice President.'

'Good morning, Rose,' Ellen smiled.

'I'm not *already* here, Rose,' Lazenby said. 'I'm *still* here.'

'Yes, Director. Just so I know, is anything I'm seeing here happening?'

'No.'

'All right. Director, I thought you ought to know the breakfast television shows are saying the crowds around the Capitol got a lot bigger overnight, and there are reports that a lot of them may have weapons.'

Everyone in the room was suddenly more awake.

'What kind of weapons?' Lazenby asked.

'They're not sure. One reporter says she saw handguns. And several of our agents monitoring the situation there called in to say the same thing.'

'Jesus Christ.'

'Yes, Sir. The Chief of Police is now saying the situation is out of his control. I'm having it taped for you.'

Kelly bit her lip. 'Frank was right,' she said.

'Wonderful,' Lazenby said. 'Why in the hell didn't Bryson call us? Why in the hell didn't our agents call sooner?'

'I don't know, Sir. Anything else I can do? Do you need coffee?'

'No, thank you. We're about through. But I need Dean Ken Hunt's home telephone number in Houston.'

'Right away, Director,' Rose said, on her way out of the office.

'Kelly,' Lazenby said as soon as she had left, 'get Ellen out of here and into a Yugo. Have a second Yugo follow you. And stay well out of range of the Capitol. I'm not sure exactly how you're going to do that, but try.'

'Yes, Sir,' Kelly said, getting to her feet and stretching.

'Wait one moment, Kelly,' Ellen said. 'Ted, Raul, would you both please face me and raise your right hands?'

Lazenby and Gutierrez looked at each other.

'Can we know why?' Lazenby asked.

Ellen smiled.

'If I'm going to be President in exile, I'm going to need some help in place right away, and there may not be time to do this later. So if you wouldn't mind…'

Both men faced the Vice President with their right hands raised.

'Mr. Lazenby, on a provisional basis, and assuming it becomes necessary, will you promise faithfully to execute the office of Vice President of the United States, and General Gutierrez, will you on a similar basis promise faithfully to execute the office of Secretary of Defense of the United States, and will you both promise to uphold the Constitution of the United States, so help you God?'

'Ellen,' Lazenby asked quietly, 'doesn't the Senate have something to say about this?'

'Yes,' Ellen Trevathan replied. 'And I'll ask them the first chance I get. Right now, we have other things to do. So, I need to know. Are you with me or not?'

44

AFTER HE AND Kelly had escorted Ellen Trevathan safely back to her residence, Raul Gutierrez asked Kelly to drop him off, still in disguise, at his office. He changed back into uniform, ordered vast quantities of strong black coffee and a street map of Houston, and went to work. Air transport for Ellen was his first priority. He commandeered an executive jet aircraft for a flight from Andrews Air Force Base to Ellington Field, and ordered six fighters to stand by for escort duty. Soon afterwards, he placed Andrews, Ellington Field, and other strategically important air force bases under heavy guard, and scrambled every available fighter to give Houston round-the-clock air protection. Next, Gutierrez made unobtrusive preparations to mobilize all Air Force Reservists for active duty. Finally, he came to the most difficult part of the operation. He placed a call on a top-secret encrypted telephone line to his only potential ally.

'I was wondering when you'd call,' General Terrell said. His voice sounded tense.

'It's now or never, Bill,' Gutierrez replied. 'All hell is going to break loose this afternoon. I need to know for sure which side you're on.'

Gutierrez heard the Army Chief of Staff sigh into the phone.

'I don't know what to do, Raul. I don't like what's going on any more than you do. But the Williamsburg Doctrine has been around for a long time. You and I didn't have anything to do with it, but since it is in place, we have to assume there was a good reason for it. And if two of our colleagues feel it should be invoked…'

'The Williamsburg Doctrine goes against the Constitution, Bill. You know that as well as I do.'

'Look, Raul, I'm not a lawyer, and…'

'Bullshit,' Gutierrez interrupted. 'You don't need to be a lawyer to know that the Constitution is about to be torn to shreds, any more than you need to be a lawyer to know you don't let your soldiers butcher civilians in time of war. All you have to be to know those things is a professional soldier, which is what you are.'

There was silence for some time.

'Bill,' Gutierrez continued, 'I'm going to tell you something that I'd like you to keep to yourself. I can't control what you do with it, but I'm making the request. OK?'

'OK,' Terrell replied.

'Yesterday afternoon, my office received credible information that Ellen Trevathan's life would not be safe after the vote.'

'Oh, for God's sake…,' Terrell broke in. 'They wouldn't…'

'No, listen to me. Last night I got hold of Ellen and two Secret Service Agents, and we got into disguise, looking like goddamned street people, and we went to see Ted Lazenby at the Hoover Building. He agreed with my assessment of the situation. He and I have taken steps to make sure she's safe. You need to know what you are getting yourself involved in if you side with Hessler and McGarry.'

'I would never have agreed to anything like that,' Terrell said quietly.

'I know that, Bill. That's why you have to help me here. Look, I remember what you said at that meeting we had with Latham. You were with me then. I need you to be with me now that the chips are down. You know I'm right.'

There was a long silence as Terrell weighed his options. Gutierrez closed his eyes.

'What do you want me to do?' Terrell asked finally.

'Thank you,' Gutierrez replied, the relief evident in his voice. 'First, I want you to put a blockade around Houston. I want you…'

'Houston? Why Houston?'

'That's down to Ted Lazenby. I'll explain as soon as I can. I need you to trust me on this for now.'

'OK.'

'I want all the protection you can give. I've already arranged air support. I want check points on every freeway and every road leading into the city, including every point where those roads intersect with the ring roads. I want a strong presence downtown, tanks, personnel carriers, whatever you have, and I want every building, except for two, within ten square blocks of San Jacinto and Clay Streets evacuated. The police chief is on standby to help you with that.'

'Slow down, Raul. San Jacinto and Clay. OK. What are the two exceptions?'

'South Texas College of Law and the Four Seasons Hotel.'

'OK.'

'And I want you to have all forces under your command stand by for alert, including mobilizing all reservists for active duty.'

Terrell hesitated. 'Raul, that kind of decision needs an order from the President. At the very least, I'd need something from the Secretary of Defense.'

'The Secretary of Defense is still in Russia,' Gutierrez said. 'I tried to contact him. Wade has ordered him to stay there until sent for.'

'Jesus Christ.'

'Later today, President Trevathan and her new Secretary of Defense will ratify every action you take. You have my word on that.'

'Who is the new Secretary of Defense?'

'Later. Will you do what I've asked?'

'I'm on it,' Terrell replied.

'We'll need to be in constant contact. I suggest we adopt war procedure now and continue until further notice.'

'Agreed,' Terrell said, before hanging up.

Gutierrez looked at his watch and wondered when the second American Civil War would begin.

* * *

During the hurried drive from FBI Headquarters to Andrews Air Force Base, Lazenby took the only chance he had to brief Kelly on what he expected of her.

'When you get to Houston, there will be transport waiting. Take Ellen straight to the law school. Ken Hunt has already closed the place to students and faculty, and none of his people will be there, except for a few administrators, secretaries, librarians, computer technology personnel, catering staff, the kind of people you'll need anyway. Our field office has already taken over security inside the building. You should find they've installed additional phone lines and a bunch of computers. There will be a strong military presence outside, covering all of downtown, so I don't think you'll have any problems. Everybody is staying at the Four Seasons, which is two blocks away. They've emptied about half the hotel already, and you can have as many more floors as you need there. Ellen has to get to work right away, and she's going to need as many members of the government as we can get to join her. You're in charge of making it possible for them to work, but delegate as much as you can.'

291

'Who's coming with us?' Kelly asked.

'Today, four Supreme Court Justices, the Head of the Postal Service, and the Chairman of the Federal Reserve. Tomorrow, we should have the remaining members of the Court, except for the Chief, a lot of senior military officers, the Director of the CIA, and most of the House committee chairs. That should be enough to hold things for a few days.'

Lazenby looked out of the car window.

'Nothing we can do about the Senate or the Chief Justice for now. They're stuck in the Capitol until after the vote.'

As Kelly stepped out of the car to walk to the hangar where the aircraft waited, Lazenby called her back.

'Oh, Kelly, there are two other things.'

'What?'

'In this envelope there are numbers to contact Raul Gutierrez and me at any time. We may have to go underground, so don't share them with anyone except Ellen and Jeff.'

'OK. What's the second thing?'

'I have to function as Vice President for a while. You'll take over as acting director in my absence.'

Leaving Kelly open-mouthed and speechless, Lazenby drove away. Kelly had never suffered from air sickness in her life, but spent the entire flight fighting back the urge to throw up. Ellen, on the other hand, seemed composed and, sensing Kelly's stress, made no demands on her. The Vice President took charge of the cabin crew, and spoke reassuringly to the other officials on board the aircraft, who were as worried about the families they had left behind as they were anxious about what lay ahead. Each of them had been whisked from home with no preparation and with little information, except that a national emergency was expected, during which it was important that they continue their official functions. Kelly knew that she should be playing some part in helping them cope, but she was overwhelmed. The fact that there was nothing she could do during the flight made the situation worse. She felt nothing but relief when the aircraft touched down, and she had no alternative but to take command of the operation.

On Ted Lazenby's instructions, a convoy of black limousines, accompanied by every available FBI field agent, was waiting at Ellington Field to drive the party into Houston. Houston's Mayor and Police Chief contributed a procession of police motorcycle outriders, which accompanied the group through a succession of city streets which had been closed off to traffic in advance of its arrival. The convoy attracted little attention. Things were quiet in town. Most people were in their offices and homes, waiting for the Senate's vote and Steve Wade's television address to the nation.

By the time the party arrived at South Texas College of Law, the Dean's suite on the second floor had already been prepared for the Vice President's use. The moot court room and the law library had been reserved for the use of the Supreme Court. Several large screen televisions had been installed in the student lounge, and CNN could already be heard reporting on the last phase of the Senate impeachment proceedings. Armed agents were patrolling the building. The Four Seasons had sent a large vase of flowers and a tray of fruit, with a note welcoming the Vice President to her exclusive floor of the hotel. Ellen explained the possible developments of the next several hours to Dean Ken Hunt, and asked him to serve as interim Attorney-General. Hunt swallowed hard, and asked if he could call his wife to tell her he would be late getting home.

Late in the afternoon, they gathered in the student lounge to watch the story unfolding in Washington. CNN's coverage alternated between the proceedings in the Senate Chamber and the increasingly menacing scene outside. A nervous female reporter was speaking from the main entrance to the Capitol, which was guarded by a number of police officers armed with sub-machine guns.

'We're expecting the vote to be taken within the next hour or two,' she said. 'The crowds have now spilled over from the area outside the Capitol to the surrounding streets, and they appear to be filling up the Mall. It's been many years since demonstrations on this scale have been seen in Washington. But there is no sign that the Senate has been intimidated. In fact, according to one chief aide, it has made them even more determined to press ahead with the vote, which, it now seems inevitable, will go against President Wade. There is one new development. Marines are taking up positions around the Capitol – you may be able to see some of them as our camera scans the area – and they are spreading out, surrounding the building. They are heavily armed, and we have seen several armored vehicles in the area. We're trying to get more information about this development but, so far, no one is saying anything about it officially. And we still have no comment from the White House. Apparently, they're waiting to see what happens. But we're still expecting the President to address the nation as soon as the result of the vote has been announced.'

The reporter placed a finger on the tiny microphone inside her ear.

'I'm being told that the Washington Police are advising us to move to a safer distance from the building, which we are just about to do. It looks like we have a very tense situation developing here, and no one I've spoken to has any idea what might happen next.'

45

AGENTS LINDA SAMUELS and Gary Mills flanked President Steve Wade, as he walked unhurriedly from the Oval Office to the situation room. The White House was eerily quiet. Most of the civilian staff were gone, told to stay home but remain available by phone until further notice. A team of Marine Corps specialists was working with a minimum of conversation in offices throughout the building. The atmosphere in the situation room mirrored the uneasy quiet of the rest of the White House. In one corner, a large screen television was tuned to CNN, the sound muted. On one side of the room, flanking the large conference table, several junior officers were manning computers, whose screens flashed images of the United States on to the opposite wall. Key military installations were indicated by blinking lights. Clocks on the wall above recorded the time in all the time zones around the world. Already seated around the conference table were the Marine Commandant, General Hessler, Admiral McGarry of the Navy, and the Attorney-General, Dick Latham, together with a number of lower-ranking Marine and Navy officers and civilian intelligence personnel. Martha Graylor sat, silent and alone, in a chair in a corner of the room. The occupants stood as the President entered. Taking his seat at the head of the table, Steve Wade gestured to them to sit.

'I call this session of my Emergency Council to order,' the President announced. 'It appears we have very little time. My information is that we may have less than two hours, three tops, before the Senate takes this ill-considered vote. General Hessler, your report, please.'

Hessler glanced down briefly at the notes in the folder before him on the table.

'Mr. President, I have dispatched two units to the Capitol. Their commanding officers have instructions to make sure that the public understand that the military presence is there to protect them in the exercise of their rights, and is not hostile. Many of those present are armed, and we have no information as to whether or not they are subject to disciplined leadership. Things could get nasty if they get out of control. The Washington Police have been advised not to interfere. First reports are that the units are achieving their objectives.'

'Good,' Wade said. 'And they will ensure that no one is allowed in or out of the Capitol once the vote has been taken?'

'Yes, Sir. The Senate isn't going anywhere.'

'What about response around the country?'

Hessler hesitated.

'The Marine Corps has a tradition of unquestioning obedience to orders, Mr. President. But there has been a great deal of anxiety, especially among the more junior line officers. We may lose many units. But I don't think that matters at this point. I must emphasize that we have a limited objective here, namely, to secure the White House and the Capitol until the crisis is resolved. We have enough men in place to accomplish that objective. But I must repeat the advice I have given before, that the faster we can resolve this crisis the better.'

'I understand, General,' Wade said. 'I don't think that will be a problem once the senators appreciate their situation. Our strategy is simple. The show of support we have in place around the Capitol is intended to change the minds of seven senators. That's all we need to reduce the majority to less than two thirds. We will give them time for reflection, for reason to prevail, and a new vote will be taken, one that goes the right way. I'm quite confident that will happen. The people have decided to make their voice heard.'

'I sincerely hope so, Mr. President,' Hessler said.

'Admiral McGarry, what about the Navy?'

'Not so good, Mr. President. We're pretty much split down the middle right now, but once the vote is taken, I'm afraid I may not be able to hold the line. Naval commanders can be a pretty independent bunch, and…'

'I'm not interested in the psychology of naval commanders, Admiral,' Wade almost hissed, as Hessler muttered an obscenity under his breath. 'I don't have time. What's going on?'

McGarry shrugged.

'With regard to our surface ships, we've lost the fleets almost entirely, Mr. President, in the Atlantic, the Pacific and the Med,' he replied in a subdued tone. 'The ships that are at sea are on their way back home at full speed. The aircraft carrier *Admiral Kelso* pulled out of Norfolk this morning, three days ahead of schedule, without telling anyone, and we haven't heard from it since. Maybe they're just going to wait it out, but maybe they're ready to do more than that. Either way, it's not good.'

'So, what you're saying is, you don't have any damn control at all over your own Service,' Hessler interrupted. 'What kind of outfit are you running, Admiral?'

'One that calls for a certain degree of intelligent thought,' McGarry shot back.

'All right, that's enough,' Wade intervened. 'We don't have time for squabbling. Let's get to what really matters, Admiral. What about the nuclear subs?'

'We have the subs,' McGarry said. 'At least for now. They operate on a different protocol. As long as you hold the keys to the nuclear codes, they will not accept orders from anyone else. Obviously, that's only going to last for so long. Once the word gets out about the vote, they may decide their only option is to head back to base.'

McGarry leaned forward on the table and looked nervously around the room.

'Of course, one possibility would be to make sure the word doesn't get to them for a while,' he suggested tentatively.

'You mean, we could insulate them from that information?' Wade asked.

'We could, Mr. President,' McGarry replied. 'A submarine is an isolated environment. They are cut off from the rest of the world in a way surface ships are not. Signals are strictly controlled. Even so, we could only hold them for a limited time. We could buy more time by planting some positive disinformation.'

'You mean, tell them the vote went in my favor?'

'It's a possibility,' McGarry replied.

Wade took a deep breath. 'Let's do it. Has anyone heard from Terrell?'

'He's ratted on us,' Hessler snarled. 'Same with Gutierrez, although we expected that.'

There was a silence around the table.

'Sounds like we're out-gunned,' Wade observed somberly.

'In some ways,' Hessler replied. 'But in two decisive respects we have the advantage.'

Wade looked up.

'First, we control Washington. We're surrounding the Capitol, and we're occupying the White House. The opposition isn't going to risk the kind of damage it would take to dislodge us.'

'I wouldn't be so sure of that,' the President said quietly.

'If they did,' Hessler said, 'it would only be as a last resort. It would take them time just to position themselves for the attempt and, meanwhile, the whole world will be urging restraint, which is what the diplomats like to call not having the balls to take decisive action. By that time, the situation will have resolved itself, one way or the other. Assuming everything goes well, we don't have to worry about it. If not, it gives us a chip to bargain with.'

'Besides,' McGarry said. 'We're dealing with Ellen Trevathan. She's a pacifist. She's not going to open fire on us. Not until every other possible approach has failed.'

'As I said,' Steve Wade replied, 'I wouldn't be so sure of that. What's the second thing?'

'We're in control of the nukes,' Hessler said, with a grim smile. 'You have sole charge of the codes, Mr. President. There's nothing the opposition can do about that.'

Every eye around the room was on Hessler.

'I hope, General,' Dick Latham said, his face white and strained, 'that you are not suggesting the President would use a nuclear weapon within the United States, against his own people. I can't believe you would even say it out loud.'

Hessler returned Latham's look with a contemptuous sneer.

'I'll put your lack of sophistication down to your lack of military training, Mr. Attorney-General,' he replied tersely. 'The point is not that the President would order the use of a nuclear weapon. The point is that he could. It's something we can use to keep the other side off balance. They have to make the calculation. I would remind everyone present that we're not planning a prolonged campaign here. We only need a very short-term tactical advantage, just long enough to allow the President to resolve the political situation.'

Wade looked around the room for Martha.

'What's the word on the Vice President?' he asked.

'I've confirmed that the Vice President has established Headquarters in Houston, at a law school, Mr. President, as we were told earlier,' Martha replied, her voice barely audible. 'We're not entirely sure who is with her. We know one or two members of the Court, a few

Congressmen, and her personal Detail, obviously.'

'Gutierrez or Terrell?'

'We don't think so, Mr. President. Word is they're still in Washington, though we're not sure exactly where.'

'What about Lazenby?'

'Same goes for the Director, Mr. President. He's probably still in town, but we're not completely sure.'

Wade looked at his watch.

'General Hessler, can't we prevent these people from going to Houston to become Knights of the Round Table at the Vice President's Camelot?'

'Prevent travel? No, Mr. President,' Hessler replied at once. 'We cannot.'

'But…'

'We don't have the resources. The only way would be to detain them, and we don't have the man-power to do that. Besides, if part of the idea is to avoid adverse publicity, that would be worse than letting them go.'

'I hardly think publicity is an issue in this situation,' Latham said.

'Be that as it may, as I said before, Mr. President, this is a short-term operation. I recommend we use our resources only for necessities, such as remaining in control in Washington. That's all that matters. Let them play whatever games they want in Houston. Who cares?'

The President nodded.

'Martha, are we all ready to go with the broadcast?'

'Yes, Sir, all set.'

'Good. Then let's turn up the volume on the TV and see if the Senate has got the message yet.'

'Mr. President …'

'Yes?'

'You should know that… that the Vice President is planning her own broadcast immediately following your address.'

Wade nodded.

'Yes, I'm sure she is,' he replied. 'What a field day for the press!'

He stood and faced the entire room.

'I want to say one other thing. If anyone wants to leave, if anyone feels they cannot be part of what we're doing here, I understand. I can't force anyone to get involved. But if you want to leave, do it now. An hour or two from now, I may not be able to allow it. All I require is that you keep the confidentiality of what has been said in this room. If you agree to that, you are free to go, with my thanks for everything you have done up to now. If you remain, then I must demand your absolute loyalty. Don't be afraid to speak up. Does anyone want out?'

The President's eyes fell on Linda Samuels and Gary Mills.

'What about you, Agent Samuels? Agent Mills? Will you continue to protect me?'

Linda stood. For a moment, she had difficulty in focusing her eyes. She was aware of the gaze of everyone in the room.

'You're the President, Sir. We will do our duty by you.'

'Thank you,' Steve Wade said.

* * *

When the call came, Carlson was standing as close as he could get to the top of the Capitol steps, where a line of heavily-armed Marines stood shoulder-to-shoulder, holding the crowd at bay. On hearing his mobile phone ring, Carlson turned his back on the Marines and made a space for himself to answer in the midst of the people standing around him.

'This is Carlson,' he said, holding the receiver as close as possible to his mouth and pulling the top of his coat down over it.

'Carlson, this is Fox,' the voice said.

Instantly, Carlson's mind came to attention.

'I heard you spent your vacation in France?'

'No, I prefer Italy.'

'Acknowledged. Thank you, Fox.'

'Is everything under control?'

'That's affirmative, Fox,' Carlson replied. 'Is everything under control at your end?'

'Everything's going according to plan.'

'Good.'

'Make sure you stay in contact. Things are going to move very quickly from now on.'

'Roger that, Fox.'

The line went dead.

'Good news?' Rogers asked.

'Good news,' Carlson replied. 'We're almost there.'

46

STAGE FRIGHT WAS a new experience for Ed Monahan. Before today, he had never been able to understand why some lawyers felt nervous before going into court. For Monahan, appearing in front of a judge or jury was as natural as taking a shower in the morning. Like all good trial lawyers, he experienced a mild rush as he stood to cross-examine a witness or make a closing argument, but it had never been a problem. On the contrary, he had learned to value the added sharpness of mind it gave him in his mental battles with witnesses, judges, and opposing counsel. Even during the impeachment he had felt nothing more than the usual rush. But then again, there was little for him to do, except make a few objections which the Chief Justice overruled with the kind of summary verbal blow to the head for which he was famous. Opening statements were brief and to the point. The House manager's counsel was good. Her opening statement gave away little information about the case she intended to present, so Monahan decided to reserve the substance of his defense for his closing argument. There were no witnesses. The Senate agreed with the Prosecution that they could rely on the record developed by the House Intelligence Committee. Monahan decided not to call witnesses for the defense, because he saw nothing they could usefully say. The President's only hope was that the Senate would find the evidence against him to be insufficient. And now, it was Monahan's job to persuade them of that. Monahan had won one battle. He had persuaded the Chief Justice that closing arguments should be given after the senators had made whatever statements they wished to make, rather than before. At least, this way, he did not have to worry about sixty-seven or more speeches to which he had no right of reply. Even so, what they said left him in no doubt that, if the President were to have any hope at all, this would have to be the best closing argument of his career. Like everyone else in the Senate Chamber, he was aware of the large and vocal crowd and the Marines outside the building, and he could only guess at the effect that was having on his audience. The closing argument for the House was effective. Counsel sounded confident, apparently feeling that she was pushing on an open door. Now, it was his turn, the eyes of the entire world were on him in real time and, for the first time in his life, Ed Monahan had stage fright.

'You may proceed, Mr. Monahan,' the Chief Justice was saying.

Monahan stood, took a sip of water, and walked slowly to the podium. He had no notes with him. Dispensing with notes during closing arguments was a trick he had learned early in his career. It impressed juries, and demonstrated his command of the case. He considered notes to be the equivalent of a comfort blanket anyway, a diversion for the hands, a prop to reassure the speaker that there was somewhere to turn to if his mind suddenly went blank. He had never understood how a lawyer could try a case for several days and still need notes to make his closing argument. At least, not until now. But, nervous as he was, he forced himself to rely on the techniques which had brought him so far in his career. Standing at the podium, he cleared his throat, and tried to ignore the stares focused on him, the lights shining in his eyes, and the expectant silence which pervaded the Chamber.

'Thank you, Your Honor. May it please you, Mr. Chief Justice, members of the Senate, distinguished Counsel. If you will indulge me for a moment, I must begin by saying what an honor it is for me to have represented President Wade during these proceedings. Steve Wade has served his country well during a career devoted to public service. As a prosecutor, state legislator, governor, and finally as President of the United States for two terms, he has given outstanding leadership and service. And I believe this alone should give us all pause, before we rush to judgment and condemn him in these highly political proceedings. We should be surprised, and we should be loath to believe, that a man with Steve Wade's record of public service could have done the things of which he stands accused. We should also remember that this is not a trial in the sense that we use that term in the law courts. It is a political proceeding, initiated by the President's opponents, and intended to bring about a political result. The crime of which he is accused is vague and ill-defined, and I submit to you that you should not even consider taking a decision as grave as removing from office the President of the United States without the clearest possible evidence. That evidence is wholly lacking.'

Monahan surveyed the Chamber. They were listening. His nervousness began to subside.

'The House has chosen not to present evidence from witnesses. Why – you may ask? What did they have to fear? Was it, perhaps, that they preferred not to expose the evidence to the test of cross-examination, which a distinguished legal writer many years ago called 'the greatest engine ever invented for the discovery of truth'? Whatever their motives, they chose to rely on the record of legislative proceedings in which there was no opportunity for the President to challenge what was said. The Senate agreed to that course of action. But I must point out again that now you will not have the opportunity to hear that evidence challenged, and perhaps to discover its weaknesses and inconsistencies. And I, on behalf of the President, can only do my best to expose its flaws as they appear from the record developed by the House Intelligence Committee. You don't have to look too closely to see some of these flaws. Take Harold Jeffers, for example. A man who, on his own admission, accepted three hundred dollars as a bribe not to talk about what he claims he saw in that hotel room in Chicago. But he did talk about it, didn't he? At some length. You may ask yourselves, why? Was it out of a sense of public duty? Or was it that someone, perhaps one of the President's enemies, offered him another bribe, perhaps more than three hundred dollars, to come forward with his story? We will never know, and the reason we will never know is because the House lacked the confidence to expose him to cross-examination. And Jeffers is just one example. So I submit that you must look very carefully at the evidence, very carefully indeed. What exactly does the evidence show?

'You heard that the President had an affair with a woman called Lucia Benoni, and that he lied about it. Members of the Senate, I hope we can all agree that President Wade was not the first man in public life to lie about an affair, and I seriously doubt that he will be the last.'

This was greeted with some chuckles and whispered conversations around the floor, which Monahan took to be a good sign.

'However much we may disapprove of that conduct, and let me make it clear that I do not attempt to defend it, I hope you would accept that it is not a ground for impeachment. What else does the evidence prove? Miss Benoni was also the lover of a man called Hamid Marfrela. Marfrela was a Lebanese diplomat, who was in contact with certain white supremacist groups in Oregon. There is evidence that he and some of his friends set up a company, Middle and Near East Holdings, Incorporated.

This company contributed money to an organization called the Western States Geophysical Research Institute, and that organization made contributions to the President's party. What's so remarkable about that? Nothing. Because everything I have just described to you was legal. It violated no law, no code of conduct. In fact, there is no credible evidence that the President even knew that it was going on. But the House uses those facts to build a fantasy of epic proportions. Using inference on inference, supposition on supposition, they have created an illusion that there was something sinister going on, that the President was accepting inducements to do something nameless, which they can't really even describe to you, but which, in some undefined manner, affected our national security. The question you must consider is whether there is any evidence at all to support this fantasy, or whether it is merely wishful thinking on the part of the President's enemies. I believe that, when you have asked that question, the answer is clear. This impeachment is a house built on sand, a house without foundation. Has any evidence been presented that our national security has in fact suffered? No. Has any evidence been presented to show that the President ever met, ever talked to Hamid Marfrela? No. Has any evidence been presented that he ever communicated with white supremacists? No. The whole case is speculation. You could not convict a shoplifter on such evidence in any court in the United States, let alone impeach the President.

'Now, although it is not my intention to detain you for long, I must go through certain of the evidence relied on by Counsel for the House, and deal with some of the arguments she made.'

For another hour, Monahan pulled out all the stops, picking apart every piece of evidence and every argument against the President. His stage fright was now forgotten. He was in full flow. The Senate listened attentively to every word. Finally, he was ready to close.

'And so, I submit to you that the evidence is wholly insufficient, and that it is your duty to reject the Article of Impeachment brought against President Wade. In conclusion, let me just say this. There is more at stake here than the future of Steve Wade, the career of one man. This isn't just an attack on the President. It's an attack on the Presidency. What is at stake today is nothing less than the integrity of our nation's institutions of government. Politicians may rejoice in the opportunity to heap ruin on an opponent, regardless of the cost to America. But it takes a statesman, or a stateswoman, to put Country before Party, to put the Presidency before partisan opportunism. Today, I'm asking you to be statesmen and stateswomen. I'm asking you to put America first, to safeguard the Presidency against partisan political attack. Thank you.'

Monahan made no immediate move to leave the podium. Don't be in a hurry, his instinct told him. Leave slowly and with confidence. As he was about to move, he saw the Senate Minority Leader get to his feet. Monahan stayed in place.

'Mr. Chief Justice, my colleague, Senator O'Brien, asks if it would be in order for him to put one or two questions to Counsel for the President?'

The Chief Justice drew himself up in his chair. 'Senator, I ruled that Counsel would make closing arguments after each senator had his or her say.'

'I understand that, Your Honor, but...'

Monahan knew he had no choice. He had hoped to have the decisive last word, but he could hardly deny the senators the chance to ask a question. He would have to turn it into an opportunity to make points of his own.

'Mr. Chief Justice,' he said, as calmly as he could, 'if the members of the Senate have questions and time remains, I would be glad to answer.'

The Chief Justice nodded.

'Very well. You may proceed.'

'Mr. Chief Justice,' the Minority Leader said, 'I yield to my colleague, Senator O'Brien.'

'Thank you, Senator,' O'Brien said, getting to his feet. He was holding a small notepad at which he was peering through his reading glasses. 'Mr. Monahan, the Senate is grateful to you for your excellent presentation on the President's behalf.'

Monahan bowed his head slightly, trying to remember how many times a compliment of that kind from the bench had been a prelude to disaster.

'But I do have one or two questions. Firstly, is it not true that Ms. Benoni was murdered, and that the police were satisfied that her murderer was Mr. Marfrela?'

'That is correct, Senator.'

'And is it not also true that Mr. Marfrela himself was murdered, apparently by someone connected to the white supremacist group calling itself the Sons of the Land?'

'So the police believe. I don't think that has been conclusively established.'

'Perhaps not,' O'Brien replied. 'But I am informed that many of the demonstrators who are presently surrounding this building, in an apparent attempt to influence the outcome of our vote, are in fact members of the Sons of the Land and similar groups. I wonder if you think that is just coincidental, or whether you have any comment on it?'

Monahan thought over his answer for several seconds.

'Senator, I regret that I do not have any information about that. There has been no evidence about it, and I do not think it would be right for either of us to speculate about it.'

Senator O'Brien stood for a moment, and listened to the muttered conversations which had broken out around the Chamber.

'Well, whether or not there has been evidence about it,' he continued, 'is it your position that we should just ignore it?'

Monahan swallowed hard.

'All I'm saying, Senator, is that it would be unfair to blame the President for anything like that, when it has not even been suggested that he has any connection to what's going on.'

'Perhaps that's the suggestion I'm making,' O'Brien said. 'It would be particularly unfortunate if this demonstration intimidated us into taking the wrong decision. And, I must say, I do find it intimidating, even though it will not cause me to change my vote.'

'I'm not sure what other response I can make, Senator,' Monahan replied. He looked up briefly at the Chief Justice, who nodded.

'Counsel's point is well taken,' the Chief Justice said. 'Of course, the Senate may take into account whatever it wishes in these proceedings. But Mr. Monahan is correct in pointing out that there has been no evidence to connect the President with whatever is going on outside.'

'I yield the remaining portion of my time back to the Minority Leader,' O'Brien said, returning to his seat.

Moments later, Ed Monahan left the podium. He turned to his associate, Brenda Matthews.

'Nice job,' she said. 'I think you changed some minds.'

'Not enough,' Monahan replied.

47

ED MONAHAN HAD changed exactly five minds. It was an impressive achievement, but the House still had sixty-nine votes, two more than they needed for their two-thirds majority. The vote would appear dramatic, but the result was inevitable. The procedure seemed interminable, and the television commentators played up the drama and the historical significance of the vote for all they were worth, but it became clear to all present that history was being made, that a President of the United States was to be impeached successfully for the first time. When, late in the afternoon, the Chief Justice finally announced the result, many senators and their aides bolted and made straight for the exits. They need not have hurried. They found the doors guarded by Marines, flanked by an ugly crowd of demonstrators shouting slogans. The Marines informed them, politely but firmly, that for their own safety they would not be allowed out of the building until further notice. Shortly afterwards, the electricity and water supplies and the telephone land lines to the building were disconnected. Mobile phone coverage and internet access were suddenly intermittent, if available at all.

The first female President of the United States took the oath of office in Houston, Texas, in the student lounge of a law school, standing by the vending machines and the magazine racks. Instead of a full complement of the nation's officials and a cheering crowd, she was accompanied only by a handful of Secret Service and FBI agents, her acting FBI Chief, and her Attorney-General designate. There was no parade, no inaugural ball and, after her swearing-in, the new President went straight to work. She walked upstairs to her second floor office, where Kelly Smith called Ted Lazenby and put him on speakerphone.

'Congratulations, Madam President,' Lazenby said.

'Thank you,' Ellen said. 'I think. Tell me what you know.'

Lazenby sighed into the phone. 'Well, first, for all practical purposes, the Senate is under siege,' he said. 'My guess is Wade isn't going to let them out until they take another vote more to his liking.'

Ellen sat down hard in her chair. 'God in Heaven.'

'We're in contact with them spasmodically by mobile phone, at least for now, though someone is doing their best to cut off network coverage. The land lines are down, and the electricity and water have been turned off. We don't know about food and medical supplies as yet. Hessler's boys are making sure they stay locked in there. Which is probably just as well, because there's a very large, very angry crowd of supremacists and other assorted fine citizens out there also, and they're not even hiding their weapons any more. The Marines are all that's standing between the mob and the Senate.'

There was a silence.

'Of course, what this means,' Lazenby continued, 'is that we have to revise one of our assumptions.'

'Time,' President Trevathan said quietly.

'Right. It's not on our side any more. The Senate is in an impossible situation. We have to help them, and we have to do it quickly. Raul is working on our options now with some of his people. We should have them for you in an hour or two.'

'This is all sounding rather grim, Ted,' Ellen observed.

Kelly was sure she picked up Lazenby's smile on the other end of the line.

'I wanted to give you the bad news first,' he replied.

'Feel free to continue with the good news any time.'

'Yes, Madam President. Well, Terrell is with us. So are most of McGarry's people. The only areas we can't control are the Marines and the nuclear weapons. Other than that, we have a clear military superiority.'

'Other than that, Mrs. Lincoln, how was the theater?' Ellen commented.

'Something like that. But assuming Wade would not actually use a nuclear weapon, and further assuming that no officer would obey an order to use one, we do have a decisive advantage in any foreseeable conflict. Given the use of conventional forces, Raul and Terrell have no doubt we could liberate the Senate and take back the White House, and do it quickly.'

Ellen Trevathan closed her eyes. 'But the cost would be…'

'Horrendous, yes. There would be considerable loss of life, and we would essentially have to rebuild Washington. We would probably have to reduce the White House to rubble.'

'I'm sure you've asked Raul to think of alternatives.'

'Yes, of course. His options will be designed to minimize the damage. But they will also be designed to achieve the objective.'

'I thought this was the good news section,' Ellen said, after a pause.

'There is more,' Lazenby said. 'As I'm sure you've noticed in Houston, the country is pretty quiet.'

'It's weird,' Ellen replied. 'Unreal. General Terrell's people have cleared everyone out of the downtown area. It's like a ghost town. But the local TV stations are saying it's that way throughout the city.'

'Same everywhere. We've got police on the streets everywhere, just in case. But there's nothing for them to do. Wade has miscalculated, Ellen. Other than the loonies in Washington, people are staying in their homes. The news channels are saying people are frightened and concerned. But there are no demonstrations, nothing in the streets. There's an incredible volume of chatter on all the social networking sites, way too much for our analysts to evaluate within any useful time frame, and they say it's totally impossible to define the trend at any given moment. But they have been taking large random samples, and they are all highly favorable to you.'

'Which proves your point that the demonstrations were orchestrated by the loonies all along,' the President observed.

'Yes. The other good news is that the media have abandoned any pretense of neutrality. It looks like we'll have one hundred percent support from the press, home and abroad. Obviously, everyone will carry Wade's broadcast, but they will also carry yours, and I don't think there's any doubt which way the verdict will come down.'

Ellen reflected for a moment. 'So, what you're telling me, Ted, is that if we can deal with the immediate problem in Washington, we have a good shot at uniting the country behind us.'

'We have a great shot. The two unknown factors right now are whether Wade's broadcast will change anything, and whether we can deal with the Washington mob.'

'What's the word abroad, politically?'

'Everyone's keeping quiet and waiting. It may be a while before they send out their formal congratulations, but no one's interfering. State says we have the Brits to thank for that.'

'How so?'

'Well, officially they're not taking sides, but behind the scenes, they've made it clear through diplomatic channels that anyone who tries to take advantage of our situation will get their asses well and truly kicked in short order.'

'We owe them one.'

'Yes, we do.'

'Madam President,' Kelly Smith said, 'I'm sorry to interrupt, but Wade's broadcast is about to start.'

The President nodded. 'Ted, I'll call you back as soon as I'm through with mine. We hit the airwaves as soon as Wade has finished.'

'Good,' Lazenby said. 'I'll be here. Oh, very quickly, Madam President, there is one piece of good news from the Senate.'

'What might that be?'

'Well, having nothing better to do, they thought they might as well go ahead and confirm your first appointments, myself, Raul, and Ken Hunt. And they said, if there's anyone else, just call in the names.'

Ellen laughed out loud, but then stopped abruptly.

'Do they know how serious the situation is?'

Lazenby hesitated.

'We haven't told them everything. We don't want to create a panic. Also, the press is in there with them. We thought it might be better to leave it vague for now. Even so, it's only a matter of time – a short time – before they start speculating.'

'You're afraid they might change their minds about the impeachment?'

'Right now, no. But it's a very volatile situation, Madam President. We don't know what they might do if this goes on for too long.'

'Well, tell them I really appreciate it, and I'll say thank you properly down the road.'

'Will do.'

'And Ted…'

'Yes, Madam President.'

'You're right not to say too much. But tell them we're going to find a way to get them out of their situation, and we're going to do it quickly.'

48

'GOOD EVENING,' STEVE Wade began, staring stonily into the camera in front of him. 'As you all know, this afternoon the United States Senate voted in favor of an article of impeachment against me. In their eyes, I have become the first President in our nation's history to be impeached successfully. The Constitution gives the Congress the right to bring impeachment proceedings against a President, and there is then a trial in the Senate. If the President is convicted of treason or other high crimes and misdemeanors, then he is to be removed from office. And tonight, I want you all to know that I respect the Constitution. If I had committed any such crimes, I assure you that I would have removed myself from office. I would not have waited for proceedings in Congress, or a vote in the Senate. But I have not committed any such crimes. Recently, when I was a guest on Conrad Beckers' show, I made it clear that these allegations that have been made against me are utterly untrue. They are the work of my political enemies, who have become almost insanely jealous of the success I have had in doing the work the American people elected me to do. They can't stand the fact that this Administration has been so successful. They hate me for it. In short, I have been set up. I never met the man, Hamid Marfrela, and I know nothing about his activities. I have no connection with the State of Lebanon or with any of its operatives. I have never solicited or accepted any money or favors from anyone in Lebanon. All that happened is, I fell in love with a woman called Lucia Benoni. Now, it is true that I lied about my relationship with Ms. Benoni. I lied to you, the American people, to my closest advisers, and even to my wife. Those lies cost me my marriage, and I regret them. But that is what happened, and that is all that happened.

'Tonight, I have to do what is in the best interests of the United States. And, after close consultation with my advisers, I have determined

311

that what is in the best interests of the United States is for me to remain in the White House and carry on with my work. This has not been my decision alone. Many influential political and military leaders agree with me. I am in the best interests of America. I know that, you know it, and so do my enemies. I know I have your support, the support of the people, because you want me to get on with the job. You don't care about political wrangling. You want to see America made safe and strong, and that's what I intend to do, as I always have. But there are those who want me to leave office. Among them, to my great regret, is my Vice President, Ellen Trevathan, a woman I trusted. I am told she has left Washington, together with some of her advisers. I am told that some elements in our military are supporting her. You may hear her claim to be the new President of the United States. But I don't believe that's what you want. I believe you want the same firm hand on the tiller that you have had during the last six years. There is trouble brewing in the Middle East. Africa is in turmoil. America must take its place on the world stage. So, tonight, I call upon the Vice President and those with her to return to Washington, and help me to keep America strong. I hope that all my supporters will stand up for me now. Come out and support me in this hour of trial, just as you did in two elections. Take to the streets and show the Senate how much you care. Don't let these people get away with what they are trying to do. Show them that the will of the American people is more important than any political maneuvering. Take back your government tonight.

'There are certain short-term measures I have been obliged to take in order to maintain our national security. Threats have been made to the Senate, which is still in session in the Capitol. The cooler and wiser heads in the Senate have called for a fresh vote on my impeachment. They know they have done the wrong thing in trying to impeach me. But a crowd of people has gathered outside the Capitol. Many of them support me, but some of them intend to intimidate the Senate, as they have already been intimidated, into voting me out of office. I am told that many of these people are armed and dangerous. The Washington Police have been unable to disperse them. I cannot allow this intimidation to succeed. Therefore, I have today ordered units of the United States Marine Corps to stand guard over the Senate, and to be ready to do whatever is necessary to protect public order in Washington. I have temporarily closed the White House and placed it under the protection of the Marines also. While this crisis continues, there will be daily press briefings, and I have assured our allies abroad that we will not allow the crisis to interrupt our work on the many serious issues we are facing. I am confident that we will resolve this crisis speedily and that everything will be back to normal within the next few days. In the meantime, I need your support. I am your President. You need me. America needs me. I am here, and here I will remain. Thank you, and God bless America.'

* * *

In an office in the White House, Dick Latham turned to face General Hessler as the President's broadcast ended.

'We'll never get away with this,' he muttered.

'Well, Mr. Attorney-General,' Hessler replied, 'it's too late to worry about that now.'

* * *

At the same time, in his office in *The Washington Post* Building, Harold Philby shook his head.

'He's lost it,' he said to Mary Sullivan. 'He has finally lost it.'

'Is that what you want me to write,' Mary asked. 'That the President of the United States has lost his sanity?'

'Write the truth, Mary,' Philby replied. 'What did you see this evening?'

* * *

Across town, in front of the Capitol, where the crowd had been watching Steve Wade's speech on a huge television screen erected for the occasion, loud cheering broke out, Wade's name was chanted and, on George Carlson's phone command, shots were fired into the air.

'This is it, Dan,' Carlson shouted to Rogers over the cheers and the chants. 'It's all going to fall apart. This time tomorrow, we will be in control.'

'Why doesn't Fox give the order?'

'He will. Soon. All we have to do is be ready to move.'

* * *

Fighting an urge to run for dear life, Ellen Trevathan adjusted her hair one last time as she sat in the chair behind Ken Hunt's desk, listening to the producer count her down.

'Ladies and Gentlemen, good evening,' she said, forcing her voice to remain calm. 'Tonight I address you for the first time as your President. I know you didn't vote for me as your President. But I became President by the operation of our Constitution earlier today, when the Senate

313

voted to impeach former President Steve Wade. And I have become President during what may be the most serious crisis in our nation's history, a crisis every bit as serious as 9/11, a crisis every bit as serious as the attack on Pearl Harbor, a crisis every bit as serious as our Civil War. So tonight, I want to be as honest with you as I possibly can. I wanted to become President one day. I intended to seek my party's nomination at the end of President Wade's term of office. But, much as I wanted to be your President, I never wanted it to be like this. I have no idea whether Steve Wade did the things he has been accused of. I have no means of knowing. I worked closely with President Wade for several years. I always had a high opinion of him. Otherwise, I would never have agreed to run for office as his Vice President. In all frankness, I would never have believed him capable of the things he has been accused of. That's why I stood by him during the impeachment. But the question of whether he was guilty or innocent was not mine to judge. That is the Senate's job. The Senate held a trial, and determined that President Wade was guilty of high crimes and misdemeanors. Whether or not I agree with them, whether or not you agree with them, does not matter now. Whether you or I want Steve Wade to continue in office no longer matters. I need you all to understand that, once that vote was taken in the Senate, Steve Wade ceased to be your President, and I became your President. All of this happened automatically, by operation of law. Those of you who do not want me as your President will have the opportunity to vote against me in two years' time, when our next election is held. If I decide to run which, I have to tell you, is a big 'if' right now. That is what our Constitution provides for. That is the way we do things in America because we believe, as we must, in the rule of law. Until the next election, I am your President, and it is my intention to act as such.

'Steve Wade, however, does not believe that. He has seized control of the White House, your White House, and he refuses to leave. I don't know why or how this has happened. But I must be frank with you about how serious this is. There are a few high-ranking military officers who believe that they have the right to decide who becomes President, and Steve Wade has enlisted the support of these officers. I want to make it clear that the overwhelming majority of the members of our armed forces are loyal to the Constitution. But there are a few who are not, and these few have taken control of our most important public buildings in Washington – the Capitol, the Supreme Court, and the White House itself. They are keeping your senators imprisoned in the Capitol, and are depriving them of food, water, electricity, and contact with the outside world. Their intent appears to be to coerce the Senate into changing its mind about the impeachment. I must tell you that former President Wade retains control of the codes governing deployment of our nuclear weapons. I must also tell you that, based on intelligence reports, many of the people gathered around the Capitol at the present time are not, as Steve Wade claims, members of the public engaged in a lawful protest, but members of right-wing supremacist groups whose aim is to do harm to your Government.

'These events have produced a very grave situation, which cannot be permitted to remain unresolved. In consultation with my new Secretary of Defense, Air Force General Raul Gutierrez, and other advisers, I have taken a serious decision. They involve all Americans. First, I have communicated to Steve Wade and those supporting him the following ultimatum. He is required to vacate the White House, and call on those military units supporting him to surrender peacefully, not later than forty-eight hours from the start of this broadcast, that is to say eight o'clock, Eastern Standard Time, on Thursday. All those who comply with this ultimatum, including former President Wade, will be dealt with fairly under the law. If this ultimatum is not complied with, I will take whatever action may be necessary to restore constitutional and democratic rule to the United States. Such action may have a heavy price, but it is one we must be prepared to pay. You can help by remaining in your homes and keeping the peace in your own communities. You know, as I do, that one man, however popular he may be, cannot be allowed to hold our country, our Constitution, to ransom. When I next address you, it will be from the White House, and as a President who is in complete charge of the affairs of the United States. Until that time, I thank you and wish you well.'

49

THE MEETING BEGAN as soon as the television crew left. Moving to the sitting area of Ken Hunt's study, the President, Hunt, Kelly, and Jeff made themselves comfortable, and waited until the secure call from Ted Lazenby and Raul Gutierrez had been patched through on the speakerphone.

'Congratulations, Madam President,' Lazenby said. 'Great speech.'

'Thank you,' Ellen replied. 'I was shaking like a leaf.'

'It didn't show. You looked and sounded like the President. I'm proud to be serving under you.'

'Thanks, Ted. You understand we're committed now. I've given the ultimatum. There's no way back now.'

'No. But I don't think there ever was.'

'What's going on at your end?'

'Our intelligence from the White House is that there are very few people left in the building. Most of the staff were sent home before Wade's speech. We have Wade, Latham, Hessler, and McGarry, and a bunch of Marines, plus a couple of Secret Service Agents, one or two administrators and a chef, and that's about it. The grounds are swarming with Marines. The place is heavily defended. Oh, and…, God, Ellen, I hate to have to be the one to tell you this, but they…'

'Tell me what, Ted…?'

'They found Martha Graylor…'

Ellen turned her head away. 'Oh, no,' she said quietly.

'They found her in her office. She'd overdosed on sleeping pills. She left a note, something about everything being too much for her, and she couldn't go on. I'm sorry, Ellen. I know you were close.'

Ellen held her head in her hands for a few moments and bit her lip, recovering her composure.

'OK, what about the military situation?'

'We have you protected pretty well. General Terrell is cooperating fully. He's moving more troops into position around Houston. You may notice a few more tanks on the streets in the next few hours. Nothing to worry about, they're on our side. We're flying reconnaissance missions in the area around the clock. We have a carrier and a couple of subs in the Gulf of Mexico, but they're not showing any hostility. We've picked up a few coded messages and private tweets that suggest the Navy is coming over to you, if it was ever otherwise. McGarry's not exactly supporting us yet, but there's no evidence that he's trying to screw us either. It may be that he knows the game is up. So I'm happy with your security, at least for now.'

'What about Washington? What about Hessler?'

'Same as before. They have very little support. Even Hessler's people are having second thoughts. But the people they have on the ground are hard-core. And they still have the Sons of the Land pinch-hitting for them outside the Capitol. They were watching the speeches on the big screen, and they were pretty enthusiastic about Wade. But it's just noise, no movement so far. We have agents everywhere, so we'll get a heads up if that should change. We still can't do much about the Senate. But we do have the other members of the Court, except the Chief, of course, plus several more heads of department flying out to Houston tomorrow.'

'So the Senate is still in trouble?'

'Yes, Ma'am, I'm afraid so.'

'We have overwhelming superiority, but they have the nukes, and they can make us destroy Washington to force them out.'

'Right. We can take the White House and the Capitol back, but it's going to be a bloodbath, and there's no way around that.'

'And I just promised on national television to do exactly that less than forty-eight hours from now.'

'We agreed we had no choice, Madam President,' Raul Gutierrez's voice joined in.

'Yes, we did,' Ellen said. 'But we're talking about a possible civil war here, and if there's any way to avoid a civil war, we have to find it. I'm open to suggestions. Ted, I'm assuming from what you said, the information you have, that you still have a line open into the White House?'

'Yes. They're keeping a phone line open for now at least, but there are no guarantees.'

'So, there's some hope of negotiating. Who are you talking to?'

'Dick Latham.'

'Has he given you any reason to think…?'

'No. None at all. Our discussions have been strictly factual. They're not acting like people who know they have a deadline.'

'So, what we have to figure out,' Ellen said, 'is who would be the most effective negotiator in this situation – assuming they want to talk to us.'

'My vote is for Raul,' Lazenby replied. 'This is a military standoff, and Raul is a military man. If anyone can convince Hessler he's in a hopeless position, he can. My suggestion is that we shouldn't try to deal with Wade directly. He's a crazy man, and there's no way he's coming out voluntarily. But maybe we can turn his people against him. If they think it's a lost cause, they may start to desert him.'

'What about that, Raul?' Ellen asked.

'I agree there's no point trying to get to Wade,' Gutierrez replied. 'But the military side is up to Hessler, and I don't think there's much negotiating with him. Madam President, it's entirely possible Hessler thinks he has the advantage because they control the nukes.'

'He would actually contemplate telling Wade to use nukes? Is he out of his mind?'

'He's a psychopath in uniform, Madam President, and he has to be desperate by now. Wade too. I wouldn't put anything past them at this point. That's why I think we have to find some way to talk to them that doesn't come from a military position, and we have to find it quickly.'

'Such as…?'

'Well, it seems to me this is a constitutional issue as much as anything. Maybe Ted would have more success making overtures to Latham.'

'I doubt it,' Lazenby said. 'When I talk to Latham, he sounds like he's scared shitless. I can't see him standing up to either Hessler or Wade.'

There was a silence.

'I do have one suggestion,' Gutierrez ventured tentatively.

'Go on.'

'It sticks in my gullet to suggest it, but if you were to offer an amnesty to all military personnel below the rank of colonel, you might get them to turn on Hessler and his henchmen. These are experienced officers. They're not stupid people. It must have dawned on them by now that they are backing a losing horse.'

Ellen shook her head.

'These are officers in the armed forces of the United States, Raul.

They knew what they were getting into.'

'I'm just making a suggestion, Madam President…'

'I know.'

'Madam President,' Jeff broke in. 'May I?'

'Go ahead, Jeff.'

'General Gutierrez, is there a way to spread the word that an amnesty might be on the cards, without the President actually saying so?'

'You mean, spread a rumor?'

'Right.'

'Sure. It would be the easiest thing in the world. All we have to do is use the networking sites and drop a leak or two to the press. The CIA would pitch in and help, too. Technically, this isn't their jurisdiction, but they've been itching to get involved. This would be right up their street.'

Jeff looked at Ellen, who raised her eyes to the ceiling.

'All right,' she said. 'But it has to be deniable. I don't want to commit myself to amnesties right now.'

'Understood.'

'All right. Back to negotiations. I don't think we have a consensus yet.'

Kelly leaned forward in her chair.

'Mr. Vice President, do you happen to know whether Linda Samuels is one of the Secret Service Agents who's still in the White House?'

'I think she is,' Lazenby replied. 'I have the names here. Just a moment. Yes, Linda Samuels and Gary Mills. Why do you ask?'

'She might be a useful contact. I've known Linda all my life. I can't believe she supports what Wade is doing. She has to be there just out of personal loyalty.'

'Don't underestimate her personal loyalty, Kelly,' Ellen said. 'I talked to her before she went to jail, remember?'

'I remember, Madam President,' Kelly replied. 'But she and I are very close, always have been. I was thinking, I might just be able to get to her.'

Ellen thought for a moment.

'Ted,' she said decisively, 'get that line into the White House patched through to the law school here, so we can use it whenever we have to. I want you to start talking to Latham as soon as possible. I'm also going to have Kelly make an approach to Agent Samuels. We'll have two things going at once. Let's hope one of them works.'

'Will do,' Lazenby said.

'Madam President,' Raul Gutierrez said, after a silence, 'we have to assume at this point that negotiations may not succeed. I need your permission to finalize the plans for retaking the White House and the Capitol. And in light of the possible nuclear threat, I believe we have no option but to choose an option which is fast and decisive.'

'How fast and decisive?' Ellen asked nervously.

'We can rebuild the White House,' Gutierrez replied. 'But we can't rebuild one of our cities after a nuclear attack. I'm prepared to accept the first possibility if we can prevent the second.'

The President held her head in her hands. 'Can you guarantee that we can prevent the second?'

There was a silence.

'No. I believe it's highly unlikely. Maybe even unthinkable. But I can't guarantee it.'

'God help us all,' Ellen said. 'Go ahead, Raul. Put whatever you need to in place. But nobody moves without my order.'

'Understood, Madam President.'

'Jeff,' Ellen Trevathan said when Lazenby and Gutierrez had rung off, 'make sure the television people are ready to go night and day. I need to be able to broadcast at a moment's notice.'

'I'll see to it,' Jeff said, leaving the room.

The President turned to Kelly.

'Agent Samuels struck me as a woman of principle, Kelly. I admired the way she stuck to her guns, even if it was misguided.'

'Yes, Ma'am, she is.'

'I don't know why, but I think she may hold the key to this thing. Let's not waste any time.'

50

'HEY, LINDA, WHAT'S going on?' Kelly asked quietly.

The phone conversation with her friend had taken more than an hour of delicate negotiation to arrange. But now Kelly installed herself in Ken Hunt's office with a pot of coffee. Dick Latham was designated to negotiate on behalf of Steve Wade. Before she allowed negotiations to be opened, Kelly insisted that she should be alone during the call, and that no one should listen in on or record the conversation. The White House had insisted on the same conditions.

Ellen Trevathan had returned to the hotel to rest for an hour or two, and Ken Hunt had driven home for a brief reunion with his wife.

'Oh, much the same,' Linda replied lightly. 'Well, not really. How about you?'

'I'm fine. I can't say I like the weather too much down here in Houston. Too muggy. I'm kind of hoping I can get back to Washington before too long. Are you doing OK?'

'Yeah, I guess. Except for Bob, but you know how that goes.'

'Now what's he done? Still trying to tempt you back?'

'Not exactly. He and the bimbo have named the day. They're planning an October wedding. Nice for them, huh?'

'Oh, God, Linda. I'm sorry.'

'Yeah, well, what are you going to do?'

Kelly took a sip of coffee and allowed some time to pass.

'Yeah. We have a difficult situation here, Linda.'

'No shit.'

'Yeah. Maybe you and I could do something to help. What do you think?'

Linda laughed.

'That would be something, wouldn't it? Kelly and Linda. The old team. We always used to say we were going to change the world. Remember? When we were in college? We used to sit up all night figuring out how to put the world to rights.'

'I remember. We solved all the world's problems several times over.'

'If only they'd listened to us.'

'Right. No more war, hunger, crime. Peace and prosperity for the whole world.'

'What a deal.'

'Yeah,' Kelly said, smiling. 'Those were good times, Linda. I miss them.'

'Me too.' Linda's voice sounded sad. 'That was before we got involved in all this shit.'

Kelly took a deep breath.

'What if we could just help to save America? That would be a pretty good start, wouldn't it?'

Linda sniffed.

'We were college kids, Kelly. It was all so simple back then. I don't even remember what we thought the answer was.'

'Neither do I. But perhaps we could work it out again.'

'I'm not sure there are any answers, Kelly.'

'There might be. It's worth a shot, isn't it? What if we could get together? Do you think we might be able to work something out?'

Kelly heard Linda give a deep sigh. 'Get together?'

'Yeah. Why not?'

Linda hesitated.

'Kelly, is this an official approach? I mean, from Trevathan?'

'I have authorization, yes. But it's still between the two of us.'

'I'm only authorized to speak to you over the phone.'

Kelly planted her feet firmly on the floor. The time had come for the part of her strategy she had not confided to the President. She felt her stomach tie itself in knots.

'I know. But I think it would be better face to face, Linda, just like in the old days, sit down together, work things out.'

'I don't know how we could do that, Kelly. I can't leave the President. Gary Mills and I are the only agents he has left to protect him.'

'Fine, so get me in there. I'll come to you.'

As she said it, Kelly raised her eyes to the ceiling. There was a long silence.

'Jesus, Kelly, I don't know how I could do that. The White House is under military command now, and I'm right at the bottom of the food chain.'

'I assume the White House is ultimately under Steve Wade's command. Isn't it? I mean, as far as you're concerned, he's still the President, right?'

'Yes, he is.'

'So he gets to decide who gets into the White House and who doesn't. You're close enough to him to have his ear. Why don't you run it by him?'

'You're suggesting I should go to the President, and say I want a visit from an old friend, to talk over old times, and would it be OK for her to come to the White House?'

'No. I'm suggesting you tell him that the Acting Director of the FBI has asked for a meeting to discuss the situation before the deadline expires.'

Linda gave a little squeal of delight. Kelly smiled. Just for a moment, she had heard the Linda she had always known. Just for a moment, she had dropped her guard. Linda was genuinely pleased for her.

'Kelly, you're Acting Director? Way to go, girl. When did this happen?'

'Lazenby conferred it on me just as I was about to leave for Houston. I haven't had much time to think about it. But I do have official status, and I do have President Trevathan's authority to negotiate. It's a chance, Linda. Things are going to get seriously out of control before long. There'll be nothing either one of us can do then. If there's anything we can do, now is the time to do it. All I'm asking for is the chance to talk.'

Linda hesitated. 'I can't give him up, Kelly. He's my President.'

'I'm not asking you to give him up, Linda. He's going to have to make that decision for himself. All I'm asking for is the opportunity to talk. Me and one agent, Jeff, probably. No one else.'

'How is Jeff? You guys doing OK?'

'Yeah, we're doing fine.'

'You always were the lucky one.'

Kelly grinned. 'Hey, I gave you a chance, remember? When we were at the D.C. Police Headquarters that time. You were the one who said 'no'.'

'One of the many fine decisions I've made about my life.'

'You've made a lot of very fine decisions in your life, Linda, and don't you ever forget that.'

'Yeah, well…'

'So, what do you say, girl? Shall we give it a try?'

It was some time before Linda replied.

'I'll do my best to speak to the President and Mr. Latham about it, Kelly. I can't promise anything, but I'll get back to you.'

'You're doing the right thing, Linda. Thanks.'

'Sure. Love you.'

'Love you.'

* * *

Kelly hung up the phone, got to her feet, and walked slowly into the anteroom to the dean's office, where Jeff was waiting for her, reclining on a sofa with his eyes closed. As she closed the office door gently behind her, he opened his eyes, and sat up.

'How did it go?' he asked.

'I got to first base,' Kelly replied. 'She's going to try.'

'OK. So, now what? You want to report to the President?'

'No. Let her rest for a while. We'll tell her when we get a definite response one way or the other. Did you work on the arrangements?'

'Yes. General Gutierrez has his personal plane standing by at Ellington Field with an escort. We're all set for the flight into Andrews, and from there we'll have an Air Force helicopter available. We can set it down on the White House landing pad. That should mean we don't have to worry about the crowd outside, just the Marines inside.'

'Great, Jeff. How about Justice Finnis?'

'Waiting for us over at the hotel. You want to go see him now?'

'You have the paperwork?'

'Got it.'

'OK. Let's go.'

Despite the late hour, and the sense of urgency she felt, Kelly could find energy only for a slow pace as she and Jeff strolled hand-in-hand along the short city blocks from South Texas College of Law to the Four Seasons Hotel. Light rain was falling, but after so many hours spent inside the law school, they found it refreshing, and gave no thought to opening an umbrella. There were no longer any ordinary guests at the Four Seasons. The manager had relocated those who were there when the crisis broke to other hotels in the city. An armored personnel carrier stood guard outside the main entrance and uniformed military police officers were stationed at either side of the entrance, providing a stark contrast to the uniforms of the regular doormen. Kelly and Jeff presented their identification, were admitted, and made their way through the lobby to the bank of elevators. They rode in silence to the eighteenth floor, then walked the short distance to the room where United States Supreme Court Associate Justice, Jeremy Finnis, was in temporary residence. The Justice was expecting them. Although it was now well after midnight, he was dressed in a suit and tie. Despite his small stature, Justice Finnis had an imposing presence which fully supported his reputation as one of the country's leading legal minds. Opening the door, he graciously ushered them into the living room of his suite.

'Well, Madam Director,' he smiled at Kelly, 'this is a rather unusual request. I never thought I would be asked to issue warrants. That normally happens at a rather lower level.'

'Yes, Mr. Justice,' Kelly replied, returning the smile, 'but these are unusual times.'

'Indeed they are. Do you have the applications?'

'I have them, Mr. Justice,' Jeff replied.

'Good. Have a seat while I take a look.'

Jeff produced a bundle of papers from his briefcase, handed them to the Justice, and sat beside Kelly on the sofa. One of the law school secretaries had prepared them earlier, using forms supplied by the clerk of the local federal District Court. Justice Finnis seated himself nearby in a comfortable armchair, donned his reading glasses and, without undue haste, perused the documents he had been given. Having done so, he gazed into space for several seconds, removed his glasses, set them down on a small coffee table, and sat forward in his chair, clasping his hands together.

'So, if I understand correctly, Madam Director, I am being asked to issue warrants for the arrest of a former President of the United States, a former Attorney-General of the United States, and a member of the Joint Chiefs of Staff, in addition to…'

'A search warrant for the whole of the White House, yes.'

Justice Finnis rose and, holding the documents, walked slowly around the room towards the window. Outside he could see the dark, cloudy sky and the yellow sodium lights of the city stretching apparently without limit into the distance.

'Off the subject for a moment, I don't suppose there's any news about the other…'

'The other Associate Justices are safe, Mr. Justice. They're on their way to Houston. Of course, the Chief Justice is still in the Capitol. We have no reason to believe he has been harmed.'

'His heart hasn't been too good over the last few years,' Justice Finnis said. 'I hope he has his medication with him.'

'We're doing everything we can.'

'I know,' Justice Finnis replied.

'You should be able to sit as a Court in a day or two if you need to.'

The Justice nodded. 'Realistically, what chance is there that these warrants will ever be executed?' he asked.

Kelly rose and joined Finnis at the window.

'Mr. Justice, there are certain aspects of our plans I'm not at liberty to disclose at this time, but I assure you it is my intention to execute every one of them. As to probable cause…'

Justice Finnis stopped her.

'Oh, you hardly need to persuade me about probable cause,' he said lightly. 'Anyone who's been breathing during the last few days knows there's probable cause. All the same, you'd better swear to it formally. Based on the information supplied to you, do you believe there is probable cause to believe that the offenses named in the applications have been committed by the persons named, and that evidence may be found at the location named to support the charges against those persons? Do you so swear, so help you God?'

Kelly raised her right hand. 'I do, Mr. Justice.'

Finnis turned, and walked to the writing desk by the window. Picking up a pen, he carefully signed each application. Jeff walked over to the table, took the applications back, and replaced them in his briefcase.

'Please return copies to me when you get the chance.'

'I will, Sir,' Jeff replied.

'Have I done the right thing?' Finnis asked, with a smile.

'I believe you have,' Jeff replied. 'Thank you, Mr. Justice.'

'No, thank you,' Justice Finnis replied. 'Both of you. As a Justice of the Court, I'm not supposed to express opinions about what might become a pending case one of these days but, as an American, I want to say I'm glad for what you're doing and I wish you God speed. When we spoke earlier, you wouldn't tell me much about what's going on, Agent Morris, but I have enough marbles left to figure some of it out for myself. Oh, I won't say anything, of course. But it seems to me that there may be a certain amount of danger involved in what you're proposing to do. I hope you will both be careful.'

'We will, Mr. Justice,' Jeff replied.

'Thank you, Mr. Justice,' Kelly said.

They shook hands, left the room, and walked back along the silent carpeted corridor to the elevators, where they stood for a moment without pressing the button.

'Nothing we can do now till Linda calls back,' Jeff said.

'No.'

'So, where do you want to wait it out?'

'My room,' Kelly said. 'That's where they'll call as soon as she calls the school.'

'Sounds good, Madam Director,' Jeff grinned.

Kelly leaned against the wall and smiled.

'"Madam Director",' she mused. 'That's the first time anyone has called me that. Was he really referring to me?'

'Unless there was some other woman in the room I didn't see,' Jeff said. 'It sounded pretty good, didn't it?'

'Yes, it did,' Kelly said. 'But it's going to take some getting used to.'

'Can I still call you 'Kelly' in bed?'

'I'll think about it.'

She pressed the call button. The elevator in which they had come was still on the eighteenth floor, waiting to take them elsewhere.

'Whatever you call me, Jeff, I'm not sure it's going to cut any ice with those people in the White House.'

'Maybe it will,' Jeff said, holding the door for her. 'Maybe someone still cares about the institutions of government. Our job may be to figure out which one of them it is.'

51

'AND I'M telling you, I don't give a damn what your orders are.'

'Easy, Sam,' Senator Joe O'Brien said quietly.

He gently eased the Chief Justice back into his chair. O'Brien's own blood pressure was rising fast, but he remained calm enough to realize that the colonel and lieutenant they had been trying to negotiate with for the last hour were holding all the cards. O'Brien also knew, as did his colleagues, that the Chief Justice's heart condition was not being helped by the mood of confrontation. The small supply of his medication he had with him had run out, and one or two senators who had medical training were expressing concern. O'Brien had tried to persuade Sam Mayhew to relax, but the feisty head of the Supreme Court was having none of it. Used to picking fights with counsel in the courtroom, he did not seem to appreciate that he could not do the same with the military officers who now sat opposite him. The meeting had not gone well. Like the Chief Justice, the colonel was not a diplomat. The Marines, it seemed, had their orders, and not even the Senate or the Chief Justice of the United States was going to prevent them from carrying them out. Prospects of resolving the situation any time soon did not seem good. And O'Brien was receiving some very disturbing reports from Frank Worley, whose mobile phone was still receiving some messages, about what was going on in the outside world. Unlikely reports, perhaps even unbelievable, but disturbing nonetheless. He sensed that time was of the essence, but he remained powerless. At last, the Chief Justice subsided into his chair. O'Brien decided to try one last time.

'Colonel, I think we at least have the right to know whether your orders came from President Trevathan, or whether she authorized them,' he said.

The colonel seemed unimpressed.

'My orders came directly from my Chief of Staff, General Hessler,

Senator. It's not up to me to question a direct order, and you can be sure I'm not about to. In any case, there's no way I would let you out there right now, because we are not in control on the ground. I couldn't guarantee your safety.'

'If the only problem is the crowd, I don't see why it's such a big deal. Disperse them.'

'We can't do that, Senator.'

'Why not, for God's sake. You're the Marines. You ran up the flag at Iwo Jima. I can't see why…'

'With all due respect, Senator, this is not a wartime situation. Those people out there are not the enemy. They're citizens engaging in a lawful protest.'

'Lawful protest, my ass. They're holding the Senate hostage.'

'Be that as it may…'

'It's not a lawful protest, for Christ's sake, it's a lynch mob. They're carrying guns, and they're threatening us with violence. Disperse them. Don't you have water cannon, plastic bullets?'

'Dispersing them would be a police action, Senator. The military doesn't have police powers unless the President declares a state of emergency and asks us to step in. That has not happened, as far as I'm aware.'

'You need a declaration of a state of emergency, when an armed mob imprisons the Senate in the Capitol?'

'In addition to that, Sir, if we did try to take action, and the crowd resisted, there would be the potential for an incredible loss of life. We have superior fire power, but we are greatly outnumbered. We might not even be able to hold them.'

O'Brien shook his head in disbelief.

'Can't you send for reinforcements?'

'I have made the request, Sir. The Washington police are standing by a short distance away. But you have to understand that there are thousands of people out there, many of them armed. The sight of more fire power might panic them. If they get excited and start a firefight, we're out of options. So, right now, we're trying to keep the situation calm.'

'Well, it's not very calm in here. The Chief Justice is not well.'

'I'm fine,' Sam Mayhew interrupted.

'Sam, let me, please,' O'Brien continued. 'Another thing I don't understand is why the electricity and water are cut off. We've already had one or two people take nasty falls down the stairs, we have a couple of staff members trapped in the elevators, and I don't even want to describe the state of the bathrooms. What are they playing at, for God's sake? Heads will roll over this when we get out of here, I promise you that.'

The colonel and the lieutenant exchanged grim glances.

'As I understand it, Senator, some of the demonstrators arranged some pretty sophisticated sabotage. I'm not sure how. But you're not the only people in town without those amenities right now. I know they're working on the problem, and I'm sure it will be fixed before too long.'

'We're supposed to have back-up generators.'

'I understand, Sir.'

O'Brien looked at his colleagues. None of them seemed to have anything useful to add. Even the Chief Justice seemed subdued. None of it made any sense to O'Brien. His gut told him that there was something very wrong. It should not be this easy to incapacitate the Senate. The crowd had brought the government, or at least part of it, to a complete standstill. Then, a thought came to him. What if this was not an isolated incident? What if they had done the same to the other branches of government? What about the Supreme Court, just a few blocks away? What about the White House? What about the President? Frank had picked up some story about her setting up Headquarters in Houston. Nonsense, of course. Why the hell would she do that? Or was it nonsense? And suddenly, as O'Brien put the various pieces of the puzzle together, the reality of the situation dawned on him with a clarity that made his blood run cold. The presence of so many armed people outside the Capitol was no coincidence. Nor was it a spontaneous protest on behalf of Steve Wade. He was witnessing a *coup d'état*. Not only witnessing it, but he was also one of its victims. Steve Wade was gone, but who, if anyone, had taken his place? Who was running the United States? Whoever they were, it seemed they controlled the military. And, at least for now, they controlled the Senate. O'Brien sat down heavily in a chair, feeling the eyes of the marine officers fixed on him like the little red dots that mark a target for a rifle. With a massive effort, O'Brien took a deep breath and tried to control himself sufficiently to begin to think of a way out.

'So, Colonel, am I to understand that you have no suggestions as to what might be done to resolve the situation?'

'As I said before, Senator,' the colonel replied, 'the only course seems to be to wait it out.'

He seemed to hesitate.

'Well… I suppose there is one thing I might suggest… But it's hardly my place…'

'If you have anything to suggest, go right ahead and suggest it,' O'Brien said firmly.

'Well, Senator, it did occur to my lieutenant and myself… well, it's pretty obvious that those folks out there are supporters of President Wade.'

'So…?'

'And we were thinking that, if the vote had gone the other way, we probably wouldn't have the problem we do now.'

The man's audacity took O'Brien's breath away. It was some moments before he could respond and, looking around the room, he saw that his colleagues were having the same reaction.

'Are you…, are you suggesting that we change our vote?' he asked.

The colonel coughed awkwardly.

'I'm suggesting you *announce* another vote,' he replied. 'Whether or not you *take* another vote is up to you.'

'For God's sake,' one of the other Senators exploded.

'You asked for a suggestion, Senator,' the colonel said. 'I've given you one. Whether you follow it is up to you. Frankly, even if you did, there's no guarantee that the crowd would disperse immediately. They might decide to throw an impromptu street party. But it might increase our chances of getting rid of them.'

O'Brien held up his hand to restrain the other senators, all of whom seemed ready to weigh in with howls of outrage.

'I think, Colonel,' he said, 'that my colleagues and I need to take stock of our situation, and try to figure out what to do next. If you would excuse us.'

'Yes, Sir,' the colonel replied. He nodded to the lieutenant. Both rose smartly and left the room. Two Marines stood outside the door, waiting to escort them back outside.

'For God's sake, Joe,' the Chief Justice began, roused to action again.

O'Brien restrained him with a touch on the shoulder, and turned to face the other senators.

'Just a moment, Sam. I don't know whether you understand what's going on here,' he began quietly. 'But I think I do.'

'I'm glad somebody does,' Senator Alan Boswell replied angrily. 'Because I sure as hell don't.'

O'Brien threw up his hands.

'We're prisoners, my friends. Prisoners. Those people out there aren't there to protest. They're there to seize power. And the Marines aren't here to keep them out. They're here to keep us in.'

'What?' Boswell shouted.

'Hear me out, Alan. Think about it for a moment. Wade is gone. We impeached him. We have several thousand armed people on the street. The Marines won't lift a finger to help. We're getting this story about Trevathan getting the hell out of Dodge, and Wade still being in the White House. But we don't have any real idea what's going on. And we're completely cut off. For all we know, the whole of Washington could be in their hands.'

'Of course Wade's still in the White House,' Boswell said. 'There hasn't been time for him to leave. That doesn't mean he's trying to hang on to power.'

Senator Kate Green shook her head.

'I'm not so sure. Joe may be right. I'm sure your aides got the same story mine did, Alan. Trevathan's in Houston because she has to be, and nobody knows whether Wade is going to leave or not.'

'That's ridiculous,' Boswell protested. 'How could he not leave? My aides told me all this stuff was coming from Lazenby. He's a loose cannon. Who knows what the hell's going on?'

'Well, something is,' Kate said.

Boswell turned back to Joe O'Brien.

'Are you really saying that Wade is trying to hang on to power, even though we've impeached his ass?'

'At this point,' O'Brien replied, 'I almost hope that's what I'm saying. Because if not, some other people are trying to take power, and I don't even want to speculate about who they might be.'

'Whoever they are,' Kate Green pointed out somberly, 'they've got Hessler with them.'

There was a long silence.

'God in Heaven,' Boswell said. 'What the hell are we going to do?'

'I guess we could follow the colonel's suggestion,' Kate Green said tentatively. 'Send word out that we changed our vote. Make up some procedural crap about the first vote being invalid. The press people here would go along with it. They're in the same boat we are. Once they restore order, no one would hold us to any announcement we made under duress.'

O'Brien shook his head firmly. 'Once who restores order?' he asked.

'Good question,' Kate admitted.

'Whatever the situation is outside, it might only make it worse.'

'I can't see how,' Boswell said. 'But I don't think it's a question for us. I think we should go back to the Chamber and report back on our meeting, and I think we should let everyone know what the colonel said.'

'I'm not sure we ought to bring it up,' O'Brien said. 'I really don't think we should be encouraging our colleagues to think that way. I don't want to be responsible for it.'

'We could treat it as a suggestion of last resort. Offer it only if no one has a better idea,' Kate Green said.

O'Brien nodded. 'I can live with that.'

He looked around at the other senators and the Chief Justice, who nodded their agreement.

'God bless democracy,' he added ironically.

'Come on, Joe,' Boswell said. 'You know we don't have any real choice.'

'OK. Let's go,' O'Brien replied.

* * *

'With all due respect, Mr. President, I don't see what we have to gain by letting her in here.'

General Hessler was leaning across Steve Wade's desk in an effort to make his point more emphatically, but he was not sure that anyone was listening to him. The former President had his head turned to one side. The other occupant of the room, Dick Latham, seemed completely out of it. He was sitting wearily in an armchair, appearing almost to ignore the conversation. The White House's unreal quietness was getting on everyone's nerves. The corridors and offices were almost empty. Agents Linda Samuels and Gary Mills patrolled the halls, and marine guards patrolled the grounds, but the occupants of the Oval Office hardly noticed them. The nerve center had shifted to the situation room, some distance from the Oval Office, in which a group of senior marine officers supervised a network of sophisticated computerized tracking devices providing information about military movements throughout the world. In the situation room, printers worked ceaselessly, television and computer screens provided immediate access to news and weather information. But none of this reached the Oval Office, except for the occasional report deemed important enough to require Hessler's personal attention. The Oval Office seemed strangely detached from reality, a head without a body.

'We have to talk to someone,' Wade replied eventually. 'It's not good politics to ignore an offer to talk. That's not what the American people want. They are looking to us to resolve this situation. If Trevathan wants to talk terms, we should listen to her.'

'They're not asking us to listen to her,' Hessler said. 'They're sending some young woman…'

'That young woman happens to be the Acting Director of the FBI, General,' Latham interrupted, apparently taking a renewed interest in his surroundings.

'That title is not legal,' Hessler rejoined, 'and it doesn't conceal the fact that we are being asked to deal with the minor leaguers.'

'That's the way it's done,' Latham insisted. 'I would have thought, with your experience, General, you would know that. You don't bring in the big guns until the deal is ready to be done. You don't expose them to the risk of failure.'

'And they want her college buddy, Agent Samuels, to talk to her?' Hessler snorted contemptuously. 'The two girl friends are going to negotiate for us? Sounds like a typical Trevathan idea to me.'

'It's a damn good idea,' Latham said, getting up slowly. 'Agent Samuels is very loyal to the President. She went to prison for him. She's not going to give anything away. And Kelly Smith is a very smart woman. You don't get to be Ted Lazenby's personal assistant without having what it takes, believe me.'

'And it gives us cover,' Wade added. 'While they're talking, we're making other plans, or carrying out other plans. We look like good guys for talking to them, but we're also pressing forward with our agenda. And we can buy more time by saying we have to consider very carefully any suggestions that they may make. I don't see a downside to it.'

Hessler stood up straight and faced Steve Wade.

'All right, Mr. President, if you put it like that, I guess I don't have an objection. But you do understand that once she's in, Miss Smith can't leave, and neither can anyone she brings with her.'

Dick Latham turned around sharply to look at Hessler.

'What the hell do you mean by that?'

'Just what I said,' Hessler snarled viciously. 'Anyone we allow into the White House will get a first-hand look at our operation. We can't allow the other side to gain access to that kind of intelligence. It's not secure.'

Latham pushed himself up out of his chair and walked decisively towards Hessler as if to confront him.

'I don't believe this,' he said angrily. 'You're seriously proposing to kill the woman, you're going to murder her?'

'I'm drawing attention to a regrettable operational necessity.'

'Are you out of your fucking mind?' Latham screamed. 'Steve, would you get this psychopath under control, for Christ's sake?'

'It's not murder, Mr. Attorney-General,' Hessler replied. 'In case you haven't noticed, we are in a state of war. The disposal of enemy agents is a normal incident of war. I don't expect you to understand that, but that's the way it is.'

'That's bullshit,' Latham shouted. 'We are not at war. Smith is not an enemy agent, and she's not going to go anywhere near our operation. She'll have a marine guard every step of the way. We're not going to let her anywhere near the operations room.'

'It's not secure,' Hessler repeated. 'Who cares, anyway? By the time anyone asks what happened to her, we will have the entire Senate under threat of immediate invasion, and we'll have a battery of nuclear weapons trained on Houston. Kelly Smith will be the last thing on Trevathan's mind, I guarantee you that.'

Latham looked hopelessly at Steve Wade.

'Steve, come on. For God's sake.'

Hessler smiled. 'Do you really think it's up to him any more?' he asked.

Wade turned even further round in his chair, his back to the other occupants of the room.

'I have to leave security matters to General Hessler,' he said quietly. 'I have other things to consider.'

'The hell you do.' Latham walked up to Wade's desk and brought a fist crashing down on it. 'I didn't sign up for this. I'm a prosecutor, for Christ's sake. I'm not about to condone murder.'

'You don't have any choice, Mr. Attorney-General,' Hessler said.

'The hell I don't,' Latham replied, heading for the door. 'You'll damn well see what choice I have.'

'May I remind you,' Hessler said quietly, without turning round, 'that there are a number of Marines outside that door, who will carry out any order I give them without questioning it. I strongly advise you not to test my patience.'

Latham stopped at the door, turned, and gave Hessler a look of pure hatred.

'I'll be in my office, Mr. President.' He left the room.

Hessler switched on the radio attached to the collar of his uniform.

'The Attorney-General will be accompanied at all times until further notice,' he said.

'Yes, Sir,' a voice responded.

'Well, I think we're in agreement, Mr. President. I'll give the word that Smith and one other agent may pay us a visit.'

Steve Wade turned his chair back around. 'When do we move on the Senate?'

'I recommend we put my forces on alert when Smith arrives. At the end of the discussions, we allow her to call Trevathan to say we're still talking. We go in when their defenses are down.'

'Very well. And the nuclear weapons?'

'I'll get started on redeploying them now. Once they are in place, you can talk to Trevathan any time you want and make sure she understands what she's up against.'

Wade drummed his fingers nervously on his desk. 'I hope she gets the message.'

'Ellen Trevathan is a lightweight,' Hessler said contemptuously. 'She can't stand the idea of force. Not since her first peace conference in 1964. She's the one the Williamsburg Doctrine was made for. She'll fold like a stack of cards.'

'Let's not forget that, right now, you're the only member of the Joint Chiefs who still supports the Williamsburg Doctrine,' Wade said. 'McGarry seems to have become unreliable. Ellen can count on a lot of support if it comes to a fight.'

'There will be no fight, and McGarry will be back once he figures out they can't stop us,' Hessler insisted. 'We're holding all the cards. Once the Senate reverses its vote, they'll be back on board. Without that vote in the Senate, Trevathan has no legitimacy.'

'We can't hold the Senate hostage forever,' Wade said. 'This depends on the people, not the Senate. I'm not hearing about too many people taking to the streets. I'm a popular President. What is wrong with these people? Can't they see what we're trying to do here? Can't they see we need their support? That's what's going to get Ellen's attention, when she sees that the people are behind me.'

'We have the people that count on the streets,' Hessler said. 'Here in Washington. Lots of them. Once we take the Senate, they'll make their views known soon enough. The people want what they always want, Mr. President. They want a quiet life. They want to see this thing resolved, so they can get back to their beer and football. And that's what we're going to give them by this time tomorrow. Besides, Trevathan knows what would be involved in trying to retake the White House. There won't be a White House any more, and she's not going to do that. Now, if you'll excuse me, I'll go and get things started.'

Wade nodded. Hessler left the Oval Office. Two Marines stationed outside the door came to attention and made as if to follow him. Hessler shook his head.

'Stay here and guard the President,' he ordered. 'Don't let anyone in without my permission.'

* * *

As Senator O'Brien followed his colleagues wearily back into the Senate Chamber, Frank pushed himself up from the floor and walked over to join him.

'How did it go?' he asked.

O'Brien shook his head. 'Not good,' he replied. 'You'll hear all about it.' He took one step forward, intending to take his seat, but then abruptly turned back.

'Frank, is there any way, any way at all, to verify these stories we've been hearing? They seem unbelievable, but…'

'You think there may be something to it, Senator?'

'I'm beginning to think so. I'm afraid our colleagues may be on the verge of making a big mistake, but without some more facts, I don't see any way to stop them.'

Frank's eyes suddenly opened wide. 'You mean they're thinking of…'

'That suggestion has been made to us… Maybe.'

Frank ran his hands through his hair. 'Perhaps there is a way. I'm not sure how much longer my phone is going to hold out… I wonder if… ? Give me a moment, Senator.'

O'Brien nodded and made his way slowly to his seat. Frank ran to a corner of the Chamber where he hoped there would be marginally less noise, and with a silent prayer dialed a number. The phone seemed to ring for ever, but just as he was about to give up, his call was answered.

'Kelly Smith'.

'Kelly, thank God. It's Frank.'

Unable to sleep or relax, Kelly and Jeff had walked back to the law school and were waiting by the phone in Ken Hunt's office. Kelly was sitting in the Dean's chair, alternating between nodding off and suddenly being wide awake. The sound of her mobile phone made her jump.

'Frank? Where are you?'

'I'm in the Capitol with Senator O'Brien.'

Kelly gestured to Jeff, who, also now wide awake, ran over to kneel by her side and listen in on the call.

'Listen, Kelly, I'm not sure how much juice my phone has left…'

'What's going on in there?'

'That's what I have to tell you. We're being held hostage by Hessler's marines…'

'Yes, I know…'

'The problem is, no one really knows what's going on outside. There are all kinds of rumors flying around. The Senators don't know what to do, Kelly. Senator O'Brien thinks they may be about to take another vote on the impeachment.'

'Jesus Christ,' Kelly breathed. 'Where does Senator O'Brien stand on that?'

'I don't think he wants to do it. He's asked me to try to get some more facts. You were the only person I could think of. I don't know how much time we have left. Conditions are pretty bad in here, Kelly…'

Kelly looked at Jeff anxiously.

'Frank, listen, you were right to call. I can't tell you everything, for security reasons. What I can tell you is that President Trevathan has taken the oath of office. She is safe, and she is in charge of the legitimate government.'

'In Houston? That's the rumor around here.'

'Yes. I'm here with her. Wade is still in the White House, and he and Hessler are trying to prevent Trevathan from taking over. But it's not going to work. I know you have some Marines to worry about, but most of the military is supporting Trevathan. We have a plan in place, and we expect to have everyone safe soon. But here's the thing, we really need the Senate to hold firm.'

'Can I tell Senator O'Brien I've talked to you?'

'Yes. Tell him he has to reassure the Senate that we're doing all we can. I can't say any more now, but President Trevathan has promised to get you all out of there, and that's what we are going to do.'

Kelly heard the sigh on the other end of the line.

'Thank you, Kelly. I'll do what I can.'

'I know you will.'

There was an embarrassed silence.

'Just in case, Kelly… I… I want to apologize for being such an asshole.'

Kelly smiled. 'It's not necessary.'

'How is it going with… Jeff, is it?'

'Yes. Fine. How about you? Found someone to have a future with?'

Frank laughed. 'Still looking. Somehow, it doesn't seem so important right now.'

'Yeah, I know. Frank…'

'Yes?'

'Thanks.'

The phone beeped several times, then went dead.

Kelly looked at Jeff.

'We'd better speak to the President,' she said.

* * *

'This is Fox. Are you hearing me?'

'I hear you spent your vacation in France?'

'No. I prefer Italy.'

'Hearing you loud and clear, Fox,' Carlson replied. 'Go ahead.'

'The Marines have been put on alert. When the time comes, your people will storm the Capitol. The Marines will put up a show of resistance, but will be unable to prevent the crowd from entering the building. No shots will be fired. I expect you to be responsible for that. If they are fired on, the Marines will return fire, but their rules of engagement are that they are not to fire unless fired on. This is to be an action by the people, not the military. The world's press has to see that the American people are taking back their institutions. But nobody is to move before time. Is this clearly understood?'

'That's affirmative,' Carlson replied.

'Good. And you understand what is to happen once you're inside?'

'The Senate is to be persuaded to change its vote.'

'Yes. And as soon as that happens, you call me, and wait for further orders. Once you are secure in the Senate, you may have your people take a few other buildings, just to make the point, the Supreme Court, the Library of Congress, whatever you want. Tell your commanders to make sure the press get a good look at what's going on. But the same rules apply. No shooting. Understood?'

'That's affirmative. How long…?'

'Not long. There are a few things to take care of, political matters, nothing that need concern you.'

Fox rang off abruptly.

52

'WE'RE IN,' Jeff said, hanging up. 'The helicopter has clearance to land on the White House landing pad. They require the pilot to call in with an E.T.A. at five minutes, and then two minutes out. They have assigned us a special frequency for transmissions.'

Ellen got up from her desk, walked over to Kelly and Jeff and placed a hand on each of their arms.

'I don't like this,' she said.

'We have to do something, Madam President,' Jeff replied. 'We don't know how long we can hold things in the Senate. The alternative is to mount an all-out frontal attack on the White House now, and you're not ready to do that yet.'

'It may be a trap.'

'Possibly,' Kelly said. 'But they have nothing to gain by doing anything to us. Besides, Linda would have warned us.'

'Linda may not know,' the President observed.

'They want to talk,' Kelly said. 'They could have just refused to let us in. I think the worst-case scenario is that they will use the time to plan their next move, which they will do anyway. But so will we. And General Gutierrez said the more time we could buy him, the better.'

'And they have agreed that you can be in touch with me by telephone?'

'We made that a non-negotiable condition. We'll report whatever happens, of course.'

'I've been keeping my eye on the television, Kelly. I don't like the look of that crowd around the Capitol. Something's fixing to blow there.'

'"Fixing to", Madame President?' Jeff smiled. 'You've been in Texas too long already. We need to get you back to Washington.'

'My fault,' Ken Hunt grinned. 'I haven't learned to watch my Ps and Qs around the President yet.'

Ellen managed a tired smile.

'Fixing to, is about to, whatever,' she said. 'The point is, as Jeff said, we don't know how much time we have. And, Kelly, if things get out of hand in Washington, I'm going to take action. I will protect the Senate. So if I call and tell you to get out of the White House, you get out right away, and you come back here, no questions asked. All right?'

'Yes, Ma'am,' Kelly replied. 'Let me suggest we have a code for that, so we don't give them a heads-up.'

'How about I say'we're 'fixing' to do something? It's not a phrase I'm likely to use accidentally again, now it's been pointed out to me.'

'Sounds good,' Kelly said. 'Dean Hunt, you make sure you hold her to that. No 'fixing to' unless you mean it.'

'You got it, Kelly,' Hunt replied.

'We need to get going,' Jeff said. 'As it is, we're not going to be there before the middle of the afternoon.'

'We're out of here,' Kelly said.

'I wish you God speed,' Ellen said. 'I will be praying for you, and I will never forget this.'

* * *

'Quite a reception committee,' Jeff said nervously, as the helicopter pilot hovered his craft above the White House grounds. The area was crowded with uniformed Marines brandishing assault rifles.

'It's like something you'd expect to see in Colombia,' Kelly answered.

'You want me to set her down?' the pilot asked. His voice crackled through Kelly's headset. Kelly had stipulated that they would not actually land until she had the chance to assess the situation on the ground. She was not sure exactly what it was she was expecting to assess. She had no real alternative. This was the point of no return. She looked around one last time.

'That's affirmative,' she replied.

The helicopter descended slowly and gracefully, coming down softly on the landing pad. Kelly and Jeff unbuckled their seat belts. Jeff grasped the small briefcase tightly as they left the helicopter, keeping their heads low until they were clear of the main rotor blades. A marine captain and two guards approached from the direction of the entrance to the White House. The captain saluted smartly.

'Director, Agent Morris? I'm Captain David Manning, United States Marine Corps. I've been assigned to escort you into the White House.'

At the word 'Director', Kelly glanced at Jeff and raised her eyebrows.

'Thank you, Captain,' Kelly answered.

'Ma'am, I'm required to ask you to check your firearms,' Manning continued. 'Please hand them to these Marines.'

Kelly nodded briefly to Jeff. It was what they had been expecting. Without protest, they handed over the automatics they had brought with them.

Captain Manning glanced at the guards.

'You can wait,' he ordered curtly. 'I'll take it from here. Radio control that we're on our way in.'

'Sir. Yes, Sir,' one of the guards responded.

'This way, Ma'am,' Manning said, leading the way at a brisk pace across the lawn. At the entrance he stopped. He turned, suddenly less confident.

'You'll be met inside,' he said. 'I'll wait until they arrive.' He took a few steps in the direction from which they had come, and then stopped abruptly.

'OK,' Kelly said.

It was just a gut feeling, but Kelly knew she was right. Was it something in Manning's manner, his hesitation, the way he had looked at her, the fact that he had called her 'Director'? She was not sure. But whatever it was, it was real, something was on offer, and she had to take advantage of it.

'Captain Manning, may I speak to you for a moment?'

'Yes, Ma'am.'

Manning walked back to join Kelly and Jeff, and stood facing them with his back to the White House lawn, where the curious marine guards stood at attention, keeping the small party in their gaze.

'I'd like to ask you a question,' Kelly said. 'Are you aware of any, shall we say, rumors that may have been circulating among your Marines recently?'

She saw Manning swallow hard, turning his head slightly to each side in turn, as if expecting someone to creep up on him.

'I don't know what rumors you mean, Ma'am.'

'Oh, I think you do. I mean rumors about what will happen once this crisis ends.'

'About what will happen?'

'To officers such as yourself. Once President Trevathan has ended the crisis.'

Manning looked away.

'Obviously, any officer would have to be worried about the consequences of decisions he may have taken, any questionable orders he may have obeyed.'

Manning seemed uncertain. He was shifting his weight uneasily from foot to foot. Kelly wondered whether he had been sleeping well recently, or whether he had been lying awake at night wondering what lay in store for him. She had given him a chance, but she could not make him take it. There was not much time, but she must not rush it. She waited, allowing him to find his balance.

'Ma'am, are we…?'

'We're completely off the record. I give you my word.'

Manning nodded.

'Off the record, Ma'am, there has been a rumor among the officers and men here, that Pres… that is, Miss Trevathan has offered an amnesty to officers below a certain rank, in the event that she does become President. I don't know where it came from.'

He hesitated. 'Is it true? Do you know?'

Kelly felt Jeff's eyes on her. She took a deep breath.

'Captain Manning, Ellen Trevathan is already the President of the United States,' she replied. 'Whether or not any amnesty is to be granted is up to the President. It's not something I can officially confirm.'

'I understand that,' Manning said. 'But …'

'Let me finish,' Kelly interrupted. 'What I'm saying is, I can't confirm or deny anything officially. But there is one thing I can tell you. Ellen Trevathan is a woman of her word. You can take that to the bank. Do we understand each other?'

Slowly, Manning raised his eyes to meet Kelly's and nodded.

'Yes, Ma'am, we do. Thank you.'

'Good,' Kelly said. 'I'll remember. And I will leave it to your discretion whether or not you pass on our conversation to anyone else.'

Manning seemed poised to ask another question, but he had no time. Linda Samuels and Gary Mills were making their way to the entrance from inside the building. On seeing them, Manning saluted again and returned to his duties on the lawn

* * *

For several long moments, Kelly and Linda stood and looked at one another. Then, without a word, they walked into each other's arms and embraced. Kelly held Linda for some time. When she released her, she noticed that tears had formed in her friend's eyes. Hurriedly, Linda wiped her nose with the back of her hand. She stepped across to Jeff and kissed him lightly on the cheek.

'I'm sorry,' she said. 'I should do the introductions. Kelly Smith, Jeff Morris, my colleague, Gary Mills.'

With silent nods, Kelly and Jeff shook hands with Gary.

'Why don't we sit down?' Linda said, leading the way into a spacious conference room which had been furnished with coffee and water.

'This is awkward,' Linda began, once they were seated around the mahogany conference table. 'I don't know how to…'

'First,' Kelly said, 'we're not recording this. Are you?'

'No,' Linda said. 'This is off the record.'

'Good,' Kelly said. 'I asked for this meeting, Linda, so why don't you let me make a start, and everyone else can join in as they need to. Is that OK?'

'Sure. That's fine.'

'Jeff and I are here in our capacity as federal agents,' Kelly said. 'But we're also here at the request of President Trevathan, to see if we can't find some way out of this impasse. I need to make it clear that, while we have authority to negotiate, we would have to get the President's agreement to whatever might be proposed.'

'So would we,' Gary said. 'We would have to get the President's agreement.'

Kelly was about to respond sharply, when she felt Jeff's hand on her arm. He laughed pleasantly.

'All right,' he said. 'Look, it's obvious that we take different positions here as to who the President is, and I don't see anyone backing off right now. So why don't we agree to call them 'Trevathan' and 'Wade', or 'Ellen' and 'Steve', for now? We all understand no one's conceding anything. It might make things run smoother.'

'Fine with me,' Gary said. Kelly and Linda nodded, Kelly with some reluctance.

'All right,' Kelly said. 'I have two things to say to begin with. First, I understand that Wade was a very popular President, and I understand that he thinks the Senate has treated him unfairly. Maybe they have. But the thing is, Linda, we have to be ruled by the Constitution and, according to the Constitution, Wade is gone. That's black-letter law. Once the Senate votes, Wade is gone.'

'What's the second thing?' Linda asked.

'Trevathan controls the military.'

'Some of the military,' Gary Mills corrected. 'Not including the nukes.'

'The nukes are irrelevant,' Kelly responded quickly. 'No American serviceman is going to use nuclear weapons against his own country.'

'Maybe, maybe not,' Gary said. Something in the tone of his voice made Kelly's blood run cold.

'We're quite sure of that,' she said, with a little hesitation.

'I wouldn't be, if I were you,' Gary replied coolly. 'Guess where some of those weapons are pointed, as of this afternoon?'

There was a long silence. 'I don't believe it,' Jeff said firmly.

'Is that true, Linda?' Kelly asked.

'I believe so,' Linda replied. 'That's what I'm told.'

Her face had become very pale.

'It's a bluff,' Jeff said. 'Wade would never do that. What hope would he have of being President if he did that? It's bullshit.'

'You're not listening to us,' Gary said.

'Damn right, I'm not listening to that,' Jeff replied.

Gary exhaled heavily. 'No, you're not hearing what we're saying.'

'What Gary means,' Linda jumped in, 'is that you assumed we were saying that Wade pointed the nukes at the United States, and that any decision to use them would be taken solely by Steve Wade. We didn't say that.'

Kelly and Jeff looked at each other in horror. For some time they could not reply.

'It's Hessler, isn't it?' Kelly asked eventually.

'Yes.'

Jeff snorted, shaking his head.

'I don't get this. Wade is claiming to be the President of the United States. My understanding is that the President has sole control of the nuclear codes. How could Hessler…?'

'It's not that simple, Jeff,' Gary interrupted. 'Wade has very few options here. At the beginning, it seemed that the Joint Chiefs would all support the Williamsburg Doctrine… well, all except Gutierrez anyway. But Terrell wouldn't play ball, and then McGarry dropped out. That left Hessler as Wade's only senior military adviser. Obviously, Wade has been taking his advice, and he has given Hessler a lot of leeway on strategy.'

There was another long silence. Kelly could hear her heart beat against the silence of the room.

'In any case,' Linda said, 'you couldn't retake the White House

345

without destroying the building, and considerable loss of life. We know that Trevathan is not about to do that. She doesn't like guns.'

Kelly leaned forward in her chair.

'Linda, if Wade and Hessler believe that, they are making a serious miscalculation.'

'Oh, come on.'

'The Institution is more important than the building, Linda. Trevathan will take it back, or take the ground it stands on back, whatever the cost. And she'll do it tomorrow. You have her word on it.'

'What were you saying about the Senate?' Linda asked, after she and Gary had remained silent for some time.

'I said that after the Senate vote, Wade was gone as President.'

'What if the Senate took another vote, and came up with a different result?'

'You mean, under duress, with Hessler's Marines and that mob of white supremacist yahoos holding guns on them? You think that qualifies as a vote?'

'Trevathan could question it in the courts,' Gary Mills observed, with a careless shrug. 'But Wade would remain President.'

'I don't see that,' Jeff said. 'He's not President now. The only vote so far has been to remove him. The Constitution doesn't say the Senate can put him back into office again.'

Before Gary could reply, Linda leaned forward, and put her hand on his arm.

'Kelly, what do you mean 'white supremacist yahoos'?' she asked.

Kelly looked at her closely. 'Oh, don't tell me you don't know who they are.'

'As far as I know, they're citizens,' Linda said.

'Well, yes, they are citizens, unfortunately,' Kelly replied. 'They're also white supremacist yahoos, organized by the Sons of the Land. Remember them?'

'Bullshit,' Linda shouted angrily. 'Why can't you people deal with the fact that Wade is a popular President, and the people have turned out to support him. It's the people who will be taking back the Senate, Kelly, not any white supremacists.'

Jeff moved forward in his chair, but Kelly shook her head.

'Linda, you remember when we had dinner that time? You wanted to tell me how uneasy you were about some of the things that were going on here in the White House, and I was telling you how crazy things were at the Bureau because we were tracking all those protests?'

'I remember.'

'Well, what we were actually tracking were car loads, van loads, truck loads of people coming to Washington from out West. It was a highly organized operation. We didn't see it coming until it was too late, because there were so many vehicles involved, vehicles that are now parked all around Washington. If you'd been out of this place recently, you would have seen them. That whole thing was orchestrated by the Sons of the Land. And those were also the people Hamid Marfrela was working with. So suddenly, here we have Wade getting impeached, and the Sons of the Land showing up in force to try to help him out. Do you see where I'm going with this?'

'So, you're saying Wade set all this up?' Linda asked eventually. 'You're saying there never was any mass movement of the people at all?'

'Well, what did you think, Linda?' Kelly countered. 'Don't tell me you bought the story that you and Gary are part of some glorious stand on behalf of the American people? That Wade is some icon the people have to protect against political assassination by the Senate? God in Heaven, Linda, after all the years I've known you, you're not going to tell me you fell for a load of crap like that?'

Linda stood, her face set, her hands clenched furiously. 'It is not a load of crap,' she shouted. 'How dare you…?'

'Take it easy, Linda,' Gary said.

He leaned forward across the table.

'How sure are you of this?' he asked.

'The Bureau has been monitoring the Sons of the Land for several years,' Kelly replied. 'We have a lot of intelligence on them. We even had an agent inside their organization for a while, but they found out about him. We lost him, Gary, and he was a good man. But, as a result, we were ready for them to make a move of some kind. When the impeachment started, we saw a convoy of vehicles leaving their compound in Oregon. We watched them every step of the way to Washington. Other convoys joined them. Unfortunately, they got wind that we were on to them and broke up, so we had to try to watch each vehicle. Even with satellite coverage, we lost track of some of them. Until they got to Washington. But we have agents in place, and these agents have positively identified George Carlson and Dan Rogers, who are known to be the commanders of the Sons of the Land. They are on the steps of the Capitol as we speak. Now, OK, maybe Wade didn't orchestrate this himself. Maybe someone else did. But the fact remains, the Senate is being held hostage by a bunch of thugs.'

'The Senate is being guarded by the Marines,' Gary Mills said, but his voice lacked conviction.

'Guarded?' Kelly asked. 'Or intimidated?'

There was a long silence.

'This isn't getting anywhere,' Linda said eventually.

'It has to get somewhere,' Kelly said. 'And it has to get somewhere fast.' She looked at Jeff, who nodded slightly. 'Wade's organization is falling apart, Linda.'

'It doesn't look that way to me. You've been out there in the grounds. You've seen the pictures on television. I don't see anything falling apart.'

'That's because you're not hearing what those Marines out there in the grounds of the White House are saying.'

'What do you mean?'

Kelly leaned forward in her chair.

'It seems that there have been rumors circulating. They're saying that Trevathan is prepared to grant an amnesty to junior officers and enlisted men if they give her their support. They're thinking about it. They're having second thoughts about carrying out some of the orders they've been given. Clearly the law is on Trevathan's side, so I don't think it's going to take them very long to figure out what to do, do you?'

'That's bullshit.'

'No, it's not. I've heard the rumor myself.'

'If so, Trevathan planted it. It's just bullshit.'

'Whoever planted it, it's working. And Trevathan would have every reason to be grateful to anyone who defends the Constitution, even if that wasn't their original decision. Including you, Linda. Including you, Gary.'

Gary Mills sneered. 'You think you can turn us around? Is that why you came here?'

'I came here to talk,' Kelly replied. 'But, since we're on the subject, I wouldn't want to see the two of you go down with the ship. You're both very loyal people, but your loyalty has been used, betrayed. If you stay with Wade, the story is not going to have a happy ending.'

Gary shook his head. Linda was looking down at the table. Both seemed suddenly subdued.

'There's one more thing,' Kelly said. 'I know you're loyal to Wade. But, from everything you've said, and everything we know, this isn't about Wade any more. It's about Hessler. I don't think Wade has any more control than you do. Not any longer. Do you really want Hessler running the country?'

Linda looked up.

'And it's one thing to go to the mat for Wade,' Kelly continued. 'It's another thing to give it to Hessler.'

Linda seemed ready to respond, but Gary stopped her.

'Can we take a break?' he asked.

'Sure,' Kelly replied.

'It will give us a chance to talk over what you've said, and see if there's any point in continuing this.'

'OK. How long do you want?'

'Let's say fifteen minutes. Help yourselves to coffee.'

Abruptly, he and Linda left the room.

'What do you think?' Jeff asked. 'Did we make an impression?'

'Hard to say,' Kelly replied, reaching for her mobile phone. 'These Secret Service types are hard core. At least they want to think about it.'

She dialed a number and was immediately connected to Ellen Trevathan's office.

'What's happening, Kelly?' the President asked. The tension in her voice was palpable.

'All I can say is, we're in and we're talking. We're on a break. I can't say anything more right now.'

'I'll be waiting,' President Trevathan replied. 'Is there anything I can do?'

'Yes,' Kelly replied. 'If you haven't done it already, would you please declare a state of emergency?'

53

WHAT A BITTER irony, Senator Joe O'Brien reflected, that after serving for more than thirty years in the Senate, he had finally realized a dream he thought would always elude him. He was speaking on the floor of the Senate, and he had the complete attention of a packed Chamber. There had been many occasions when he would have given a very great deal to have all his colleagues hanging on every word he said. But that hardly mattered now. What mattered was that he had their attention, and that it was crucially important that he keep it. Part of his hold over them, he knew, was anxiety, and part was sheer exhaustion. The air-conditioning had been off for hours, the Chamber was hot and stuffy, it felt as though they had been locked in for ever, and the extreme physical discomfort was affecting everyone. The senators took what little ease they could in their seats. Those who did not have seats in the Chamber, the aides, and journalists, slumped wherever they could, briefcases, television cameras, microphones abandoned at their sides. The journalists knew that they were witnessing a great story. What they did not know was whether they would survive to tell it. They were also unsure exactly what the story was. Ellen Trevathan had not lifted the news rationing imposed by Ted Lazenby, and the only word reaching the Senate via the few mobile phones and laptops still working was that there was a crisis, the precise nature of which was unclear. Only Senator O'Brien, relying on Frank Worley's conversation with Kelly, had, or thought he had, a little hard information. The journalists were guessing. Once the siege was lifted, the race for the prize-winning scoop would begin. If they had the energy, and if they were still in one piece. The Chief Justice, regardless of the fact that the impeachment proceedings had ended, and that he no longer had any constitutional function to perform in the Senate, had resumed his seat in the Speaker's chair. No one seemed to mind. The Senate was ready to accept direction and guidance from anyone prepared to give it.

Unsure of what to do in the midst of so much chaos, Ed Monahan had kept his seat at counsel's table.

'So, I guess the bottom line,' O'Brien concluded, 'is that we are being asked to regard ourselves as prisoners in this building until whatever situation is developing out there resolves itself. It's not an attractive proposition…'

'Damn right,' a male voice broke in.

'But I'm not sure what else we can do. If anyone has any better ideas, I'd like to hear them. But I must warn you that anything we decide to do will have to be accomplished without the aid of the Marines. And there is a very nasty-looking mob out there. So, whatever we do, we need to give it some serious reflection.'

O'Brien stopped to invite reaction to what he had said. He caught Kate Green's eye, and nodded to her almost imperceptibly.

'I agree with Senator O'Brien,' Kate said in a firm voice, standing in place without moving to the podium. 'Whatever the situation is out there, it's obviously very dangerous.'

'That's my impression also,' Alan Boswell added.

O'Brien wondered how the discussion would proceed. The Senate had no presiding officer. It was now long past considerations of protocol and rules of procedure. There was no longer any question of precedence in taking the floor, or yielding time. Under any ordinary circumstances, with the usual restraints removed, the senators would have been climbing over each other to speak first. But no one seemed anxious to take the lead. After a prolonged silence, Tom Danvers, the senior senator from West Virginia, an elderly man with a shock of silver hair and a stately, dignified bearing, slowly approached the podium.

'Senator O'Brien,' he began, the effect of the heat and fatigue obvious in his voice, 'I understand that the situation out there is dangerous. And the whole Senate is grateful to you and the other senators who have been trying to get what information you can, and trying to find a way of dealing with it. But I believe it would just be wrong to lie down and allow ourselves to be held hostage here. President Trevathan needs us to function as a Senate. And it goes against principle to allow one of the branches of the legislature to be held hostage by a bunch of terrorists, which is what those folks are. We just shouldn't allow it. That's what I have to say.'

Danvers paused, trying his best to look combative despite his own inner feelings of disquiet. Several senators shook their heads, and there was some murmuring.

'Well, that's all very well, Tom,' one shouted out. 'But what exactly are you suggesting we do? Send them a message that we're not going to stand for it? What if they say 'no'?'

Danvers drew himself up to his full height.

'No. I'm suggesting that we exercise our right to walk out of here,' he said with conviction. 'Hell, there's a hundred of us, plus our staff, and the ladies and gentlemen of the press. What are these terrorists going to do, shoot us all? Shoot the entire Senate?'

'Hell, Tom, if there are some of my constituents out there, some of them just might,' a senator called out, to general laughter.

Danvers did not join in the laughter.

'With all those Marines out there? I don't think so. I was a Marine myself in my younger days, and I don't believe I would have let that happen if I were in their position. Look, we did our duty today. We voted on the impeachment. Now I want to go home and see my wife, have dinner. Let's just get the hell out of here, Ladies and Gentlemen.'

Danvers's words were greeted by a substantial round of applause. Several senators shouted their agreement.

'What do you think, Joe?' one asked.

Danvers moved away from the podium slightly to allow O'Brien to approach, but showed no sign of resuming his seat.

'I'd like to agree with Senator Danvers,' O'Brien replied, 'but it's just not possible. For one thing, I don't believe the Marines have the capability to protect us. There are too many of us, especially if we all run out of here in a hundred different directions. It would very likely precipitate a fire-fight, which could result in a huge loss of life. I don't believe that risk is justifiable.'

'I'm willing to take that risk,' Tom Danvers insisted. 'It's a matter of principle.'

Quite a number of senators applauded and cheered. O'Brien felt his stomach begin to churn again. He took a few deep breaths to calm himself.

'And in any case,' he continued, 'I'm afraid leaving is not an option. Physically, I mean.'

He paused.

'What do you mean?' Danvers asked.

'I mean the colonel made it pretty clear that the Marines will not allow us to leave, at least for now.'

'What?' Danvers asked, incredulously.

'It's not up to the colonel,' a senator shouted before O'Brien could reply. 'It's a matter for us to decide. Is this guy seriously telling us we can't leave the Capitol? Hell, I think that constitutes a contempt of the Senate, right there.'

O'Brien closed his eyes.

'Well, maybe it does, Bill,' he said. 'But what exactly are you going to do about that? You want to send the Sergeant-at-Arms to arrest him?'

To O'Brien's relief, this produced some laughter.

'Look,' he continued, 'I agree with Tom in principle. This shouldn't be happening. But it is. I also think the Marines have our safety in mind here. Obviously, there's some serious disorder going on outside. They're the experts, and I don't see any point in forcing the issue, when we may be able to leave without any problem in a little while.'

'That depends what you mean by 'a little while',' another senator observed. 'Judging by what you just told us, the colonel didn't hold out much hope that this would end any time soon.'

'I think we have to accept that Ellen Trevathan and those working with her are doing all they can,' O'Brien replied. 'I don't see any reason to doubt that. We need to be patient and hang in there; give them time to work it out.'

Danvers moved back to the podium, making O'Brien shift to one side.

'So, if I'm understanding you correctly, Senator O'Brien,' he said, 'the Marines had no solution to propose to us except to wait it out?'

O'Brien looked uneasily at Kate Green. Before he could reply, Alan Boswell got to his feet.

'Well, that's not exactly true,' he said.

O'Brien looked down in irritation. 'Shit,' he muttered to himself.

'Do you want to tell them about it, Joe, or shall I?' Boswell was asking.

O'Brien looked for help to Kate Green, but Kate merely shrugged her shoulders. They would both have preferred not to raise the issue but, with so much at stake, they had already agreed that the Senate was entitled to hear everything.

'Be my guest, Alan,' O'Brien replied.

He stepped back as Boswell made his way forward to a heavy, expectant silence.

Boswell gripped the podium tightly.

'The colonel did have one suggestion,' he said tentatively. 'And I think I'm right in saying that those of us who were there agreed we should bring it to your attention, not recommend it, you understand, but at least give you the option of thinking about it. He suggested that, since most of the hooligans out there are apparently supporters of Steve Wade, they might be persuaded to go away if they were given the impression that we had reversed the impeachment vote.'

To O'Brien's surprise, Boswell's words were greeted with almost total silence. Kate Green raised her hand, then stood.

'The colonel also said that couldn't be guaranteed,' she pointed out.

'That's correct,' Boswell confirmed.

The silence continued.

'You said, 'if they were given the impression',' a senator asked eventually. 'You mean, put out a statement to that effect, rather than actually do it?'

'Yes,' Boswell replied. 'For one thing, I think there would be serious questions of legality surrounding any actual vote we took under the present circumstances. The Constitution says we can impeach the President, but it doesn't say we can put the President back into office after he's been impeached.'

He looked behind him at the Chief Justice.

'At least, I believe I'm right in saying that?'

'I wouldn't want to comment on the record,' Mayhew replied, 'in light of the fact that if such a thing actually happened, it would certainly come before the Court eventually, but off the record, I would say you are probably right.'

'So, the idea would be just to issue a statement,' Boswell continued. 'We would repudiate it the moment the siege is lifted. I don't believe anyone would hold it against us in the circumstances. I'm sure our colleagues in the press would help us.'

O'Brien had now lost the floor. With some alarm, he realized that Boswell was going a little further than just providing information. Boswell actually thought there was some merit in the idea. Animated conversation broke out all around the Chamber. The senators huddled in small groups. Some aides, suddenly springing back to life, moved in to join them. The journalists also woke up, extracting pens, notepads, and tape players from their discarded briefcases. After some time, Boswell turned and approached the Chief Justice, who nodded his agreement, and hammered his gavel down several times with enough force to cause the hubbub to die down.

'Ladies and gentlemen,' Boswell said. 'If I may have your attention. It seems we are not following strict procedure just now, which may be just as well. I would suggest that any senator who wishes to speak on this issue should be free to do so, and that we should then take a vote. If that meets with your approval...'

Joe O'Brien stepped quickly up to Boswell's side, interrupting him.

'Senator Boswell, I think you and I agree that we mentioned the possibility of making a statement because it was our duty to report back on everything that had taken place during our discussion with the Marines. But I don't believe we for one moment thought it was the right thing to do...'

'That doesn't mean we can't vote on it,' a voice shouted from the back of the Chamber. 'It sounds like a damn good idea to me.'

To O'Brien's dismay, a chorus of voices shouted agreement.

'There's no guarantee of anything, even if we did issue a statement,' O'Brien protested.

But his voice was now uncertain, and was almost lost in the renewed conversation. With his long experience of the Senate, Joe O'Brien was well able to recognize an emerging consensus when he saw one, and he was seeing one now. He looked hopelessly at Frank, who was sitting on the floor near the podium. He shrugged and shook his head.

'You did your best, Senator.'

Ed Monahan had been listening to the argument from his seat at counsel's table with a mixture of concern and disbelief. As he saw the consensus build, he did something he would never in his wildest dreams have imagined himself doing. He rose abruptly from his seat, strode to the podium, and half pushed Senator Alan Boswell to one side, at the same time raising his right hand in supplication to the Chief Justice. He saw Sam Mayhew look at him closely and then, to his surprise, nod almost imperceptibly and gavel for order. Order took some time in coming, especially when the senators saw who was standing at the podium.

'Mr. Chief Justice, Members of the Senate,' Monahan began hesitantly. 'I realize that this is probably out of order. In fact, I'm sure it is. But you were kind enough to listen to me for quite a while over the last few days, and I would ask for your further indulgence, just for a few minutes, because I have something to say which I believe is important. So, please, listen to me for just a moment.'

Out of the corner of his eye, Monahan saw that Senator Boswell was looking none too pleased. But his audience gave no such sign. He decided to continue until he was interrupted.

'Now, you all know that I represented President Wade, and tried my best to stop you impeaching him. So you know which side I was on in that debate. But things have changed now. Because of your vote, Ellen Trevathan is now President of the United States. With all respect, you can't put the clock back. There's no way to undo what you did and put Wade back in office, which is what those people out there want.'

'That's not the suggestion,' a senator called out. 'The idea is to *say* that we…'

'I understand that, Senator,' Monahan interrupted, fearful of being drowned out in a sea of protest. 'But hear me out. That isn't just a mob out there. Those are intelligent people, people smart enough to have orchestrated whatever is going on. And those people are probably more than smart enough to figure out that you would not, and could not, have taken a vote to reverse your position on the impeachment. If that's the case, the only thing you're going to achieve by spreading a false rumor is to make them even more angry than they are now. At best, nothing changes.'

Monahan saw a large number of senators began to nod. No one was disagreeing. Boswell's consensus was beginning to die as quickly as it had been born. Ed Monahan decided to add what was really on his mind.

'But the most important point is, that if you did put out a story like that, it might jeopardize whatever President Trevathan and her advisers are doing out there. We know from Senator O'Brien's Chief of Staff that the President is in Houston. We're not sure why, but I think it's a pretty safe bet that it's not so she can enjoy the climate.'

'Hey, not so fast there, young fella,' the senior senator from Texas drawled, breaking the ice and drawing some sympathetic laughter towards Monahan. 'Ain't nothing wrong with Houston.'

Monahan smiled, despite his anxiety.

'I'm sure that's true, Senator, and I didn't mean to disparage your home town. But my point is, I think we have to assume that the President is in Houston because it's not safe for her to be here in Washington. Now, we may not know all the details, but one thing we do know. She needs all the help she can get. If you suggest that the Senate has capitulated, it may send a message to her enemies that her support is falling away, and it may encourage them to go even farther than they have. So I believe you have to hang tough now, for the sake of our Government, for the sake of our Constitution. I beg you, don't go along with this idea.'

Monahan waited only for a moment before resuming his seat. The conversation resumed, but only momentarily. To everyone's surprise, Sam Mayhew gaveled again and, once he had induced silence, he walked slowly to the podium and took the floor himself.

'Ladies and Gentlemen, it's probably just as much out of order for me to interrupt the Senate's proceedings as it was for Mr. Monahan. Now, this may be the first time I've agreed with him since this whole thing started, but since he took the risk of speaking up, I guess it's probably all right for me to do the same.'

There was a little laughter, dying quickly away.

'Mr. Monahan is right. If you release this story of a vote that was never taken, everybody will find out the truth eventually, that's true. But 'eventually' is not the problem. The problem is here and now. I believe President Trevathan is in a good deal of trouble right now. Like you, I don't exactly know why. But I have been made aware that my colleagues on the Court have gone to Houston with her, so I have to assume that the danger goes beyond the President herself, and is reaching out to our Government as a whole. So, in my estimation, whatever is going on is of a very grave nature. If you undermine the President's position now by releasing a story that you have been pressured into changing your vote, it might give her enemies, the enemies of America, perhaps I should say, just enough encouragement to make a decisive difference. I want to get out of here as much as anyone else. But I believe it to be our duty, mine as well as yours, to stay and to support the new Administration.'

After almost a full minute of silence, Senator Joe O'Brien walked to the podium and stood alongside the Chief Justice.

'I don't believe there's any way to argue with what the Chief Justice has said,' he observed gravely. 'I guess, if necessary, we can take a vote, but I sincerely hope that will not be necessary. Anyone who feels it is, please raise your hand now.'

Not a single hand was raised. From his seat at counsel's table, Ed Monahan nodded to Sam Mayhew. For the rest of his life, Ed would believe, and would tell everyone he could, that he distinctly saw the Chief Justice of the United States wink back at him.

* * *

For just a moment, the colonel experienced an absurd flashback to a movie he had seen as a child with his father, a diehard fan of old Westerns. Who had the hero been, John Wayne, Randolph Scott? He could not remember. But he remembered the scene in every detail. The hero, the cavalry officer, and his companions were trapped in the ruins of their fort, cut off from their reinforcements, just waiting for the Indians to attack again. 'It's too quiet out there,' the script had told the officer to say to his sergeant. And, sure enough, the officer had been right. The Indians were just picking their moment. The colonel had the same feeling about the situation which confronted him now. Something in the mood of the crowd had changed. The chanting and shouting had largely subsided. Most of the crowd surrounding the Capitol seemed to have turned to face the Marines head on, and the occasional flash of metal suggested that their weapons were barely being concealed any longer. There was a mood of expectancy, almost as if they were waiting for a command. They were too quiet. And too organized. Unobtrusively, he gestured to the lieutenant to join him.

'Lieutenant, order your men to prepare to fire a warning shot over the heads of the crowd. But they will not fire without my command.'

'Yes, Sir.'

'I don't want any accidents, here, Lieutenant. Remember, General Hessler's orders are that no one in the crowd is to be harmed.'

'With one exception, Sir, I believe.'

'That's correct. Does Sergeant Hendricks still have Carlson in his sights?'

'He's never let go of him, Sir.'

'Good. But not until General Hessler gives me the order, and I pass it on to you.'

'Yes, Sir.'

'Dismissed, Lieutenant.'

'Yes, Sir.'

But the lieutenant did not immediately move away.

'Sir…?'

'Yes, Lieutenant.'

'I'm not trying to question General Hessler's orders, Sir. But if they do rush the building, and we do nothing…'

'I'm aware of that, Lieutenant. As I am sure is General Hessler. I'm assuming there's a plan to cover that eventuality. But it's important not to act prematurely here. If we do, we could endanger lives unnecessarily. I'm sure General Hessler is doing everything he can to be cautious, as should we. Our job is to follow orders, Lieutenant.'

Unconvinced, the lieutenant saluted.

'Yes, Sir. Thank you, Sir.'

54

Linda Samuels and Gary Mills entered the room quietly and took their seats.

'It seems we've reached an impasse,' Gary observed.

'I can't accept that,' Kelly replied. 'There's too much at stake here.'

'There's word that the Senate may be about to revisit the question of the impeachment vote,' Gary said. 'If that happens, Wade remains President, and Trevathan will have to make whatever deal she can.'

'I don't believe that,' Jeff said. 'What is the source of your information?'

Linda and Gary looked at each other without replying.

'Don't tell me. General Hessler,' Kelly said acidly.

'It doesn't matter what the source is,' Gary responded. 'That's the word that's going out, and that's the word which will be passed to the Marines and to the President's supporters outside the Capitol.'

'If you do put that word out,' Jeff said softly, 'whatever blood is spilled out there will be on Hessler's hands. Yours too.'

'Hessler's manipulating the whole situation,' Kelly said animatedly. 'Jesus, Linda, can't you see that? This isn't about Wade and Trevathan any more. It's about Hessler. Wade is just as much a pawn in his hands as you are.'

'General Hessler is doing his duty, Kelly, just as Gary and I are,' Linda replied. To most listeners, Linda's voice would probably have sounded the same as it had earlier in the meeting. But Kelly had known Linda for too long not to notice the difference in her tone. The conviction which had been there before had gone. It was as if she were repeating her arguments by rote. Gary Mills now represented the voice of conviction. Kelly wondered what they had discussed during the recess. She decided that a weakness had arisen in the opposition camp. She did not know how or why, but she knew that it must be exploited.

'Tell me how you see this going, Linda,' Kelly suggested.

'I don't know what you mean.'

'Well, OK, let's say for argument's sake that Hessler's people and the crowd outside the Capitol close down the Senate. That still leaves almost the entire military working for Trevathan, not to mention the House, the Supreme Court, and the Agencies. Some time tomorrow, Trevathan will order the military to retake the White House. It will be a mess, but there's no doubt that they will succeed in doing it. It's just a matter of superior forces. How do you see it going from there? For Wade? For you?'

'I don't think Trevathan will do that,' Gary Mills broke in. 'And you're forgetting about the nukes.'

'That's a bunch of crap,' Kelly replied, 'and you know it. And my question was directed to Linda.'

Reluctantly, Gary held his tongue. But Linda did not respond immediately.

'It's not a bunch of crap, Kelly,' Linda said.

It was said weakly. She now knew the truth. Kelly instinctively sensed a breakthrough. She knew now was the time to press home her advantage. But she was not given the chance.

'Well, yes, it is a bunch of crap, in a manner of speaking,' a smooth male voice said from the door on the far side of the room. He had entered so quietly that no one in the room had sensed it.

'But that's politics, isn't it, Agent Samuels? Most things in politics are a load of crap, when it comes right down to it. But it hardly matters, does it? You see, in the end, it's all about power. And sometimes, if you want power, you have to take whatever help you can get, wherever it may come from, crap and all.'

The four negotiators stood up and looked in the direction of the voice.

'Mr. President,' Linda muttered.

'Welcome to the White House, Agent Smith, Agent Morris,' Steve Wade said. 'I hope everything is to your satisfaction, and you find your visit useful?'

'We're making some progress, Mr. Wade,' Kelly replied evenly.

Wade smiled.

'I will overlook your ungracious failure to accord me the proper title, Miss Smith. I'm not a small-minded man.'

'I accorded you your proper title, Sir,' Kelly replied.

'Kelly…' Linda whispered.

Wade gestured as if to wave Linda away.

'No. Don't be concerned, Agent Samuels. Agent Smith's failure to follow protocol is unimportant in the circumstances. Now, where were we? You were saying something about a load of crap, if I remember rightly.'

Kelly looked briefly at Jeff, whose gaze seemed to be frozen on Steve Wade.

'Is it your intention to join in the negotiations, Mr. Wade?' she asked.

'No, no, I don't think so,' Wade replied, laughing. 'I was just passing, and I overheard what you were saying, and it struck me as rather funny.'

'Really?' Kelly rejoined. 'In what respect?'

Wade spread his arms out wide to either side. 'In every respect,' he said. 'The whole damn thing. The Senate thinking it can impeach me when I've done nothing wrong; thinking they can get rid of me when I'm the most popular President in history; Ellen Trevathan, the peace-maker, thinking she can storm the White House with all the king's horses and all the king's men, and take over from me. It's all funny. Downright hilarious, in fact.'

Wade continued to smile, as he took a seat at the table. Kelly and Jeff resumed their seats, followed by Linda and Gary. Linda could not take her eyes off Wade. She had never seen him like this, seemingly not taking the situation seriously, perhaps even detached from reality. From the time when Julia had left the White House, Wade had not been himself, and as the impeachment crisis lurched along, he had become more and more withdrawn, remote, at times inaccessible. But what she was seeing now was a new level of disfunction, and she could not begin to guess how she was supposed to react to it. An image of Hessler in a very different light came to her and would not go away.

'Now, why doesn't someone explain to me what I have to do to get Ellen Trevathan off my back?' Wade was asking.

'I'm afraid there's no way to do that,' Kelly replied. 'But by agreeing to step down peacefully now, you could avoid a great deal of unnecessary bloodshed and damage. I know that would count for a lot in whatever decisions President Trevathan might make once this is over.'

'I could just as easily say the same to her,' Wade countered. 'I know how to be magnanimous.'

The smile seemed to be frozen on his face. Something about it made Kelly feel cold. All at once, she began to see what Linda had seen, how tenuous the man's grasp on reality had become. She cast about desperately for inspiration. Out of the corner of her eye, she saw Jeff's gaze shift a little. She glanced across at him and knew that he had seen the same things she had. Jeff leaned forward across the table.

'If I understand you, Sir,' he began, 'your reason for wanting to remain in power is because that's what the people want. You're popular, you were elected to a second term in office, you should be allowed to finish it. Am I correct? I mean, is that what we should report to Ellen Trevathan?'

Kelly looked closely at Wade, and saw him connect with Jeff. 'Attaboy, Jeff,' she said to herself.

'That, plus the fact that I did nothing wrong,' Wade replied.

'And all those people out there at the Capitol? I don't mean General Hessler's Marines, but all those people who are out there protesting? That's a spontaneous demonstration by the people, to show how much they care, to show that they want to keep you in power?'

'Certainly. What else?'

Kelly looked at Linda, who was suddenly looking pale.

'The Director was claiming, Mr. President,' Linda said, 'that…'

Wade turned to face her.

'Who was claiming?' he demanded.

'The… I'm sorry, Agent Smith,' Linda replied nervously. 'Agent Smith was claiming that the people supporting you at the Capitol are thugs organized by a white supremacist group. I pointed out that she was wrong, of course. But it might help to move things along if you would confirm that personally, you know, just so that we can get past it and move on.'

Wade laughed again.

'Oh, for God's sake,' he said. 'You see how much you people need me? You see how naïve you're being? What does it matter who they are? What does it matter what groups they may be members of? They are the people, and they are about to ensure that the will of the people is carried out.'

'You mean, they're there to intimidate the Senate into taking another vote, this time to keep you in office?' Kelly interposed.

'That would not be my choice of language,' Wade said, with a nod in Kelly's direction. 'But essentially, that's what the people seem to have set out to achieve. And I'm sure you will agree that whatever agents the people may choose to act in this matter, those agents are acting on behalf of the people. The people want me, Miss Smith, and the people need me. That is why I cannot leave. The people will not allow me to leave.'

Wade began to laugh quietly. Everyone else remained silent.

'Mr. President,' Linda said. 'Before I go on with the negotiation, there's one thing I need to know. Can you deny for us that you played any role in bringing white supremacists to Washington in advance of your impeachment?'

Wade did not respond immediately, but continued to laugh to himself. Linda looked anxiously at Gary Mills, but he did not seem to want to make eye-contact. Eventually, Wade appeared to consider the question.

'I wanted to make sure that the people were heard,' he replied. 'That's all. I don't handle the details. That's up to Hessler. I'm the President of the United States, for God's sake.'

Linda had risen slowly to her feet. Her manner was serious and intense.

'And is it also true that these white supremacists are the same people who were involved with the Lebanese agent, Hamid Marfrela?'

Steve Wade threw his hands in the air in apparent exasperation.

'Whoever the fuck Hamid Marfrela was,' he replied to the room at large. 'I keep telling you I didn't know him. Why won't anybody believe me?'

'Yeah, imagine that,' Jeff Morris muttered.

Kelly took a deep breath. It was time to roll the dice.

'All right,' she said, as authoritatively as she could. 'Before we go any further, Mr. Wade, I have to advise you that I have a warrant for your arrest...'

Jeff's eyes opened wide as he turned to face her.

'What?' Gary Mills shouted, in disbelief.

'The charge is one of treason. I have a duty to advise you that you have certain rights. You have the right to remain silent...'

'Oh, for Christ's sake,' Gary shouted.

'If you give up that right, anything you do say may be used against you in a court of law.'

Steve Wade threw his head back, laughing hysterically. Linda remained completely silent.

'You have the right to an attorney. If you cannot afford an attorney...'

Abruptly, Wade stopped laughing.

'I have a goddamned attorney,' he shouted, 'and much good it's done me. You want me to answer your question, Agent Smith? OK, I'll answer it.'

'Mr. President,' Gary Mills interrupted, 'perhaps you should…'

Wade brought his fist crashing down on to the table.

'I'll answer,' Wade repeated. Suddenly, he dropped his voice, appearing calmer. 'After all, it's not going to make any difference.'

Kelly suddenly became very cold again. 'What do you mean?' she asked.

Wade snorted. 'You're not going to be able to execute your warrant, Agent Smith, and you're not going to be in any position to repeat anything I might say to any court.'

Kelly felt Linda look across at her.

'I'm sorry, what exactly do you mean, Mr. President?' Linda asked.

Wade shifted a little in his seat.

'It wasn't my choice,' he ventured, almost sounding apologetic. 'It was Hessler's decision. He said it would be insecure to let the two of you leave. It's an operational matter. I have to leave that kind of decision to him. It's nothing personal, you understand.'

Instinctively, Kelly's hand moved to where her side-arm should have been. She tried to withdraw it without being noticed. As she did so, she noticed that Linda's face had turned from pale to deathly white.

'Kelly,' Linda said, 'I swear to you by all I hold sacred, I had no idea…'

'I know,' Kelly replied.

Linda turned back to face Steve Wade.

'It's true, isn't it?' Linda asked quietly. 'You used those people, those white supremacists or whatever the hell they are, to try to stay in power. You and Hessler.'

'I don't care who I have to use,' Wade shouted. 'Why can't you people understand that? Who cares whether it's the Lebanese, or the Sons of the Land, or the Lions Club of America? If they can help do the will of the people, yes, I will use them.'

'You've lost your mind.'

'Perhaps I have, Agent Samuels. But I'm still the President.'

Linda had stopped listening to him. 'You bastard,' she continued in the same quiet voice. 'I went to prison for you.'

'For which I was appropriately grateful.'

'And now it looks like I've committed treason for you.'

'Words, Agent Samuels. Hot air. By this time tomorrow, none of this will matter.'

'And, on top of everything else, you're telling me that you're going to kill my best friend. Is that what you're telling me?'

Steve Wade smiled a smile of pure contempt.

'Some people are expendable, Agent Samuels. Including, I'm afraid, you and your best friend, the would-be Director. I'm afraid that's just the way power works. By this time tomorrow, this whole affair will be over, and none of these little distractions you're talking about will matter a damn. Not to me, not to anyone else. And if a couple of people had to die along the way because they were foolish enough to become involved in a conspiracy to overthrow me, well, that's how these things go sometimes.'

In the terrible silence which followed the final revelation of Steve Wade's insanity, Kelly saw the whole thing in her mind's eye before it happened. She made a hopeless effort to push herself up out of her chair. But there was absolutely nothing she could do about it. Both Linda Samuels and Gary Mills were far too fast, far too well trained, for anything to be averted. All Kelly could do was watch the events which followed, as if in an endless slow-motion sequence, events which, in actuality, could have taken no more than a couple of seconds. Watch, and uselessly scream Linda's name. With practiced ease, Linda drew her service weapon and, from a range of just a few feet, placed two shots with clinical accuracy side by side in the middle of Steve Wade's forehead. Without a sound, Wade slumped backwards in his chair, instantly dead, the force of the bullets not quite enough to topple him out of the chair, but more than enough to detach substantial parts of the back of his head. A mere instant later, true to his training, and without independent thought, Gary Mills drew his own weapon and shot Linda twice in the region of the heart. The gun fell from her hand and, after snatching briefly at the edge of the table, Linda collapsed on to the floor. Kelly at last came out of her chair and fell to her knees, her breath gone, and her eyes beginning to glaze over. Vaguely, she saw Jeff walk over to Gary, who seemed to be standing frozen, as if in shock, and disarm him. Climbing unsteadily to her feet, and holding on to the table for support, she slowly maneuvered herself past the chair containing the body of Steve Wade, to where Linda lay slumped on the floor. Slowly, Kelly lowered herself to kneel by her friend. Shocked and disoriented as she was, one look was enough to tell Kelly that Linda was almost gone. For the last time, Linda opened her eyes. Kelly took her hand and, just for a moment, experienced the false hope of a look of recognition.

'Kelly,' Linda whispered, fighting for breath through the trickle of blood which had begun to emerge from the corner of her mouth, 'I have to go. If you see Bob…'

'Linda, hang in there with me, please…'

'No, Kelly, listen. Listen. It's too late. Tell him I'm not taking him back this time. Tell him, this time, it's over. Kelly, I love you.'

'I love you too, Linda,' Kelly replied. But, as she spoke the words, realized she would never know whether Linda had heard her or not.

* * *

A few seconds, or hours, or weeks later, Kelly hardly knew which, she heard Jeff's voice shouting across the room to her, telling her to pick up Linda's gun. Mechanically, she obeyed. She was still on her knees by Linda's body. Turning in the direction of Jeff's voice, she saw that he was holding Gary Mills' weapon and pointing it at the same door by which the President had entered, however long ago that had been. Gary was sitting motionless in a chair by Jeff's side. Looking up at the door, Kelly saw in its frame the figure of General Hessler. He had a nine-millimeter Glock pointed directly at Jeff. She knew that she somehow had to put her grief and shock aside, she needed to make the most massive effort of her life. Standing slowly, she forced her hands to point Linda's gun at Hessler. But, despite her determination, her hands were shaking, and her eyes were wet with tears. Hessler smiled at her grimly, then looked across to the chair which contained the body of Steve Wade. He stared at the body for a few seconds, before shaking his head dismissively.

'Useless fuck,' he muttered. 'All talk and no balls. You know, he actually thought he was still going to be in charge when all this is over. Well, at least now we're through negotiating.'

'That's correct, General,' Jeff said. 'It doesn't matter what the Senate does now, does it? Ellen Trevathan is President of the United States, and you're under arrest for treason. Take two long steps further into the room, place your weapon on the ground, and take two steps back again.'

Hessler laughed. 'Well, you do seem to have me outnumbered,' he said. 'Two to one. Depending, of course, on whether the lady could actually use that weapon she's holding.'

As she stared into Hessler's eyes, Kelly relived the moment when Linda fell, mortally wounded. And then, unable to control her thoughts, she began to relive another occasion when she had seen friends die. She saw herself back in that godforsaken factory in the Bronx. She saw the storage room near the main gate. She saw herself dive for cover with Joe and Tina, as the bullets flew all around them. She relived the endless waiting for the sound of the sirens that meant back-up was on the way. She relived the sound and the fury of that terrible night, the sharp crack as the bullet entered Joe's skull, Tina's imploring screams as she waited to die, lying on the ground by Kelly's side. There had to have been something she could have done differently. This time she would do it right.

'You'd better believe she can, and will, General,' Kelly replied. 'Without a second thought.' Her hands were steady now, and her voice held a deadly calm.

'Well, then, I am outnumbered,' Hessler said, with a smile. 'But not for long, I think. In fact, here come my reinforcements now. Now it's my turn. And, since I'm not in a patient mood, let me advise you both strongly to drop your weapons, and do it now.'

Half turning to the entrance leading to the garden, Kelly saw that Captain Manning had entered the room. He had drawn his own side-arm, but he had also seen Steve Wade's body, and seemed shocked, and uncertain what to do. Behind him stood a lance-corporal and four Marines, all holding assault rifles. Manning looked at Hessler.

'With your permission, General, what is going on here?'

Hessler nodded towards Kelly and Jeff in turn.

'These traitors shot President Wade, Captain. Have your men disarm them and take them into custody.'

Manning looked at Kelly questioningly. But it was Gary Mills who spoke.

'No, they didn't,' he said quietly, turning towards Manning. 'Agent Samuels shot him. And I shot her. I'm sorry.'

'You shut your mouth,' Hessler said. 'Don't listen to this moron. I'm telling you, these people came in here under cover of negotiating, and they shot President Wade.'

Manning looked around the room and took a deep breath. 'With all due respect, I don't think so, Sir.'

Hessler turned his weapon and took aim at Manning.

'What did you say?' he demanded.

'I disarmed Director Smith and Agent Morris myself when they arrived, Sir. They didn't have anything to shoot the President with.'

Hessler swallowed hard.

'It's obvious what happened then. They took Agent Samuels' gun, and they used that to shoot the President,' he offered lamely. 'They shot her, they disarmed Agent Mills, and then they shot the President.'

Without turning Linda's gun away from Hessler, Kelly addressed Manning.

'Captain Manning, what Agent Mills told you is correct.'

Manning nodded. 'Yes, Ma'am. I know.'

'Good,' Kelly said. 'Then I need your help. I am the Acting Director of the FBI. I have a warrant for the arrest of General Hessler on a charge of treason. I need your help to execute it.'

Hessler snarled in Kelly's direction. 'She's crazy. Obey my order without delay, Captain. Detain these people and take them into custody.'

Out of the corner of her eye, Kelly was able to see Manning's hesitation all too clearly. The Marines standing behind him also seemed transfixed, waiting for someone to make a decision for them. Kelly knew that Manning was all that now stood between America and a second civil war. She tried to find words to tell him, but just as she opened her mouth to speak, the officer in Captain Manning took over.

'I'm sorry, General Hessler,' he said. 'I can't carry out your order, Sir. It's over now. Please place your weapon on the floor, Sir.'

'Fuck you,' Hessler shouted. 'If you don't obey me, I'll have you shot, you impudent little cocksucker…'

'Marines,' Manning shouted, even more loudly than Hessler, 'disarm the General. And if he resists, shoot him.'

The lance-corporal's eyes opened wide, and he swallowed hard, but he obeyed Manning.

'Sir. Yes, Sir. Marines, take aim. On my command, forward march!'

Levelling their assault rifles at Hessler, the Marines awaited the lance-corporal's order, which was only a second in coming.

'Forward march.'

'Thank you,' Kelly said, under her breath.

'No, you fucking don't,' Hessler snarled, extending his arm and his Glock in the direction of the approaching Marines. 'I'll have you all shot, you insubordinate assholes. In fact, I'll do it myself.'

'No, you won't, you psychotic bastard,' Jeff said. He took several bold steps forward, and put Gary's gun right against Hessler's head. 'Try anything, and you're the first to die. You have my word on that.'

Before Hessler could reply, the Marines were on him. After a momentary hesitation, he permitted the lance-corporal to take away his gun.

'It doesn't matter,' he muttered, as much to himself as anyone else in the room. 'There's nothing you can do to me. The Williamsburg

Doctrine has been part of the procedure since the Sixties. I did what was right for America. Fuck you all. You can't touch me.'

'We'll see about that,' Kelly replied quietly.

The Marines surrounded General Hessler and led him away.

'Thank you, Captain,' Jeff said, the relief evident in his voice.

'Yes, Sir,' Manning replied. 'What else can I do?'

Jeff looked at Kelly, who had slumped into a chair, and knew that, for now, he had to take command.

'Do you have any way to contact the Marines on duty outside the Capitol?'

'Yes, Sir. My colonel's in command there. We're in constant communication by radio.'

'Secure?'

'Of course, Sir.'

'Contact your colonel immediately. Tell him Wade is dead. Tell him that President Trevathan has declared a state of emergency, and that you are temporarily in command. Order him, and the Marines who are with him, to defend the Senate with any and all means at their disposal. Then get whatever reinforcements you can to Capitol Hill, ground troops, helicopters, whatever. You're the expert. Whatever you think will help.'

'Yes, Sir. Should the Marines move in and disperse the crowd, Sir?'

Jeff considered for a moment.

'Are those big TV screens still in place and operational around the Capitol and down the Mall?'

'As far as I know, Sir.'

'Good. In that case, order them not to take action for now, except to defend the Senate if necessary. But they should stand by to move on your command. After you've done that, alert all sections of the military to the fact of Wade's death, starting with any units in charge of nuclear weapons.'

Manning hesitated. 'There is one thing, Sir…'

'Go on.'

'The 'football'.'

'The what?… Oh, you mean…'

'The box containing the nuclear codes, Sir. It's supposed to remain within the reach of the President at all times. If I'm to give out news that President Wade is dead…'

'Where is the 'football' now?'

'It's secure, Sir, but we need to get it to President Trevathan.

Especially if the news of Wade's death is going to be made public, and word gets out abroad. We don't want to be caught with our pants down.'

Jeff put a hand up to his forehead. 'Oh, God, this is out of my league.'

Manning smiled. 'If I might make a suggestion, Sir?'

'By all means,' Jeff replied, returning the smile.

'There's talk that President Trevathan has appointed Mr. Lazenby Acting Vice President, and that he is still here in Washington. Is that correct, Sir?'

'As far as I know,' Jeff replied cautiously.

'In that case, Sir, President Trevathan can execute what's called an Article Twenty-Five in favor of the Vice President. It would allow him to take control for a limited period of time until the President arrives back in Washington. It would really help to know that is in place when I contact the various units. Just so there is no question as to who's in charge.'

Jeff nodded. 'Very good, Captain. I'll see to it.'

'Yes, Sir. Anything else, Sir?'

'Yes. Please take Agent Mills into custody, and have someone bring us our side-arms.'

'Yes, Sir.'

Captain Manning turned to leave the room, taking Gary by the arm. 'Oh, and Captain…'

'Sir?'

'This isn't your highest priority. But when you get a chance, send some of your men to arrest Admiral McGarry and Attorney-General Latham. The charges are the same as in General Hessler's case.'

Manning smiled.

'It will be my pleasure, Agent Morris.'

55

SUDDENLY, THEY WERE alone, and the room was silent. Jeff walked over to the chair in which Kelly was sitting, removed Linda's gun from her lap and placed it on the floor. He knelt beside her and held her as she wept silently. After some time, Kelly looked up.

'I did it, Jeff. I killed her.'

'No, you didn't.'

'If I hadn't played on the doubts she was having… I saw it while we were talking. She had started to see what was going on. I thought if I could …'

She lowered her head against his chest. Jeff kissed her gently on the forehead.

'And you were right. But there was no way you could have foreseen what she would do.'

He kissed her again. 'She did it for you.'

Kelly looked up.

'It was after Wade told her he planned to have us killed. That was the final straw. She couldn't see any other way out.'

'She must have known what Gary would do,' Kelly whispered.

'Yes.'

Jeff allowed her a minute more to pour out her tears.

'Kelly, listen. I know this is hard for you. But I need you to function. We have to call the President.'

Abruptly, Kelly got to her feet. 'Oh, God, yes. Where's the phone?'

'I'll get it.'

As he did so, a Marine entered the room carrying their weapons, placed them on the table, saluted, and left. Jeff nodded to him. Kelly was dialing the number. Ellen Trevathan answered immediately.

'Kelly, thank God. Are you OK? What's going on?'

With an effort, Kelly composed herself. 'We're fine, Madam

President. We're still at the White House.'

She hesitated.

'Look, there's no easy way to tell you everything that's happened. But you need to take action without delay. There are some things I'm going to have to explain to you later…'

'That's fine, Kelly,' Ellen replied. 'Talk to me.'

Kelly took a deep breath. 'Well, first, Steve Wade is dead…'

Kelly heard the intake of breath on the other end of the line.

'It was nothing to do with us,' she continued. 'His own people turned against him. I'll tell you more later. The important thing is, whatever happens in the Senate, you are now President, and the mob has no basis for saying otherwise. Not that they ever did, but…'

'I understand, Kelly'. The President's voice betrayed her profound shock. 'What else?'

'General Hessler is under arrest, and the other conspirators soon will be,' Kelly said. 'But the most important thing is, a Captàin Manning has taken charge of things here for the Marines. He is doing his best to make sure they can protect the Senate, but the situation there is very volatile. The Marines are outnumbered. We have reinforcements moving up, but they're playing a very dangerous game.'

'What should I do?'

'Madam President, I think it's time for you to speak to the American people,' Kelly replied. 'The big TV screens are still in place, and they can patch you through. I know it's asking a lot, but if you can talk to them, you may be able to make them see sense. You should also make sure your broadcast reaches the military.'

'No problem,' Ellen replied. 'We can do that.'

'The other thing is…'

'The 'football'? I know. General Gutierrez had that figured out. Ted Lazenby should have the Article Twenty-Five declaration by now. I'll be on my way to Washington as soon as I can arrange to leave here. Was that what you were going to say?'

'You read Captain Manning's mind,' Kelly said.

'Good, then let's talk after my broadcast. You two stay put and take care of yourselves.'

'We will, Madam President. And good luck.'

'Thank you, Kelly. Good luck to us all.'

* * *

Kelly and Jeff watched the broadcast with Captain Manning in the situation room, which he was now using to coordinate the defense of the Capitol. Other TV sets had been placed so that the Marines on duty in and around the White House could also watch without leaving their stations. It seemed to Kelly that Ellen Trevathan had aged visibly in the short time since their last meeting. She understood exactly how the President felt.

'The first thing I have to tell you,' Ellen began after greeting the viewers, 'is that former President Steve Wade died this afternoon in the White House. I very much regret that I do not have access to all the details of his death at this time. I am told that he died as a result of a confrontation involving members of his guard. Although I have no further information right now, I can assure you that no one in my Administration was responsible for his death in any way. I can also assure you that, as soon as I return to Washington, I shall ensure that there is a full inquiry into the circumstances, and I undertake to make the findings of that inquiry public, whatever those findings may be. For now, I am sure you will join me in mourning the loss of a great public servant and, in my case, an old and dear friend. I have one other particular regret, which is that the urgency of the situation did not permit me to convey the news of Steve Wade's death personally to the former First Lady and her children before announcing it on national television. Julia, wherever you are, if you are watching, I am truly sorry that you had to find out about it like this. If there had been any way to avoid it, I would have taken it.

'Now, I must address myself to a nation which has been brought to the brink of a second civil war. In doing so, I am speaking to the whole nation, but of course particularly to those citizens who have chosen to make their views known by protesting in such large numbers outside the Capitol and in the surrounding areas of Washington. To you, I have to offer both a message of hope and a warning. First, you must understand that I am speaking to you now as your President. I became your President as soon as President Wade was impeached by the Senate. I know some of you wish that had not happened. That, of course, is now academic. As soon as President Wade died, the Presidency would have passed to me automatically, even if he had not been impeached. As your President, I cannot and will not tolerate the continued siege of the Senate. Not only has it caused enormous hardship to the senators, their staffs, the Chief Justice, and the many journalists imprisoned in the building, but it cannot be tolerated in a free society that the government, or any part of it, should be held hostage. Peaceful demonstration is one thing. Armed intimidation is quite another. This is not the time to apportion blame for what has happened, and that is not my purpose in speaking to you. I am sure many of you came to Washington for what you considered to be good reasons. But whatever your reasons may have been, it is now time to go home. You will have your opportunity to judge my Presidency at the next election, and I will welcome your judgment at that time. But I will not allow you to dictate the course of events by force. Therefore, I am giving you notice now to lay down your weapons and go home. Anyone who does this is free to leave, and will not be arrested or harassed by the military or the police. Simply put your weapons on the ground, and walk away. That is all you have to do.'

Ellen paused for effect.

'I must tell you that, because of the gravity of the situation, there will be extremely serious consequences if you do not do as I have asked. I have determined that the situation at the Capitol constitutes a clear and present danger to the national security of the United States, and I have declared a national state of emergency. The armed forces are now completely under my control. Some factions of the military were opposed to me, but the officers in charge of those factions are now under arrest, and I have the loyalty of all our men and women in uniform. I have ordered the armed forces to use all necessary means, including the use of deadly force, to defend the Senate from any violence or threat of violence which may be offered to it. If you look around you, you will see reinforcements beginning to arrive, on the ground and in the air. I assure you that you are no match for these military units. I have further ordered the use of all necessary means to disperse the crowd holding the Senate hostage, unless the crowd immediately begins to disperse, and has taken substantial steps to vacate the area around the Capitol within ten minutes of the end of this broadcast.'

Ellen softened her voice.

'I don't want to use force against my own people. No President would. But I will not be intimidated or prevented from exercising the authority of my office by mob violence. I promise you, I will be as good as my word. Before I go, let me just add one last thing. I know that most of you are good, law-abiding people who love your country. By now, I am sure you realize that you have been deceived and led astray by a handful of people who do not have the same interests as you do, and who came to Washington, not to support our government, as they pretend, but to overthrow it by force, if necessary. Do not try to take action against these people. I will do that soon enough. But walk away from them. And do it now. God bless you, and God bless America.'

* * *

In silence, Kelly and Jeff walked upstairs from the situation room, through the West Wing, and out into the fresh air of the Rose Garden, where a light rain had started to fall. Captain Manning followed a little way behind them. The three stood looking up into the sky, enjoying the freshness of the rain on their faces.

'Do you think she did it?' Jeff asked, eventually.

Manning looked at his watch.

'We'll soon know,' he said. 'If we get to ten minutes from now, and we haven't heard an almighty big bang, or lots of people shooting at each other, we're probably going to be OK.'

56

Three months later

As KELLY AND JEFF were shown into the Oval Office, President Ellen Trevathan and Vice President Ted Lazenby stood to greet them. Lazenby shook hands with Jeff, then, ignoring Kelly's outstretched hand, pulled her into a giant bear hug.

'How are you doing?' he asked gently.

'OK,' Kelly replied quietly.

Ellen hugged both Kelly and Jeff, and seated them in front of her desk. She remained standing, leaning against the desk.

'Was it good to get away for a while?' she asked.

'Fantastic,' Jeff replied. 'Another six months of that, and I might even start feeling normal again. I had no idea how much stress I'd accumulated. How are you doing, Madam President?'

'Better with every day,' Ellen replied. She turned to Kelly.

'How was Linda's funeral?'

'Beautiful,' Kelly said. 'Beautiful. And the hardest thing I've ever done in my life.'

Ellen nodded sympathetically. 'I'm sure.'

'Her parents really appreciated your message. They understand you couldn't say it publicly, but I know it meant a lot to them.'

She hesitated.

'Of course, they asked me…'

'Linda's not going to come out of the inquiry too badly,' Ellen said. 'At least by comparison with others. Once the facts are known, I think people will understand, even if they don't agree with what she did. I wish I could say more.'

'I know,' Kelly said.

'How is Gary doing?' Jeff asked.

'Still in the psychiatric wing at Mount Sinai,' Ellen said. 'Still under a suicide watch. The doctors say it's going to take some time. They're doing everything they can.'

'Is he going to be prosecuted?' Kelly asked.

Ellen smiled, pushed herself upright and walked back behind her desk to take her seat.

'No,' she said. 'And the reason I'm smiling is that, technically, you should have had some input into that decision. But I was sure it was one you would want to delegate, not to mention that you would have been a witness, so I had Justice take a preliminary look at it. We can't really say anything officially until after the inquiry, but everybody seems to agree that no useful purpose would be served by bringing charges.'

'I'm glad,' Kelly said.

She shifted uneasily in her seat, joining her hands tightly in front of her.

'While we're on that general subject, Madam President, I did get your message. Look, I'm really flattered, but I can't…'

'Why on earth not?' Ellen asked, smiling. 'I didn't extend the offer in order to flatter you. You're my number one choice for the job. You more than proved yourself while you were Acting Director. As far as I'm concerned, you're the natural choice to succeed Ted.'

'Amen to that,' Lazenby agreed.

Kelly sat up as straight as she could.

'It's just that… well, being Acting Director in an emergency is one thing. But when it comes to the job itself, there are many people much better qualified and much more experienced. It would cause all kinds of jealousies and resentments. There would be all kinds of political fall-out.'

'Why don't you let my people handle that?' Ellen suggested.

'I don't mean political in that sense, Madam President. I mean, within the Bureau.'

The President raised her eyebrows in Ted Lazenby's direction.

'Kelly,' he said, 'when the President mentioned to me that she was going to nominate you for Director, I took some soundings myself within the Bureau. There may be a little grumbling, but then, there always is. There was quite a bit when I was appointed. That's something you just have to live with. It's the same with any high-profile public appointment. But the people who matter feel that it would be a slap in the face for the Bureau if you were not nominated. After all, when did the Bureau last have a national hero, or heroine, in its ranks? Let's face it,

Kelly, we haven't looked this good in, well, God knows when. So, when the President asked for my opinion, I said she could not possibly make a better choice.'

Jeff laughed and took Kelly's hand. 'See, I told you,' he said.

Kelly smiled.

'I'm still worried. I just don't want it to be a problem for you, Madam President.'

'It won't be,' Ellen replied firmly. 'I've already told the Senate Leaders that they are welcome to give me any early feedback they pick up from their members. I promised them that, if it seemed to be a real problem, I would offer you the choice of withdrawing. But so far, everything is overwhelmingly positive. I'm confident that you'll sail through the confirmation hearing. The rest is up to you. Assuming you want it…'

'I'm just in such an emotional state right now…'

'I understand,' Ellen said.

'If I could have a little time…'

'Of course. There's no real rush. I was going to suggest announcing your nomination in a day or two, but we don't have to. I haven't assembled much of a staff yet. We may even have someone to work with you by the time you decide.'

Kelly gently released Jeff's hand, stood, and made her way towards the window to look out over the garden.

'What a mess this has all been,' she said, almost inaudibly.

Ellen also stood.

'Yes. But it could have been worse,' she said. 'At least those people put their guns down and went home. We got the Senate and the Chief Justice out safely. And the only shots fired were the ones fired here in the White House.'

'Thanks to your speech, Madam President,' Jeff said.

'Thanks to many things, including what the two of you did,' Ellen rejoined.

Kelly looked back at Ted Lazenby.

'Do you think we will ever figure out what really happened?' she asked suddenly. 'Do you believe Steve Wade was mixed up with Lebanese agents and white supremacists? I kept asking myself, while I was at Linda's funeral, what it was all about, and none of it makes sense. I just wanted to know why I was watching my friend's coffin being lowered into the ground, what it was she had to die for, and I couldn't make sense of it. I couldn't find any answers.'

Lazenby pulled his hands through his hair.

'I'm not sure we'll ever know the full story,' he replied. 'But we did make a little progress while you were away. The Agency and the Bureau both spoke to George Carlson at some length. I decided not to tell you about it while you were involved with Linda's funeral, but you'll find copies of the reports on your desk when you get back to work.'

Kelly looked up in surprise. 'The Sons of the Land guy?'

'The same,' Lazenby said, smiling. 'They picked him up at the Capitol as the demonstration was breaking up, and he's been talking his head off ever since.'

'Carlson's talking?' Kelly asked. 'Wasn't he a mercenary? I'm surprised they got any cooperation out of him.'

Lazenby laughed.

'They didn't at first,' he said. 'But during a separate military debriefing, it came to light that Hessler had given orders to a marine colonel at the Capitol that Carlson was to be taken out. It occurred to me that it might be interesting to pass that information on to Carlson, and see how he reacted. So, I suggested to our agents that they introduce him to the colonel. I think it's fair to say he didn't appreciate it very much.'

Kelly's eyes opened wide. 'Hessler was going to have Carlson killed? Why?'

'Because he knew too much. Hessler was the Sons of the Land's contact in Washington, Kelly.'

Kelly leaned against the wall. 'Hessler was 'Fox'?'

'Exactly.'

'Sonofabitch,' Kelly exclaimed. 'Oh, God, I'm sorry, excuse me, Madam President…'

Ellen laughed.

'That's OK Kelly.'

'Anyway,' Lazenby continued, 'when they confronted Carlson with the colonel, and he realized how close he had been to going to the big compound in the sky, he started singing, and he sang a good long song.'

'And implicated Hessler?' Jeff asked.

'Hessler, and some other people,' Lazenby said, 'but curiously enough, not necessarily Steve Wade.'

Lazenby walked slowly to a chair and made himself comfortable.

'Hessler's acquaintance with the Sons of the Land goes back quite a way,' he began. 'Long before any of this started. Hessler hasn't talked at all, by the way, at least not yet, but preliminary indications are that he's seriously crazy. It seems he's had this obsession for years: America is going soft, America is being sold short by the politicians, time the military took control, and so on. Which, of course, is pretty much the same message the Sons of the Land were putting out. Anyway, according to Carlson, Hessler approached him out of the blue one day. None too gently either. Carlson happened to be in Washington for some nefarious purpose or other. Hessler has him followed, has him accosted on the street, and bundled into the back of a car, Al Capone style, and driven off at high speed to some secret rendezvous. At this point, Carlson figures he's history, his enemies have caught up with him. But it's his lucky day. Instead of being rubbed out and having his body dumped in the Potomac, he finds himself drinking whisky in a shack out in the boonies somewhere with a senior general, a general in the real army, talking about the good times in Africa, man to man, old campaigners sharing war stories, and so on.'

Lazenby stood and poured himself some coffee from a pot on a side table, then resumed his seat.

'And the upshot of all this is that Hessler suggests they keep in touch, because if there is truly a God, their day will come. The day will come when Hessler will find a way to bring down the government and replace it with someone worthy of America, presumably himself.'

'My God,' Jeff said quietly.

'Yes. Carlson's role, of course, is to build up his operation and prepare for the big day. So they establish a protocol for secret communications, and Hessler becomes Fox. A few years go by, and they have a couple of strokes of luck. The first is, Hessler gets himself appointed to the Joint Chiefs…'

'And that's something we're going to take a hard look at,' Ellen Trevathan observed bitterly. 'Believe you me. I want to know how that happened.'

'Right. And the second piece of luck was that, in his new capacity, he discovered the Williamsburg Doctrine.'

'What was all that about?' Jeff asked.

'I can answer that,' Ellen replied. 'I've had one or two very intimate conversations with General Terrell about it. It was a classic piece of mid-1960's Cold War paranoia. You have to understand, that was the height of the military machine's influence. If there's a red spy under every bed, and communists are taking over the whole world, you have to try to impose your own form of order on everything. These people actually thought that they were important enough to bypass the Constitution in the interests of military control. They had a meeting in Williamsburg, all hush-hush, of course, and they came up with this pernicious nonsense, essentially denying the Presidency to anyone who wasn't a white male who shared their obsessions about military supremacy. Then the Sixties ended. Terrell says that, after that, until Hessler came along, no one took it seriously. It was buried away in the archives and never mentioned, except for laughs over a few drinks. But Hessler saw it as a lot more than a funny story. He actually believed it could be used.'

She shook her head.

'It's history now,' she concluded. 'You can be sure of that.'

'So,' Lazenby resumed, 'eventually, Hessler got the break he had been waiting for. He had been trawling for opportunities to compromise Wade in some way or other. Carlson said Hessler had a pretty impressive network of contacts, and somehow he came up with Hamid Marfrela. Marfrela was ambitious, he liked money, he liked the high life, but he was still pretty low level, and he was desperately anxious to impress his masters back home in Lebanon. And he was quite prepared to get his hands dirty with a little intrigue, if he got the chance. So, naturally, Hessler found him interesting, and he sent him to Carlson to see what could be arranged. He probably had in mind some Lebanese involvement in the Sons of the Land's activities, stirring up trouble, what have you. But it was Carlson who stumbled on the real gold dust. At some point during the discussion, Marfrela mentioned his connection to Lucia Benoni and, of course, through her, to Wade.'

'What was Marfrela's connection to Benoni, exactly?' Kelly asked.

'Money and violence, not necessarily in that order,' Lazenby said. 'Carlson said Marfrela was a sicko, got his kicks beating up women. Once he found that Benoni was a compatriot, and she had a direct link to Wade, he pounced on her and wouldn't let her go. He set her up in an apartment, gave her money, sent her abroad to buy clothes, told her she was serving her country, and eventually brought her back in to spring the honey trap. But the interesting thing is, Carlson doesn't think she ever came up with anything concrete they could use. He thinks she liked Wade, and didn't want to hurt him.'

'Maybe that's why Marfrela killed her,' Kelly observed. 'Maybe she wasn't playing ball, and he ran out of patience.'

'Either that, or it was just for kicks,' Lazenby said. 'Carlson never found out. Either way, he and Hessler were pretty mad with Marfrela. Mad enough that Carlson had Marfrela killed, though that was partly to protect the Sons of the Land's position.'

'Nice people,' Jeff said.

'Aren't they? Of course, losing Lucia was a blow for Carlson and Hessler. But it wasn't the end. The story wouldn't go away. Mary Sullivan was playing it for all it was worth in the *Post*, and the opposition, with their damned Committee, was all over it, and before they knew what was happening, there was talk of impeachment. In some ways, it was worse for Wade with Lucia and Hamid dead than it would have been with them alive. The whole thing just kept looking more and more sinister.'

'Not helped by the fact that Steve kept lying about it,' Ellen observed.

'But Carlson and Hessler actually thought, just because that was happening, that they could march on Washington and take over?' Kelly asked. 'It's breath-taking.'

Lazenby looked at her seriously.

'That's something you're going to have to take a harder look at than I did, Madam Director,' he said. 'I admit I never would have thought a crackpot organization like that could have succeeding in doing what it did. The level of support they had was frightening.'

'That's the lesson for us. We're going to need better intelligence about groups like that,' Kelly agreed. As she was about to say something else, she suddenly halted. 'Carlson didn't say anything about…?'

'About Phil Hammond? Yes, I'm afraid he did. They were on to him, and he admitted they killed him. He wanted me to know that it took a long time, and Phil was very brave.'

Kelly put her head in her hands. 'Those bastards,' she whispered.

Jeff stood, walked over to her and put an arm around her shoulders.

'So, where did Steve Wade really fit into all this?' he asked, after a prolonged silence.

Lazenby thought for a while. 'You and Kelly were the last people to see him alive. What's your read on it?'

'It seemed to me he'd completely lost it,' Jeff replied somberly. 'He was virtually incoherent. He was talking like he thought he could rule the world. It was like something out of a bad B-movie.'

Lazenby nodded.

'That's what I would have expected. Without Hessler controlling him, he would have been lost. Once he was impeached, he would have walked away.'

'You think that was the whole story, that Hessler controlled him?'

'I think so,' Lazenby replied. 'You only have to look at what happened in the final days. Ellen couldn't even get in to see him. That must have been Hessler.'

He walked over to join Kelly and Jeff.

'There's no real evidence that Steve Wade did anything wrong except cheat on his wife with Lucia Benoni. If he had come clean and admitted it, the whole affair would have died away, as similar things had in the past. But he lied about it and, after he had painted himself into that corner, things started to spiral out of control. There are two murders. The Oregon connection comes to light. The *Post* picks the story up and won't let go of it. Julia leaves him. His political opponents pounce. And so on and so on. He starts to come unglued and, when he does, there's Hessler waiting in the wings, offering him a way out. By this time, Wade's defenses are so far down he even buys into the Williamsburg Doctrine. And, before anyone really realizes what's happening, it's all got so far out of control that there's no way back.'

There was a long silence as the four occupants of the Oval Office stood looking out over the garden.

'Well,' Ellen Trevathan said eventually, 'I suppose the lesson is checks and balances. Checks and balances, and the power of removal. Once we entrust too much to any one man – or woman – there's always the danger that things will go wrong. We just never knew how wrong they could go.'

Kelly took Jeff's hand.

'I think the lesson is, how fragile everything is,' she said quietly.

'Fragile?' Ellen asked.

Kelly smiled.

'It was something Linda said to me once when we were in college,' she said. 'It was late one night. We were talking about whatever our cause was at the time, saving the whales, or the elephants, or the starving children in Africa. And I just remember her saying how fragile everything was. I didn't really understand what she meant at the time. But I do now. She was talking about herself. As well as I knew her, I never knew how fragile she was.'

Ellen Trevathan nodded.

'I think fragile is a good word for life,' she said. 'But life has to move on, and we have to move on with it. I have a busy day today, Kelly. Why don't you get settled back in, and I'll be hoping we can start work on plans for your confirmation in a few days' time.'

Kelly nodded, then added, 'I think that what I was trying to say earlier is that I'm just taking a new look at my life, wondering what I'm doing, and why I'm doing it, when everything can fall apart so easily. I feel like I'm in a small boat, out in the middle of the ocean, without a compass. I have a few points of reference, one or two stars to steer by, like Jeff, thank God. But I'm not sure where I am or where I'm going any more.'

'I know that feeling,' Ellen said. 'I've been there myself recently. All I can tell you, Kelly, is that, eventually, you sight land. In the meanwhile, don't lose sight of the stars.'

'I won't.'

Kelly turned and smiled, present in body. But her mind was elsewhere, as it seemed to be so often; in a factory in the Bronx, in a conference room at the White House, at a graveside in Minnesota. She knew Ellen was right. All she could do was wait for the sight of land. She hoped it would come soon.